D1713501

An Agent of the King

N.J. SLATER

Copyright © 2010 Nigel Slater
All rights reserved.

ISBN-13: 978-1502455536

DEDICATION

To my long suffering partner, with apologies for so many days listening to the keyboard clicking.

CONTENTS

CHAPTER 1

EGYPT 1798

Archibald Fitzwilliam Lewis Dexter, always known to his friends as Archie, leant against the less than sturdy rail running up to the bow of the Royal Navy frigate, HMS Leander. Leander was known as a 4th rate, the smallest and most vulnerable of all the Royal Navy's warships. Along with many of the three hundred and forty strong crew he was scouring the shimmering horizon keenly for the first telltale sign of the sails that might at last reveal the presence of the French fleet.

From Toulon to Cadiz, Admiral Nelson had searched in vain for them. Somewhere in the constantly shifting heat haze of the late afternoon, Napoleon and his warships were carving their way through the deep blue water of the Mediterranean, en-route the Admiralty believed, for Egypt.

Nelson's squadron had arrived off the Egyptian port of Alexandria several days ago but found it bereft of French warships. Convinced both he and the Admiralty had been mistaken he made haste for Naples, where re-supply could be made. Leander had been belatedly dispatched back to Alexandria to warn the British Consul of the presence of a potential French invasion fleet.

Enjoying a brief moment of solitude, Archie had time to ponder on the turn of events that had lead to his arrival on this small warship, as another turning point in history appeared to be waiting just over the horizon. Ostensibly, he had been attached to Nelson's staff as an intelligence officer, in another career saving move instigated by his omnipotent father. Once more it had been said, Archie had allowed his moral weakness to shame the family. In his heart he accepted that was true, but with a wry grin he knew he could never change and would want life no other way.

With the sun beginning to set, the sheer magnificence of the spectacle enveloped him and his spirits soared. He gazed in childlike wonder as the burning red orb appeared to settle into the darkening waters on the horizon. He realised that he had stood almost motionless for nearly two hours, not really acting as a lookout at all, because his mind had been preoccupied by one expanding and troubling thought. There simply was no way fate alone had brought him to the position he now found himself in. Here he was spearheading a vital mission to impart a grave warning to the British Counsel in Alexandria, he Archibald Dexter, surplus staff officer to Rear Admiral Nelson, not even an officer of the Royal Navy. Scandal and disgrace, followed by the irresistible pressure of the family name riding to the rescue, had seen to it that he was here on this warship.

Were these just the inevitable consequences of fate toying with his life? Was he simply caught up in the ever-changing, unpredictable twists and turns that bind all living things together? He laughed out loud at the ludicrous notion. He knew for certain that this was not fate but the hand of man guiding him to his destiny. Surely he was the only officer in the fleet, if not the entire Royal Navy, who had once lived in Alexandria, spoke the local language, could converse in French, courtesy of his French governess and even got by in conversation with the Turk and Spaniard too. Someone knew without doubt that

Napoleon meant to attack Egypt and use that as a stepping-stone to India. Nelson was the only hope Britain had of stopping Napoleon's invasion and heaven help him he thought with a chuckle, Archibald Dexter was central to that scheme.

The Leander sailed on alone, quietly cutting through the water into potentially lethal danger. Though armed with fifty cannons, she was still considered out of date and with no place in modern warfare as a ship of the line. For Archie the sounds of the timbers creaking against the strain of the sails, accompanying the swish of the passing water invoked a feeling of intense excitement, as though riding a living beast. A soldier by trade, he nevertheless enjoyed days like this, as a romantic at heart he knew deep down that he was sailing into the pages of history.

The ship's captain, Thomas Thompson, had taken his orders from Rear Admiral Nelson with what Archie felt was an irrational swell of pride, seemingly unaware or careless of the risks of sailing on alone. Nelson and the remainder of the squadron continued to hunt for the French fleet whilst heading for resupply and Archie sincerely hoped that they would be successful. The prospect of Leander sailing head on into the French fleet alone was not conducive to restful nights.

Looking to starboard, he could still discern the dusty smudge blurring the horizon even as the sun set. North Africa, a land of cultured barbarity his father had told him, when as a boy the family had journeyed to Egypt. Previously his parents had left him in boarding school when they travelled overseas but as the young Archie was no great scholar and his father believed the world at large was the greatest teacher a boy could have, at the age of thirteen he had found himself in Alexandria. He lived in Egypt until his father's illness forced their return to England some three years later.

Strolling aft he found Mid-Shipman Percy Farthing, a strikingly ugly, almost hunchbacked young man, a result Archie was sure, of too many generations of close breeding.

'If the moon rises into a clear sky then we'll make Alexandria tonight,' he bellowed as Archie approached. He had but one volume to his voice, appallingly loud!

Archie approached more closely before replying, 'I do hope so and I'll feel happier knowing Leander's heading back to the safety of the squadron.'

'So it's true then, you're staying in Alexandria?' Farthing asked, his tone barely concealing his amazement that anyone should prefer the dangers of dry land to the safety of the sea.

'Yes, the Admiral is still absolutely convinced that Napoleon sees Egypt as his next target and from there onwards to India. He wishes me to ensure that the Consul makes no mistakes and prepares not only for his own safety but warns those brigands who rule the place, to give them time to prepare a welcome for the Frenchies,' he answered, ending with a hearty laugh.

Looking quizzical, Farthing laughed too, 'You don't expect a bunch of savages to trouble the Frenchies do you?'

'If the tribesmen have a mind to, then they will bleed Napoleon dry amongst the sands, believe me. If they're fool enough to treaty with Napoleon or meet him in open battle then they will be slaughtered. The Arab horsemen are second to none and at their own game in the desert, who knows how it will end?'

'Will they fight?' asked Farthing, doubt evident in his voice.

'Good God yes, over anything and against anyone. They'll happily hack each other to bits, let alone an invader from the infidel north. Oh yes, they'll fight all right but whether it will do them any good I guess we will see soon enough, unless the Admiral succeeds where he has so far failed.'

The moon did indeed rise into an inky black, diamond encrusted sky, only a segment but white and bright, allowing the Leander to anchor within the main harbour of Alexandria on the night of the 29th of June 1798. Archie was rowed ashore, along with Lieutenant Hardy who bore Nelson's official dispatches. The oarsmen secured the small boat and along with four sailors provided as escorts, the two officers ascended a flight of rough hewn steps to the quayside.

In the harsh moonlight, the low, dun coloured houses, separated by rough dusty streets, appeared shuttered and quiet. Memories flooded back for Archie as he remembered how squalid much of the town was, with only small areas of wealth and prosperity dotted amongst the dwellings of the poverty stricken masses. Minaret's and the occasional date palm provided the only break in the low skyline.

The Consul's residence itself was someway inland from the harbour where dozens of fishing boats crowded the waterfront. The stench of fish and general filth was almost overpowering in the fetid night air. One of the sailors had made this journey before so was able assist Archie in picking their way through the narrow streets lined with ramshackle houses, some of several stories almost touched on their upper floors cutting out much of the moonlight.

The streets were largely deserted, though a few old men sat in their doorways, drinking thick, black coffee and whiling away the night hours. Twice Archie wheeled around; convinced he could hear footsteps on the dusty, unmade roads. The smells of the distant harbour, the odours of spicy food and human filth, assaulted his memory and despite being unsure of where he was, he felt excited and strangely at home. Time was becoming distorted, the present was mingling with so many days he thought long past, recollections of boyhood adventures, times of running wild and free, that seemed so real once more.

The sailors carried oil lanterns to light their way as they cautiously walked into the heart of the town. They moved from pools of bright moonlight into patches of pitch darkness, as the streets twisted and turned their way up from the sea. Now and again they crossed an open square, passing under the shadow of sparse date palms. Beneath one, a man lay in a drugged daze, rhythmically snoring, undisturbed by the group passing by.

As the small party rounded a corner into a wider tree lined thoroughfare, they were violently assaulted from an arched doorway. The sudden, ferocious violence shattering the peace of the night was stunning to the senses, in a heartbeat the quiet sub-Saharan night was ripped apart by the noise and vicious hatred of a fight to the death. Three men in local garb lunged at them with long curved sabres. Reeling back as a sword sliced the air, Archie saw in horror the head of one of the sailors all but cleaved from his body and heard the sickening thud, as the lifeless corpse fell to the ground.

Reacting with commendable speed another of the sailors, Jenkins, Archie recalled, a hefty, simple lad from Wales, blocked a sabre thrust with his hastily drawn pistol, only to have the sword pulled back and stuck six inches deep into his stomach. As he roared in agony, his pistol went off in a blinding flash and his attacker's lean, bearded face exploded in a welter of gore and bone.

Another of the sailors received a fearsome sword blow to his arm but fired his pistol as he fell, the ball hitting his assailant in the centre of the chest, felling him in an instant, though he continued to thrash around on the hard ground, making a high pitched squealing noise.

The third attacker grabbed at Hardy's bag, the dispatches inside from Nelson clearly the target of the assault. Archie punched the man in the face so hard he heard and felt a finger snap. Whilst he struggled to draw his sword and the attacker fell back still clutching the bag, the night was suddenly torn apart once more by a vivid flash and ear splitting bang, followed by a blood curdling scream as another of the escorts discharged his pistol at point blank range into the Arab man's stomach.

Then as suddenly as the dreadful assault had started, it was over. Two of the sailors were dead, another grievously wounded and three locals lay bleeding to death in the dust of the street. His heart pounding, his stomach threatening to rebel at any moment, Archie took stock. Looking around he was surprised to see two men slinking off into a narrow side street, what their business was he could not be sure but under the blue white light of the moon, he could see clearly that they were European.

'Sir, we must go quickly, there may be more of them buggers,' the youngest of the group of matelots managed to get out, his face ashen in the moonlight. Lieutenant Hardy looked as stunned as the rest of them, his mouth moved but no words were uttered. Archie knelt by the fallen men, one clearly dead, the other almost there. Archie took Jenkins hand just as he heaved weakly and died. The man with the deep cut to his arm was showing amazing powers of recovery so Archie came to a decision.

'We're not leaving them to the human jackals that walk these streets, no more than we would in London. I'll carry one, you the other,' gesturing at the young sailor to help.

'First reload all the pistols and then make haste, we're only one street short of the Consul's residence,' he added, with more hope than confidence in his voice.

Staggering under their burden, the two men carried their fallen comrades and encouraged the injured man to keep up. Hardy had recovered his composure somewhat and with pistol drawn, covered the party's rear. At the end of the road stood a small square, flanked by houses far grander than they had seen so far. These were the houses of rich merchants, one of which had been taken as the British Consul's residence some years ago. By convention it should offer sanctuary, but in these troubled times, Archie could not be certain.

The large oak doors took a fearful pounding and there were a number of calls to open up in the name of the King before an Egyptian servant answered, opening the door just a few inches to peer outside. With no ceremony, the anxious party forced their way past him into the courtyard within, Hardy slamming the door closed and throwing the large iron bolts. When two female servants appeared, their screams ensured the rest of the household was swiftly woken.

*

Archie forced his eyes to open against their will. Something was wrong, very wrong and he sat bolt upright, panic gripping him like a vice. He was laying in almost complete darkness but what else was it that he struggled to comprehend? He slumped back onto his firm bed again, the lack of motion after weeks at sea, that was it. He laughed out loud at his foolishness even as the first recollections of the past evening's horror came back to him.

His troubled thoughts were interrupted by a polite knock on the door, followed by the entry of an old man, stooped with age but still over six feet tall, he had a kindly but worn face with skin the texture of ancient leather. Moving almost silently in soft slippers, he opened the thick wooden shutters and let in a flood of light, the sky azure blue and cloudless.

'Young master Archie, so good see you, my, oh my, how fine have you grown?' he announced in thickly accented English, slapping his hands together, a gleeful smile lighting up his face.

'Fahrouk, how the devil are you?' Archie exclaimed, leaping from the bed careless of his nakedness and clasped the old man in bear hug. 'I didn't think you could possibly still be here. Where were you when we arrived last night?' he cried, joy fairly bursting in his heart.

'Attending my sister, alas she is not well and as the master is away I am not needed here. Young Master, such trouble you bring with you, why do my brothers treat you so badly,' the old man whined, clearly distressed that

Archie had been so ill-treated.

'Alas my old friend these men were no common thieves in the night. They were sent to relieve me of letters for his Excellency and two brave men died to save me,' he added, tears welling in his eyes. Six hours of fitful sleep had not helped dull the memory of how close to death he had come last night.

'Please, I must dress and return to my ship. As his Excellency is away, I must speak with my ship's Captain'

'Captain Thompson is downstairs Master Archie, he wishes you to join him,' Farouk explained, gesturing to a young boy standing at the threshold of the door to bring in the bowl of water and shaving utensils he was struggling to carry.

Twenty minutes later, somewhat reinvigorated, Archie came down the stairs. As if by magic his uniform had been cleaned and pressed so he made a presentable sight as he stood to attention before Captain Thompson. The Captain rose to return his salute, glanced awkwardly at Archie's unshaven chin but bade him be seated at the large table that had been prepared with a breakfast fit for an Englishman. Archie looked across at old Fahrouk in admiration at his remarkable ability to serve a full English breakfast in Egypt, just as he had during his father's time in Alexandria.

'My God Sir but that was a close call,' Thompson announced. 'Two fine men down, blast those French dogs. Now eat and then we shall make our plans. I've a dozen men armed and ready at the gates should there be any more trouble, so we shouldn't be disturbed.'

'Sir, I'm grievously sorry for what happened. I feel I should have thought it more of a possibility, for this is a lawless place at the best of times. How is Smith Sir?' Archie asked quietly, fearing more bad news.

'The Surgeon has saved his arm and he is resting as we speak. Fortunately the sound of gunfire carries on the night air, so we knew there was trouble and the shore party made good time once they had received directions. You all did well last night but the question is what to do now?' he asked, before attacking another egg with enthusiasm. No seafarer could pass up the chance of fresh food and even as they ate, through the open door, a Midshipman could be seen gathering eggs in the rear courtyard, with the young boy's enthusiastic assistance.

'I can travel to Cairo Sir, but I cannot see what good Baldwin will do there,' Archie volunteered.

'No need, Hardy has already left with two men and local guides and heaven help him,' Captain Thompson answered.

'It may be better if I try to make contact with either Ibrahim or Murad Bey myself Sir. I met them when I was sixteen, just before leaving for England. They have houses here in Alexandria but spend much of their time in Cairo or just roaming the desert. If Napoleon comes then they can be counted on to fight him but it must not be on his terms or they will surely fail,' Archie said, with a final certainty.

'If Nelson can only find the blasted French at sea then none of this will be necessary, I hate the idea of trusting a load savages to fight our war for us' Thompson huffed. 'We must go find this Mohammed El-Koraim chap, calls himself sherif would you believe! We must make him prepare however he can in order to meet Bonaparte and defend this place if possible. Then I must seek an audience with these Bey fellows.'

'This is their country and they will make Bonaparte pay dearly for his adventure. Sir, Napoleon has already taken Malta, if he's coming to Egypt then his arrival is imminent. I would not want to presume Sir but without delay someone must warn the Bey's people and surely the Leander must rejoin the safety of the squadron? I have met El-Koraim and grew up with his son, he will listen to me.'

'You're right young man. I believe you're possibly the only hope we have of giving these people fair warning. Can I leave you some men? They can protect the house at least,' Thompson asked while helping himself to a succulent peach. 'It's good fortune indeed that you were along for the ride, eh my boy? Someone somewhere knows a great deal more than they are saying I reckon?' he added flatly.

'If... no, when Bonaparte comes then he will probably take this house and a few good men will be lost. Sir, I know these people here and can lose myself amongst them, which is why I took the liberty of not shaving before breakfast, for which I apologise,' Archie explained with as much sincerity as he could muster, knowing how important these matters were to Naval Captains.

'No matter, you're right. Decided then, Leander sails at once. Midshipman Hollis,' he bellowed. 'You'll be all alone here Dexter. You know it'll be weeks before Nelson returns, if at all,' he warned in more hushed tones.

'I know Sir. This was my home for three years, I have many friends here who will not fail me, if I can but track them down. I'll warn the Marmeluke rulers and help them all I can until Nelson arrives,' Archie stated bluntly and with considerably more confidence than he felt.

The next half hour passed in a frenetic whirl of activity as the sailors parceled up all the fresh food the household could spare and when eventually they were ready to leave, Thompson turned to Archie once more.

'Take great care young man, at best I think your native friends will slow Bonaparte down a little but if Nelson fails to sink him at sea then I fear Egypt is lost. Good luck to you and I hope to have the pleasure of your acquaintance once more,' he added gruffly.

'Thank you Sir,' Archie replied, coming to attention. 'When the fleet returns to these waters, if they should see three fires burning closely together on the shore that will be my signal to you to make speed toward them for whatever help I can give you or indeed you can give me,' he added with a nervous grin.

All too soon he found himself alone in the courtyard, the great doors securely bolted. The sounds of the bustling streets beyond seemed muted and distant, the shaded garden was cool, despite the power of the fierce morning sun.

'Fahrouk!' he shouted,' quickly man, where are you?'

As always, the old man was by his side in an instant. He never seemed to grow tired of the demands made of him and served with a perpetual smile.

'Fahrouk, my old friend, bad times are coming to your land. The French seek to conquer Egypt for themselves. The British Navy searches for them at sea but if they fail then they will come. I must warn your rulers so they can prepare themselves,' Archie explained as the old man listened intently.

'Master, El-Koraim is at his palace here in Alexandria. Murad is camped in the sands away to the east. I can take

19

you to El-Koraim's palace but I cannot get you inside,' he said sorrowfully.

'Just get me to the door and I'll get inside. Now, I need clothes for clearly I have enemies here in Alexandria and it's no place for an officer and a gentleman. Also can you find the house of the French Consul in Alexandria?' he asked, a faraway look crossing his face as his mind raced to formulate some kind of a plan.

Within an hour he had dressed in loose flowing robes and a head towel, fashioned into a rough turban around a small hat, effectively disguising his European features. Given time, the sun and his growth of a beard would complete the illusion. On his feet he wore a battered but serviceable pair of leather slippers. He flatly refused the old man's insistent requests to accompany him after discovering a youth in the kitchen who it was said knew the city like his own backyard.

By mid morning he was ready and with the boy leading the way he left by a side gate set deep into the courtyard wall where it ran along a narrow side street, little more than an alleyway in reality. Five minutes later the boy slowed, tugging insistently at Archie's robe.

'There is the grand house of the French men,' he exclaimed, beginning to point before Archie quickly restrained him.

'Let's walk around these streets,' Archie told him in his still faltering Arabic.

Together they walked three sides of the house, bigger by far than the British Consular residence. Typical ostentatious revolutionaries Archie mused. Satisfied, he asked the boy to lead him to the Sherif's palace, the French could wait, but he had not forgotten last night or the two men lurking in the shadows.

The palace was small by European standards, situated at the end of a tree-lined avenue, flanked by two small mosques. From this slight rise in the ground, Archie could see across the town, mostly low rise disheveled buildings shimmering in the intense heat of the day. In the distance he could just make out the city walls at the Rosetta Gate, surely he thought no match for the French army. In places, the city walls stood tall and mutely defiant but elsewhere they had all but fallen to the ground in ruins, silent testimony to the decay rife in this country living under feudal rulers, loyal to a distant pasha in Cairo, who in turn held fealty to a faceless man a thousand miles beyond.

The gates to the Palace's outer courtyard were open but four guards in Marmeluke cavalry dress stood stiffly and almost at attention. Archie strode up to them, unwinding his headgear as he went. The appearance of his European face brought them forward, keen eyes looking him up and down but offering no obvious threat. This was a peaceful country right now, for a short while at least.

'I come from the British Pasha in the town with grave news for his mightiness Mohammed El-Koraim. Please I must speak with his man, his trusted one,' Archie stated boldly, struggling to recall the local language he had once excelled at.

'Why do the British send a man in rags? Where is the British Sherif, he has been to this house many times. Why does he need you and this boy to run his errands?' the taller of the guards huffed.

'Because he is in Cairo,' Archie said firmly, whilst advancing a few paces, 'and this is urgent. You tell El-Koraim's trusted man that Baldwin Pasha's man has grave news. There may be no El-Koraim's palace to guard soon, a great and powerful enemy comes to this place, now go!' he bellowed, hoping that parade ground shouting worked the world over. The guard sent an underling running into the courtyard and as the sun beat down, Archie stared at the guard and the guard stared back. Incongruously, beautiful music drifted from a high window in the palace and still they waited.

'What is this madness,' a voice boomed from the shadows as a short, rotund man in gaudy robes bustled out into the sunlight. 'Whoever you are just go away, what do you mean by… disturbing the peace… of this… morning,' the little man blustered falteringly. Totally bald, his head appeared like a raison, set with jet black eyes and a cruel, thin mouth cast into what appeared to be a permanent sneer.

'Have we met before Englishman?' he asked more quietly, now studying Archie closely.

'Sir, we have but I was then more a boy than a man. My father is Quentin Dexter, then Pasha for his Majesty King George. Father and I enjoyed the hospitality of your master and I remember the efficient service provided by you good Sir, on many occasion,' Archie enthused, warming to his task as the language and culture came back to him.

'A pleasure indeed,' El-Koraim's factotum replied and with a shallow bow he gestured for Archie to proceed inside, snapping his fingers and pointing the boy towards a small door, where no doubt he would find servants to mingle with. It was so nice to see the class system at work the world over Archie thought, with a barely concealed grin.

He was ushered across a wide courtyard and through a maze of passages to a considerably larger walled garden. Lush fruit trees, heavy with lemons, provided shelter from the fierce sun and only the soft buzz of insects broke the silence, for no sounds from the town beyond found their way inside this inner sanctum. In the far corner, a table was laid out on a dais and seated upon large, beautifully crafted cushions were three men, the largest of whom was Mohamed El-Koraim, in all but name the Mayor of Alexandria. Archie noted the presence of the ornate table, a rare item in even the most lavish of Egyptian households. He realised that El-Koraim still held onto delusions of grandeur and pretentions of status beyond his relatively humble position

Archie was led up to the group and introduced with a flourish by the man he recalled went by the name of Ut. To his astonishment, El-Koraim recalled him straight away and leapt to his feet to greet him, in English.

'Archie the man, Allah be merciful, your father is good with his manhood, yes?'

'He is indeed, 'Archie replied in El-Koraim's native tongue, feeling that the more practice he had here with friends, the better.

El-Koraim was a giant bear of a man, resplendent in the finest gaudily coloured silk shirt and turban. Around his ample girth, a sash of scarlet complete with scimitar set off the ensemble.

'What brings you to my door, not to see me I guess, but surely Tasmina, hey?' he guffawed and punched Archie none too gently on the arm. Archie reeled theatrically from the blow, impressed by the man's power of recollection. 'She's in Cairo but now you are the real man, she comes running I should think,' he bellowed, clearly amused at Archie's embarrassment upon being reminded of how he had lost his virginity years ago.

'Sit down and take food with me. What is this grave news you speak of?' El-Koraim asked as he sat down heavily, dismissing his companions with a casual wave. Before Archie could continue, a cloud crossed the man's face and his eyes darkened. 'Was the attack in the street of Murat anything to do with you? I assume you arrived on the warship that even now leaves our port?'

'Alas it was and two brave men died so that I might live and bring news from the great British sailor Nelson. Your land is in danger as never before. What do you know of Napoleon Bonaparte your Excellency?' Archie enquired respectfully.

'You know, word spreads far and wide of his victory over the weak people of Italy. Your father told me of the terrible things in France, the rulers put to death, wholesale murder of many people. This Bonaparte, he cannot want anything from this land surely?' El-Koraim said, the smile now gone from his face, a look of worry clouding his eyes.

'My country believes Bonaparte will come here within weeks. He will seek to launch an expedition from here to invade India, to steal Britain's trade,' Archie answered. Choosing his next words carefully, he added, 'he's a very powerful man and his army is strong, armed with many cannons. He's swept all before him but he's never encountered such people as your Excellency commands and if you fought him using the desert as your friend then he may be ruined.'

'Where do I find this accursed swine, I'll cut him to pieces for my dogs and lay his army to rest in the sand,' roared the Sherif of Alexandria, standing now, in exactly the display of arrogant defiance Archie had expected and dreaded. Standing himself and trying to remain calm, he looked the huge man straight in the eye.

'As you did with my father, I beg you to trust my word Excellency. This man Bonaparte has a dangerous army but he will be surprised by the welcome your tremendous soldiers will give him. You must not stand and fight though or his cannons will cut you down. I beg you, use your land, draw him into the heat of the desert and wear him down until the vultures finish him.'

'A wise head on a young man's body,' laughed the ruler of Alexandria. 'Now, where will I find this Bonaparte?'

'That's the difficult part. His Navy is certainly close by so scouts must look for him all along the coast. He may even be landing as we speak!'

'So be it,' El-Koraim roared, before firing off commands to unseen men in the shadows of the house. From what Archie could understand it involved paying anyone who saw warships off the coast a ransom in gold for the information but little else of substance.

Satisfied by his success and exhausted by the events of the last twenty-four hours, Archie settled once more into the cushions and began to eat as though he had never seen food before. Slowly roasted meats, stews and a bewildering array of fruits were laid before him. There was more food spread out on this one table than most local families would be fortunate enough to eat in a week. El-Koraim moved about the palace rattling off endless orders and dispatching messengers, including those he sent to the Marmeluke rulers of Egypt, Murad and Ibrahim Bey.

When he returned, Archie quizzed him about the French presence in the town. It transpired that there were over twenty members of staff at the Consul's house, including two recent arrivals, young men who had already come to the Sherif's attention. They had spent many days at the waterfront, paying fishermen for trips into the bay and further along the coast. They had also made themselves a nuisance amongst the women of the town and whilst high on hash or opium they had scandalised the locals with their behaviour.

Reluctantly Archie bade El-Koraim farewell, promising to return at sundown. For several hours he immersed himself in the bustle and thrum of the streets. The markets were alive with colour and smell, a thousand voices all vying to be heard. An abundance of foodstuffs and other wares were on show to be purchased by the few inhabitants with money to spend. Traders and beggars tugged at his sleeve but he had long ago learnt the art of ignoring them.

He pressed on all the way out to the city wall, dismayed at its lack of height and crumbling stonework. This once great structure would hold Bonaparte for perhaps half an hour, he realised.

After following the wall for some distance and noting the gates of sun-dried and weakened wood, he made his way to the waterfront. The mass of fishing boats and assorted small craft could not have been in starker contrast to the small warship still slowly picking its way out of the teeming harbour. Towed by three rowing boats, Leander was making her way to the relative safety of the open sea and Archie found himself whispering a private wish that she would rejoin Nelson with all speed.

He reeled and nearly missed his footing, when amongst the crowd of quayside loafers he spotted two men in European dress, the same two men from the moonlit street where bloody murder had been done.

Dressed as he was, it was no trouble at all to lounge upon a barrel of tar and watch both the Leander's stately progress towards the open sea and the two men. Like waterfronts the world over, Alexandria's was littered with the dregs of society. Beggars, who were all but naked in rags, lingered in the hope of stealing rather than finding work. Small groups of young children, some actually naked, skipped through the crowds, stealing from the unwary, who occasionally gave futile chase.

After a short while, the two Europeans headed away from the wharf and sauntered back into town. The taller of the two was clearly in charge, his slightly chubby companion showing obvious deference during their animated conversation. The tall man was slender in build with his head perched upon a long, thin neck. His boyish face and blond hair were partly concealed by what looked like a somewhat battered, English straw boater. Archie was able to follow them with ease and it was no surprise to him that they made their way back to the French Consul's house and passed inside by way of a side gate.

He found a place to sit and waited for them to leave but it was a fruitless task and after several uncomfortable hours he returned to the British Consuls residence. There he spent a nervous and inactive afternoon before leaving for El-Koraim's palace just as the sun began to settle in the dusty sky. He had once more dressed carefully in local attire but remembering the two men on the quay, he armed himself with his two pistols and a borrowed dagger.

The evening was to prove a memorable one for it was as though time had stood still and all that was missing was his father holding court and his elegant mother to be the centre of attention as ever. They talked of times gone by and Archie learned news of Karim, El-Koraim's youngest son. The same age as Archie, they had grown into young men together and along with another local boy they had led a riotous existence of wild adventurers in this exotic land. Karim he learned was now a wealthy spice merchant operating his own fleet of ships and was the proud owner of splendid houses, from Palestine to Spain.

Archie ate more than his fill and smoked a little too much hash, so when shrieks and yells woke him, he was still a guest of El-Koraim. Awake in an instant, a pistol in one hand, a dagger in the other, he rushed into the courtyard where everyone seemed to be running in circles and all talking at once in a crazed babble. It was barely dawn and for some reason the world was in turmoil. Seeing Ut sprint past, Archie grabbed him by the loose folds of his robes and pulled him to a stop.

'It's too late Master they have come, the French are in the harbour. His Excellency has taken command of the city and vows he will defend it to the death,' he stammered.

'Where is he, El-Koraim, where has he gone?' Archie demanded.

'The harbour, the French are in the harbour, thousands of ships, we are doomed men,' Ut shrieked, on the verge of hysteria.

Archie ran toward the harbour just as fast as his legs would carry him. The hash had given him the most awful throbbing headache and he was so thirsty he could cry but on and on he ran. At the quayside, crowds had gathered to stare in awe at the ships, not actually in the harbour but less than half a mile out to sea. Perhaps hundreds but not quite thousands he thought. Swallowed up by the seething mass of people, he watched the fleet hold its position offshore for several hours. Some of the ships appeared to be moving slowly westwards, for what purpose he could not imagine.

He made his way back to the palace in a terribly ill frame of mind. All that Nelson had hoped for was lost. Somehow the Royal Navy had missed the French yet again and now, laughing out loud, Archie realised that he was their token effort in the defence of Egypt.

Back at the palace, El-Koraim was strangely calm. He debriefed Archie in a most surprisingly military manner. He had, so he assured him, arranged for the five hundred strong garrison to defend the city wall. Messengers had been sent once more to the Beys, begging them to ride to the defence of the city. Bedouin leaders had been suitably bribed to scout along the shoreline for the French vanguard, though they both knew murder and pillage would be foremost on their minds, rather than any form of military reconnaissance.

Archie returned once more to the waterfront and mingled with the teeming crowds of nearly hysterical on-lookers. Viewed through the glare of the strengthening sun, the French fleet seemed to have grown in size. It still appeared to him that there was a general shift in their position slowly westwards but without his spyglass he could not be certain. He was no expert but he was sure at least two of the big warships were eighty-two gunners. Further out to sea were countless other vessels, transports he concluded, bringing infantry and the dreadfully efficient French artillery, even cavalry he supposed?

His head was spinning with ideas, wild, impetuous and mostly suicidal. He needed to do something as the feeling of impotence was just too hard to bear. He thought that if only Nelson were to return today, the victory would be absolute. Alas Nelson was probably still en route to Naples and would not return for weeks, if at all. What if Captain Thompson failed to persuade Nelson that the attack on his men confirmed Napoleon's plans? Archie felt he must do something or he would surely go insane with the terrible frustration.

He contemplated taking a horse and some Marmelukes along the coast, but he knew that was folly as the Bedouin had already been paid to scout on El-Koraim's behalf. He did however idly dream of seeing their first encounter with the French, for some of the tribes in these parts took barbarism to new depths.

A thought struck him like a thunderbolt and he leapt from the bale he had used as a vantage point. He pushed through the crowds, making his way towards the long straight road leading to the square dominated by the house of the French Consul. He had no idea how but he was determined to find someone from that house who was privy to Napoleon's plans.

The once grand square had seen better days but the French Consul's house remained stylish and well maintained. The streets around the house were alive with movement, anxious people going about their daily lives but embroiled in even more animated conversation than usual. Women moved in tight little groups, their high pitched chatter clear, despite their heads being swathed in material that left only their eyes visible. Barefoot and not decently clothed by European standards, they moved through dusty, excrement smeared streets, intent on their private business.

Small groups of poorly equipped soldiers moved with some purpose at least but certainly not urgency. Finding a low wall to lean against, Archie slumped to the ground and tried to merge into the background.

The hum and buzz of the street fascinated him as he observed life passing him by that morning. In a European city, panic would have gripped by now but not here in Alexandria. He could not decide if this was stoicism or more likely a complete lack of understanding at what the arrival of Bonaparte meant for them. The shabbiness of the few soldiers on the streets was no reassurance to him but perhaps the local people had more in the way of blind faith. Just as a small woman, with an even smaller child, struggled by with their impossibly high piles of bright linen, the front door to the French residence opened.

Two local men and the taller European hurried from the doorway and crossed the busy street, heading directly for him. With his heart pounding in his chest, Archie waited until they were almost upon him before he began to make a move, just checking the action in time as the men rushed past and strode away along the busy thoroughfare. Such was the adrenaline rush Archie could hardly stand on shaking legs but stand he did and working the cramps out of his limbs he ventured to follow the men through the crowds.

It was fortunate the European was so tall or Archie would never have kept the party in sight, as they weaved between all manner of human obstacles and courtesy it seemed of the short, rotund Arab, navigated the labyrinthine streets. Archie had no idea where they were within minutes and began to hang back a little, wary suddenly of blundering into a dead end and springing some kind of trap.

Almost without warning, the group of men ducked inside a low gateway set in a long featureless wall, the gate slammed shut and they were gone. Feeling nothing but frustration, Archie walked on to the next corner and found a small market where he was able to mingle with the crowds and wait. The market was selling foodstuffs and aromatic spices that caught his senses, brightly coloured and stored in tall earthen pots. Scattered all around were fruits and strange shaped vegetables, which if they had English names then he was not aware of them.

He was captivated by the clamour and garish colour surrounding him just as he had been when as a youngster he walked these very streets all those years ago. Filthy people dressed in stinking rags, mingled with soldiers and extravagantly dressed merchants. It was in these streets that years earlier he had enjoyed wondrous adventures with good friends such as Karim and Sullieman. The memory overwhelmed him as he allowed his mind to wonder where his childhood friends might be now.

Sullieman had been a year older than him and by way of a series of escapades they had become blood brothers, moving easily together from boyhood to young men in the startling and exciting world that Egypt was, for the privileged few. Sullieman's father was a rich and powerful merchant trading across the Mediterranean Sea and beyond to India and some said, even China.

In an instant the memories burst as the three men walked into the market, now in the company of four other locals. They spared no glance in Archie's direction and he confidently trailed in their wake once more. Within minutes he was passing along streets that were familiar and as they were less crowded, he felt sufficiently assured to allow the group to move some way ahead. Suddenly a sixth sense told him the party had stopped around the next corner, so tightening the robes over his face he took a deep breath and more cautiously strolled onwards.

With some small measure of surprise, he found himself emerging from a narrow alleyway directly opposite the British Consul's residence. The Arabs were in a huddle some way down the street, whilst the Frenchman was engrossed in what appeared to be polite conversation with Farouk, at the front courtyard door. Archie was stunned by this development and only by an immense force of will did he keep walking by.

Unsure of what to do next, he walked around what he was confident was a complete block and moved once more towards the British Consul's house. The gate was closed now and there was no sign of the Frenchman. However, one of his Arab companions was loitering by an alleyway and as Archie continued walking casually by, he noticed a second Arab, sat in the sparse shade of a fig tree that somehow clung to life on the dusty street corner.

Fighting a rising tide of panic, Archie strolled past, keeping alongside a bent old man, hoping to be taken as his companion or perhaps son. He tried with every beat of his heart to think, breath and walk like a local, busy but not rushed. Certain after a while that he was not being followed, he made his way once more to the house of El-Koraim. Cursing under his breath, as he approached the Palace he noticed not one but two of the Frenchman's companions, clearly watching the gates. This ability to pick faces from a crowd was a talent he had known since childhood and he was never more grateful for it than now.

He walked on, uncertain of what to do next, a sick feeling settling into the pit of his stomach, his heart racing painfully. The slow realisation dawned on him that he was truly alone here and may have just become someone's prey! Had the French spies monitored the departure of the British closely enough to realise one man was missing?

He returned to the French house, play them at their own game he thought, settling down to watch, just in time to catch a remarkable spectacle unfold. The pounding of horse hooves and the shrieks of people desperate to escape being crushed into the dirt of the road heralded the arrival of some twenty mounted Marmelukes, splendid figures on their compact horses, snarling stallions which they reined to a clumsy halt before the great house's main gate. In the midst of the cavalry was El-Koraim himself seated on a large chestnut stallion, streaked with sweat and flared of nostrils, in perfect harmony with its rider.

Flushed in the face, El-Koraim leapt from the saddle with surprising agility and strode to the gate. Drawing a long curved sword, he pounded the gate with the weapon's ornate hilt before pausing a while and eventually placing the weapon back beneath his robes. By the time the door was answered, he struck a dignified pose once more and after presenting his credentials was admitted, the large gate closing firmly behind him.

Archie was intrigued and alarmed in equal measure. Praying to all the Gods he knew, he hoped El-Koraim had not just launched a one-man strike at the heart of the French presence in Egypt. Almost laughing out loud, he imagined the scenes as El-Koraim demanded an explanation for the arrival of the French fleet and presumably requested their immediate departure.

Almost two hours passed by as the sun beat down on the anxious but curious crowd. The cavalry were restless but showed no signs of action and as the heat of the day reached its most intense, everyone began to wilt in what shade they could find. Eventually El-Koraim emerged, as red faced and angry as when he had entered, shown off the premises by the same tall Frenchman Archie had followed earlier. Now he was certain, this was the same man who had lurked in the shadows watching assassins cut down the brave sailors.

As the gate closed and the horsemen saddled up and began to leave, Archie pondered his own predicament and did not like the conclusion he reached. Both houses in which he could seek sanctuary were being watched, a sinister Frenchman seemed to dog his every step and to cap it all Napoleon Bonaparte and an invasion fleet lay off the harbour.

*

As the day's heat finally began to relent with the arrival of evening, Archie at last had a semblance of a plan in his mind. The French would surely land at dawn and before then he needed somewhere safe to lie low. Clearly El-Koraim's and the British Consul's residence were being watched, either for him or perhaps more likely, Lieutenant Hardy. He had forgotten about the young officer, presumably now in Cairo but certainly unaware of the fleet's arrival off the coast.

What he also needed were his weapons, telescope and money, which meant getting back into the Consul's house.

If nothing had changed since his childhood then he knew how that could be done.

The wait for nightfall felt interminable but eventually the setting sun turned the sky first a deep blood red then a ghostly purple twilight bathed the town before finally with surprising speed night fell, the heavens pitch black, sprinkled with millions of diamond-like stars. Not bothering to check for the watchers lurking in the shadows, he approached the house from the rear. He climbed the low wall of a neighbouring house, startled momentarily when a dog growled someway off in the gloom of an unseen yard. As quickly as he dare, he shuffled along the wall to the old twisted tree that seemed to grow out from under the very stones of the wall itself.

Slowly he inched up its rough trunk and stretched for the long bough he remembered from his childhood. Too noisily for his comfort, he swung out along it hand over hand until he was astride the rear courtyard wall of the house he had once called home. He half scrabbled and half fell down the wall into a small shrub. He remained motionless, ears scanning the sounds of the night. Somewhere a baby cried and a young girl sang a haunting melody that held his attention for some minutes.

Cautiously moving to the kitchen door, he let himself in. With no light to guide him, he stumbled along a corridor in search of Farouk, desperate not to cause an alarm that might alert the watchers outside. Suddenly Farouk appeared in the gloom, a long knife just visible in his hand.

'Farouk it's me,' he blurted out, 'I need help, I'm being hunted!'

'Master Archie, Allah be praised I was sure you were

dead. The French are here in the harbour,' Farouk whispered. 'They're waiting outside to capture you and Lieutenant Hardy,' he added. 'They think you are both out of the city but say you should surrender to them when you return.'

'Not a chance old friend. I'll sleep here tonight but tell no one else in the household that I'm here. I'll leave at dawn but I need money and somewhere in the city to hide,' he pleaded.

'My brother's house in Il-Koarat is empty, for he's away in Cairo. There is money I can get you and guns if you need more.'

Archie felt a surge of relief and the sudden overwhelming need for sleep, long and deep.

'Go quietly to your room Master Archie and I will bring you food and money. I shall wake you just before daylight, so you can climb that tree once more,' he added with a chuckle. 'How your father never found out that you spent your evenings outside the house with your friends, I will never know?'

Archie squeezed the old man's arm and made his way to his room. He packed both of his pistols, ammunition and a spy-glass into a small bag. He tried to wait for Farouk but exhaustion overwhelmed him and he fell into a trouble free sleep.

Almost instantly it seemed, he lurched awake as Farouk gently shook him. The faithful servant gave him a small bag stuffed with money to wear under his robes. He also gave him a battered leather satchel overflowing with food, some of which Archie devoured hungrily as he dressed.

He embraced Farouk warmly and shouldered his bags, whilst his two loaded and primed pistols he tucked into his belt concealed by his robes. His naval issue sword he left behind but he carried a curved dagger nearly a foot long and a miniature stiletto blade Farouk implored him to take.

'Thank you Farouk. Make sure the staff all know what to say if asked about me. Trust no one that you would not trust your very life with. The French will attack at dawn, of that I'm sure. El-Koraim will have no chance to stop them, Alexandria will fall and Cairo too I expect. It will be hard for Egypt but the French only want to have a base from which to move on to India. They will soon be gone,' Archie explained.

'Take great care Master Archie. I will look out for you visiting the shelter of the garden each night, an hour after darkness falls,' Farouk said, bidding him farewell.

Archie pocketed a crude map Farouk gave him and made his way out by the kitchen door. It was more of a challenge to get back out over the wall but eventually he managed it and disappeared into the warren of surrounding streets. It was almost daylight by the time he found Farouk's brother's house. The crude key took an age to open the door set deep into a crumbling wall but soon enough he was safely inside.

As daylight arrived, he opened the rear shutters and explored the humble but clean house. Beyond lay a small courtyard, which to his relief nothing overlooked. Sitting at a small, roughly hewn table, he ate some of the food he had carried with him and began to rack his brains for a way to see El-Koraim.

His reverie was shattered by the rumble of distant cannon fire. Heart racing, he leapt to his feet, grabbing everything he needed before he left the sanctuary of the house, heading towards the sounds of a fresh volley of cannon fire. Muffled as it was by distance, he could still discern that it was fire emanating from the city, rather than rounds coming in. Citizens were running in all directions, amid much shrieking and hollering. There was yet another shot, this time from a lone cannon and he tried to home in on that sound.

In the distance he could see the city wall, lined with not only soldiers but also men, women and children all of whom seemed to be waving at something and putting up a fearful noise. Away to his left rose a majestic granite column, a relic from the days of Imperial Rome. He pondered whether it could be climbed, as it would make an ideal vantage point but instead he continued to head toward the sound of the guns.

Reaching the city wall, he scrambled up a steep, crumbling stairway and stared open-mouthed at the sight before him. Under the bright morning sun, just out of musket range, were thousands of French infantrymen. Risking drawing attention towards himself, he took his spyglass and scanned the massed ranks of soldiers.

Relieved to a small degree, he saw no cannon, nor cavalry. Clustered together in the distance was a group of officers and there, the centre of attention, he saw so clearly that he felt his heart miss several beats, was Napoleon Bonaparte. As he watched, the group dispersed and as somewhere along the city wall a cannon fired once more, he knew the attack was coming. Astounded, he saw the single cannon ball bowl over a rank of soldiers, nearly half of whom lay writhing in agony or still and broken on the ground as the dust cleared.

Just then the clean, bright air was cut by a series of bugle calls. The French army pulled itself together and separated out into a number of columns, all heading for the meager defences of Alexandria. Drums beat a terrifying, insistent tattoo and the infantry came on and on, amidst a steadily rising cloud of swirling red dust.

The solitary cannon fired once more, felling a dozen more of the leading soldiers but a rattle of desultory musket shots from the defenders appeared to hit no one. Several columns headed towards where the western harbour's fort, lying in a semi-ruined state, stood mute guard. Another column marched through the sand and town rubbish heaps toward the Rosetta Gate, a once proud structure now held fast by sun tormented wooden gates, barely supporting their own weight. Still more columns marched on toward the wall right where Archie stood watching.

It was time to get to safety, so he pushed his way through the crowds lining the wall and made his way to the ground. He darted into a dark alleyway and made his way into the labyrinthine streets and their momentary illusion of safety. Gunfire erupted, echoing all around him down the once quiet streets. Screams and shouts competed with the cacophony of small arms fire and the crash of what would be the final cannon shot ringing out. Confused and mortally afraid he made his way along the largely deserted streets and was soon completely lost.

Finding himself by the harbour once more, he looked back towards the town, only to see dozens of French infantrymen streaming out into the open from the tight maze of streets, driving ahead of them a handful of local militia who soon fell to the ruthlessly efficient French skirmishers. Archie followed the crowd, who were now panicking and running in and out of the tiny streets fringing the water. The French were regrouping, so Archie was soon out of their sight but still trapped within a swirling crowd of terrified humanity. The noise was deafening, the babble of human panic, the screams of terror as children became separated from parents, the bellowing of helpless and hapless adults. The sounds, he remembered, it was always the sounds that came back to him in the night, the din of battle, the cries of fear and the screams of pain followed by the dreadful silence death.

By the time he reached the eastern harbour, the crowds had thinned somewhat but a burst of firing drew his attention to the narrow strip of land leading to Pharos Island. He was truly astonished by what he saw next. A group of twenty dismounted Marmelukes were falling back in good order, pumping sporadic fire from ancient looking firearms into a tight column of advancing French infantry, felling half a dozen in the process. French musket fire dropped several Marmelukes to the stone floor before the diminishing group reached the fort. To Archie's amazement, he now saw that the motley band was lead by El-Koraim no less and after taking two more casualties, the little group reached the sanctuary of the fort.

The French now advanced in open skirmish order but no fire came from the fort's walls. Not until the attackers were less than thirty yards away, taking what cover they could behind the detritus of the quay-side, did a row of weapons appear along the upper wall. At first there was a bright flash and then a cloud of white smoke rolled out from the fort and hung a while in the still air, followed by the crash of the volley which killed at least four Frenchmen and wounded several others. The soldiers pulled back out of range, to be joined by ever increasing numbers of reinforcements.

Archie decided it was time to return to his sanctuary until the situation calmed down. He headed into the city now seemingly overrun by French soldiers, who to a man appeared determined to ignore the civilians, who mostly hurried out of their way, darting into any available doorway or alley.

Working his way down narrow streets and into the hostile tangle of alleys forming the most rundown section of town, he scurried round a corner and came face to face with three French soldiers who seemed startled but not hostile toward him. Before anyone had chance to speak, the small, dark skinned Sergeant staggered backwards with a surprised look on his face, glancing down at the open gory mess of his chest, before crashing to the ground. Archie flung himself left into an alleyway, the soldiers moved to their left too, crashing through the doorway of a small house. Cowering in the shadows, Archie heard screams and cries from within the house followed by gunfire.

A few moments silence was followed by hysterical shouting from somewhere within the house. Open mouthed, Archie watched two young men plummet head first from the roof onto the road below, to lay still, twisted grotesque rag dolls, bleeding profusely into the dirt. More shouts from above preceded the body of a young woman crashing down onto the ground. Groaning hoarsely, she writhed in pain for a short while, blood pouring from puncture wounds all over her body before she stiffened and then lay still.

Before Archie could react, the French soldiers burst out of the door, back into the street, the first man casually spearing the girl once more with his bayonet. Archie moved without thought, without questioning, the familiar terrifying rage building fast within him, the fire burning in his head, a scream trying to force its way past his dry lips. He drew his pistols and unseen in the shadows, opened fire. The first shot took the bayonet wielding soldier in the side of the head, killing him instantly. Firing left handed his aim was untrue and the next shot buried itself in the second soldier's shoulder. He charged straight at Archie, screaming curses in vilest French. Archie easily parried the wild charge and kneed the soldier in the side, whilst trying to get his dagger free from under his clinging robes. As the soldier slammed the butt of his weapon into Archie's ribs, he at last got his dagger free. The first slash went wide but the second caused the soldier to drop his weapon in pain and Archie reacting on instinct, buried the dagger into the man's chest, snapping the blade clean off. The soldier fell against him and they fell in a perverse embrace, the Frenchman twisting and turning for a few moments before lying still.

Archie forced his way out from under the body and tried to stand. Shock kicked in, his heart was racing uncontrollably and his stomach heaved painfully. He collapsed, retching into the sandy drifts at the base of the wall. Reeling from the violence of the last few minutes he collected himself, picked up his fallen pistols and after a last glance at the ripped and broken young bodies, staggered down the road. After a few turns, he forced himself to calm down and take stock. Breathing deeply and slowly, he hurriedly rearranged his robes to cover the large blood stain on his front.

Making his way along the strangely quiet streets, he

contemplated the absurdity of life. He detested organised religion and could not bring himself to believe there was a God but if by chance there was then he was far from benign. How else could it be, that on a beautiful, warm sunny day, a devout young girl had in a few short minutes, passed from life to being hurled from a roof and butchered on the tip of a bayonet?

Fortunately he encountered no one else in the last few minutes of his journey to his refuge and soon he was bolting the door securely behind him. As the shock began hitting him again he collapsed sobbing to the floor. Trembling, he tried to rationalise the last few hours, feeling very scared and utterly alone. What had been a wild adventure until now was suddenly a deadly serious matter. If he was caught now, he would be executed out of hand as a murdering spy. Nelson was weeks away and may not return at all he admitted to himself once more.

'Pull yourself together man,' he raged to the empty house. He knew that as many times before, he had only himself to rely upon and one wrong move would spell disaster.

With shock fading to exhaustion, he slipped into an uneasy but deep sleep where he lay. When he awoke, stiff and bruised on the cold, sandstone floor, darkness had fallen. He listened for the sounds of the Alexandria night but silence mocked him. Rising shakily, he stood for a while in the courtyard, looking upwards at the myriad stars. Finding the remains of his food, he ate every last morsel, not a clever move he realised too late. He retrieved his pistols, cleaning and reloading them by the light of a small oil lamp and searched for a replacement for his knife. In a small cupboard he found a fearsome if slightly

44

rusty, curved dagger, almost a small sword. He cleaned it thoroughly and put it with the rest of his small arsenal. He took everything upstairs and collapsed on the small bed where in an instant he was sound asleep once more.

*

He woke with a start, leapt from the small cot like bed and stood in the centre of the room, a pistol in each hand. His heart was hammering in his chest; sweat glistened on his skin as the rays of sun squeezed past the ill fitting shutters. Several anxious minutes passed before he relaxed and finally recalled where he was and the series of horrors had befallen him in the last few days.

Taking several deep breaths and stretching so hard his spine audibly cracked, he put down the guns and walked slowly from the house to the small private courtyard and relieved himself in the hole that sufficed as a toilet. The courtyard was cool and quiet, the sounds of the waking town muffled by high sandstone walls and two tall but scraggy date palms. He was desperately hungry, his stomach rumbling painfully so he returned to the house. A few meagre pieces of fruit already on the turn in the hot, dry climate had to suffice.

After washing and dressing in clean robes, he tried to keep busy with domestic chores, laundry to be done and floors to be swept. He kept it up for over an hour before he relented and formulated a plan of action. He concluded that there was no option but to blend in with the populace, live a simple life, spending as much time as possible in the safety of his borrowed home. He had convinced himself that Bonaparte would have little trouble controlling the city and would if the citizens cooperated, just leave them be and move on.

Food was a pressing need, so taking a deep breath to steady his nerves, he left his sanctuary behind. On a whim he also left his guns hidden in the bedroom, reasoning that the French may well have set up checkpoints and the discovery of British issue pistols would spell his certain execution as a spy. Once more he wondered if Lieutenant Hardy was riding to the rescue with the Marmeluke hordes in tow. Not likely he concluded and as each hour passed Bonaparte would grow stronger with each boat load of forces he landed.

The streets were alive and bustling with life once more. He wondered at the local people's ability to accept their fate. Small knots of French infantry were on most street corners but seemed strangely relaxed and in the nearest market he saw soldiers paying for fruits rather than looting. The realisation that Bonaparte had decided to pacify the population rather than subdue them gave his spirits a lift. He purchased what he hoped would be a couple of days supply of fruit and vegetables. He ate his fill of a hot spicy stew made from stringy lamb and other things mostly unidentifiable but he left the market in good heart.

Somewhat aimlessly he walked the streets and more by accident than design found he was approaching the French Consul's house once more. A significant crowd was in attendance, not exactly held back but certainly kept in place by a triple rank of French Guardsmen, Napoleon's elite fighting force and personal guard. Clearly the French leader had made this his headquarters.

The crowd was made up of a cross section of town's people from rich merchants and their attendants, to dirty filthy urchins, the smell of whom was only now beginning to seem less than evil to Archie's sensitive nose. As subtly as he could, he began to work his way through the melee until he found himself standing crushed up against a hunchbacked old man. The man had two young women with him, both covered head to toe in black, only their eyes, bright and alert pools of darkness revealing their youth and vitality. More unsettling he found himself nose to nose with surely the biggest, ugliest French Imperial Guardsman in Africa. Avoiding eye contact Archie squinted through the small gaps between the impressive ranks of soldiers.

He was alarmed to see a small detachment of dismounted Marmeluke cavalry lounging outside the front doors, with half a dozen scowling Guardsmen in attendance. He had just begun contemplating an explanation for this development when the big doors burst open and there he was, Napoleon Bonaparte himself, personally seeing El-Koraim to the door.

The crowd fell silent momentarily before an intense babble broke out, rising in volume, close to hysteria in places. The soldiers grew tense then with a quick glance, followed by a half wave, half salute, Bonaparte was gone. El-Koraim mounted his magnificent horse and with his escort in attendance, approached the crowd.

'People of Alexandria, listen to me well. I am still your Sherif and we will prosper! No one will steal your goods and no man will take your women or your sons. We will live with Allah's hand to guide us. Go about your business with no fear in your hearts,' El-Koraim bellowed, without the slightest hint of doubt in his voice.

Archie was dumbfounded. How had El-Koraim even survived, let alone been taken into Bonaparte's confidence? Everything he had heard of Bonaparte was clearly true. In a single masterstroke he sought to control this city through its own leader. Bonaparte had plans way beyond Alexandria and it seemed he had the good sense not to oppress the place by force. However, within the crowds he had heard talk of executions taking place in town squares as reprisals for futile pin prick attacks upon the invaders.

After El-Koraim and his escort had left, Archie was drawn once more to the waterfront and soon he was casting his eyes over a remarkable vista. The harbour was crammed with ships of every size, from stately warships to barely seaworthy hulks that had carried Napoleon's supplies the length of the Mediterranean. A swarm of small boats ferried supplies from the French ships to the shore, whilst those vessels alongside the quay itself, disgorged their cargo directly, some with the help of recently constructed wooden cranes.

Cannons by the dozen were building up on one quay he noted with dismay. Mountains of stores were growing, as locals eager to please and earn money no doubt, helped to carry the chattels of an army away into the town.

Amongst the myriad of small boats weaving around the harbour, Archie watched a group apparently selling to the French ships. He saw food being eagerly hauled aboard, fish, fruits and vegetables of all kinds. Cloth too was being bought, brightly coloured and exotic to the Western eye. The little ships were watched keenly by the ships officers, still wary in this alien world but they did nothing to intervene. The flotilla moved with a kind of organised chaos amongst the French fleet, seemingly under the direction of one slightly more substantial vessel, which required the strength of eight men to propel it around the harbour's crowded waters in lieu of its furled sails.

This boat was currently at the stern of the biggest warship in the harbour and Archie was drawn to the sight of one of the Arabs in animated conversation with an officer who held considerable rank, judging by his uniform braids. Fascinated by this little drama, he followed the boats progress as it weaved its way to the next warship, where the same Arab hailed the ship now towering majestically above him. An immaculately attired officer leant over the side and once more a shouted conversation ensued. After a while a sailor lowered a rope and a hessian wrapped parcel was hauled aboard with some difficulty by three men.

Intrigued, Archie determined to follow the vessel but was disappointed to see it heading for the harbour entrance. He moved as fast as he dared to keep up, actually beating it to the end of the harbour's short protective wall. Finding himself alone, he watched as the crew started to raise small sails in order that they might catch the gentle offshore breeze, which was trying in vain to move the stifling heat of the morning.

The little boat began to pick up speed and as it passed beneath him, the man who was clearly its skipper glanced his way. Sullieman! Was that why he had been drawn to watching the little boat, some kind of subconscious recognition? His heart raced, adrenaline coursing through his body and before he had time to think, as the boat passed by less than four feet from the wall, he felt his body leap and fall through space in a kind of sickening slow motion. Gravity took charge and slammed him into the boat, felling two burly crewmen. In an instant he was

49

pinned and blows rained down on him as daggers were swiftly drawn.

'Sullieman my friend, my friend,' he shrieked, 'it's me Archie, Archie!'

Dazed by a fist striking his face with the power of a hammer, he only partially heard the shouting of commands to unhand him but then everything froze in time as still held by many hands he looked up into the smooth, still boyish face of Sullieman Al-Ateef, without doubt the best friend Archie had ever had. Still partly concussed, he was hauled to his feet and embraced in a near life threatening bear hug, kisses raining down on his cheeks as he looked into the tear filled eyes of his saviour.

'By Allah what is this? My old friend, I thought you English said good morning and shook hands before leaping into any old passing boat,' he said, barely able to contain his excitement. 'I know you promised to visit but like this?'

'It's a long story my friend but needless to say I am more than grateful to see you,' Archie explained, a smile beaming from his face, feeling genuine happiness and some degree of relief at this turn of events. 'We must talk in private and now,' he added in hushed tones, switching briefly to English.

'Come then,' Sullieman said, guiding him towards a small covered area at the stern. The little vessel was now making headway beneath its sail and the crew seemed to have got over the sudden interruption. To a man they were all involved in working the little boat as it headed out into the shimmering haze of the open sea, whilst casting just an occasional wary glance at their surprise guest.

Sullieman fired off some orders and soon he and

Archie were feasting on dates and peaches, washed down with tar like coffee. Archie related his adventures as succinctly as he could but Sullieman like all Arabs loved a yarn and demanded more and more detail, becoming highly excited when he heard of Archie's encounter with French infantrymen in dark alleys.

'El-Koraim has done well to make a kind of peace with the French. That will save the city much trouble. Some have tried to fight and paid a terrible price, it's a time to bend with the breeze, for now,' Sullieman said in measured terms. 'Of course whilst there is peace, there is money to be made,' he added with a laugh that shook his entire body.

Sullieman had taken over his father's business interests after the old man was murdered in a blood feud when the family refused to pay a disputed debt. Such things were common place in Egypt, as was the revenge Sullieman had exacted. As the vessel continued along the coast, Sullieman explained in calm and dispassionate terms how he had systematically removed this other family, whilst absorbing their lands and businesses into his own empire. Archie was not remotely concerned; this was the local way, in England not that long ago, such a dispute would have ended in a duel on Blackheath. The result would have been the same, death and dishonour and to the victor the spoils.

As the diminutive vessel made its way, first out to sea until the coast was just a brown smudge on the horizon and then turned eastwards, Archie and Sullieman chatted like overexcited schoolboys. Archie insisted they speak Arabic as his life depended on his ability to blend into the local population. Only after about an hour of slow progress in the gentle breeze did he broach the subject of their destination.

'My father lost his house in Alexandria but I now have a wonderful farming estate in Palestine,' Sullieman explained. 'I still have the family home in Malta too. Do you remember the weeks we spent there my friend?'

'Heavens yes I do,' Archie assured him with a warm smile, basking in shared memory, 'Napoleon has taken Malta, so they say,' he added, his smile fading.

'No matter,' Sullieman said with confidence, 'we're going to a small island village. I say village, in truth it's little more than an encampment with a tiny harbour where my boats can rest up between trips across the sea. My father lost the grain-stores in the feud he had with Abbas shortly before his death but I make a good living my friend, spices, expensive textiles, anything that is treasured,' he added somewhat enigmatically.

Archie felt his euphoria slipping slightly, life had changed for his old friend and for some inexplicable reason this worried him more than it seemed to be concerning Sullieman.

As the sails finally began to fill out in the stiffening breeze, they began to make steady progress and after a few more hours Archie spotted land ahead. They were around five miles from the Egyptian coast when they approached the low lying but fertile island. It was around three miles in length, by two in width, supporting a surprising number of palms. The scrubby land between was essentially sand bound together with coarse grasses and reeds. Looking toward the mainland he could see numerous smaller islands and by the appearance of the horizon it was clear they were now lying off the delta of a substantial river.

The natural harbour they were entering was crowded with tiny fishing boats and everywhere was a bustle of activity. On the shoreline, a ragged collection of small stone houses made up a somewhat decrepit village and in the trees beyond, he could just make out Bedouin style tents.

They tied up alongside two similar vessels, amid much shouting of greetings and demands for news. The conversation swirled over Archie as he tried desperately to keep up. Everyone knew that the French had arrived and the overriding concern seemed to be how much gold they might have brought to spend.

Sullieman led Archie through the village and a short distance later they came to the tents.

'It's no castle for sure but a home nonetheless, for as long as you need it,' Sullieman said quietly, with a genuine smile.

Archie looked around at the tented village, taking in the industrious scene where men and women laboured over a variety of boxes and vessels, bales of bright coloured silk, textiles from India and barrels of oils and liquors. Beyond them, somewhat incongruously, several women were packing dozens of small marble statuettes into crates. Here was a veritable treasure trove of goods as would be found on most quaysides in these parts, except they were not in any coastal town, they were hidden away on a small island off the coast. Unusually the stevedores and warehousemen in this operation all carried daggers, swords and even pistols.

Smuggling was almost a family tradition for many in this part of the world, so Archie was surprised to feel quite so shocked at this revelation. He watched Sullieman go about his business with frequent glances in his direction, spreading the word that here was a friend.

For the remainder of the day, Archie dozed in the soporific heat but as the evening came he sought out Sullieman and the two men took off on a tour of the island, sharing reminiscences and if truth be told both avoiding the subject of what next? It was Sullieman that felt the urge too strong to resist in the end.

'So what next eh Archie, what next?' he asked, the ever present smile alive and in no way fixed to his boyish face. 'An officer in His Majesty's Guards creeping around with an Arab...trader. What would the General think? 'he added in a stage, mocking tone.

Archie looked pained, not really knowing what to say and somewhat astonished that Sullieman knew so much about his life after he had left Egypt. Smuggling was a crime the world over, smugglers were usually little more than pirates but he loved this man as a brother. Not only that, he needed him as though his life depended on it, which of course it did. Reaching the shoreline once more, they sat upon the upturned hull of a wrecked fishing boat in silence, savouring the slight cooling of the still, heavy air and stared out into an empty, calm sea.

'So, what's to be done my friend, the French are my enemy too. They've taken my country, though that said they're going to be good customers,' he added, a faraway look upon his face. 'Don't get me wrong, I'll make money from them but I want them gone. Tell me this, when will your Navy's fleet return? We saw them depart, some said for Corfu!' Sullieman asked, watching Archie closely.

'Soon I hope, unless I've been abandoned,' he answered, with what he hoped was an easy air. His heart thumped as he tried to control his expression, whilst desperately trying to decide how far to trust his friend. 'If Nelson returns, he will not be able to do much anyway,' he added. 'He has a squadron at his command, no more.'

'Then join me Archie, we will supply the French pigs with wine, women and hash, make our fortune and watch the Bedouin bleed them in the desert sands. I hear that already they have Frenchmen captive further along the coast.'

'Don't ever underestimate Bonaparte because few in France who did, lived to tell of it.'

'He does not know this land, the land itself will devour him,' Sullieman insisted.

'Maybe so, maybe so, 'Archie pondered, 'as for me, I must await Nelson's return and if two months pass then I'll make my own way to Naples. For now though I will accept your hospitality my friend,' he added with a rather forced smile.

'Excellent and so you shall. We shall have adventures anew. We have good food here and even better women,' he said with another belly laugh.

Archie thought this show of bravado was wearing a little thin. Sullieman's family fortunes had taken a severe knock that much was clear. A fugitive from his own lands, a wealthy merchant once but now little more than a smuggler and effectively an outlaw. That said, Archie could think of nowhere he would rather be right now and the situation might yet be turned around. As for Bonaparte, if he could not be defeated, he could at least be taught a lesson or two, if only Nelson returned in time.

The next day, he sailed back to Alexandria with Sullieman and his little flotilla of boats. A healthy trade was made with the many French ships still at anchor in the harbour. Whilst sharing in the work of passing supplies up to the larger vessels, Archie's keen eye noticed that maybe half or more of the warships were no longer present. He scanned the crowded waters and counted just six warships riding at anchor, with one more tied up against a stretch of crumbling, almost decrepit harbour wall. If his memory served him well then it was the 3rd of July, just two days since Napoleon arrived in Egypt. He wondered if Napoleon felt safe enough to send his warships away or whether he was so insecure that he had ordered them to safer waters.

'Sullieman, where have the warships gone to?' he asked, once all the fruit and fish had been handed up to the French, in exchange he noted, for local currency.

'Maybe the eastern harbour, we can look on our return but the waters there are very shallow,' he replied. He too scanned the array of ships, still numbering in their hundreds, both in the harbour and riding at anchor in the calm Mediterranean waters offshore. 'They're mostly empty now, see how high they ride.'

A cursory glance was all Archie needed to see that his friend was quite correct in this. He was convinced that the warships would remain nearby but where had they moved too. At last he felt he had a mission, something useful to keep him occupied.

Sullieman wanted to go ashore, so Archie joined him, taking the opportunity to return to his lair to collect his pistols and a few other possessions. Sullieman met up with two thickset and taciturn men at a busy but run down market. Sensing his presence was not required Archie wandered to the waterfront and confirmed that only a few dozen small French freighters lay at anchor in the eastern harbour. By the time he returned to the market, Sullieman was alone and in high spirits.

'Good news Archie. The French have issued a decree that has prevented all looting and they have bought currency for gold'

'Why does this please you so?' Archie asked, already half suspecting the answer.

'Because they will need to purchase more gold than they have and I will sell it to them for whatever they wish to trade,' Sullieman said with a glint of avarice in his eye and a wry smile of amusement spreading across his handsome features.

Archie slapped him hard across the back, genuinely enjoying his friend's company in these dangerous hours. Surrounded by French soldiery, he should have been afraid but nothing of the kind, he felt he was blending in, bearded and sun browned already, no one would take him for an English soldier thousands of miles from home.

As they made their way back to the boats in the company of locals wheeling handcarts laden with provisions, his attention was drawn to the French infantrymen or rather the almost total lack of them. The dusty, dung strewn streets separating the semi-derelict sandstone and mud hovels were once more dominated by locals. By the time they reached the harbour once more, he was convinced that the number of soldiers patrolling the streets had dramatically reduced. Could Bonaparte have already begun his advance into the Egyptian hinterland he wondered?

The little group of boats maneuvered they way through the still crowded waters of the harbour, passing the two armed sloops now standing guard at the entrance. The

French sailors ignored them as they made their way out to sea, yet Sullieman ordered the little group to sail straight ahead, northwards until they were over the horizon before turning east and beginning the trip back to their island base.

They were back by early evening and made their way through the fishing village and to their tented encampment. As the sun slowly sank toward the horizon, the evening promised much as Sullieman was in high spirits and drink was soon flowing including bottles of the finest French brandy. A lavish spread was prepared, the odours of lamb roasting on spits making the waiting almost too much to bare. With fruit and vegetables recently bought in Alexandria, the women of the camp provided a fine feast.

As the moon rose into the star studded sky, Archie and Sullieman shared a second bottle of brandy, Sullieman lamenting that they had no hash in the camp but more would be arriving tomorrow he was certain. They had been joined by two voluptuous women and Archie was soon comfortably cosy by the roaring fire. He was entangled with a woman called Sheriti who was matching the men glass for glass, as the brandy bottle slowly emptied. She stood a little less than six feet tall, possessed of long powerful legs and a full bosom. Her round, smooth face, framed by thick dark hair, seemed to be permanently lit by a radiant smile. By the flickering firelight, her African beauty captivated and entranced Archie with her irresistible aura of sensuality.

The night passed into tomorrow and Archie found himself with a light head, in high spirits, heading unsteadily towards his tent, Sheriti clinging to his side. The moonlight barely penetrated the inner reaches of the tent and it was in a surreal gloom that the two lovers stripped each other naked amongst the cushions and luxurious silken blankets. Both were practiced in the arts of love and yet Archie was taken aback by the sensual power of the woman's body as he found himself between her muscular thighs, his fingers and tongue eliciting moans of pure delight as he caressed her damp, heavily downed sex.

Sheriti expertly caressed the contours of his rigid erection, administering the most exquisite pleasures with her full lips until long before he was ready, he cried out, arching his body in uncontrolled ecstasy yet never once breaking contact with the core of her womanhood. Relentless he worked for her pleasure until finally she was driven almost beyond reason with orgasmic convulsions, striving to prolong such deep and overwhelming pleasures, almost smothering him with her flesh, giving off the most guttural, feral noises he had heard in a long while.

Much later they were woken by firstly distant rumbles and then sonorous crashes of violent thunder that shook the ground, great bolts of lightning blazing through the tent's thin walls, serving to illuminate their love making with a white hot, stark majesty. Archie was in raptures as they were briefly illuminated then plunged into darkness once more, what a sight to behold he thought, joy singing in his heart, all his troubles momentarily forgotten.

The vivid flashes of light afforded him tantalising brief glimpses of Sheriti crouched on all fours, her pendulous breasts swinging free, her voluptuous backside, round and firm, spread wide as he thrust the full length of his thick erection time after time, deep into her wet sex, the feeling of raw elemental power transmitting itself through the storm's energy to his swollen organ. He laughed out loud, roaring with pure youthful delight as he spurted his seed into her welcoming body.

Exhausted, they lay in each other's arms, dreamily listening to the rhythmic tattoo of the torrential downpour on the tent. For the first time in days he forgot that he was alone, surrounded by Napoleon's army and facing death with the first wrong turn. Soon the warmth of Sheriti's body lulled him into a deep, untroubled sleep.

*

He woke to find he was alone, the early morning sun shining brightly enough through the canvas to blind him, while unseen hammers drummed against the rear of his eyeballs. As he stood, his balance nearly failed him and his stomach fought with his will power but he made it outside to find the camp largely still asleep. Roughly wrapped in his robes, he staggered through the sparse palms and long grass to the shoreline where he stripped naked and ran into the water. Swimming out nearly a hundred yards in an easy but powerful stroke, he turned and floated for what seemed an eternity, trying to make the pain in his head go away before swimming slowly back to the gently sloping beach.

He lay naked in the sand, warmed by the sun and slowly the pounding in his head relented. For a dark haired man, his lithe and well muscled body was largely hairless and had always been a source of fascination and attraction to his lovers over the years.

Memories of the previous night began to surface and a smug smile spread across his face. He flexed his aching back in the sand and allowed himself a mighty yawn. He allowed an image of Sheriti to form in his mind and adrenaline seeped back into his blood stream once more.

'Archie, I have news!' he heard Sullieman call. It was all he could do to raise his head in order to watch his friend walking down the beach but noticing the agitated group of men accompanying him he reluctantly wrapped his robes around his now blissfully warm but sandy body. Somewhat embarrassed, he hopped about trying to remove some of the gritty coating which was already itching maddeningly.

'The French warships,' Sullieman shouted eagerly, 'they're in Aboukir Bay!'

This got Archie's full attention and he sprinted toward Sullieman and his ever present lieutenants.

'Aboukir Bay, where is that?' he asked.

'Not far at all, forty minutes with a fair wind,' Sullieman informed, as eager as Archie to go and see.

'If you remember, I said we must go to Palestine, I have business in Jaffa and father's house is there. We can sail close to the bay and see what the French are up to. If you're right then your Nelson will not return for many weeks, so all we can do is watch and wait eh?'

'When we return from Palestine they may be gone but if not I must get a closer look. Nelson will need to know as much detail as I can give him. He cannot save Egypt from Napoleon but he can still deal him a heavy blow,' Archie told his friend enthusiastically, barely able to contain his rising excitement.

'I'm told that the French are nearly prepared to leave for Cairo, maybe even today,' Sullieman said. 'It seems this Bonaparte is an impatient man.'

'Don't worry my friend, it's not Egypt he wants, his prize is India,' Archie assured him. 'He'll not have it all his own way if the Beys react to the danger in time,' Archie added, 'and if Nelson returns whilst Napoleon's fleet is exposed, well who knows then.'

Together they returned to the camp and after hastily packing, set off with around twenty other men to the little harbour and the boats that waited there. Soon they were at sea, four boats and the largest no match for a Royal Navy sloop in size.

They worked their way along the coast, running against a feeble breeze and Archie scanned the shoreline with a beautifully made telescope lent to him by Sullieman. Minutes stretched into hours and on the smaller boats, oars were brought out to supplement the failing wind.

Eventually he was just able to make out a small fort on a prominent headland. Already the heat was making the air shimmer and the view through the telescope was little more than a blur. Fortunately the gentle movement of the boat on the calm sea did not make the matter worse. As they cleared the headland, he could make out masts, how many it was impossible to say but from what he could see he was prepared to accept that the bay contained a substantial part of the French warship fleet. Whether any of the freighters were still in attendance he could not say, but he thought it unlikely.

As they continued along their way, the view into the bay was obscured by a low lying island. In places it was little more that a shoal and he could see the white water of breaking waves. To the landward side and the western end of the island, vegetation had established a foothold including a number of substantial looking palms. From this distance he struggled to estimate its size but it was some minutes before his view of the bay returned. This time he counted four masts, two of which had sails unfurled.

All too soon the views of the bay fell behind them and Archie was left to sit back against the ship's rail and enjoy the trip. Though he knew there was nothing he could do and should Nelson return then he would most likely find the French fleet on his own, he nevertheless felt he was neglecting his duty. He comforted himself with the thought that Captain Thompson had assured him that Nelson would not return for at least a month. If he recalled correctly then his adventure in Egypt had only lasted four days so far.

As things turned out, his stay in Palestine was to last far longer than he or Sullieman had intend that it should. By the end of what turned into a sojourn lasting nearly three whole weeks, Archie was set fair to burst with frustration. This was despite experiencing a wonderful new land, as Sullieman tended to his business interests.

They had feasted well with Turkish traders through many long nights. Several of these business meetings degenerated into wild bacchanalian orgies with prodigious amounts of potent drink being consumed. This was usually followed by reckless and in Archie's case, successful gambling sessions on the outcome of sports ranging from cock fighting to Turkish wrestling bouts, several of which he took part in, successfully betting against himself to lose and surprising his hosts with his strength and skills.

It was with some sadness and a fair measure of trepidation that he said his farewells and boarded the small boat now laden down with textiles, spices and intricately carved jade jewelry. All the boats rode perilously low in the water as they made their way back along the coast. The land and towns of Palestine were so much finer than the widespread poverty and squalor of Alexandria. It was not only the prospect of what lay ahead as they sailed back towards Napoleon and his invading army that accounted for Archie's reluctance to be sailing away.

As the hours passed, he had a sometimes heated conversation with Sullieman about what was the best course of action. However he finally won a grudging acceptance that if the chance arose then they should assist Nelson to engage the French fleet. Sullieman was all for doing his bit to help Napoleon spend his gold reserves, whilst waiting for the Marmelukes and the desert sands to eventually defeat the French army. Archie eventually persuaded him that his life would be made much easier if the French warships were resting on the sea bed.

To this end, as the little flotilla approached Aboukir Bay, they passed much closer to the barrier island. Archie scanned the barren strip of land with the spy glass and saw not only movement but what appeared to be ramparts. A brief glint of light caused him to flinch and put the scope down just in case the watchers were themselves being watched. Sullieman needed no telling and began to put distance between them as fast as the stiff offshore breeze allowed.

'I need to get onto that island, tonight,' Archie announced, with far more confidence than he felt.

'That's plain crazy, why would you do that?' Sullieman joked, though one look at Archie's face told him his friend was never going to be dissuaded.

'Nelson could be here within days and if he can ambush the French at anchor we can turn this defeat into victory. That island guards the entrance to the bay and you must get me onto it tonight.'

'You've caught the sun my friend,' Sullieman said with a resigned grin.

*

It was gone midnight by the time Archie jumped lightly from the rowing boat that had carried him to shore. After a bitter argument, he had persuaded Sullieman to let him go ashore alone. Armed with his pistols and a pair of daggers, he moved stealthily through a scrubby, grass capped dune and slipped into the inky blackness of a small stand of palms. It took him nearly an hour to creep across the small island and reach the low lying, seaward side.

For the previous half an hour he had caught the occasional glimpse of torches burning some way off in the distance like indistinct fireflies and crawling through the last few hundred yards of cover, he caught the first whisper of voices. His heart was drumming loudly in his chest, his stomach churning as adrenaline coursed through his veins. For the hundredth time he cursed his recklessness because capture meant certain death, shot as a spy at the very least. Still he inched forward because he had to be certain as to what threat this small garrison posed to the Royal Navy squadron, when at last it showed itself.

The coarse grass and scrub was almost at an end but against the phosphorescence of the gently breaking surf, he could make out the line of an unnatural ridge. Just beyond, visible in the flickering torchlight was a row of five tents and close by them was the answer to all his questions. He could just discern the dulled metal, reflecting the yellow light of the smoking torches, two enormous mortars, short-barreled and pointing at a steep angle toward the night sky. These weapons would be formidable opponents to any attacking force passing close by and very difficult to hit as they lay below the level of any warship's guns. He knew they would have to be neutralised if and when Nelson made his appearance.

Peering into the gloom of the bay he could see nothing despite straining his eyes for five minutes or more. He was certain the French ships would still be lying at anchor but none were showing any riding lights. Just then for the briefest moment, in the centre of the bay a light flashed and then was gone, some carelessly revealed lantern no doubt.

The journey back across the island was as hard as his outward trip. He could not afford to relax just in case the French had patrols out. In the event they had none, obviously feeling secure in their control of this part of Egypt at least. A good few hours of darkness still remained when Archie reached the boat. He was rowed expertly back to the sailing boat and the party stole away into the inky back night.

The next morning Sullieman was up and ready to leave by dawn. He had much to trade with the citizens and occupiers of Alexandria. Archie travelled with him but went exploring the bazaars and markets on his own, absorbing the chatter around him. Napoleon he quickly learned had left weeks before with most of his army, great columns of infantry, some cavalry and many artillery pieces had been seen leaving the city. A General had been left in charge of Alexandria and its garrison, but under El-Koraim the apathetic residents were by and large simply getting on with their lives.

He joined the aimlessly milling crowd gathered in the road outside the French Consul's residence and briefly caught sight of the tall, thin Frenchman once more as he left the house with a small escort of soldiers. He tried to take in more of the man, noting the small scar on his chin, the mole on his cheek and the swagger in his gait. Archie slid deeper into the curious crowd until the mysterious man was out of sight. Realising the risk he was taking he abandoned his plans to sneak into the British Consul's residence and see Farouk.

Back at the old harbour, he quietly slipped aboard Sullieman's boat and watched the unloading completed. Mountainous heaps of stores on the quayside were being snapped up by locals but only after a French Quartermaster had purchased the lion's share. Sullieman dealt personally with the rotund little officer before climbing aboard the boat with a bulging satchel of currency.

'Ready to leave?' he asked with a twinkle in his eye. 'Bonaparte has gone to Cairo they say. Word has it El-Koraim has paid the Bedouin to act as the eyes and ears of the French army, but trust me, they'll have taken the gold and scarpered,' he added laughing.

'El-Koraim will also profit well from all this no doubt,' Archie added with a cynical snort.

'Too true and I hear the Bedouin have already been buggering Frenchmen out in the desert. They released some prisoners and their tales have terrified the whole French army,' Sullieman said lightly then more gravely,' but a frightened soldier will stand and fight.'

'How can we find out if Nelson is coming?' Archie wondered out loud. 'Do any fishermen work the waters out toward Malta?'

'It'll be hard to get that information before the French do,' Sullieman concluded as his crew cast off. 'You can rest assured that everyone, including Bonaparte, knows the English will come, so the second they do we'll know about it and if there's time to help, we will. After all, your Admiral will need food too eh?' Sullieman said with his irrepressible and infectious good humour.

Archie could not help but laugh himself at the thought that this was truly what life meant for Sullieman, a quick sales drive, never mind the invasion and a clash of navies, just bring forward the customers.

Two more days passed without incident, Archie having persuaded Sullieman to send out a boat in the morning to head north a while to look for Nelson but to no avail. He did at least have a plan of sorts now and Sullieman had agreed to give him some men to help. When the time came for a showdown, Archie knew his friend would be there with him and sadly he thought, would most likely die by his side.

The 1st of August 1798 dawned clear and bright. Everyone went about the camp's business as usual and as every morning, the little flotilla of boats set off to sell their wares. On this morning they sailed to Rosetta where they rendezvoused with a Moroccan vessel and took delivery of various items of cargo. Archie thought it best never to enquire exactly what Sullieman traded in. As on every day, two boats went to Alexandria to buy and sell goods, the most important purchase being food.

Archie had spent another memorable night with Sheriti and he had to admit that though she was maybe fifteen years older than him, he was becoming very fond of her. There were perhaps twenty women in the camp and village combined, many younger than Sheriti but none had that most rare allure that she possessed.

Having decided to remain in camp, he whiled away

some time exploring the small island and as the midday heat became too much to bear he sought Sheriti's company once more. He made his way down to the little harbour to find her, with a view to retreating to his tent with her one more time. Sullieman's boat he noticed was fairly racing into the harbour ahead of a stiff breeze, Sullieman standing on the bow like a bizarre figurehead, with his hand shielding his eyes giving the impression of noble salute.

'Archie...Archie...come on man!' he bellowed across the water, as soon as he caught sight of his friend. 'They're here!' he shouted, in a state of high excitement.

He could only mean one thing so Archie rushed down to the water's edge to greet him. As soon as the boat ground onto the shallow sandy beach, Sullieman leapt ashore.

'We left Alexandria maybe two hours ago and on the horizon, heading this way were at least a dozen warships. I don't know for sure if they were British though, can we sail to meet them?'

'We can try but if we missed them we wouldn't be able to help. No we must go, whilst we still have time, land on that island and make our way across it so we can attack those French guns as Nelson arrives. If we land at the eastern end then we can remain unobserved.'

'Okay, as we agreed, two boats and ten men go ashore. We must leave now or it'll be too late, your Navy will be there before us,' Sullieman announced before firing off a string of orders.

In a remarkably short time the two boats were being launched once more. Fully crewed and with a fearsome bunch of men, armed to the teeth, they hoisted their sails. Archie had never seen Sullieman's men in action but they had always seemed to him little more than pirates and today they seemed to be spoiling for a fight.

As they moved away, he scanned the little crowd that had gathered but he could not see Sheriti anywhere and with a sickening feeling in his stomach he reluctantly accepted that he may never see her again. With an effort of will he turned away and concentrated on matters that were coming to a head, truly this was do or die and to the romantic fool in his complex, contradictory character, this was a day to live for.

The little boats made good speed ahead of the freshening breeze and by the sun's position, Archie concluded that it was around four o'clock when they made their landing on the eastern end of the barrier island at Aboukir Bay. If any of the French crews had spotted them, no alarm had seemingly been raised. The French warships were riding at anchor, exactly as they had been weeks earlier. Archie sincerely felt for the crews roasting aboard those stinking ships. Sullieman had not been asked to provision them, so he wondered where, if anywhere, they were getting fresh food from.

The heavily armed band made their way stealthily across the most overgrown half of the island. Eventually Archie called a halt and imploring the men to stay lying down and silent, he and Sullieman crawled forward. Reaching the last small clump of bent palms, Archie could see all the way to the island's western tip, across open ground, broken only by low, grass topped dunes.

He gazed at the French camp, a tranquil scene under the searing afternoon sun. To the two large mortars had been added a pair of field artillery pieces, all set within a sandy revetment that partially hid their presence from the sea. Five small tents were dotted around the camp, leaving Archie to wonder exactly how many Frenchmen were present. Most were sheltering from the sun, leaving what appeared to be a watch of just three men.

The two friends lay under the cruel sun for what seemed an eternity, watching a scene of serene inactivity. One of the Frenchmen rose and stretched, yawning expressively. Looking out to sea, he shielded his eyes from the sun then clambered atop the sandbank they had constructed to protect their guns. He jumped back down and walked casually to one of the tents, soon to reappear, now carrying a telescope and in the company of a man who was clearly an officer. Both men climbed the sand bank with some difficulty and took turns with the spy glass.

Archie put his own telescope to his eye, prepared now to risk a dangerous reflection. Sails! On the horizon were sails and mastheads, two of them to be precise. He passed the scope to Sullieman.

'Three ships coming this way,' Sullieman whispered,' why don't those fools react?'

'They can't be sure they're not friendly can they...and nor can we either.'

'I can make out four masts now so it must be the ships we saw this morning, let's just hope that it's your Admiral eh?' Sullieman hissed, giving Archie an almost playful nudge.

Suddenly the French officer came to a decision. His shouted orders carried clearly to the two men and Archie knew that a stand to had just been ordered. Half-naked men spilled out of the tents, trying to dress whilst shielding their stinging eyes from the glare of the late afternoon sun.

71

With impressive speed though, chaos became order and one of the field pieces was made ready. Within minutes the crew members were all in position and after a last look through his spy glass, the officer raised, then dropped his arm. With a ground shaking crunch the gun fired, white smoke enveloping the gun and crew before being carried off in the breeze. With practiced ease the crew reloaded and fired once more. The warning signal given, the rest of the guns were quickly made ready.

'Go get the men but come back carefully,' Archie ordered,' we must wait until the guns are actually attacking our ships before we make our move.'

They had what seemed a dreadfully long wait as the first two warships sailed majestically ever closer. To Archie and his soldier's mind set, everything seemed to move in a curious and frustrating slow motion. An hour or more had passed since the warning shots from the island guns. The two French ships that he could see clearly, had unfurled signal flags and set sails but still rode at anchor. As the two leading British warships finally slid past the island, showing great restraint, the gunners waited until the first ship was almost past before opening fire.

The colossal roar initially stunned the waiting men, followed by a billowing cloud of smoke momentarily obscuring the gun emplacement in its entirety. Archie and his party moved forward at a running crouch, Archie praying these two ships would not return fire and catch them in the open. The French gunners were hastily reloading their weapons unmolested by return fire. It was impossible to judge if the British ships had received any hits in the opening engagement. By the time the second volley rang out from the French guns, the first ship was safely past. Smoke hung heavily in the air and the gunners were franticly reloading as Archie and his ragtag army charged into the French encampment, surprise absolute.

Showing discipline that would have done a Guards regiment proud, Sullieman and his men ran with Archie until they were no more than thirty yards from the French guns. Some knelt, most stood but all had no qualms about opening fire before most of the French gunners even realised the danger from their rear. Archie knelt and hoisted up the fearfully heavy musket, a locally built copy of the 'Brown Bess'. He squeezed the trigger and only when the smoke cleared did he see his target, the French officer, squirming on the sandy floor. A ragged fusillade of shots cut the air like a burst of fire crackers, the stench of gun smoke acrid and painful in his nostrils as he watched gunners fall right across the camp.

He ran on, trying to sling his musket at the same time. One of the gunners was trying to prepare his own musket but was felled by a ball smashing into his leg. Archie drew one of his pistols and fired, missing a gunner armed with a long straight sword. Scrabbling for his second pistol, Archie fired just as the man charged at him with the sword held high. His shot caught the soldier high in the chest and he fell as though poleaxed. The heavy ball fired by the Light Dragoons issue pistol was lethal at less than twenty feet, now armed only with his dagger, Archie ran on.

'Stop...stop...now!' he yelled at Sullieman's men, as the remaining Frenchmen raised their hands in desperate surrender. One chose flight and was shot at point blank range by one of Sullieman's savage looking sailors but the rest restrained themselves. Within minutes they had captured the half dozen remaining gunners, trussed them up with strips of their own uniforms and then set about looting both the men and their camp.

Archie left them to it and looked across the water in awe as more of Nelson's warships sailed into view. Suddenly he remembered the orders given to his beach party and looked away to the east. Sure enough three, thick black columns of smoke rose into the air, now all he could hope for was that the signal would be recognised and he would get the chance to rejoin the squadron. First however, Nelson's ships had to be victorious.

He set off at a slow trot along the water's edge to find a vantage point and watch the battle unfold. Time was passing and as far as he could tell not one shot had been fired by either Navy. Minutes ticked by as the leading Royal Navy warships slowly closed on the anchored French fleet, while yet more warships silently entered the bay. This encounter was going to be decided right here, that much was obvious.

Eventually, the first two Royal Navy vessels sailed slowly between two of the French ships and with an ear splitting crash, an exchange of fearsome broadsides began. For the first time in many weeks, Archie was quite delighted to be separated from his companions. There was no romance in cowering in a floating coffin, wondering if the next cannon ball to strike the hull would launch foot long splinters through the air to rip your body to pieces. He had not prayed in years but he began right there on the beach, it certainly could not hurt he thought.

The battle raged for hours and continued as night fell. The roar of cannons was incessant, as was the destruction continuous. As ships were partly, then completely dismasted, they drifted aimlessly but still fired their surviving guns. The dark bay was illuminated by one of the biggest ships, well ablaze. All Archie could do was to speculate that it was French, purely on account of its size. The normally ebullient Sullieman was unnervingly quiet; his men too, despite having liberated a quantity of brandy from the French camp. To all the men on the beach that warm summer's night this was a new experience, to be witness to slaughter on an epic scale.

Several more hours passed and the bombardment continued with little signs of abating. After what Archie estimated was nearly four hours of continuous battle, there came across the water, first a vivid orange flash, followed closely by an unearthly thump that shook the ground and moved the very air the small party breathed. They all stood and watched in dumbstruck astonishment as flaming debris arced through the night sky, landing with a whoosh in the sea or a crump as some unfortunate ships were struck and set alight. In the flickering light of the fires they could see that the explosion had removed one of the ships and of course it's crew, from the battle forever.

For a while, the cannon fire slackened but over the next few hours it steadily intensified once more. By the light of burning timbers, two ships could be seen leaving the bay but the party on the beach could only speculate as to their nationality. As the cannon fire diminished, Sullieman decided they should leave and ensure the prisoners were secure before they made their return to the landing point. One of his men knew the form and successfully spiked the French guns. The survivors of the attack were herded into a tent which was roughly tied shut to ensure they stayed put, for a while at least. Anything of value and all the looted firearms were shared out and the raiding party, unscathed to a man, began the return journey across the island.

Reunited with the boat crews, they made fast the booty and amid much back-slapping and sharing of brandy, everyone looked to Sullieman and Archie for the order to take to the boats. The first fingers of dawn's, suffuse grey light were just stealing over the horizon and Archie could make out a ship that appeared to be heading in their direction. He had it in his spyglass straight away and urged calm.

'Get the boats off the beach but no more... I'm sure...yes I think it's the Leander, the frigate I came from England on,' he assured the nervous men.

As the warship approached to within five hundred yards, the beach party watched as an anchor splashed into the clear, blue water and shortly afterwards a rowing boat began to make its steady journey to the shore.

'Archie my dear friend,' Sullieman said with a shaky voice,' this looks like goodbye once more. It's been such a grand adventure let's hope the Gods have more plans for us eh?'

'It will be so Sullieman, I feel it in my bones,' Archie managed to get out, tears welling in his eyes.

'There'll always be a place for you here and this Napoleon will be gone soon. I'll bankrupt him before too long.' Sullieman joked.

'Don't underestimate him. The French can be vicious bastards when riled!' Archie warned, holding his friend in a tight grip.

Glancing out to sea he saw the rowing boat was now only a hundred yards from the beach. Six sailors toiled over the oars and crammed in amongst them were six

Marines. He gave his friend a last tearful, rib crunching hug and with a sad smile added, 'Please say goodbye to Sheriti, no make that farewell, until we meet again, she's a true Egyptian wonder.'

Sullieman slapped him on the back and they giggled together like school boys once more. Archie looked across at the rowing boat approaching the beach, a marine now standing on the prow, ready to jump ashore. The man suddenly executed a slow forward roll over the bow into the water, a bloom of crimson blood smearing the surface around his body.

A ragged volley of shots rang out causing Sullieman's men to fan out with impressive speed, preparing their weapons. Archie hit the sand as around a dozen French infantrymen emerged from the tree line, struggling to reload their muskets as they closed on the beach, staggering through the deep, clinging sand of the low dunes.

Sullieman's men opened fire, getting around six shots off, felling three Frenchmen but still the remainder came on. The Marines opened fire with a disciplined volley, which at a range of little more than thirty yards dropped five more of the French infantry onto the sand. The survivors turned and ran with their still unloaded weapons useless. They had opened fire at too great a range and paid the price of their impetuosity.

Archie had prepared his musket but had no targets then in a heart stopping moment he saw, barely visible amongst the running infantry, the tall, thin civilian who had dogged him ever since his first night in Egypt. He was dressed in light coloured civilian clothes, incongruously set off with an infantryman's stovepipe hat. Hurriedly Archie fired from a prone position and as the gun smoke cleared he saw the man, clearly wounded, being dragged to safety by two of the soldiers.

He found himself surrounded by Marines, franticly reloading their muskets. Sullieman and his men boarded their boats and with no small difficulty manhandled them off the beach. Satisfied that the French were not about to launch a second attack, the Marines and Archie clambered aboard the rowing boat and as one unit the sailors pulled on the oars to back off the beach.

Archie risked standing in the boat to give Sullieman a wave, which was heartily returned, before a Marine ordered him to stop rocking the boat. Reluctantly he complied as he watched his friend turn to direct the little boat to sail away from them. Undoubtedly spurred on by this timely reminder that the French were certainly not defeated in Egypt, the oarsmen rowed hard for Leander. In no time at all, Archie was scrambling back aboard the warship that had brought him to such an adventure and undoubted danger but a miraculous reunion with his childhood friend.

The crew of HMS Leander worked at a frantic but disciplined pace to prepare her for sail and by the time Archie had got his bearings, the vessel was slowly making way.

'Captain Dexter Sir, welcome back aboard and with Captain Thompson's compliments, would you care to use my humble quarters to make yourself presentable and then attend him in his cabin if you please,' rattled out a proud looking Midshipman Farthing.

'Good to see you again,' Archie replied jauntily, following him below.

A little under an hour later he found himself not standing before but sitting with, Captain Thompson in his private cabin at the ship's stern. As he gave a cold, factual account of his adventures and an assessment of Napoleon's grip on Egypt, he found himself pushed to elaborate by Thompson, a man who was clearly a romantic at heart and who was enjoying such a fantastic tale of daring do.

Archie was not afraid to praise Sullieman and his men, whilst glossing over their smuggling activities. He felt sure that having a good word from the Royal Navy might one day keep Sullieman from the gallows. The Leander was carrying Nelson's dispatches to be returned to London and Thompson insisted that Archie formulate a written report of his one man campaign against Napoleon.

Over the following days the Leander sailed on under azure blue skies. Archie, in the fortunate position of having no role in sailing the vessel, was able to relax and take the opportunity to write a formal report of his adventures since leaving the ship behind, just over a month ago. As he wrote, he reflected on the astounding good fortune that had seen him not only survive but also play a small part in Nelson's triumph.

Days passed under variable, light winds and the Leander made little progress in her passage. Two weeks had passed and Archie was bored to distraction as they approached the island of Crete. The strong sun produced almost unbearable conditions below deck, even for an officer. The heat, combined with the awful stench of men's bodies, hot timber, rotting food and tar, meant that he spent as much time on deck as possible. Thus he was idly passing the time, leaning on the rail watching a school of long silver fish, when the cry went up.

'Sail Ho!' hollered a man perched almost at the very top of the mainmast, 'astern and gaining!'

To a man, the crew on deck peered toward the ship's stern. At deck level, Archie could just make out the faintest smudge as a spyglass was quickly taken aloft.

The call came back down, 'It's a warship, dead astern and under full sail!'

There followed an anxious few hours and a number of course changes but it became clear that not only was the mystery ship gaining on the Leander, it was also following each change of course. Captain Thompson had no more sail to use, so there was nothing more he could do except sail the ship as efficiently as he could. The crew, depleted by injuries from the recent battle, made the ship ready for combat once more. The consensus of opinion as the ship slowly overhauled them was that she was French and coming for them.

While the crew frantically worked to outrun their pursuer, Archie had nothing to do but deal with the churning terror building in his stomach. He had watched the battle in Aboukir Bay, witnessed the senseless slugging match that was naval warfare. To his mind there was nothing a man could do to prevent his own death, as the lethal iron balls struck the ship. Worse still, he would not even have the distraction of fighting to help him stay sane. The tension built inexorably within him as the gap between the two ships slowly closed.

Several hours passed before the crew of the Leander had identified their stalker as a seventy-eight gun French warship. With less sail, the Leander could not out run her and battle was inevitable.

As the French ship closed to within five lengths of them, Captain Thompson decided to take the initiative. The French ship would eventually pass two hundred yards off Leander's starboard side. Thompson had the Leander steer sharply to starboard across the bows of the French ship. As the ships crossed, Thompson ordered first the foreword guns and then the aft guns on the starboard side to open fire. The bow of the French ship offered a small target but she was hit, railing and parts of the foremast crumpling under the heavy iron balls. The fight had begun.

The two ships tacked and turned, broadsides rang out and the death toll mounted. Archie found himself a musket and began trying to pick off enemy sharpshooters, perched high in the French rigging. He tried and largely failed to blot out the horror all around him. The constant hammering of the guns shook the deck and his innards turned to jelly as renewed terror gripped him. Blinding smoke stung his eyes and then came the crunching, violent crash as cannon balls struck the ship beneath his feet. Rigging crashed to the deck, crushing those sailors not already torn apart by cannon balls. He saw one of the officers cleaved in two, his lower body standing mockingly for just a second, as his torso was blown clear into the sea.

For what seemed an eternity the two ships hammered at each other. Archie had just felled an officer on the French vessel when he heard a sickening scream and saw Mid-Shipman Farthing fall to the deck, right alongside his Captain. He ran to the young man, who was still screaming fearfully before suddenly falling strangely silent. Blood was pouring from a gaping wound in the young man's chest. Archie and a sailor half carried, half dragged the wounded man below deck in search of the surgeon. They found themselves walking straight into a vision of hell. Where the surgeon worked, dead, mutilated bodies lay alongside the pitifully whimpering and ear piercingly shrieking wounded. Most had limbs missing or foot long shards of wood protruding from their destroyed bodies.

They attracted the blood soaked surgeon's attention and heaved the unfortunate young man onto a trestle table. Suddenly conscious and with a burning determination in his still bright eyes, the young man grabbed Archie's shirt front.

'The dispatches Sir, get them from the Captain's desk, throw them overboard, we are lost...lost,' he shouted, struggling to be heard above the cacophony of dying men's screams and the thundering guns.

'Do something for him, anything please,' Archie pleaded with the cadaverous looking surgeon and then made his way shakily to the Captain's cabin in the stern.

He staggered on quivering legs along a dingy companionway, just as the Leander took another full broadside. The hull shuddered under the impact, smoke and dust filling the air, choking him as he tried to keep his footing aboard the rolling warship. Somehow he reached the Captain's spacious cabin and slipped inside.

He looked around, struck once more by the contrast of the relative luxury, the leather chair behind the colossal desk, the neat cot, pyjamas correctly folded on the soft pillow. The only things awry were some fallen papers and broken glass from the shattered windows in the fantail. On the desk was the wooden box containing not only Nelson's dispatches to the Admiralty but his own report, none which he thought the French should read. As the Leander lurched once more and swung violently to port, he grabbed the box, smashed the lock with his pistol and hurled it and the papers through the broken window and away into the sea.

Heading towards the door, he took one last look around and then as he felt the Leander come to a stop, he made his way back down the companionway, drawn to Mid-Shipman Farthing's side, unable to bear the thought of the young man dying alone, as die he surely would.

Half-way there, a painful, crashing percussion shook his body to its core, as the ship absorbed yet another broadside. He felt himself pirouette at lightning speed, his left arm whipped violently around him as he was spun into the wall. The noise inside his head as it struck the hard timbers was even louder than what would turn out to be the final broadside now firing from Leander's guns. Lights, bright and whirling, danced before his eyes before inky blackness descended mercifully over him and his body surrendered to a glorious, warm feeling of peace.

When he came to, he realised he was not dead but immediately wished he was. He was lying on a table, back in the hell's kitchen amongst the screaming, whimpering casualties of the battle but he struggled to understand why he was there. His fuddled mind realised that the ship was stationary and the guns had fallen silent. He was just beginning to work out the meaning of all this, when a thunderbolt of burning agony raced up the inside of the bones in his left arm and proceeded to tear his brain apart. He screamed, so loud and so long, that his throat felt like it had ripped open. He lifted his left arm and looked in horror at his hand, hanging in two pieces, cleaved down the middle as though by a surgeon's knife.

'Hold still old man,' the calm voice of the surgeon, David Wilkes urged him, 'it will have to come off you know!'

'No... no way... bind it together, it'll heal, I know it will,' Archie begged him, his head spinning, the pain coming in nauseating waves, never ending and growing with each passing moment, as they broke on the shoreline of his very sanity.

'It will not heal, believe me it'll kill you! Hey you there, I need you,' the Surgeon shouted to a gore soaked sailor,' hold him down.'

At that very moment, French sailors burst into the room, punching and kicking British sailors and the helpless wounded alike. Wild eyed they eagerly grasped any bottles of medicinal rum they could find, even snatching the surgeon's saws and knives. One man aimed a punch at the surgeon himself, knocking the poor man to the deck. Archie struggled to reach his pistol, the rage building in him as never before. He would kill them all he vowed but he was so weakened, he could do nothing to prevent a French sailor from calmly taking the weapon from him, too weak even to speak. The blood-lust in the French sailors was fading and with their booty gathered in, they left the dead and dying behind. The surgeon slowly came to his feet, looking around for his stolen tools and anyone who could help him with his patient.

Archie, delirious with pain and shock, tried to fight the Surgeon as he attempted to examine his smashed hand. Desperate, the Surgeon cocked his fist and the last thing Archie felt was a crushing blow to his chin.

*

CHAPTER 2

LONDON 1804

The open cab came to a slightly hesitant halt amongst many others pulling up before the impressive frontage of Devonshire House, nestled in its own spacious grounds in London's Piccadilly. The home of William Cavendish, the 5th Duke of Devonshire was on this late spring evening, the setting for one of the society events of the year. A tall, dark haired man stepped lightly down from the carriage and watched as it slowly moved away into an area where numerous other carriages were waiting.

Elegantly dressed and moving with an athletic grace, the man showed his ostentatious, gold embossed invitation to the footmen at the open doors and made his way inside. He followed the line of servants along a wide corridor, illuminated by hundreds of candles and as many oil lamps again. As he walked, he was watched by the stern faces of the Duke's ancestors, cold lifeless eyes glaring down from within heavy gilt frames.

Carried along in the tide of guests, he admired the beauty of the tall, raven-haired woman ahead of him, whilst trying to concentrate on picking out one particular face in the crowd. Dressed in a tight fitting long black coat and fashionably high collared white shirt, set off with an outrageously lurid cravat, he flattered himself that he was attracting a number of admiring glances. Somewhat controversially, he favoured the tight dark trousers that were all the fashion, courtesy of London's famous dandy Beau Brummell.

At the door to the immense ballroom, a footman made to take his hat and gloves. The hat he handed over in but he ignored the man's entreaty that he should remove his white gloves. He took the small ticket and simply glided past the flustered young man before skillfully avoiding the extravagantly dressed master of ceremonies who was announcing the guests. The Duchess of Devonshire sat with her husband on a small dais at the end of the room, waiting to be personally introduced to the chosen few.

Taking a proffered drink, he forced himself to mingle. The early evening passed in a pleasant haze of small talk and mild flirting with a curvaceous young lady, who was almost as tall as he was. A stern faced older woman hovered at her shoulder and when he invited the young lady to dance, she intervened with a well timed observation that the girl's uncle was waiting to talk to his favourite niece. Flushing with embarrassment she was whisked away, leaving him to resume his scan of the crowd, so many couples now whirling and weaving around the dance floor, a surreal kaleidoscope of colours and motion under the flickering lights.

He had just taken another drink from a passing tray bearer, when his attention was drawn to the man being introduced to the Duchess at the far side of the room. The man was tall, almost slender in build, devastatingly handsome, with unusual naturally blonde hair. He had at once the appearance of a feckless youth and a serious, somewhat intense young man. He was in fact thirty two but looked some ten years younger, especially when as now, dressed in a style both debonair and risqué.

'Well, well and what a pleasant surprise good Sir,' a sweetly provincial accented voice, whispered in the distracted man's ear.

Whirling round he found himself in the company of a petite young woman, dressed in a dazzling navy blue ball-gown, extravagantly trimmed in fancy lace works. Looking down at her perfect, almost elfin face, framed by lustrous, chestnut brown hair, he was unable to avoid casting a quick glance over her expansively exposed and bountiful breasts. He found his breath momentarily caught, quickly recovered and put a name to the vision.

'Cordelia...my heavens, you are a delight on the eyes indeed,' he said, whilst taking and kissing her tiny gloved hand.

'You have been a stranger of late, you naughty man, it has been what, six years or more since you last paid your compliments, off fighting some dreadful war I heard,' she twittered merrily, enjoying his discomfort. She struggled to recall the details of the story, but The Times had labeled him a hero, as had King George no less. She knew that he was a bounder, a cad, doubtless a liar and a cheat and yes, she knew for sure she would fall in love with him in an instant, given just a modicum of encouragement. Suppressing a grin she recalled that she had heard that he was the most skilful of lovers and how she longed to shake off the dreadful propriety that held back women of her standing in society.

'I've been back in London for two years now, surely it's you that have been distracted my dearest Cordelia,' he whispered mischievously.

'As I'm certain you well know I have been in Spain with father but we've been forced to return for a while, the people have turned quite beastly. Damn that jumped up Bonaparte and all his little men,' she cursed, tears welling up in her eyes.

'Don't worry, you're safe in London and don't for one minute think that these rumours of invasion will amount to much,' he assured her, gently touching her arm, hoping that she would not read the lie behind his smile.

'He's evil, all those poor families forced to live on charity in dreadful hovels across London. I hate them and their vile revolutions,' she hissed, the anger genuine and heart-felt.

'Hardly hovels my dear but I know what you mean, now come please, let's dance.'

As he guided her gently towards the dance floor, he swept the crowd for the blonde man and sure enough there he was, paired with a statuesque woman of some years his senior, whirling with commendable grace across the floor.

'Cordelia you look majestic as ever my dear,' he opined, taking her petite hand. As they danced, she chattered on about mutual friends and her longing to return to Spain but he was barely listening, his attention held by that handsome blonde head across the dance floor.

'I said, are you listening?' he heard her say, smiling up at him. 'Father will be furious when he sees me with you,' she added, the sparkle in her eyes suggesting her amusement at the prospect.

'Oh never mind him dear, he never likes anyone who gazes upon his beautiful daughter,' he said lightly. Looking down at her, a sudden lustful feeling gripping him, she really had blossomed into a stunning young woman whom he should most certainly have bedded, had she not been the daughter of one of the most ferocious men in the Kingdom.

'Oh you really are quite my most favourite wastrel you

know,' she laughed. 'I'm almost tempted to run away with you for a night of unbridled lust, just to watch my father blow his top.'

In such a manner he passed a most delightful, flirtatious evening of fine food and drink in magnificent surroundings, spent he realised in rather naughty and now suddenly grown up company. The evening included becoming reacquainted with Cordelia's father, who was surprisingly pleasant. From inherited wealth in Somerset, Sir Greville Hendricks had become Lord Hendricks on the death of an uncle he had never met and was now a fulltime politician and close ally of Pitt. He also counted the tall man's father as a close friend and therefore was privy to most of his faux pas, of which there had been many over the years.

Once more on the dance floor with Cordelia, he sought in vain to catch a glimpse of the tall blonde man. He rather awkwardly moved Cordelia around as much of the ballroom as possible in order to find the missing dandy.

'Father seems to have forgiven or forgotten your sins, you lucky man,' she laughed.

'Sins... surely not,' he replied casually, sparing her luscious form only a brief glance as he scanned the dance floor with increasing desperation.

'Sins I say Sir,' she mocked. 'Sent down from Oxford then almost court-martialled by the Guards and ever since, what, spending your allowance on loose women and wine eh?'

'Not fair old girl or true, hurtful actually,' he protested gently.

Suddenly he caught sight of the blonde man just as he was passing through a doorway in the far corner of the vast room. It seemed the man could not help himself pass a furtive backwards glance as he made his exit.

'Would you excuse me my dear, call of nature.' With a swift kiss to her hand and a look that was rather more dismissive than he intended, he left her somewhat flustered and alone amongst the gaily dancing throng.

He moved easily but swiftly between the swirling couples on the dance floor. Once through the doors to where the bathrooms were located, he glanced briefly behind him and then walked hurriedly along the corridor, before bounding up a gracious curved stairway, three steps at a time. Following a building plan held in his head, he moved rapidly along another long hallway, again lined with more miserable looking ancestors of his Grace. Moving silently over the deep, burgundy carpet, he came to a dead end and with a quick look back, he entered the room on the left, almost but not quite closing the ornately carved and gilded door behind him.

He waited, the faint sounds of the ballroom still reaching him as he stood in the darkness, a mild scent of expensive perfume teasing his nostrils. This was clearly a lady's bedroom, oh the scandal he thought with a grin, not just any lady's bedroom but Lady Devonshire's herself. He took deep, regular breaths but he could not slow his pounding heart. Minutes passed and impatiently he waited.

At last, he saw the door across the hall opened slightly and then after a cautious pause, the blonde man slipped out furtively, closing the door gently behind him. Pausing for a count of twenty, he came out into the hall and set off in pursuit, spotting his quarry once more as he reached the foot of the stairs. By the time he reached the ballroom, the blonde man was clear across the dance floor, ungallantly excusing himself from a doe-eyed young woman and continuing his rushed exit towards the main entrance of the house.

Cordelia tried to intercept her erstwhile dance partner but he manfully ignored her and left her furious in his wake. By the time he reached the main door of the house, the blonde man had already left but he caught the briefest glimpse of him in a carriage, drawing away from the house. He made a furious hand signal towards his own diminutive carriage and with a crack of his whip the driver bid the horse to fairly race across the front drive and pick up his passenger. Within seconds they were away into the deepening gloom, the driver's eyes locked onto the wildly swinging carriage lamps of the blonde man's ride.

The streets of this area of London were wide but dark, the traffic light. The two carriages made their way slowly along the poorly lit road, the moonlight making only the slightest impression on the otherwise impenetrable darkness between the sparse oil lanterns. Occasionally they would pass other carriages whose headlights cast a dim glow to see by or they passed through a pool of pale yellow light reaching out to the edge of the road from a door left open, perhaps to ventilate the smoke filled rooms of an ale house or theatre.

Without warning the first carriage came to a halt and the blonde man jumped down. Slipping inelegantly in the inevitable pile of horse excrement, he crossed the road, heading for the open door of a tavern. The tall man slid down from his own coach and followed the man inside, discreetly utilising a door on the opposite side of the small, corner building.

The low ceiling and thick, rolling clouds of blue

tobacco smoke made it difficult to see more than halfway across the single room. There was a good-natured crowd in attendance and the noise level was unbearably high. The alehouses of this part of Holborn were considered quite respectable and generally safe for a stranger to enter. Presently, with a foaming mug of ale in his hand, he made his way around the crowded room until he located his quarry, sitting alone in a corner alcove. Positioning himself on one corner of a long bench occupied by two elderly gentlemen, he waited and watched.

Ten minutes passed before he was rewarded with the sight of another man joining the blonde man at his table. The new arrival was young, perhaps twenty-five years old, slight of build with a long mop of greasy hair, half obscuring a dreadfully pockmarked face. While listening to the blonde man's rapid fire speech, he gulped at a mug of ale, spilling almost as much as he managed to slip past his lips. All the while his head turned, left, right, left, right and back once more. One very nervous man, thought the observer idly.

Suddenly the blonde man was standing, a small leather document holder passed quickly across to the younger man, who snatched it up and slipped it under his coat. Not one to stand on ceremony, he poured more of his ale down his throat, the rest down his front and spun on his heels toward the door. The tall man followed, noting the once fine dandy had slumped back into his seat with a dazed and infinitely sad look upon his handsome face.

The young man hurried down the dark side street, huddled close into the walls of the shops he passed. The tall man moving with long easy strides, rapidly caught up with him and satisfied himself they were alone on the quiet, pitch-black street.

'You there, hand that over in the name of the King,' he said in a quiet but menacing tone, whilst grabbing the man's collar.

Expecting resistance, as the smaller man lashed out at him, he aimed a powerful blow to the side of his head. The young man staggered but recovered with surprising speed and plunged his hand inside his coat. In the gloom the concealed pistol was never clearly visible but the tall man lashed out once more, this time with his left hand, catching the man's face, shattering his jaw in three places, teeth and blood spraying through ruined lips.

The force of the blow had utterly stunned the man but on reflex he continued drawing his pistol. In a heartbeat the other man's right hand slipped a long thin blade up into the young man's chest. Hearing the pistol fall to the ground, the tall man held onto the rapidly dying man in a tight embrace against the window of a cobblers shop. Leaving the blade buried to the hilt, he put two fingers to his mouth and let out a piercing whistle into the darkness.

His small carriage came clattering down the road and shuddered to a halt. The driver leapt down and between them they bundled the dead body aboard and in less than a minute were moving off once more.

Desperately trying to slow his breathing and prevent himself throwing up, he let the rage subside. Breathe...breathe... he told himself and gradually his racing heart slowed perceptibly. As the carriage clattered along to nowhere in particular, he regained control of his body, fighting a desperate, irrational urge to defecate or vomit, he was not sure which.

'Tom...head toward the river, somewhere quiet,' he

ordered the driver, his voice somewhat shaky. Carefully he removed the blade from his victim, the hiss of air from the man's punctured chest was almost his undoing and only by taking extended deep breaths was he able to control his nerves. He cleaned the thin blade on the dead man's coat and returned it to the concealed sheath in his belt. He then quickly recovered the leather folder and methodically removed everything else he could find in the man's pockets.

What followed was a harrowing and surreal journey through the dark London night in the company of a dead man. He did not even know the man's name and yet he had just cut him down in a respectable London street. He had no doubt though that this man had intended to kill him where he stood, so as he tried to unwind, he felt his conscience was clear. However the rage, that terrible, frightening rage was still there, getting stronger and it terrified him more each time it made its presence felt.

The night was growing chilly and even the violent motion of the cab as it crashed and bounced over the rough London roads could not prevent him from falling asleep, as his body relaxed after its lethal encounter. Such had been the speed with which tonight's operation had come to its climax there had been no time to make an elaborate plan beyond capturing the man who received the package. The office simply did not have the manpower to spare more than the two of them, so a disaster was always possible. However, the evening had been something of a coup and if he were allowed to carry through all his plans then the rewards would be momentous.

The carriage came to a stop, snapping him from his reverie. With the aid of Tom, his driver, he managed the unsavoury task of getting the dead man out of the carriage and over the low wall before letting the unfortunate soul fall into the river. With no backward glance they climbed back aboard and set off into the night once more.

*

As Tom was turning the carriage to leave the Thames embankment, some of the most powerful men in England were sitting down in a private room at the exclusive Brooks Club, on London's St James Street. The elegant surroundings suited these men perfectly as they were the very epitome of solid, timeless, establishment figures. The Prime Minister, William Pitt, did the honours and handed out expensive cigars to his fellow diners. They had eaten well on the finest game London had to offer at this time of year and after a seemingly never-ending series of courses, their appetites were well satisfied.

Throughout the club, highbred gentlemen were retiring to private rooms, where more than likely over a game of whist, they would broker business deals or manipulate the future of whole countries whilst consuming the very finest brandy, French of course.

Pitt sat down in a high backed leather-clad chair and whilst preparing his cigar, studied his companions closely.

Seated opposite him was Lord Hawkesbury the Home Secretary, next to him Lord Harrowby the Foreign Secretary and finally Viscount Melville the First Lord of the Admiralty.

'That was a fine meal Hawkesbury, I have only tasted finer game pie at your own dinner table,' Pitt asserted, through a cloud of acrid blue, cigar smoke.

'The cook here is quite exceptional and of course since the Prince of Wales has taken to frequenting these hallowed halls then the standards just get higher,' the Home Secretary replied, whilst still struggling to light his cigar to his satisfaction.

'Are you all right Harrowby?' Pitt asked. 'You've appeared distracted all evening. Nothing wrong I hope?'

'I do apologise gentlemen,' the Foreign Secretary replied, sitting up straight and putting his watch back into its pocket.

'You've checked that watch every ten minutes since you arrived,' Pitt observed with a rather uneasy smile.

'To tell the truth, I'm expecting a dispatch by courier and will enjoy my brandy and feel my digestion ease once he has arrived.'

'Anything we should be worried about old boy?' Melville asked lightly, catching the Prime Minister's eye.

'Far from it, I hope,' Lord Harrowby replied warily. 'The truth is that it concerns what we've been discussing all evening. I'm confident that by the end of the evening I will be able to satisfy you all just exactly how urgent the reinvigoration of the Third Coalition really is.'

'Well I don't think anyone in this room doubts that, it's just the rest of Europe that seems to question Bonaparte's intentions, they're scared of their own shadows. Every one of them fears provoking him. What a ludicrous notion that is. Can they not see that what Napoleon cannot persuade people to give him, he will simply take for himself?' Pitt stated bluntly.

'Well I think history will judge that we gave it our best shot at the conference of Stockholm. I've had two replies to the counter proposal we agreed upon taking office but I still await Cavendish's thoughts. You know that I really value his judgment and I'm sure it will be in accordance with our own ideas. He has such wonderful insight, I know he will come up with something fresh,' Pitt added.

Lord Harrowby shifted uncomfortably in his chair and despite having prepared himself with a stern mental note to refrain from such an action, once more the watch came out, the click as it opened sounding like a gunshot within the confines of the small room. All eyes were drawn to the time-piece and Pitt looked sternly across at him, fortunately a discreet knock at the door saved all from further embarrassment.

'Sincere apologies Prime Minister, my Lords,' the Head Steward began as he bowed slightly. 'Lord Harrowby I have been urged most strongly to pass this letter to you immediately,' he added and handed a wax sealed note to the Foreign Secretary before withdrawing, closing the heavy oak door with barely a sound.

'Would you excuse me,' the Foreign Secretary said as he broke the seal.

'Good Lord yes, if it makes you less twitchy, the wait will be worth it,' Pitt joked, trying to lighten the tension which had by now gripped them all.

Lord Harrowby read the note quickly, then once more, taking care this time not to miss a single word. He rose and tossed the paper into the fire, where it flared briefly and then was gone. Pausing for effect, he turned to face his audience, noting their rapt attention and if he was honest, secretly relishing this moment of triumph.

'Prime Minister I have received the gravest of news,' he began. 'A short while ago, the son of a peer of this realm, broke into the private chambers of the Duke of Devonshire and made off with his Grace's response to the Conference of Stockholm. The document was taken from the Duke's home and from there handed over to a man believed to be an agent of France,' he continued, now beginning to enjoy immensely himself as all three men leapt to their feet in perfect unison.

'What...good God no...but how?' Pitt spluttered.

'My God, you're not serious, the bloody nerve of it. What had Devonshire written I wonder?' Viscount Melville whispered.

'Gentlemen, gentlemen, please...' Pausing once more, Lord Harrowby continued. 'The document was handed over in a tavern in Holborn but recovered a few moments later by a man from Sir John Marshall's office. There never was any real danger, the document was a forgery, as we had learned of the execution of this plot earlier today and made a substitution.'

'Who is this traitorous dog?' raged the Home Secretary, 'I'll see him hang by dawn.'

'Oh God no, please don't tell me I know the man?' Lord Hawkesbury begged.

'Who is it Harrowby?' Pitt asked his voice deliberate and calming. 'I suppose it was bound to happen. London is awash with French agents and assassins, from low lives and sailors, to the aristocrats we took in but who've now found a lost loyalty to their homeland. I imagine it was one of these so called French gentlemen who befriended and then twisted one of our own against us?'

'Prime Minister, would you forgive me if I refrain from naming this man just now?' Lord Harrowby asked quietly. 'I don't know how he came to be working for the Bonapartist rabble but Sir John will find out, in that we can trust. More importantly, now we know he's a traitor, we'll be watching him and there are plans for him gentlemen, big plans so I am led to believe.'

He returned to his seat, trying to mask the relief he felt, yet savouring the confusion around the table. Foreign affairs had always been a game, the ultimate high stakes gambling for the most part. Now, he and Great Britain were about to play the greatest hand in history, a hand that could quite literally win or lose the whole world.

'Talk to me Harrowby, I have a feeling I'm missing out on something here,' Pitt said slowly, just the faintest trace of menace in his voice.

'Prime Minister, I take it we all agree that the active participation of all the parties of the Third Coalition is the only guaranteed way of stopping Napoleon, once he has finally made his move?' Lord Harrowby said confidently, to a wave of nodded heads.

'Thus it seems that the other countries of Europe need a nudge in the correct direction. They are not willing to see the worst of Napoleon. Always they convince themselves that he has no ambitions to conquer Europe for himself. He plays a waiting game, that way he grows stronger as we grow weaker. While he shows no signs of outward aggression, our chances of a strong alliance grow fainter. Tonight we have seen how important this is to him. He must at all times know what is in our hand so that he can continue to bluff us all. Eventually even Britain's readiness will be so weakened that he will have his moment to strike. With no alliance in place, he will have the advantage and the outcome could be too close to call.'

'How can we manipulate this situation?' Pitt asked. 'Bonaparte has only to avoid an aggressive posture and those weak fools in Europe will forget he even exists.'

'We think we have found a way to persuade the rest of

Europe that Napoleon is preparing to make his move. We honestly believe we can force Napoleon to make a premature alliance that will persuade even the Prussians that he is making himself strong enough to take on the World.'

Only the ticking of the mantelpiece clock broke the silence that followed. The Foreign Secretary let it drag for effect before continuing.

'For now, I implore you to keep this amongst the four of us only. We have a plan to force Napoleon into a premature alliance with Spain!'

The most powerful men in England sat in silence for a moment. It was Pitt that finally broke the mood.

'If this works then the Coalition will most certainly be assured but so gentlemen, will war with France!'

*

Archie Dexter woke slowly, squinting at the bright light that somehow found its way through the tiniest of gaps in the heavy curtains. The noise of the city street outside was intrusive, as London life continued to run at fever pitch. The interminable clatter of horse hooves and the accompanying rattle of iron shod wheels competed with raised voices of street vendors and people simply trying to make themselves heard. It was mornings such as this that made him long for the country life once more but for now he knew it was not to be.

He had slept well last night, considering that the previous evening he had cut down a man in a quiet London street and then dumped his body into the River Thames. That man was an enemy of the King and to Archie's way of thinking that was enough to condemn him to death.

He tugged the small, ivory handled bell-pull beside his

bed. He slept alone in his gracious four-storey townhouse situated in London's Mayfair. The house, barely three years old, had been a gift from his father. This was generous indeed as his father had more than once despairingly told his errant son that he was no longer to be considered the fruits of his loins and to prepare for penury in later life as he was not getting a brass farthing by way of allowance or inheritance. However, all that was before Archie returned to England as a wounded war hero, to be decorated by the King and feted by no less than Admiral Horatio Nelson.

As he awaited the arrival of Cedric Protheroe his manservant, he pondered life's vicissitudes. His father owned a good deal of Kent and a fair parcel of Sussex too. Born into privilege, the young Archie had been a troubled boy from an early age. Highly intelligent but unable to accept the word of any teacher as gospel, he questioned everything from the existence of God, to the benefits of a knowledge of Latin grammar.

With his father's posting to Egypt had come the taste for adventure that would mould the remainder of his life. To find an atheist cynic and romantic adventurer in one man was quite unusual. Combine that with a pleasure seeking hedonist and old fashioned royalist who would die for his country and you had a man who was almost unique.

Upon his reluctant return from Egypt he was sent to Eton. There he soon found that his desire to question his teacher's words rather than stimulating debate merely provoked a rage that frequently resulted in a beating. While still at Eton he discovered a passion for gambling that was to be his undoing on more than one occasion. At the ripe old age of seventeen he could pass for older and often gained access to a notorious gentleman's club in nearby Windsor.

Card games passed many a night of the young Archie's life and he became very skilled in the art of gambling on the turn of a card. However the element of chance always brings about a man's downfall and when he tried one desperate gamble too far, the night ended with him losing the school's stables and all the horses within to a Portuguese grain merchant. Archie was expelled without delay and returned home in disgrace.

'Good morning Sir...er Archie, sorry,' Cedric Protheroe stuttered from the bedroom doorway. Bearing a tray of tea and muffins, he slid gracefully into the room. He placed the tray upon a side table and drew back the curtains, flooding the room with light and yet more noise.

'Good morning Cedric and a sunny one too I see,' Archie replied, pouring his own tea and tucking into a hot, buttery muffin. His inability to wait for his man to pour the tea was a constant source of irritation to Cedric and Archie knew it.

'I've laid your clothes out for you and will prepare your bath shortly. Will you be going out straight away? 'he enquired.

'Yes I must leave soon, sadly,' Archie replied through a mouth full of muffin. If he was honest, he would prefer to sit in his private garden and finally get to read Wordsworth's new collection of poetry.

Cedric was a damn good man he decided, he would not like to spend his days waiting on someone else in this fashion. Slim and handsome though cursed with a slightly hangdog look, Cedric was a man who was always immaculately turned out and always appeared inwardly distressed at those who failed to maintain his high standards. Archie had befriended him in a French prison following the attack upon HMS Leander. He was a well educated man, who had been forced to leave his comfortable Sussex school at just fourteen years of age after his father disappeared on an expedition in Africa. He had washed up in the Navy and had two ships shot out from under him, eventually ending up a prisoner in a converted fort close to Nice. The regime was brutal, with a sadistic Commandant who broke every rule of decent behaviour. Cedric was repatriated after years of incarceration, arriving in England aboard the same ship as Archie. With no family and having no home to call his own, they had travelled to Kent together.

Once home, to Archie's eternal surprise and embarrassment, he was welcomed by his father, now glowing with pride at his wonderful son. Glancing at the stump of his left arm, he wondered for perhaps the thousandth time, what price had to be paid to earn a fathers respect!

He continued to ravenously attack his breakfast, though he had slipped into a somewhat reflective mood. Last night had been the culmination of a considerable amount of work by many people and whilst it had succeeded in preventing the French intelligence apparatus in London from obtaining vital papers, it showed once more the incredible depth of their activities. Simply put, London was awash with traitors and spies.

Thousands of refugees from the Revolution had been welcomed into London society but with the burgeoning population of French nationals had come the problem of keeping track of those who were in London for a more sinister purpose. The Aliens Act had sought to bring some kind of control but Archie knew it was too little too late. He wondered, as he rose and slipped into a silk robe, if England would ever again be so kind as to offer a home for refugees, only to have a minority of them turn and bite the hand that fed them. Never, he concluded, a lesson learned surely.

A while later, he lay stretched out in his bath, the very height of luxury he always reminded himself. As a man who had endured great hardship, unlike his peers he never took such luxury and privilege for granted.

Following his expulsion from Eton, his father had somehow secured him a place at Magdalene College, Oxford. It was whilst at Oxford that he discovered a true passion for reading, especially the controversial.

He loved to read any works that challenged ignorance and idolatry. He sought out the published works of scientists such as Hutton, who challenged the very age of the earth itself and thus disputed all that the Bible had told man to believe for centuries.

Studying classic literature also excited his imagination with tales of intrigue and betrayal, filled with lusty hidden messages of sexual and social depravity which he knew mirrored life in Georgian England, where private pleasures were indulged in as never before.

Sitting alongside these books in his private study were the controversial and some said depraved writings of De Sade and others. Needless to say his own so called depravities had once more caught up with him and he was sent down for accruing serious gambling debts and being caught naked in the college chapel with the Dean's servant.

Upon returning to his bedroom and dressing, it occurred to him that his whole life had been a series of calamities, mostly of his own doing. Yet again though, his father had ridden to the rescue and secured his son a commission in the Life Guards.

He had served with distinction in Holland but bored with garrison life back in England, he had succumbed once more to his dark side as his mother lovingly described it. On the verge of being cashiered, if he was lucky, an appearance before a court martial if not, his father had intervened for the last time and secured him a post away from the Army's eyes, to serve on Nelson's personal staff as an intelligence officer. In light of the way things turned out he was still not sure how coincidental that posting was or indeed how contrived his downfall had been. Now though, he was feted as a hero but had paid a very high price for redemption.

As he concluded dressing, he fitted a prosthetic hand to the stump of his left arm. Made by a craftsman who normally produced fine clocks, this wood and metal hand was quite unique. Carved from finest mahogany, it had the exact dimensions of his missing hand. Each finger could be bent at the knuckle and midpoint and then locked in position by way of a tiny internal ratchet. It was attached to his forearm by a fine leather sheath running almost to the elbow and was so tightly secured it had never worked loose in countless fights, dances and amorous encounters. As he put on a pair of woollen gloves, he felt its solid rigidity and remembered last night how the unfortunate French agent had been pole-axed by his blow.

An echoing rap upon the front door told him that his faithful assistant Tom had arrived. Ignoring Cedric and his pleading eyes, he put his own long, dark coat on and settled a tall stovepipe hat upon his head. Cedric fairly sprinted across the hallway to ensure he made it to the large front door first in order to hold it open, somewhat ostentatiously for his master.

'Thank you,' Archie sighed,' I shall be out for the day and please inform cook that I'll dine at my club this evening, though I will be home this afternoon.'

'Very good,' Cedric replied, 'and please take care,' he added under his breath as he closed the door.

'Morning Tom,' Archie said cheerily as he clambered aboard the small carriage, 'we need to go to Ludgate Hill please.'

'Very good Sir,' Tom answered his voice a rich bass baritone with a thick Yorkshire accent. 'Do I take it we're going t' chap from last neet's place then?'

'We are indeed, he was carrying a few interesting papers, including a boot makers bill with an address that I hope is his home.'

'Best yer not be seeing Sir John fust Sir?' Tom queried, forcing his way out into the flow of traffic.

Archie knew he was right but impatience got the better of him as always. He looked at the broad back of the stocky, utterly dependable Yorkshireman and realised once more how lucky he had been in his choice of assistant.

It was just past nine o'clock on a beautiful spring morning and the roads were already crowded with a dangerous mix of passenger vehicles, drays and wagons, through which almost suicidal pedestrians dashed. The wealthiest men and women in London were about their business and the noise and clamour was almost unbearable. Within a few hundred yards, Archie's carriage had almost run down a gentleman in his city finest, two newspaper sellers and been hit by the horse hauling bales of hay to a local grandee's stables.

Tom skillfully wove through the melee and turned east into Oxford Street. Many new buildings had been finished in the last few years and a good number more were under construction. Archie looked out at the array of coffee houses, shops and theatres. He remembered not more than a few years had passed since the area either side of the road had been open fields with just a scattering of fine houses.

Tom took him on a wide circuit through Holborn, coming close to the scene of last night's drama. Archie looked ahead at the looming eminence of St Paul's cathedral. The magnificent structure towered over all its surroundings, including Wren's parish churches scattered throughout the city. He was always awestruck by the superlative engineering that had produced what he considered the finest building in London. In the same heart-beat he was staggered that man could build such a folly in order to worship a supposedly benevolent God, while in the surrounding streets, every day mothers would die in childbirth and young girls would sell their bodies in order that they may eat.

The carriage lurched awkwardly as Tom took a left turn, north towards Newgate. The traffic in the road slowed to a crawl as the carriages pushed their way by brute force through a restless but cheery crowd that spilled across the thoroughfare. Archie marveled once more at human nature as Tom used the horse to drive a passage through the mass of adults and children. The crowd, mostly made up of working people and assorted vagabonds, were massing outside Newgate prison to catch a glimpse of the day's hangings.

Tom pulled to a halt just to the rear of Saint Bartholomew's Hospital. Archie struggled out of his long coat, exposing worn and tattered clothes. Removing the stovepipe hat he donned a torn, tweed cap. Stepping down from the carriage, he glanced around at the relatively quiet street. Satisfied that no one was paying him any particular attention, he transferred some of the grime from the spokes of the carriage wheel to his face. He scuffed his already tattered shoes into a pile of horse dung and pulled on a pair of ragged, woollen gloves.

'You watch yer sen Sir,' Tom cautioned.

'Worry not, I will,' Archie assured him, exposing the butt of a pistol, 'but if you hear my friend here, you come running eh?'

'Aye, I will but I don't suppose this 'ovel 'as a number so yer'll take some finding.'

'The house just here is number one, so count along to fifteen, that's what I'm going to do,' Archie answered cheerily as he set off.

Within just a few yards the whole atmosphere had changed. The street narrowed, with buildings leaning over cutting down the sunlight. He walked slowly down the road, took a left turn and shortly, just yards past a small butcher's shop; he turned right and entered a darker and more dangerous world. The narrow street would barely take a cart in two directions at once. It was largely unmade and strewn with stinking rubbish. The neighbourhood had an all-pervading smell of rotting horse dung mixed with old food and stagnant water.

Even these narrow streets were alive with humanity,

dirty, rough looking people but none showed the slightest hostility towards him. The only attention he received was from two rather grubby young girls who vied for his affections from a secluded doorway. He gave them a wink but no smile, his disguise was holding up but he had long ago learned that his full set of teeth would mark him as an outsider in a place such as this.

By a process of elimination, he found number fifteen and pushed open the dry, neglected looking front door. Beyond was a gloomy entrance hall and to the left a stairway which he warily began to climb. A clinging smell of dust and damp assaulted his nostrils as he made his way up to what he expected to be the top-floor rooms. The stairwell echoed to the sound of the streets and the rooms behind the four doors on each landing. Behind one a baby squealed, with glee he thought rather than hunger, as a girl sang a lilting refrain in order to settle the infant. Behind another door was what sounded like an old man, ranting and raving insanely, all adding to the melody of life in this tiny part of London.

Finally he reached the top landing and one final door remained. He took the worn key and turned it in the surprisingly well-oiled lock. Once inside he quickly locked the door behind him and careful made his way in the dark to the window. With the shutters open, he looked around the dead man's home. Just one room, a bed in one corner, a battered wardrobe, a small table and an incongruously ornate leather armchair made up the furnishings. To one side was a grimy fireplace, soot stained and littered with ash, over which hung a filthy, blackened cooking pot.

It was exactly as he had expected save for the dozens of paintings hung on the walls and stacked all around the room. Medium to good quality works he judged and almost certainly all were stolen.

He quickly searched the room and in the bottom of the wardrobe full of clothes, he found what he was looking for secreted within in a small oak chest. Using a smaller key recovered from the dead man, he opened the box and carried it over to the window's light. It contained half a dozen folders of papers, each with a name on the front. He recognised only one name and quickly opened it. He felt his eyebrows shoot up as he read the first pages of the dossier, detailed and intimate in its nature.

Some of the pages were handwritten notes, he assumed made by the dead man, filed away with clippings from newspapers and periodicals. In this small folder was the biography of a traitor, a biography of the blonde man who had tried to steal one of his own country's most important secrets. The other files were presumably the details of other traitors either hooked or still waiting to be reeled in.

The rap on the door almost made him drop the papers. His heart raced as he put the box down and drew his pistol. The knock came again, only louder this time. Time stood still, only his thumping heart and the sound of the baby crying in the rooms below intruded into his thoughts. Minutes stretched and eventually he was convinced the caller had given up. Moving to the door he listened intently but could only hear the sounds of life in the other rooms, mingling with shouts and cries from the street below.

Moving quickly, he stuffed all of the folders into his waistband and buttoned his threadbare jacket up tight. Cautiously opening the door he peered into the gloomy stairwell. Satisfied it was safe, he locked the door and quickly descended the stairs. Adrenaline coursed through his body and he fought the urge to run all the way back to his carriage. Once he was safely aboard, he instructed Tom to drive to an address in nearby Aldgate.

*

The man who had knocked on the dead man's door was Arnold Pickles, a man of ill repute and fearsome reputation. He was thirty-eight years old and had spent ten of those in prison. As a child he had been an expert sneak thief but his undoubted talent had not stopped him being caught many times. As an adult he graduated to house breaking and not without some success. Prison spells did not deter him nor slow his climb up the criminal social ladder. These days he considered himself both a respectable brothel owner and a specialist fixer. If you wanted something stolen, he knew a man who could, if you wanted someone killed, he knew a man who would.

He made his way to a coffee house just off Oxford Street. Through the crowd and thick palls of pipe smoke he managed to find who he was looking for and sat down at his table. The man seated at the table made a casual gesture to a dour looking waitress and a second cup of thick coffee appeared, as if by magic.

'By the look upon your face, is it safe to assume you were unsuccessful?' the other man sneered. He was a very tall and rakishly thin man, whose once handsome, somewhat pale face, seemed to be twisted into a perpetual scowl of anger. It was in fact the look of a man in almost constant agony, an insistent nagging pain deep within his right thigh.

He spoke English with the accent of a man educated in a Home Counties boarding school, choosing his words

111

with great care and immaculate diction. None of his English social contacts would ever have guessed that William Hibbert was in reality Jean Henri Thiebault, head of the extensive French intelligence operation in London. Pickles certainly had no idea who he really worked for and was one of only two English people in London who Thiebault had direct contact with in furtherance of his espionage activities. Utilising a labourious series of cut outs and intermediaries was inefficient and time consuming but he was confident that this had kept him from exposure for nearly two years. He believed that as far as the British authorities were concerned he was simply a trade attaché at the French Embassy in London.

'No one was 'ome guv, 'Pickles answered, with the familiar feeling of unease this cold fish of a man before him always engendered. When Hibbert had come to him with his proposal, Pickles knew immediately that David Reynolds was the man for the job. Reynolds was a fence for stolen art but also a consummate blackmailer.

'Pray tell then, what news from your man in Bow Street?' Thiebault asked quietly.

'Nothin' doin' guv, the Runners 'aven't got 'im that's for sure,' Pickles answered reluctantly.

'I don't like this one bit but never mind for now, just keep trying his home and ask around but quietly though, 'Thiebault insisted.

'Don't you worry, he ain't 'ard to find normally,' Pickles replied with a chuckle.

'Just find him and ask if he has the letter for me to read. Now, moving on to another matter, did you have any luck finding that artist friend of yours?'

'Artist Guv?' Pickles replied, a curious look crossing

his face, followed swiftly by a grin as he realised what his companion alluded to. 'Oh sorry, artist indeed, yes I did and he can do those, er paintings of the passports by next week.'

'Good man, now run along and you can reach me in the usual way should you find our mutual friend,' Thiebault said with a contemptuous and dismissive wave.

Left alone with his thoughts, Thiebault felt a crushing wave of disappointment. The missing man was, so Pickles had assured him, an expert at compromising people and thus laying them open to blackmail. Thiebault had no idea who Pickles man was or how he had worked his magic and nor did he want to know.

However he had made it happen, this man had succeeded in securing the services of an English gentleman. The gentleman had been placed in no position to refuse the devastating order that he should steal from the private residence of the Duke of Devonshire. The audacious plot should have landed Thiebault an intelligence coup that would have sealed his reputation forever. By now he should have possession of a document outlining the proposals and objections of the major powers in Europe to the operation of an alliance against his master, Napoleon Bonaparte.

Carefully lighting a long, clay pipe, he pondered his misfortune. Because of the need to avoid compromising himself and his network of often unwitting spies, he was also unaware of the identity of the gentleman thief. Until this morning, Pickles had known nothing of last night's operation and he was still unaware of any details, save that Reynolds or the thief had something important to hand over to Thiebault. The problem was clear enough though, if the thief still had the stolen papers, only the missing Reynolds knew his identity. Smiling wryly, Thiebault thought, 'hoist by mine own petard' as the English would say.'

His own security was watertight, of that he was certain, so either Pickles man had betrayed them or his English thief had met with misfortune, even potentially he had been caught in the act. This was an uncomfortable thought but Thiebault was confident nothing would lead back to his door. He finished his coffee, grimacing at the bitter taste. Standing stiffly, he winced as the nerve in his thigh shot fiery pain into his groin and he was forced to draw a deep breath before he made his way unsteadily out to the street to find a cab. Squeezing and jostling his way through the throng of pedestrians, he let their conversations wash over him. Amongst the daily trivia and complaining, three times in less than five minutes he heard snatches of chatter about Napoleon and invasion. Truly the level of paranoid fear in London was exceptionally high.

Hailing a cab, he settled back in the seat, adjusting his leg to a comfortable position. As they rattled along over the uneven and in places, barely paved streets, he mused on the English people. The casual contempt in which they held the French had been a national trait for centuries. Yet the Revolution had produced an outpouring of sympathy resulting in hundreds, perhaps thousands of aristocratic French citizens being given refuge in the city. Thiebault marveled at the British spirit of fair-play and their idiotic logic.

As the cab made its way down Oxford Street, past busy food shops and theatres, he gazed upon an array of new buildings springing up across what had recently been muddy fields. Politicians planned and conspired for war, the people feared it deep in their hearts, yet they continued to build for a future and reveled in excess and light-hearted frolics at every opportunity. Perhaps, he thought, it would be better to leave this crazy race alone.

*

Archie slipped into a discrete side door of a substantial residence occupying a corner plot of Manchester Square in London's Marylebone. Since the passing of the Aliens Act, all foreign nationals were obliged to register with the government's Aliens Office. The converted house was the base for a small, secretive section of this department working to counter by any means necessary, the increasingly violent and hostile activity of French agents in London.

Despite himself, Archie waited nervously outside the office of Sir John Marshall, a frighteningly efficient man who suffered no argument and was obsessively dedicated to protecting his country. The loss of two out three of his sons in fighting with the French had left him surprisingly un-embittered but nevertheless resolute and where necessary, utterly ruthless. The dark oak door swung open and Sir John's secretary ushered Archie inside. The sallow faced youth took Archie's coat and guided him towards an open door leading to Sir John's inner sanctum.

'Sit you down young man,' Sir John ordered in a surprisingly quiet voice, without lifting his eyes from a copy of The Times. 'Tell me about last night and spare no detail,' he demanded.

Archie related the events of the previous evening, whilst Sir John appeared to continue reading his newspaper. Undeterred he continued, noting with a small sense of satisfaction when his superior flinched ever so slightly at his expression 'had to skewer him with my stiletto.'

'The man had enough papers in his pockets to allow me to locate his house Sir John and I took these files from a locked trunk hidden in his wardrobe. They are I believe the dossiers on The Honourable Charles Lyell, traitor and five others, traitors in waiting or agents of the French already.'

Sir John was at last distracted from his reading and as he looked over the buff coloured wallets, the names written on the covers caused his eyebrows to arch ever higher upon his wrinkled forehead. He took the folder marked with Lyell's name, untied the dirty red cord and began to examine its contents. With some apparent difficulty he read some of the notes and glanced at the newspaper clippings.

'Good Lord but some work has gone into this, has it not?' he mumbled to himself. 'Gambling, whoring and spending his poor old father's fortune. However, so what I say, half the dandies in London get up to worse. Why has he betrayed his country then?'

'I agree there has to be more Sir and I'd like the chance to find out what it is. If we have the Runners bring him in then certainly we've caught a traitor but if you would allow me some time then I think we might have a man under our influence that we can use to our advantage,' Archie said carefully. 'Likewise the others, rather than move on them, let's find out who it is that they have been...er... persuaded to work for and why,' he continued.

'Someone has gone to a lot of trouble with all this,' Sir John ventured, opening another folder. 'I've met this old fool and I know he was once a confidant of Arthur

Wellesley's father. What possible skeleton could he have rattling in his wardrobe that would make him work for the damned Frenchies?'

'Maybe they don't know they're working for the French Sir?' opined Archie. 'It's another reason to work on Lyell. It could be that these people have been blackmailed by this man Reynolds into carrying out a service without knowing why or for whom.'

'Dastardly clever if that's the case,' Sir John answered, now looking Archie straight in the eye. He then continued to flip through the papers in the folder, stopping suddenly.

'God Lord, the old dog has been seeing Lady Martlesham's daughter! She can't be more than eighteen years old.'

'Everyone has an Achilles heel Sir,'

'Really…everyone, I wonder? So, why should we spare Lyell the gallows then young man?'

'Three reasons Sir. First, he may lead us to the Frenchies who paid Reynolds to do their dirty work. Secondly, we may be able to turn him against the same French interests if they can be persuaded that he's not been compromised. But third and most importantly, we might use the same screw on him ourselves.'

'By heavens that's a dangerous game indeed.' Sir John cautioned.

'Only for him and he's due a day at Newgate anyhow,' Archie countered, warming to his task. 'With Lyell, there's another compelling reason not to send him for a short drop just yet. He's lived in high society in Spain, speaks fluent Spanish and French by all accounts and from what I've seen and read he's a bold and fearless adventurer. According to the newspapers, he's explored new regions of the Southern Americas where he consorted with the ruling families and brought gifts back to be presented to the Spanish King. It seems to me he may be of more use alive than dead, for now at least.'

'Very well, find out what his weakness is but nothing must lead back to here, you understand?' Sir John added with sudden steel in his quiet voice.

'Don't be concerned Sir, Protheroe will ensure that Lyell has no idea who his tormentor is until we're ready,' Archie finished, with a grin.

'You've done well,' Sir John stated enthusiastically,' and so much more will be expected of you and others before this year is over. The country faces a peril as we've never seen before. Worldwide war is coming but right here, right now, underhand and vicious men are already plotting our demise. This must not happen, you understand?'

'A new kind of secret warfare is developing, a war of terror and conspiracy within our own land,' Sir John continued. 'If we lose this battle then we might just lose the whole war. This will be a clash of the greatest power blocks the world has yet known. Never again will conflict occur on such a scale. It will be the war to end all wars and we must win it!'

'That we must Sir,' Archie agreed, though he was under no illusion that the coming war would see an end to all wars. Nations would continue to fight for supremacy across the globe just as long as nations existed, of that he was sure.

Sighing inwardly he thought to himself, let the future take care of itself, he would just do his best to survive the present a while longer. Right on cue so it seemed, he felt a stabbing cramp in the thumb of his left hand, which on reflex he reached to comfort, recoiling as ever when he felt the hard wood and metal contraption on the end of his arm.

As he dismissed him, Sir John handed over Lyell's folder. Archie sat himself at a desk in the outer office, gladly taking the offer of a cup of coffee made by one of the office clerks and began to read.

*

The Honourable Charles Lyell was at that very moment taking tea in his comfortable house in Haymarket, adjacent to His Majesty's Theatre. Born into great wealth, Lyell was by turn a self-obsessed dandy and a fearless traveller, an adventurer lauded by the popular press and pursued by eligible society ladies day and night. Right now he was a very frightened and almost broken man.

Slumped in an arm chair, alone in his oak panelled study he stared into a low fire, the ticking of a quite monstrous grandfather clock the only sound to be heard. So focused was he on his predicament that the hustle and bustle of the busy street outside had faded from his conscious thoughts. His tea went cold and his hot buttered scone remained untouched as he feverishly played over events in his mind. Each and every time these daydreams ended in his death.

Archie was fascinated by the man as he read the file, prepared so diligently by the late unlamented Reynolds. An article in The Times described how Lyell and a group of friends had conquered some of the highest peaks in the Sierra Nevada, a snow capped range of mountains in the south of Spain. The very next year, according to the article, Lyell had journeyed to the southern Americas where he had explored rainforests in the hinterland of

Brazil.

Archie liked to think of himself as something of a Renaissance man and if he was honest a bit of a pleasure seeker. Since childhood he found himself questioning the literal word of the Bible. To challenge religious dogma and society's norms excited him, a man of honour and breeding but an intelligent man who was convinced that he had but one time on earth and by any means possible, he was going to sample life's adventures. The more he read about Lyell, the more he began to like him. This realisation steeled his resolve to find out what the man was doing consorting with French agents and if possible, allow him to redeem himself in the service of his own country.

Lyell took a fresh cup of tea and read The Times with little real interest. His head was pounding with a maddening intensity, the result of a sleepless night, as he read of his friend Beau Brummell who had become embroiled in yet another scandal, this time with the wife of Lord Evelyn. Lyell let out a little chuckle but it just made his head hurt even more.

Closing his eyes against the morning sun he tried to relax but all he could see was that evil little man and his threats, his dreadful threats. What would he want of him next, that was the terrifying question playing on Lyell's mind as he knew that no blackmailer ever took just one hit at his target. Troubling him just as much was the question, what on earth was it that he had been forced to steal?

Archie continued leafing through Reynolds dossier on Lyell, coming to a couple of pages of handwritten notes. It was no surprise that Lyell was a member of the exclusive Whites Club in St James or that he attended race meetings with astounding regularity. His eye though was drawn to the second page where there was an address in Marylebone, set in the exclusive new Portman estate. There was no clue as to who lived at the address but the underscored words 'GOT HIM' suggested that this address was possibly the key to this mystery. Time will tell he thought but for now he had a night out to plan, with the Honourable Charles Lyell.

That evening found the two men preparing to go out on the town, less than half a mile separated their homes, both in fashionable areas of the capital. Lyell had taken a light supper at home at around five o'clock and with the assistance of his valet was preparing for a night of bacchanalian excess. Dressed in the elegant opulence favoured by his closest friends, he was certain he would cut quite a dash about town on this fine evening.

With the invaluable assistance of Cedric, Archie was dressed in restrained but elegant style, dark pants and frock coat, set off by a scarlet and vermillion cravat. However with the aid of Cedric's more esoteric skills, it was unlikely even Archie's own father would recognise him this evening. His thick hair was combed tightly backwards and the skillfull application of theatrical bushy sideburns, a goatee beard and pale make-up helped aged him by some ten years. Pince-nez spectacles and a gentle lowlands Scottish accent removed the final vestiges of an Eton educated man of Kent and introduced London society once more to the charming but somewhat reticent Donald Ross. To those who asked, he was the eldest son of a wealthy fish merchant who divided his time between Scotland, London and Esbjerg in Denmark.

Gaining entry to Whites exclusive gentleman's club as the guest of an absent member, Archie was soon mingling with a sizeable selection of London's elite. Three of those members present were acquaintances of Archibald Dexter but were completely taken in by Donald Ross He glided in and out of conversations in the lounge before dining alone on what he had to confess was the finest veal in London. Lyell he noticed had arrived with a group of hearty and already slightly drunk young men, who proceeded to eat dinner in an embarrassing raucous fashion.

With dinner enjoyably concluded, Archie joined a group of men in the lounge and with brandy flowing and talk of invasion and London property prices, as if by magic a pack of cards appeared and before long he found himself embroiled in play, enlivened by ever increasing wagers.

Eventually bored of the game he rose from his comfortable leather chair and prepared a pipe whilst warming his back before one of several fireplaces in the large room. He strolled casually around the opulent, oak panelled rooms and corridors, in search of Lyell. He soon found him in a small area just off the dining room, leading the shouting and hysterical chatter at a game of dice.

Unobtrusively he settled into an armchair to watch the game, from time to time distracted by an elderly gentleman who it seemed was fascinated by the Scottish fishing industry. With consummate skill, Archie's alter ego fielded questions and made small talk with the old man on a subject he knew only from a battered old volume hidden away in the extensive library he kept at home.

Despite the distraction, he was able to gather that Lyell was a gambler of some considerable courage and skill. Slowly but surely he took his friends for a mounting tally and by the time they decided to quit whilst losing, he reckoned that Lyell was ahead by a hundred pounds.

Archie had taken the time to peruse the club book where bets on everything from Napoleon's next lover to the likelihood of snow at Easter were recorded. He noted that Lyell refrained from such ridiculous wagers, the results of which were totally beyond the gamblers control. If Lyell had an Achilles heel, gambling debts were not likely to be the cause.

Gradually the group fell quiet as the night's excesses started to take their toll. After a time, Lyell began checking his large gold watch with ever increasing frequency. One by one his friends began to doze in their soft armchairs and without a word, Lyell rose and made to leave. Archie excused himself from his new friend and left the room. Lyell was already receiving his hat and cane in the lobby, so Archie swiftly but discreetly requested his own hat and coat.

Outside in the gloom of the barely lit street, Lyell waved toward a cab whose apparently inattentive driver ignored him. Another parked across the road quickly set in motion and Lyell clambered aboard. The first cabbie seemed to come alive and with a deft crack of his whip turned across the road and picked Archie up.

'Don't lose him Tom, whatever you do,' Archie implored his faithful assistant.

'Don't you worry I won't. He ain't goin' ome though is 'e?'

'He is not, Marylebone perhaps?' Archie wondered aloud.

This was confirmed when a short while later they arrived in the area of London most recently developed by property speculators. They stopped short of Lyell's cab, watching as he dismounted and walked down the quiet street, glancing back at his cab, now executing a turn in the street. Modern oil lanterns cast their gentle yellow glow across the newly laid street. Lyell retraced his steps before rapping on the door of a substantial terraced house, one of a graceful curve of new townhouses.

Lyell gained swift admittance, the door attended by a doorman inside the house. Archie boldly walked up to the same door and knocked. The door opened at once and he was admitted by a giant of a man whose formal evening dress could not disguise the fact the he was probably a prize fighter by trade.

'Ah bon soir Sir, we 'ave not had the pleasure or I would surely have recalled,' purred an elegantly dressed, handsome woman, who rose from a chaise-lounge set in one corner of the elegantly furnished lobby. Archie believed the French accent was genuine, even if the warm greeting was perhaps not. Of Lyell there was no sign.

'Come in Sir, welcome to Madam Bouvier's house of instruction. Four Guineas Sir ensures repentance,' she continued carefully as she glided toward him, arms spread wide. 'Allow me introduce you to a companion.'

'Four Guineas is indeed a substantial guarantee,' he replied easily, handing over some crisp bank notes as she guided him through a double oak doorway. His heart pounded with excitement, in for a penny in for a pound, well four Guineas he mused. The things I do for England he concluded with a barely suppressed grin.

He was led into a sumptuous lounge. Dotted around the room on sofas were several young girls and a handful of more mature women, some sharing brandy with gentlemen ranging in age from their twenties to seventies in his estimation. At a signal from Madam Bouvier, a tall woman in her forties, dark skinned and raven-haired, moving with an immeasurable sensual grace, approached him bearing two brandy snifters.

'Would you care to sit with me, my name is Anneliese,' she purred.

He soon found himself curled up with the woman on a gold and burgundy sofa, making small talk and sipping surprisingly fine brandy. Of Lyell there was no sign and when eventually Anneliese rose, he followed her as she headed toward a corridor leading to a flight of stairs.

'Lead the way my dear' he replied in his gentle Scottish accent and followed her somewhat nervously. Glancing around he still could not see Lyell, so he decided with that he had better just do his duty, espionage could wait awhile.

The woman led him into a palatial bedroom lit by two oil lamps and a low fire. Without further pleasantries she issued a stern command that he stand and strip before her. This he dutifully complied with and could not fail to notice her eagerly taking in his smooth, muscular physique, her eyes lingering on his rapidly swelling penis. She glanced briefly at his prosthetic hand but said nothing.

With no more small talk she looped a silk cord around his right wrist and pulled it tight. Another cord she tied around his left bicep. The free ends she threw over the upper frame of the four-poster bed and secured them tightly, stretching him to stand tall, hands high above his head. He glanced toward her and saw she had shed her robe and was now dressed only in an exquisite red basque of finest lace. In her hand she held a short, birch switch. Her legs he noted were long and powerful, her small breasts squeezed high by the lingerie. She was making his heart race as she moved toward him in the subdued lamp light.

'To stop, simply repent your sins,' she whispered in his ear, running her soft hand down his back to cup his firm round buttocks and then with no more hesitation and none too gently, she brought the birch down across the backs of his thighs. He gasped despite himself and then the birch fell again and again. She thrashed him harder and harder across his back and buttocks until he was writhing in pain, swinging helplessly from his bound wrists.

With no spare flesh on his athletic body, the beating quickly turned his skin bright scarlet. He began to let out a deep grunting groan with each blow. Minutes passed with no let up, if anything there was an increase in both the rhythm and strength of each cut of the birch. As the blows concentrated on his backside he began to lose control and let out a squeal with each painful lash. Twisting and turning in a perversely ecstatic agony, he glanced at his tormentor. Her body shimmered with perspiration and her eyes flashed wild and excited, gasping with effort, as she thrashed him again and again. Eventually, he cried out that he repented all his sins.

Gasping for breath, his body felt as though it was on fire. His heart hammered in his chest as he swung painfully from his bonds, his trembling legs almost giving way beneath him. He felt Anneliese reach around him and grasp his twitching erection in her slender, delicate hand. Firmly she pumped the hot rigid flesh and almost immediately with a howl of delight he spurted uncontrollable jets of semen onto the bedspread. Only Annaliese's impressive strength prevented him from having to take his full weight on his bound wrists. With practiced dexterity she untied him and lowered him to the bed.

'Impressive Donald, please call on me again anytime,' she said handing him the remains of his brandy. With no further word she dressed and made to leave.

'Do you know a friend of mine, Charles Lyell?' Archie asked, knowing this was taking an enormous risk.

'No, but men have so many names,' Anneliese replied with a short, pretty but slightly cynical laugh.

Archie struggled to his feet and rummaging in his discarded jacket gave her a guinea tip. She blew him a kiss and closed the door behind her with just a hint of a backward glance. Archie finished dressing, his body ablaze with a pain dulled by the intense sexual release.

He descended the stairs on shaky legs, passed through the now deserted lounge and exited to the lobby with still no sign of Lyell who must have moved quickly to somewhere private.

Bidding the ever present Madam Bouvier good night, he was just moving to the front-door, held open by the hulking doorman, when another previously unnoticed door opened and an elderly gentleman came out into the lobby. Through the briefly open doorway he saw into a second luxurious candlelit lounge. Sure enough there was Lyell, seated on the floor leaning against a couch, his head being gently stroked like a contented pet cat.

Just before the door closed, Archie got a good look at the startlingly handsome man who was with Lyell and cast his eye over the other young and mostly outrageously dressed men in the room. Lyell's companion was dark skinned, very slim and heavily made up giving him a distinctly effeminate appearance. This was Lyell's big secret and smiling broadly Archie stepped out into the street.

'You might have had him Reynolds but he's mine now,' Archie announced to night triumphantly.

The ride home over the poorly maintained roads was distinctly uncomfortable but he suffered in silence, relishing his triumph and basking in a slightly guilty sensual haze. Gentlemen of breeding had been going in secret to such houses for generations. Along with other so-called houses of ill-repute, walloping houses were common place in London and usually the preserve of the rich elite. Lyell's perversion though was a closed and illegal world. Molly houses were an all together more secretive world. With sodomy still a capital crime, some things were best kept secret. Without a doubt Lyell had been well and truly caught in flagrante!

*

The next morning, Jean Henri Thiebault was finishing his breakfast alone and in low spirits. As his personal maid Marie cleared his plates, he prepared himself mentally for some unpleasant questions from the Ambassador. Though he had gone into little detail, he had promised the loathsome man something of a triumph upon his return from Paris. Why the Ambassador had been summoned, Thiebault could not discover, not a happy state of affairs for the Head of Intelligence.

Marie fussed over the table some more, clearing the last of the plates but leaving him his coffee. She moved his papers to one side and swept the crumbs into her pinafore. She had worked for Thiebault for many years, since the dreadful final days of the Revolution in France.

As Marie returned he continued to read his papers, in particular one regarding a promising new agent recruited

128

in a coffee house close to Horse Guards, home of the British Army's High Command. Marie bent over to sweep the hearth and over the papers, Thiebault was afforded first a glimpse of smooth white thigh and then a magnificent expanse of curvaceous breasts. He returned quickly to his reading, suppressing his emotions he immersed himself in his work once more.

Several hours later he was ushered into the Ambassador's office and served strong, sweet coffee by a junior clerk. Left alone he took in the opulence of his surroundings, in particular the paintings and fine oak furniture, looted from the greatest houses in France. Vive la Revolution he muttered cynically as he rose to greet the Ambassador, Monsieur Albert Gironde.

'Sit, sit. You look a little grey Thiebault, the leg giving you trouble?' Gironde asked, with apparently genuine warmth in his voice.

'It is, as ever I fear Sir. How was Paris?' Thiebault enquired with real concern in his voice as he longed for his native Paris everyday he was absent.

'Not good I'm sad to say. Sedition is everywhere you look. The people are taxed mercilessly and yet they have insufficient food to feel full when they go to their beds. If it was not for their childlike adoration of Napoleon then we would feel the sting of a new revolution for sure,' Gironde answered solemnly.

The two men continued to share their concerns for their homeland and its poor downtrodden people. In the room directly above them, Marie idly cleaned the fireplace in the office of a clerk who was currently at work elsewhere in the building. By a quirk of acoustics, she was able to hear every word of the conversation taking place in the

Ambassadors' office.

She had been Thiebault's personal maid ever since as a young man, still in his teens, he had rescued her at the height of the revolutionary violence in Paris. Alongside other rioters he had stormed a magnificent house close to the Bastille. Expecting resistance they found the aristocrats had fled and the servants had joined the revolution. All had long gone, that is except Marie.

Thiebault had entered the master bedroom of the Comte du Chancel with murder in his heart. Once there he had found Marie, naked and tied spread-eagled to the aristocrat's bed. Clearly she had been beaten half unconscious and then raped, a last senseless statement of perverted aristocratic power. His revolutionary fervour was stoked to bursting point and the sight of poor Marie drove him into a murderous rage that was to be sustained for many months of bloodletting. The dreadfull shock of her attack was to render Marie speechless for nearly a year.

In truth, as soon as revolution had gripped Paris, the Chancel household had fled before their servants had chance to rise up against them. With drink in their bellies and blood lust in their hearts, a gang of the servants had attacked Marie. They all knew she had been the illicit lover of the Comte for more than a year and treated her as the aristocrat's whore they saw her to be. Despite Thiebault's kindness, Marie had been determined from that day to undermine the Revolution to her dying breath. Any doubts she haboured evaporated the day he had told her triumphantly that the Chancel family had all gone to the guillotine. She had been spying for the British for years, totally trusted and never once suspected.

Thiebault had just finished confessing to the Ambassador that he had failed in his attempt to steal documents giving the British position on a potential new European alliance. The Ambassador gave a resigned shrug and to Thiebault's relief changed the subject.

'Your friend Antoine is to visit London in the next few days. He will travel as an Irish corn merchant and you're to assist him in any way you can. He's been sent by Napoleon no less and soon journeys to Spain, where he will root out England's agent in the Spanish Court.'

'Does he know the identity of this spy? For too long now the English have known everything the Spanish Crown does, almost before they've decided to do it,' Thiebault concluded with a slight and derisive laugh.

'They're hopeless, but unfortunately Napoleon sees them as vital allies all the same. I understand the English agent's days are numbered, 'Gironde stated confidently.

'Why is Antoine coming to London first?' Thiebault asked.

'England is sending their Ambassador back to Spain and Antoine intends to sail on the same ship. Better the enemy you know and all that! It would appear that Antoine is acquainted with the family's daughter.'

'Well it'll be nice to see him once more.'

In the room above, Marie finished her cleaning and hurried to her small quarters in the attic, fortunately tomorrow was market day.

*

Marie moved confidently through the swirling, noisy crowds at the busiest market in London, Spitalfields. She carried a cumbersome wicker basket on her back and a smaller basket over her arm. As seemed to be her habit, she paused before the ornate clock tower and checked the small gold watch she kept securely under her top. A gift from Thiebault many years ago, the watch actually kept perfect time.

Henry James struggled to see through the crowds but managed to catch a glimpse of the sad looking, yet pretty lady checking the time by the clock tower. James was seventeen years old but looked closer to thirty. His face was pockmarked but handsome in a rugged manner, even with his lank greasy hair and broken nose. He moved easily through the crowd despite dragging his left leg, a consequence of stepping in front of a carriage as a small child.

He let the crowd wash past him as he moved, going with any flow he could find rather than resisting, all the while keeping his keen eyes fixed on the woman with the wicker backpack. Just then she paused at a stall piled high with potatoes and turnips. Speaking in slow but almost accent free English, she selected some fine large potatoes and the seller helped place them in her backpack. Reaching into her smock she withdrew some money, passing it to the stallholder and waiting for some change.

As the toothless old man was reaching for a few small coins, Henry James squeezed past and then was lost in the crowd. He paused to buy himself a couple of deformed carrots and drifted off through the heaving mass of humanity.

Marie shouldered her burden and moved on, pausing once more at a different vegetable stall. She glanced into her smaller basket and as ever was surprised but could barely suppress a smile, when she noticed that her shopping list had disappeared.

An hour later Henry James showed he was just as expert at placing objects into pockets, when he slid Marie's shopping list into the jacket of a well built workman as he rested on his shovel, smoking a pipe in the morning sun.

By mid-day, an official in the Aliens Office was carefully warming the sheet of paper over the heat of a candle. Over the top of Marie's shopping list, lines of neatly scribed writing began to emerge. Taking a large magnifying glass, the elderly man, a fluent French speaker, carefully translated the no longer hidden message.

*

A week had passed by when Archie next entered the dining room of Whites gentleman's club and scanned the tables, looking for just one man. He spotted Charles Lyell seated at a corner table with a thoroughly miserable look etched on his face. Archie had thought long and hard about how to make his pitch to Lyell and had finally settled on this approach, in friendly surroundings, no threats, just the inevitability of a closed trap.

'Charles Lyell?' Archie asked quietly. Lyell looked up and saw a tall, athletic looking man staring down at him through thick rimmed spectacles. He took in the slightly greying hair and long thin sideburns framing a face marked by piercing eyes and a hard looking mouth and felt instantly ill at ease.

'That I am Sir but you have me at a disadvantage I must say,' Lyell replied, rising and taking Archie's hand in a firm but sweaty grip.

'Richard York at your service,' Archie replied, allowing a fussing waiter to help get him seated at the table. 'Is there anything you can recommend old boy, I'm famished!' Richard York was another alter-ego favoured by Archie in situations where he was reluctant to reveal his true identity. A member of the somewhat wild side of London high society he was nevertheless quite well known around town and would not want his true occupation widely appreciated.

'My appetite is not so keen today but the roast beef is always divine here,' Lyell stated rather flatly. To Archie's practiced eye it was obvious that Lyell was in a blind panic, barely suppressed by the need for civility.

'That sounds lovely,' Archie said, indicating that the waiter could leave with his order, the hint being duly taken.

'I have to say that I'm intrigued to say the very least,' Lyell said quietly. 'After all it's not every day that one gets invited to lunch by a complete stranger and then have that invitation secured with a thinly veiled threat!'

'Oh, come on, not a threat surely?' Archie said with a slightly raised eyebrow.

'Your note said that you would be able to guarantee me an epic and rewarding adventure or otherwise you feared my talent would be wasted, perhaps lost forever! Would you not describe that as a carrot and a stick?'

'Well, yes, maybe so. We have much to discuss and little time as I have an assignation with a lady this afternoon,' Archie responded, with what he hoped was a disarming grin. 'A stunning proposition indeed, if I do say so myself. I met her at the Duke of Devonshire's ball a few weeks ago.'

Lyell's whole body twitched but he recovered with commendable speed, trying to look his companion squarely in the eye. As Archie rambled on about the girl,

Lyell's mind was racing, his innards turning to liquid. His eyes darted around the almost empty dining room, looking to see if anyone might be called on to give him aid.

'What exactly can I do for you Mr. York?' Lyell asked, disturbed by the slight squeak in his own voice.

'I have a wide range of business interests Charles; I can call you Charles can't I? I have a pressing need for an adventurous soul whom I can rely on to help me with a number of tasks. I need someone with a rare set of skills and who offers unswerving loyalty. I suppose what I need is a special kind of man who can get me things I'm not supposed to have or could otherwise get my hands on.'

'What…what on earth do you mean? Do you think I'm some kind of thief?' Lyell demanded, almost choking as he realised what the stranger had just said.

'Good God no Sir, you're a gentleman, everyone I've spoken to agrees. Your father should be proud of you. I hear you are a traveller, mountaineer and explorer even, I envy you your lifestyle. There are so many idle rich men in this city but you Sir have used your talents to cement a sound reputation. Oh good here comes lunch.'

Whilst the waiter served the wonderfully fragrant roast beef, Archie studied Charles Lyell closely. He saw a man who was frightened and confused but admirably restrained. He knew exactly what Lyell was thinking. He was thinking that for sure this man knew that he had been at the Duke of Devonshire's home and almost certainly knew that he had stolen from his Grace.

Lyell was on the verging of running but he forced himself to wait until he was certain that he was about to be exposed because there would be no turning back once he fled. Exile from his beloved London held little appeal.

What he could not understand was how this man knew what he had done because he was sure that York was not working for the dreadful man who had got him into this mess in the first place.

'These idle men sully the reputation of the English gentleman, don't you agree?' Archie continued, whilst chewing on a roast potato. 'Public decadence is really not the way to behave but private vices, I guess we all have those eh?'

Lyell froze, barely breathing, staring not at Archie but right through him. So he did come from those men, men who had brought him to the verge of suicide over recent weeks.

'The problem with private vices is that they don't always stay that way and then ruin so often follows. Isn't it simply outrageous the way that depravity of all kinds can be acceptable, yet always there remains something special of which nothing may be spoken, the pleasures of the molly house for instance?'

'Sit down!' Archie hissed as Lyell began to bolt from the table. Lyell, half way to his feet stared at him with huge, glassy eyes. He then followed Archie's eyes as they lowered to his waistband from which emerged the butt of a small pistol.

'Eat, please, the beef is excellent,' Archie continued quietly. He watched Lyell trying to force down some food. The mention of the molly house, the common name for a homosexual meeting place or brothel had brought Lyell's world crashing down around him. It was now that Archie was relying on the familiar surroundings to calm Lyell's panic and force the man to think logically. For the next five minutes the two men sat in silence, Archie at least, enjoying the meal.

Over coffee Lyell found his voice once more. 'What do you want from me now? Have I not done what you asked of me? Please, I beg you, I can do no more for you,' he whined pathetically.

'You've done nothing for me yet. Whatever you've done for others is passed and if they trouble you again, then I'll have them dealt with. You are too important to me to allow anyone to get in our way. If you betray me then I'll expose you for what you are then I will kill you. Your reputation will have been sullied and you'll die a broken man. Work with me and I promise you that no one will know your secrets and you will have a long and beneficial life.'

'Who are those other men? Why should I believe that I can trust you either?' Lyell sighed.

'You have my word and what's more you have no choice. You'll be watched closely, so don't run and if you do, you will be executed!' Archie told him bluntly, forcing steel into his voice.

'Oh my God, what do you want of me you swine?' Lyell pleaded.

'Go about your business, do not leave London and I will contact you when I need you. Every day at ten in the morning, go to Mary's coffee shop on Harley Street and wait for thirty minutes. If I need you I will meet you there or someone bearing my name will pass you instructions. Ensure you're not being followed and if anyone else contacts you I want to know straight away. You can leave a letter for me with Mary.'

'Who are you and what do you want me to do? Please I'll lose my mind if you leave me like this,' Lyell pleaded.

'You will just do as I say,' Archie replied, rising from the table, 'and you'll have the chance to make amends for your foolishness.'

'How do you know...things about me?' Lyell pleaded, standing too.

'I know everything about you Charles,' Archie replied with a smile and his hand outstretched. He shook Lyell's hand firmly and looked him in the eye one more time. 'This is your only chance believe me.'

*

Later that afternoon, Archie now having returned to his normal appearance, presented himself at the palatial Mayfair residence of Lord and Lady Hendricks. He fervently hoped his unannounced visit would not cause embarrassment to the family or Cordelia but he could not have been more wrong.

As soon as he was announced, Cordelia had run to his side and kissed him lightly on the cheek, much to her mother's annoyance. Slightly embarrassed, he untangled himself from her daughter and presented himself to Lady Hendricks.

'Good afternoon your ladyship, I trust you are well and do please excuse the intrusion but I had heard that you were returning to Spain within days,' Archie said smoothly, whilst kissing her proffered hand. Lady Hendricks returned his smile with warmth and a twinkle in her eye. Archie was a rogue she knew but had at last found his way and served his country with honour, though he would never be a marriage prospect for her daughter, of that she was determined.

As if she had read Archie's mind, she flushed slightly as he ran his eyes over her statuesque curves. She would not even have entertained him in her house if she had really guessed what he was thinking. Archie had always secretly admired her in the manner of a younger man's crush only more licentious in intensity. He felt that she was a gloriously handsome woman, who oozed sensuality from every pore, despite her advancing years. He was snapped from his reverie by a polite cough from the direction of the open door which lead he assumed to the gardens.

Now it was Archie's turn to feel discomfort as an icy chill of horror gripped his heart, instilling such fear that he felt at any moment his bowels would let go and mortify him with embarrassment. Caught staring lustfully at the cleavage of the Lady of the house would serve to cover his discomfort admirably.

'I'm sorry your Ladyship, it was remiss of me to arrive unannounced when you already have a guest,' Archie said, whilst straightening up and moving away from the clearly amused Lady Hendricks.

'Oh don't be so silly,' Cordelia twittered, sprinting across the room, almost dragging the young man at her side across to Archie.

'This is Sean O'Brien, a good friend of mine who I first met in Madrid. Sean this is my favourite bad apple, Archibald Dexter,' she went on, as the two men shook hands. O'Brien looked at Archie with brief hostility then quickly decided that here was a suitor who would never be more than that, after which he relaxed a little.

'Pleased to meet you Archibald,' O'Brien said with a surprisingly thick Irish accent.

O'Brien was a cheerfully handsome man in his late twenties, possessed of what Archie saw was a powerful, athletic physique, carried upon long legs that gave him a height advantage of several inches over his own impressive height.

'Have you known Cordelia long?' he asked Archie. 'I met her in Madrid after his Lordship helped me secure a goodly part of Spain's grain surplus to ship to Dublin. I thought when I left for Ireland that I would never set eyes on dear Cordelia again but not only should I find her at home in London but it seems we sail on the same boat to Spain in just two days.'

'Well, most fortunate indeed! Cordelia and I go back a long way but it seems that our ships are always sailing in opposite directions,' Archie muttered with barely concealed fury.

'Would you care for some tea Lady Hendricks?' O'Brien offered, his apparent ease amongst the Hendricks driving Archie wild with rage and fear in equal measure. For his part O'Brien was enjoying Archie's discomfort, it was always entertaining to see a potential rival suitor quite so wrong footed. Clearly this man was out of his depth and barely able to hold onto his dignity.

'Will you be staying in Spain long?' Archie enquired with a quick glance at Cordelia. She smiled back at him, clearly enjoying herself immensely too.

'Sadly only a few weeks then I must return to Ireland and arrange to hire a small fleet of ships. I do hope though that we can see something of each other Cordelia, with your Ladyships permission?'

'Oh quite so and you'll be invited to our inauguration ball of course young man,' Lady Hendricks added, warming to the task of letting Archie know where he stood, which was nowhere.

The conversation went on in much the same vein for over an hour, with the triumphant O'Brien taking every opportunity to make it very clear how much Cordelia would be seeing of him whilst in Spain. Archie fought the urge to punch him on the nose and tried to remain calm, whilst asking a few polite but probing questions about the grain business.

'Securing the harvest means I will have to travel extensively into the hinterland. I have a contact in Toledo or nearby, I forget the exact name,' he added somewhat uneasily.

'Do they have roads outside of the cities or does one travel on horseback?' Archie asked.

'Horse-back mainly though they do have mail coaches to the cities. The roads are dreadful and the heat fearsome I'm afraid or I would have invited Cordelia along, suitably chaperoned of course your Ladyship,' he added quickly.

'Cordelia is a fine horse woman but I do not think such an adventure would be suitable my dear,' Lady Hendricks interjected quickly.

'Where will you stay in Madrid?' Archie asked casually,' I hear it's a fine but expensive city'

'Might Sean stay with us mother?' Cordelia asked brightly. It was all Archie could do to prevent the word no from bursting out loud but he need have had no worry.

'I could never be so presumptuous towards your family Cordelia. There are the finest of hotels in Madrid, I shall lodge there. It's but half a mile to the Embassy I believe?' he added unnecessarily, Archie was convinced purely to aggravate him.

In this way the afternoon passed, with O'Brien enjoying baiting Archie and relishing his discomfort. For his part Archie appeared to be getting more and more jealous and determined to discover the Irishman's intentions towards Cordelia whilst in Spain. In return O'Brien was more than happy to tease him with snippets of the Madrid social scene and how he and Cordelia would pass their brief time together

Archie finally took his leave, forcing a smile as he kissed Cordelia's hand. He could not resist a subtle stroke of her delicate fingers as his eyes burned into hers, drifting blatantly over the curve of her breasts, noting with satisfaction as she blushed but did not pull away. In his heart though, there was only fear and loathing as he bade her farewell.

He caught a cab to his office, determined to see Sir John, appointment or not. Adrenaline still coursed through his veins, worry gnawing at the pit of his stomach. Sean O'Brien? Not on my mother's Aunt he thought! Antoine Pascal, French agent in actual fact.

Marie had alerted them once Pascal had arrived at the Embassy. The very next day Archie had observed Thiebault walking from the building in the company of a man matching perfectly the description of Pascal that Marie had provided.

*

'Silly question I know, but how certain are you?' Sir John questioned.

'Oh I'm certain, totally and with no shadow of a doubt. I've seen him on two occasions since he arrived in London. Saul, my agent in the French embassy gave us a flawless description. Pascal's affecting an Ulsterman's accent to cover his French lilt, yet he claims to come from Dublin.'

'Yes, once again your agent has come up trumps,' Sir John agreed. 'I hope you are sure of his safety. He's been in place far too long for comfort Archie.'

'I agree Sir but...he's safe of that I'm sure,' he reassured his superior. Only he knew Saul was in fact Marie, personal maid and cook to Jean Henri Thiebault.

'So the time has come young man. There can be no more vacillation, no more wringing of sweaty palms by our political masters. I approve of your plans in almost all respects and will seek an audience with Lord Harrowby this very evening. If the Prime Minister is persuaded then we begin tomorrow, with no going back.'

'Very good Sir but which part of my scheme meets with your disapproval?'

'Lord Hendricks and his entire family travel to Spain as planned,' Sir John said, quietly but firmly.

'Sir, I must protest,' Archie shouted, coming to his feet, anger flaring in his eyes.

'Sit down!' Sir John responded sharply. 'Agent Klaus is in mortal peril, yet he holds the key to our whole operation. Lord Hendricks knows nothing of our plans, nor does he know Klaus's identity but he does know of his existence. Pascal may or may not know Klaus's identity. Personally I doubt it but better the devil you know, so nothing must alert him to our knowledge and nothing must prevent him travelling to Spain. If the girl were suddenly not to travel then this may cause him to change his plans and we could lose him.

'But Sir, it places her in harm's way and it just feels wrong somehow,' Archie said, trying not to plead too hard.

'No more discussion. If Pascal is taken by us now or

143

just scared off then Klaus will be hunted down by a total unknown and we may not be able to prevent his exposure. Leave Pitt and the others to me, you must assume that we are getting the go ahead. Get Lyell on his way, we've already secured him a berth on the ship and I'm mindful that it sails from Tilbury in less than forty-eight hours!'

'Yes Sir,' Archie sighed, standing to leave, 'and the very best of luck with the Prime Minister.'

'Make no mistake, we are steering a course for war but this way it's a war we can win. The alternative bears no consideration,' Sir John concluded.

*

The next forty-eight hours passed in a whirlwind of frenetic activity for Archie and his men. Cedric was instructed to prepare the house for an absence of at least three months. Archie had decided he needed his manservant and his many varied skills close at hand. The unexpected meeting with Pascal had thrown his plans into some disarray but Sir John had agreed that he should go to Spain as planned.

Archie donned his Richard York persona and was waiting for Lyell in the plush Harley Street coffee shop by ten o'clock. They took seats in a relatively quiet corner and made small talk until the garrulous young waiter had served their coffee and finally withdrawn.

'Okay my nervous friend, I have job for you and who knows you might actually enjoy yourself,' Archie began. 'I need to find someone and quickly because he's in great danger from a business rival, who will quite literally, kill anyone to secure a profit.'

'Good God, what danger are you putting me in?' Lyell whined.

'Mortal danger but unless your reputation is just a cleverly woven fabrication to impress your friends then it shouldn't be anything you can't handle,' Archie hissed at him, as loudly as he dared. He noted with satisfaction that his words appeared to slap the man around his handsome face.

'How dare you, you bastard, how much of my soul do you want?' Lyell responded, a trace of self righteous anger in his voice.

'I already have every inch of it Charles,' Archie replied, somewhat relieved to see a little fight in the other man at last. 'Tell absolutely no one where you are really going, including your servants, who you will inform that you are journeying to Scotland. You are travelling to Madrid, tomorrow from Tilbury and you'll be away for perhaps three months.'

'Spain! You cannot be serious? So is this why you choose to blackmail me, in order to get me to Spain?' Lyell asked astounded but secretly just a little excited at the prospect of returning to the country he had come to love.

'Deadly serious I assure you. Be warned my friend, travelling on that boat is a member of the enemy camp. You'll undoubtedly meet a man by the name of Sean O'Brien. He's a most agreeable chap but also my sworn enemy. You must reveal nothing of me or our business but feel free to regale him with your tales of adventure and befriend him if you can. Also travelling on that boat is the British Ambassador to Spain, along with his family. O'Brien is a family friend and poses no danger to them but you must watch and listen to everything he says on the voyage.'

'Good God, what is this really all about? Why does the Ambassador travel on a passenger ship, shouldn't the Royal Navy protect him?' Lyell enquired.

'His presence conveys diplomatic protection on the vessel and he'll carry the Royal Seal, so there'll be no danger to any of you,' Archie assured him.

'What do I do when I arrive in Spain and what on earth do I tell people I'm travelling for?' Lyell asked, his mind reeling with the speed that all control of his life was slipping from his grasp.

'You can tell everyone that you are going to climb some more mountains and you must make preparations as though that's your intention. Take sufficient funds for your stay and spend your time once you arrive as though you are intending one day soon to head off into the hills. Each day at ten in the morning, take breakfast at the Café San Carlos off the Plaza Mayor. I or one of my friends will meet you there one day. They will use the codeword Bucephalus to identify themselves. You must obey them as you would me. If a messenger gives you the word Titan, you are to flee for your life and return to London by whatever means you choose.'

'This is madness, what if I refuse?' Lyell asked quietly, dreading the inevitable answer.

'Your reputation will be ruined and who knows, you may even hang! Come along for the ride Charles, it'll be fine sport, trust me,' Archie said as lightly as he could.

The two men continued to talk for several hours, working their way through a small mountain of pastries and several more cups of thick, gritty coffee. Gradually Archie was able to appeal to the romantic adventurer in Lyell and slowly he began to accept the inevitability of this extraordinary twist in his already unconventional life.

'Now go make your preparations and we'll meet again in Spain. Learn all you can of O'Brien during the voyage, for our paths will surely cross again,' Archie concluded and nearly added an instruction to watch out for Cordelia but checked himself, for he was certain Pascal meant her no harm.

*

CHAPTER 3

SPAIN

The next day, as Lyell rode in a well laden coach over the bumpy lanes of Essex, Archie was at last on his way too, travelling in a small convoy of carriages bound for Folkestone in Kent. He rode alone, with just his thoughts for company, whilst Cedric and Tom rode in the second carriage. The third carried the remainder their belongings, packed into sea trunks.

They travelled at a reckless speed, for the plan called for Archie and his party to reach Madrid well ahead of Lyell and the Hendricks family. Unlike them, they would have to endure the sparse comforts of a Royal Navy frigate, part of a squadron sailing to the western Mediterranean, from where they could harass French shipping. They would be put ashore in Portugal and make the gruelling journey overland to Madrid. The passenger ship would sail much more slowly but would dock in Santander, lying over one hundred and fifty miles closer to Madrid on Spain's north coast.

*

The Royal Navy safely delivered them to Porto, five whole days ahead of the other ship's arrival in Spain. Lyell had spent a miserable time, along with the other passengers as they were hurled about in mountainous seas for most of their journey. He had however enjoyed the last two days of the voyage, much of it in the company of the Hendricks family and their limpet like friend, O'Brien.

Lyell learned much of O'Brien's life story, blissfully

unaware that it was a tissue of lies. O'Brien was clearly besotted with Cordelia Hendricks and Lyell detected not one hint of disapproval from her parents. During many hours of conversation with the genial Irishman he committed to memory as much as he could of the man's plans for his time in Spain. What on earth York could have against a grain merchant from Dublin, he could not begin to imagine.

Once safely docked in Santander, the disparate little group took separate carriages for the dusty journey to Madrid. Though the journey was only a little over three hundred miles, the mountainous terrain and difficult roads meant for an uncomfortable experience lasting nearly ten days. Twice on the journey Lyell had found himself at the same roadside cantina as O'Brien and once the Hendricks family. In this way several pleasant enough, though exhausting evenings were passed, the bond between weary travellers unshakeable.

For his part, Lyell passed the journey admiring the towering mountains that either hovered tantalisingly on the horizon, shimmering through the heat haze or barred their way as a seemingly impassable ridge of razor sharp teeth, cutting the landscape in two. There would then follow a hair-raising and stomach churning ascent of twisting and turning tracks, all the while beckoning forward the inevitable horror of the steep descent.

Eventually the journey came to its end and the beautiful city of Madrid lay spread before him. He was once again captivated by the elegance of the city centre with its breathtaking buildings many over two hundred years old. The carriage travelled across expansive squares and clattered along wide boulevards of the city centre before moving on into cooler, shaded streets, narrow and bustling, more reminiscent of London on a summer's day.

Eventually the dust covered carriage drew to a halt outside the magnificent, almost Arabian frontage of Madrid's newest and most prestigious hotel. Almost too exhausted to walk, Lyell allowed himself to be hustled to his beautiful rooms, his luggage to be unpacked and the most modern of luxuries, a cool bath to be prepared. He generously tipped the hotel staff that had helped him, so exhausted that he barely registered the young man who informed him that he would be his personal valet for the duration of his stay.

Archie and Cedric were staying a little over a mile from Lyell's hotel, where they had taken rooms in a pleasant but simple cantina. Tom was staying in the same building but had arrived separately from them. He would shadow the two men wherever they went and would be their last line of defence should anything go wrong.

Archie had used his time to explore the city and to practice his flawed Spanish. Once the Hendricks party had arrived and the despatches his Lordship carried were read, then his mission could begin. Lord Hendricks' aide carried a number of coded messages for a member of the Embassy staff by the name of Samuel Perks. Perks was no ordinary clerk though. Using his position as cover, he was Sir John's man in Madrid and his most important job was to run an agent known as Klaus.

What Perks knew and Archie did not, was that Klaus was a high ranking official in the Court of King Charles 1V. In fact Klaus was an aide to the Prime Minister and de facto ruler of Spain, Manuel de Godoy. As Godoy twisted and turned Spain's relationship with Napoleon's France, it was frequently Klaus who was on the receiving end of his Prime Minister's frustrations and hence was privy to his innermost thoughts.

Archie had become bored after nearly a week of restless inactivity. His Spanish had certainly improved, though not enough to stop him losing heavily in a dice game several nights running. He had not been idle though and fancied that he knew much of central Madrid almost as well as he knew Mayfair.

Cedric had been keeping a watchful eye on the British Embassy for several days before finally reporting the arrival of a dishevelled party of travellers he believed to include the new British Ambassador. Archie was heartily relieved that there was no sign of O'Brien. Just the previous night his subconscious had conjured up images of the rakish Irishman repeatedly taking sweet Cordelia's virginity, first in a wildly swinging hammock and then aboard a speeding stagecoach. Oh jealous eyes what you do see, he thought with a tight grin.

Later that day in the embassy, Perks slowly and with great care decoded his messages. He was dismayed to read the last one that he examined, shocked to his very core. By far the longest message, it began well enough by announcing that an agent had been sent from England with a special request of agent Klaus. However the second paragraph telling of a new and immediate threat to the spy, unsettled him greatly.

Perks had controlled Klaus for nearly two years now and had formed a dangerously close bond with the man. Now the words he had long dreaded were written clear to see before his eyes.

"*Klaus is in imminent danger, prepare to make good*

his escape to England but not, repeat not before Klaus has obtained information for agent Bucephalus. Nothing must prevent Bucephalus from success in his mission. Klaus is to be saved if possible but is expendable."

Perks read the message twice more before burning it. He had separate instructions on how to contact this Bucephalus and would have an agonising wait until the next day before he could learn more. However he would not be idle, for he had much to prepare to ensure Klaus would not face the gallows, no matter what his orders.

*

Archie was in a relaxed mood as he strolled along a wide boulevard lined with date palms, standing tall before exquisitely beautiful sandstone buildings. The warm sun did nothing to quell the frenetic activity of the populace going about their business in the relative cool of the early morning. He felt just a slight tension, mixed with a frisson of excitement in the knowledge that at last the time for decisive and swift action was approaching.

He and Cedric had moved and were now staying in a small hotel situated on the southern corner of a quiet square, overlooking a small but ornate church. From now on Archibald Dexter would not be seen again. Being observed by Cordelia, walking the streets of Madrid, would be almost as disastrous as being found by his enemies. Richard York though had a mission to see through and now it was to begin in earnest. With his disguise in place, augmented by a large, wide-brimmed felt hat, he arrived at the Café Miguel early and took a corner table. With his refined Spanish skills he had no trouble in ordering a delicious sounding breakfast as he settled to wait.

From his vantage point he was able to watch both the side door and open frontage to the café. As eight thirty approached he was content and relaxed as a man he decided just had to be Perks breezed in. The man was short and of slight build, fair haired and sported a neatly trimmed but bushy moustache. He appeared dapper and neat without any air of pretention. Without breaking stride, he approached Archie and sat down. Archie was after all the only patron wearing brown leather gloves.

'Excuse me Sir but would you have a horse I could borrow?' Perks asked quietly.

'Indeed I do, by the name of Bucephalus no less.'

'Good morning Mr. York, Sam Perks, would you like me to order you some food?' he asked with a slightly supercilious tone.

'Already done thanks but please order for yourself,' Archie replied evenly, flicking his eyes in the direction of the approaching waiter. The order taken, the obese waiter plodded away in the direction of the kitchen.

'When I read the coded despatches, I must say I was greatly concerned. Klaus has been a faithful servant to His Majesty and if he's in mortal danger then we must rescue him without delay,' Perks insisted.

'You saw your orders, I know it's tough but we need one more sacrifice from him. We've a vital request, yes I know everyone always says that but for once it's true,' Archie tried to reassure him.

'I will not see a good man sacrificed,' Perks insisted firmly.

'My mission has the absolute priority and yes I'm sorry but that includes over your man's safety,' Archie replied as gently as he could. He had run informers and agents for years and knew how one became attached to them. He would move heaven and earth to protect Marie back in London.

'How close to exposure is Klaus?' Perks asked warily, dreading the answer.

'A French agent is in Madrid right now, with a mission to expose him. How much he knows or suspects, I don't know, save to say he's been sent from Paris with this express aim, so the presence of an agent in the Spanish Court is clearly already known to the French. I know the identity of this Frenchman and will do all I can to neutralise him before he gets close to Klaus. If he knows Klaus's identity already then I suspect we may be too late.'

'We may have another edge on this assassin though,' Perks said in hushed tones. 'I know the identity of the principal French agent inside the Spanish Court and I know where he meets his liaison. I have people who watch when documents are handed over. Perhaps we might intercede and learn what is known of Klaus.'

'Perhaps we might indeed,' Archie replied, quietly impressed, 'but first you must give Klaus his instructions and he must not be alerted to the danger he's in. Nothing must stand in the way of this request.'

'What do you need Mr. York? Klaus is due to leave Madrid in the next few days and before that he must conclude what London had said was a vital mission. Now you say your mission takes priority, which poses a problem does it not?' Perks whispered, his voice trailing off as the waiter brought a splendid looking breakfast of cold meats and bread over for the two men.

'On the face of it what I need is quite straight forward. I need either the departure date or the predicted arrival date, of Spain's next bullion shipment from the Americas.'

'What, you're not serious?' Perks replied, with a barely concealed snort of derision. 'You're not going to steal it are you?' he asked, his grin fading as he realised this was no laughing matter. 'My God, you are!' Perks said, struggling to keep his voice low. 'Why man and how? It'll start a war for Christ's sake, it will drive the Spaniards into Napoleon's camp and war will be inevitable...my God... I see it now.'

'It's really quite simple Perks, if an alliance cannot be set against Napoleon alone then surely the vacillating weaklings of Europe will have to rally against such a dangerous foe as a Franco-Spanish axis. If Napoleon is allowed to pick off one weak country at a time until only Prussia and England stand then disaster will surely follow. The great and the good in Horse Guards have told Pitt that in such a scenario we'll all need a French phrase book to order dinner at Whites by the time King George is seventy.'

'How on earth do you propose to steal Spain's bullion, its sheer folly,' Perks exclaimed, unable to prevent a furtive glance round at the rapidly filling room.

'I don't intend to and how it's to be done should not concern you either. What is vital is that the number of people who know of this can be counted on your fingers and that's how it will stay, do you understand?' Archie said, clear, cold menace in his voice.

'Do not presume to threaten me Sir! I have my orders and will carry them out, you can rest assured. Klaus can undoubtedly get your information. The question is when, because in three days time he has to travel with the High Chancellor to a town beyond the mountains. He's no choice but to go and we may have to wait until his return. There'll then be a further delay before he can get the information out through his chain of contacts.'

'I'm in no rush but every day he's exposed to danger brings the garrote closer to his neck. Make contact with him and do it quickly. Remember, this is the only priority, he is to do nothing else that risks his exposure,' Archie ordered.

'The message will get to him by midday tomorrow. The earliest he can return with our information will be the day after, failing that we have to wait until he returns with the Chancellor.'

'So be it then, now let it begin. The gold has the top priority, tell him to stop anything else he may be doing for you. I presume you have a plan in place for his escape?'

'Of course but it's too dangerous to even begin preparations until he's ready to run. He can disappear for maybe twenty four hours, no more before the hounds will be unleashed.'

*

Perks returned to the British Embassy and immediately began coding a message which would pass through several hands before being received by an office boy working in the Spanish Treasury. He would leave the small piece of paper hidden in a water closet on the building's third floor. Klaus would find the message and decode it. Perks wrote out the message exactly as Archie had instructed. After a moment's reflection, he burnt it and wrote it out again!

"Vital you find dates of next gold shipment from Americas, when it leaves and when and where it will arrive. Do not forget we still need the General's answer as soon as possible."

He placed the tiny scrap of paper into the false bottom of a small snuff box, popped it in his jacket pocket and left the Embassy. After nearly an hour he was satisfied he was not being followed and he entered the rather dingy offices of a lawyer by the name of Sanchez. Sitting at the front desk was a slight and rather weary looking young girl, who brightened markedly at the sight of Perks. Without a word passing between them he gave her the snuff box and an envelope, the contents of which exceeded half her annual salary. Her share of the money alone was more than she earned in a month.

'As quickly as possible, no delays whatsoever,' were Perks only words before with a feeling of relief he walked back out into the sunshine once more.

The girl usually went home for a siesta at one o'clock in the afternoon but today she took a detour to a café three blocks to the south. Seve, a dissolute and work-shy waiter was idly sweeping the floor prior to closing up for the afternoon. The sight of the girl and the thought of his share of the money remaining in the envelope, improved his sour mood no end.

The process was repeated twice more before late that evening, a printer's apprentice called at the lodgings of young man called Enzo. Enzo too found his spirits lifted by the caller at his door and he gratefully took the envelope and snuffbox before hiding both beneath his wardrobe.

By eight the next morning Enzo was seated at his desk in the Treasury building. Seeing that every desk appeared occupied, he took himself away to the washroom only recently installed near to where the office workers toiled in the still, hot air. Certain he was alone in the dark, slightly offensive smelling room; he secreted the small piece of paper behind a loose ceramic tile before returning to his desk. The last five minutes work had earned him nearly two months salary.

Archie, in the persona of Richard York, had seated himself comfortably in the rear of the Café San Carlos at nine thirty that morning. The small, roughly made table was set off by a bright red checked tablecloth, with clean utensils and condiments in a small rack at its centre. Ordering strong, dark coffee, he passed the time watching the few customers breakfasting, trying to follow their whispered conversations. His thoughts were interrupted by the reappearance of the waitress. She had told him that her name was Carla. She was tall, almost as tall as him, possessed of a slender body that moved as though liquid, as she expertly negotiated the cluttered little café.

'Are you sure I cannot tempt you with a little food Senor?' she purred, her dark eyes boring into him, as she placed his drink on the table before him. He could not resist a genuine smile and gave her an appraising glance that he hoped would not be taken for a leer, well not too much anyhow.

'When my business contact arrives then... here he is now,' he finished, whilst rising to greet Charles Lyell with a firm handshake. Lyell forced a smile and took the proffered seat. Food was hurriedly ordered and the girl moved on to the next table.

'How was the voyage over? I assume the weather was bad for you, as we beat you by days,' Archie asked as soon as they were alone.

'Frightful, simply frightful and though I rarely suffer with it, this time I was terribly ill for several days.'

'Did you get to know your fellow travellers during the journey?' Archie asked, anxious to hear of Cordelia, let alone O'Brien.

'One could hardly fail to, a shared ordeal and all that. I think it's fair to say that I have an open invitation to visit the Embassy any time I choose. The Hendricks' are quite delightful people. O'Brien is a rum cove though, personable enough but not what he seems at all.'

'What makes you say that?' Archie enquired warily.

'Well, for a start I don't think he's Irish at all. He says he comes from just south of Dublin, yet speaks with an Ulster accent. Do you know, on a couple of occasions I thought he sounded French. Maybe a randy Frenchie knew his mother?' he added with a snigger.

'He's a man of mystery for sure. What are his plans whilst in Spain?' Archie asked, suppressing a smile.

'He's coming to Madrid apparently. He let slip to Cordelia, the Hendricks charming daughter that he was staying with friends in Calle de Cordoba. He's here to buy grain, so he says. What is he to you and what on earth have you dragged me here for York!'

'Don't trouble yourself with that, you're here to help me and that's all you need to know. For now keep a low profile and when I need you, I'll find you or failing that I will see you here tomorrow. Now, it looks as if breakfast has arrived, tell me more about your journey?'

As they ate, Lyell opened up and talked in some detail about the journey from England. Archie was captivated by his flowing prose, especially when describing the wonderful landscape of northern Spain. He was less pleased to hear Lyell describe O'Brien's designs on Cordelia, attention that was apparently welcomed by the vivacious young lady. Unbidden images of Cordelia writhing naked beneath the Irishman flashed into his mind once more. It was the joyous smile on her face as she was so lustfully taken that he found most disturbing in these daydreams.

After nearly an hour, the two men parted company. Archie found himself warming to Lyell and was impressed by the stoic acceptance that his immediate fate was in the hands of another.

He walked through the dusty streets, carefully checking that he was not being followed. He made his way safely to the boarding house where Tom was now residing, where he updated his assistant and sent him off to scour the area around Calle de Cordoba to see if he could locate Pascal.

*

At almost that very moment, within the walled garden of the Villa St Anna, situated at the corner of Calle de Cordoba and Calle Mayor, Antoine Pascal was holding a counsel of war with his two resident agents. He was astounded by what they had to tell him, they had been supremely successful in their work whilst he had been journeying from Paris via London.

By sheer good fortune, they had been approached by one of their many informers, who in turn had put them in contact with a printer's apprentice. This young man wished to sell them the contents of messages he was passing to a spy who worked in the Spanish Treasury building. He had been passing such messages for months and by chance he had seen his next contact, a man he knew only as Enzo, entering the Treasury building. He had realised that either Enzo was the spy or more likely was passing the message to a colleague within that building.

Through a friend, the apprentice had made contact with a man he believed worked for the Spanish government but was in fact a French agent. The young man had been paid and the note he carried examined but they had still not cracked the code used to encrypt the message. That had been a week ago and they had just learned that another message had been passed along the conduit.

'No doubt the arrival of the new British Ambassador has prompted this instruction for their agent. You have done well Jean, very well indeed.'

'There's more Antoine,' Jean said hurriedly. 'We've learned that a Portuguese General is planning to betray his country to the Spanish. There is a military delegation in Madrid as we speak. Our sources tell us that no less than four Generals are here and the traitor is amongst them. The General who has sold his soul is to visit the Treasury either today or tomorrow.

'Good news for the Spanish and ultimately us but that does not help find the viper in their midst,' Pascal pointed out.

'I think perhaps it might though Antoine. Surely this spy the English have in the Court will discover the identity of this Portuguese turncoat and will tell his masters. When the message comes down the line of contacts, we will know about it. If we can find out who this General has approached whilst in the Treasury, perhaps we can identify the British spy?'

'My God you're right, this could play straight into our hands,' Pascal said, an unmistakable note of triumph in his voice. 'We must know the minute the printer receives a message from this man Enzo. You two go and keep watch on him. With the Portuguese General in Madrid this whole affair could be over by the end of the day.'

When Pascal's agents left the villa, Tom trailed casually behind them using the noisy crowd as cover. Though he had little or no Spanish, with his rapidly tanning, leathery skin and recently grown beard, he blended in easily with the busy locals.

*

Manuel Costa was a man used to the finest things in life and as he squeezed his ever expanding waistline behind his enormous mahogany desk, he was already dreaming of lunch. Sitting upright he made an effort to appear important, a little aloof yet amenable. A hectic day lay ahead and he was already regretting his decision to miss breakfast. If he felt nervous at the prospect of betraying his country once more then he certainly did not show it.

The man that Perks had codenamed Klaus had two motivations for his treachery. The first was perhaps the oldest reason on earth, greed. In Costa's case though he was also able to justify his actions in the name of revenge, which helped when the moments of doubt tormented him in the dark hours. His brother had been falsely accused of fraud and executed for the crimes of another. Costa had sworn to take his revenge, perhaps the second oldest excuse for treason.

There was a discrete knock on the door and his guest was ushered in by Enzo his clerk for the day. Costa struggled to rise but managed to respectfully greet General de Castro and offer him a seat.

By lunchtime the deal was done. Costa was authorised to make a substantial payment to the General and the treachery was sealed. Even before taking his lunch, Costa prepared a coded note and secreted it in the water closet. As he returned to his office in order to escort the General to lunch with other Treasury officials, Enzo's eyes followed him closely.

A short while later Enzo went to the washroom and recovered the note he had expected to find. This confirmed his long held suspicion that Manuel Costa was the spy working in the Treasury. Satisfied by his own attempts at espionage, he took an early lunch and with the note hidden in the tiny snuff box in his pocket, he made his way through the busy streets to the print shop in Plaza san Andreas.

Afterwards Enzo took his lunch in a small cantina and then returned to the ornate, Moorish style sandstone building housing the Treasury. Pascal's men followed him discretely the whole way. Later that afternoon, he would be followed home by the same men. All the while, unnoticed, blending in with the crowds, Tom trailed in the footsteps of the Frenchmen.

*

The next morning, a worried Archie waited impatiently for Perks to arrive at the Café Miguel. When he finally entered the crowded café, Archie had already ordered for the two of them. Wasting no time, he brought Perks up to date on developments and saw immediate and terrible fear in the man's eyes.

'My God how has this happened, what have you done?' he demanded of Archie.

'Nothing I assure you. It's clear that French agents are all over your man. They may not have his name just yet but they are obviously very close. I assume this boy is not your agent but does he know who Klaus is?'

'No. At least he shouldn't know. The messages are hidden in the building for Enzo to collect but I suppose it's not impossible that he has worked out Klaus's identity. The whole chain of messengers must have been compromised. How has this happened?'

'Who knows, but it has and right now we need to ensure that your man Klaus is safe but not before he gets my information,' Archie stated emphatically.

'Klaus will be leaving for Riaza soon. We must find out what Enzo knows and whether he's betrayed us to the French. Come, I can gain access to the Treasury building,' Perks said as he rose from his chair.

The two men walked at breakneck speed the short distance to the Treasury building. Archie waited round the corner whilst Perks used his diplomatic status to gain access. He returned minutes later, a grave look on his face.

'Enzo hasn't come in to work today. Quickly, follow me; he lives nearby, 'Perks added, striding across the busy road. 'Klaus has already left Madrid with the Chancellor so he's safe, at least for now. Don't worry I'm confident that he will get your information whilst on this trip.'

With increasing urgency in their step, the two men jostled and weaved their way through the crowded streets toward a small block of one room dwellings. Perks was unable to get an answer with his ever more urgent knocks upon Enzo's front door. Archie looked up and down the corridor relieved to note their knocks were not attracting any attention. The food smells were different but the mustiness and sounds were no different from those in similar London dwellings. Somewhere a woman was shouting at a crying child, whilst behind another thin wooden door, a couple copulated furiously and noisily.

Turning back, much to his surprise he saw that Perks had already picked the lock. The room was unoccupied, neat and spotlessly clean. Both men were relieved that there were no signs of a struggle, so in the hope that nothing untoward had befallen the young man, they left quietly. After arranging to meet up once more in the early evening, Perks returned to the Embassy and Archie walked back to his hotel, deep in troubled thought.

Early that afternoon Tom arrived at his room with yet more unsettling news. He had been watching the house of the French agents since early morning. Two of the Frenchmen had recently arrived at the house in the company of the young man they had been following the day before. With a sinking feeling in the pit of his stomach, Archie knew they had Enzo and was worried sick, despite the fact that Tom insisted that he appeared to be going along willingly.

Archie was now convinced that Enzo had betrayed Klaus to the French. Tom had still more disturbing news to impart. Around twelve o'clock, a carriage and three horses had arrived at the house. An hour later the three Frenchmen, in the company of the Spanish carriage driver had departed, laden down with supplies. Tom had not seen Enzo leave but had found it impossible to watch the door every minute of the day as he walked the street with the other pedestrians.

Archie sent Tom back to the Frenchmen's house and dispatched Cedric to find Lyell with instructions to change his appearance as best he could. Once Cedric had returned, Archie had him ensure his own disguise was all in place. Archie had let his hair and sideburns grow out but he still needed Cedric's magic touch with the dye and other little details. Finally he sent him to help Tom keep watch on the French agents lair.

Archie went for a walk to clear his head while he waited for five o'clock and his arranged meeting with Sam Perks. He absorbed the sights and sounds of the city, with its gracious old buildings, many reminiscent of cultures old and new across both Europe and North Africa. Just as in London, poverty stalked the streets alongside opulent grandeur. Walking past the door of a building dating back to the Renaissance, he watched as a fine lady of Madrid entered, completely ignoring a legless child begging for food. Nothing changes he thought and tossed the boy some coins.

He met up with Perks and they returned to Enzo's humble home. Everything was exactly as it had been before, undisturbed and to Archie's fertile imagination, no longer required. The two men left quickly and made their way to Calle de Cordoba, where they found Tom and Cedric who told them that the house appeared empty. Cedric was sent to fetch Lyell and by the shade of lemon tree, they held a counsel of war.

'The occupants of this house, which includes O'Brien,' he said glancing at Lyell, by way of explanation, 'appear to have left in a hurry. I want to see if they've left anything interesting behind.'

'Charles, I want you to keep watch while we see if we can get inside. If anyone returns, use your imagination but whatever you do make a lot of noise eh?' Archie said, trying to keep his mood light. Cedric had darkened the young man's hair and shortened it but this would not fool Pascal for a moment.

'House breaking, come on what is this all about, tell me

now or I'll go to the British Embassy and tell them you kidnapped me,' a clearly panicky Lyell blustered.

'You will do nothing of the sort young man. You're here to help us and that is exactly what you are going to do,' Cedric assured him with a crooked grin on his face. 'I'm not sure your father would be happy to find out how you tip hotel waiters eh?'

Archie gave Cedric a questioning look but his silly grin told him all he needed to know. Clearly he had caught Lyell, quite literally with his trousers down.

'Trust me Charles, this is an honourable endeavour and what's more you have no choice but to help. I like you and I'll reward you handsomely but cross me and I will ruin you, or worse,' Archie added with quiet but unmistakable menace in his voice, as he glared at the frightened, blushing man.

Perks watched closely but was unmoved. He knew exactly what was going on and had coerced many people to do his own bidding over the years. His conscience was clear watching the younger man squirm on a hook not of his own baiting for once.

Observing resignation if not defeat in Lyell's eyes, Archie gave his arm a reassuring squeeze and led the way to the subterranean side door of the house. He noted the ground floor shutters were all closed securely and no doubt the doors were locked too. There were few pedestrians walking down the narrow, rubbish strewn side-street, more an alleyway in reality. Perks quickly applied a small metal tool to the lock which was stiff with age but worn and easily yielding. With a silent prayer for an open bolt he watched Perks turn the handle. Within seconds they were inside.

Archie and Tom drew prepared pistols and they all waited anxiously for their eyes to grow accustomed to the dark. Archie led the way into a scullery and from there into a small untidy kitchen. There was no fire in the grate but food stuffs lay scattered across the rough hewn trestle table. Archie moved quickly to the stone stairs and began to climb.

Once in the hallway above, it was a little lighter but still they had to feel their way to the next doorway. Tom positioned himself to cover the front door and prepared a second pistol, he would be their first line of defence.

Quickly they searched the ground floor rooms which were clean yet sparsely furnished but nothing of interest was found. Archie became convinced the house was unoccupied and moved rapidly to the upper floor. Carefully entering the first room he came to, he found it bright and airy with open shutters. He had entered a charnel house, the horror inside almost forced his stomach to revolt. Perks could not take the vision before him and retched violently against the wall.

The young man Enzo was tied to an incongruously ornate and pretty bedroom chair. Stripped to the waist, his body was marked by a series of long burns, five in total Archie counted. His face was a mass of contusions and his throat had been cut, dried blood stained his body and much of the chair.

Archie felt his heart turn to ice, he had seriously misread Antoine Pascal. The man was clearly deranged but no matter, he was now a dead man walking. Archie would see to that personally, he promised the battered corpse.

'Why in God's name has this happened?' Perks asked his voice shaky and faint. 'How could they even suspect this poor lad knew Klaus's identity? He couldn't have told them, no matter what they did to him,' Perks whispered while appearing to shrink before Archie's eyes, as he hunched up and clutched himself tightly. His face was ashen and he rubbed his hands together uncontrollably, seeking perhaps to cleanse himself of the horror before them.

'Do you really believe that? Maybe this... caused him to name someone, anyone to make them stop. Who would he have named? Who would he have guessed at or made up, if he had to give a name?'

'Oh God no, you're right of course,' Perks wailed. 'Yesterday Enzo delivered a note that Klaus had hidden for him. Klaus must have placed it just after he had met General de Castro. Maybe Enzo linked the two events and realised Klaus was reporting on his meeting with the General.'

'Why was Klaus meeting this General? He was supposed to have no other mission but mine,' Archie asked quietly, fury building in his chest, his hand creeping unbidden toward the butt of his pistol.

'It was already arranged, it was a grand coup. Klaus had ensured it was he who recruited a Portuguese General who was looking to spy for Spain. Everything he passed to Klaus would of course be reported back to me, to either limit the damage or change the intelligence before it was passed on to Klaus's political masters in the Spanish government. In his rush to inform me he may have shown his hand to Enzo.'

'Well Enzo surely paid for that bit of curiosity did he not?' Archie retorted flatly, before turning and stomping out of the room.

They secured the house and went their separate ways before meeting half an hour later back at Archie's room.

'Who is Klaus?' Archie asked bluntly.

Perks hesitated and looked around at the others until his glare fell upon the uncomfortable face of the Honourable Charles Lyell. Perks had recognised him from the very start and knew he was a famous society dandy and freeloading adventurer.

'I'll personally vouch for all my men, including Charles. We've no more time for subterfuges and we need his help as never before. Charles, you are in the service of your King and you will rise to the challenge or you'll surely die before this day is out.' Unable to speak, Lyell chose to stare at the slightly threadbare African rug covering much of the room's floor.

'Klaus is the codename for Manuel Costa, essentially the Deputy Chancellor of the Spanish Treasury,' Perks began quietly. 'He's travelling to Riaza, beyond the mountains, where the Chancellor has a home. It's there that the final agreement will be signed for the purchase of gold from the Americas.'

Archie was more than a little impressed that Perks had recruited and successfully run such a highly placed agent, at the very heart of the Spanish government. It was little wonder he thought that recent events had almost broken the officious little man, who even now was still rubbing his hands together nervously.

'When did they leave and when will they arrive in Riaza? 'Archie asked urgently.

'They left yesterday evening and will arrive in Riaza late tomorrow. It's planned that they'll spend four days there before returning to Madrid. Once Klaus is back in the

170

capital, then you will have your answer.'

'He'll never make it back to Madrid alive for surely Riaza is where O'Brien or should I say, Antoine Pascal and his henchmen are heading,' Archie concluded. 'Charles, you know the mountains around these parts, is there any way we can beat the French to Riaza?'

'It might be possible to go over the hills and get to this place at about the same time as O'Brien, this Pascal or whatever his name may be. There's a wide valley north of here which contains the only roadway to the northern plains. I have a friend, Cortez, who's worked as a guide for me in the past. Perhaps he could take us over the narrow mountain passes and it might be possible to arrive in time to stop whatever plans they have.'

'Go now, find this Cortez and pay him whatever he asks in order to secure his services. He'll need to provide horses for the four of us and any supplies including muskets but we must move quickly,' he urged Lyell. Moving an ornate chest of drawers to one side he lifted a loose floorboard. He withdrew a small leather purse and took from it a selection of gold coins which he gave to Lyell.

'Five horses, I'm coming too,' Perks said, a determined look on his face, a little colour slowly returning to his sunken cheeks.

'Okay, let's go. Charles go quickly and find your man and if you cannot find him then you must find us someone else or we'll be forced to go alone. Perks go get what you need for the trip, speed is of the essence or we will lose not only Klaus but any chance of succeeding in our own task.'

*

Dawn the following day broke fresh and clear. Over an

171

hour earlier Archie and his companions had begun threading their way through the deserted streets of Madrid and were at last approaching open countryside. Lyell had excelled himself in Archie's eyes by finding a guide, horses and provisions before daybreak. With two spare horses in tow, enough food for three days and blankets to ward off the chill mountain air, their guide Seve Cortez was confident they would arrive in Riaza in two days. This would be only a matter of hours after the French party could hope to complete their own journey.

As the increasing heat of the day began to sap their strength, the Englishmen continued to move slowly but surely closer to the foothills of the mountains looming through the gathering, milky haze. For much of the morning, Archie and Perks rode together, with Perks anxious for news of London. It transpired that he was something of a bon viveur who missed the social scene terribly.

Archie had removed the false hair pieces of his Richard York persona having allowed the stubble to grow back naturally into impressive sideburns. He introduced himself properly to both Perks and Lyell as the strain of living a lie in such close quarters was already becoming tiresome. If their guide wondered why Lyell's blond hair was now streaked with black dye, then he kept his counsel.

By early evening the tired, dust streaked travellers were in lightly wooded foothills and Cortez made camp beside a small, fast flowing stream. Tom was the least experienced horseman and could barely walk by this time, though after some gentle ribbing, accepted his discomfort with dignity.

The men enjoyed a hearty meal under the stars but the conversation was stilted by exhaustion. By nine o'clock the whole party checked over the horses and turned in for the night. Archie lay staring up at the vast spread of space, the twinkling stars and the bright haze that made up the Milky Way. He loved being beneath the heavens, wondering whether somewhere out there, other men were looking out of their world towards the Earth. He thought it madness to preach that only on Earth would you find mankind. If that were so, whatever was that vast night sky out there for?

By the gentle light of early morning, the group threaded their way in single file along a track twisting and turning its way up a dry valley. The tough horses mostly took the terrain in their stride, only once did one of them stumble but the beast recovered quickly. As the track steepened, progress slowed to a steady plod and Archie began to have recurring doubts about their chances of success.

They exited the valley into a dense wood of pine trees which offered welcome relief from the strong sun. After another hour of steady progress they paused and ate a hearty breakfast before moving on across what turned out to be a vast tree covered plain, almost mirror flat despite the altitude they had already reached.

They pushed on through the heat of the noon sun until the exhausted horses could go on no more. They had risen above the tree line now but so steep were the bare rock faces that shade was hard to find. The sun's full force beat off the parched, arid land with relentless intensity. For a further torturous hour, in which Cortez repeatedly insisted that they were just one more corner away from shade and a mountain stream, they had moved slowly higher and higher. The men and their horses moved with heads bowed, just one more step to follow one more laboured step.

Just as Archie feared they were beaten, he looked up with surprise as he felt a sudden chill wash over him. They had turned a corner into a narrow split in the mountainside with sides so sheer, no sunlight could ever penetrate. It was at this point he realised just how high they had journeyed, for the air was frigid without the sun's warmth. Seve led them onwards though and Archie realised why, for somewhere ahead came echoing back toward them, the roar of cascading water.

When they reached a sharp turn in the valley, they saw the stream swirling over smooth rocks before plunging over a series of short vertical drops. They stopped and each held their own thoughts at this most beautiful of vistas. The noise of the flowing water, combined with the damp, cool air, was instantly reviving and the past hours agonies seemed to melt away.

They fed and watered the horses before stripping off and washing themselves down with the ice cold water. Seve cautioned against the dangers of swimming in the crystal clear pools that looked so inviting and he was right to do so, Archie knew how chilling the water could be.

They spent perhaps too long camped by the stream but when they finally moved on they felt invigorated and moved with renewed energy. For another half hour they moved deeper into the gloomy canyon. Finally Seve dismounted and for a terrible hour they were forced to lead the horses up a narrow, crumbling track, which carried them back out into the fierce afternoon sun. Their calves burned and their backs ached as they stumbled and staggered up the steep path, all the while hauling on their reluctant horses.

Just as the torment threatened to dishearten them, the view opening out ahead made their spirits soar. Before them the way eased, though the ground continued to rise gently toward the horizon, winding around large boulders and crags jutting out to form a complex, natural maze. High peaks soared above them on either side, some showing traces of snow resting in sheltered hollows. Higher still, Archie was drawn to a circling eagle, riding warm currents of air, higher and higher into the clear blue sky.

For another hour Cortez drove them on and just when they were beginning to beg him for a rest, he pulled his little steed to halt. The panorama spread out ahead of them fairly took their breath away! They were astride a ridge of rock strewn, coarse grass, looking down on the northern Spanish plains. They were at the highest point of their journey, from now on they were heading downhill.

Cortez dismounted and spoke quietly to Lyell before watering the horses.

'We're going to eat here but I'm sorry, we'll not make Riaza by nightfall. Apparently there is a thick forest at the end of our journey and we will need daylight to make our way through,' Lyell informed the others.

'Damn, that's not good news but I guess it can't be helped,' Archie replied, trying not to let his frustration show.

'The Frenchies will have maybe a day on us,' Cedric concluded, adding confidently,' but they'll have to come up with a plan to kidnap or kill this Klaus character, so it's unlikely they'll have acted before we arrive.'

'That's a good point and they will have to find him first. I know the name of the house but not its location.

Hopefully it will take the Frenchies even longer to find him. If only we knew what they intended next,' Perks said quietly.

'I doubt murder is on their mind, not just yet anyway!' Archie said, in what he hoped was a reassuring tone. 'If this Pascal is not completely crazy then he will want to know what Klaus has told you. He may even try to turn him into a double agent.'

'We must not let him fall into that madman's hands,' Perks said, the fear and anger in his voice evident to all. 'He'll not hold up to torture, so at least he'll be spared too much pain but that Frenchman I suspect is a man who enjoys his work too much to be denied.'

'Whatever the outcome, we'll make it our business to avenge that boy and rid the world of Monsieur Antoine Pascal once and for all,' Archie added with a cold tone in his voice that sent another shiver through Perks.

*

The first slivers of grey light were diffusing the sky with the dawn of a new day, as the small group of riders broke camp and rode carefully across a grass plain riven with small streams. Birdsong split the cool air into a symphony of discordant harmonies, lifting Archie's spirits immeasurably. He felt alive and vital at times such as this, at one with the world and his place in it. The romantic fool within him was alive and well, so much so, that he believed for a while that he was on one of his many boyhood adventures once more.

Within the hour they rode into the endless twilight of a coniferous forest and with the fading of the light came the commensurate darkening of Archie's mood. His thoughts kept returning to Pascal, O'Brien as he knew him and his apparently reciprocated affection for Cordelia. Whatever the outcome of the next few days, that sweet and innocent young girl was going to have her heart broken and her illusions shattered. By the end of this escapade, one of her two friends would be cold beneath the sod.

Broken only by the occasional clearing, the dark forest was unrelenting in its monotonous hold on them. They plodded slowly along in single file, conversation difficult and not really desired. Just as their stomachs were beginning to rebel, Cortez moved forward at the trot and as they rode to catch him they saw before them a vision of heaven. A lake, its water mirror smooth, surrounded by bull rushes and reeds, the rays of the still low lying sun, filtered by the trees, just beginning to dapple the surface with slivers of green-grey light.

Seve dismounted and the others followed suit. They tended the horses and then tethered them where they could graze on the long grass at the water's edge. Seve soon had a fire blazing and assisted by Cedric, began to prepare a breakfast. The others took the opportunity to wash and shave by the cool water's edge. Tempted beyond reason by the inviting cool water, Archie and Lyell stripped off and naked as the day they were born plunged into the crystal clear water.

Refreshed and invigorated, the hearty breakfast sealed a mood of optimism and hope amongst the party. They broke camp an hour later and with some sadness left the lake behind, to be swallowed up once more by the great pine forest. Climbing steadily again, Archie wondered for the tenth time or more how on earth Seve knew where he was going. That he truly did was proved positive an hour later when they emerged from the forest into a wide open valley and in the hazy light of morning, Riaza could be seen away in the distance.

The arrow straight dusty road began to feel endless as they walked slowly down a gentle slope toward the outskirts of the town. The men's clothes and the skin of their horses were dulled by a thin coating of pale brown dust, blending them in with the parched landscape and the scattering of crumbling stone houses. The first impression of the town was not good as they entered an area of hovels and shacks, seemingly occupied by screaming urchins with no adults in sight. Seve assured them that the men and women would be hard at work in the fields and vineyards all around them.

The town opened up before them after they crossed the spans of a small stone bridge. The square towers of a handful of churches were the only structures of any stature. The central plaza however thronged with humanity, bustling noisily around heavily laden market stalls.

Cortez led them away from the town centre and shortly he reined his horse to a stop outside a substantial sandstone building sitting at the extremity of long, dead-end road. This he assured them was the best guest house in Riaza, run by his cousin's sister in law. After a great deal of kissing, arm waving and general emotion, Cortez introduced them to Armanda who ran the guest house and cantina. There then followed another ten minutes of kissing and cooing as the substantially built but stunningly beautiful, raven haired woman greeted them all as though long lost friends.

With the horses tended and secured in the establishment's stables, the men retired to their small but clean rooms to wash and change into what passed for fresh clothes. Archie threw open the room's shutters and gazed out over the town toward the distant ridge of mountains over which they had journeyed so long. His moment's reverie was broken by a gentle tap on the door and then a child of no more than ten years, hustled in with a bowl of clean water and a startling white towel. With a smile as white as the linen, she fled the room with as much of Archie's dusty, sweat stained clothes as she could carry.

As he stripped off and washed his aching body down with the cool water, he continued to look out onto the town. The noise and smells drifted into the room on the breeze and momentarily his spirits sank. If they were unsuccessful today then a good man would die, perhaps a dreadful death, but if they rescued Costa, the information he held would seal this country's fate and war would surely follow. As he dressed once more in the last of his presentable clothes, he concluded sadly that war with France was inevitable come what may but at least this way England had a fighting chance of victory.

A short while later they held a council of war in the corner of the deserted cantina. Their table groaned under the weight of food and drink provided by the ever present Armanda, who had eventually retreated to the kitchen with Cortez.

'The Chancellor has a grand villa on the outskirts of town,' Perks began. 'We'll have to enquire where exactly it is though. I believe it's called Santa Rosanna.'

'Charles, perhaps you and Sam could go and see what you can find out as soon as we've finished?' Archie asked. Looking Lyell in the eye, he saw only steadfast resolve. Lyell stared back hard at the now lightly bearded man before him, trying to read his mind, seeking the truth. Now it was revealed that this was no commercial adventure as he had initially been led to believe, as a fierce patriot he was content to be doing the work of their King.

'We will enquire, subtly, perhaps at the town hall or some such place,' Lyell answered with enthusiasm.

'Good thinking and though we must remain careful, we must move swiftly for our enemies have the march on us,' Archie cautioned. 'The rest of us will do our best to find those damned Frenchies. I'm afraid that they'll make their move very soon, if indeed they've not already struck. The town will take its siesta soon, so we will meet back here at one o'clock.'

The men were ravenous and they quickly cleared all the plates before Lyell and Perks took their leave. As his companions made ready, Archie slipped into the kitchen where he found Armanda. Armanda leapt to her feet and with surprising grace, glided over to him.

'Senor have you eaten your fill? Seve tells me you speak our language well,' she revealed, standing close, her delicate hand resting on his arm.

'Not well Senorita but I get by. Thank you for the magnificent lunch,' he replied, captivated by the huge bottomless pools of her jet black eyes. She had a truly beautiful, youthful face and she smiled with genuine warmth through perfect, plump lips.

'Tell me, are their many cantina's in town? Some friends of mine rode here last week and I wondered if they might still be here,' Archie enquired lightly, his eyes roaming blatantly over her full breasts, much of which were exposed to his view by the low cut of her crisp, white blouse. He guessed she was perhaps twenty-eight years old and he noted, quite tall. Her long legs were enveloped by a voluminous skirt and her exposed ankles seemed impossibly delicate.

'There are one or two inferior imitations of my fine house, mostly by the river, on the road to the south,' she answered, not attempting to mask the contempt for her business rivals, while holding Archie's gaze.

Thanking her with a lingering kiss to her hand, he reluctantly left her and rejoined his companions. Leaving the cantina one at a time and moving through the still busy streets separately, they still kept each other in clear view. Archie had decided that three men moving together would draw far too much undesired attention in such a small town.

Pausing to buy some fruit in a busy market, he looked casually around at the people making up the noisy crowd. Strong, deeply tanned faces glanced back at him, mostly women buying food for their table from hawkers shouting and in some cases, singing to advertise their wares. Suddenly, as if from nowhere, Tom was at his shoulder.

'One of those Frenchies is behind us,' he whispered. 'I'm sure it's 'im, thickset little bastard wit' bald patch on 'is crown, he's at a stall over yonder.'

Archie turned slowly and picked out the man that Tom had spotted, purchasing cherries from a nearby stall.

'Try and alert Cedric and we'll follow him,' he ordered quietly.

There followed a tense and tiring half hour as the man meandered through the market place making his purchases. The crowd swirled and pulsated like one giant living organism, sometimes tightly packed then just as quickly there was no one at a stall except for the

Frenchman and Archie. The noisy, vibrant mass reminded him of the shoals of silver fish he had swum amongst as a child in Egypt, seemingly following unseen orders as they twisted and turned but never once losing contact with their neighbours.

The short man was frustratingly difficult to spot amongst the crowd and only his incongruously white bald patch gave him away. Archie chuckled as he realised that their salvation had been the man forgetting his hat this morning.

Eventually, now heavily burdened with hessian bags containing his purchases, the man left the market's hubbub behind and began to walk at a surprising pace down a wide, tree lined street. There was no footpath and the many pedestrians had to be nimble of foot to avoid the clattering carts and occasional ass, all burdened down with farm produce.

They crossed the river by way of the graceful, stone arched bridge they had used upon their arrival. The Frenchman kept on walking past several cantinas that were dotted along the road, just as Armanda had promised. Several times he stopped to adjust his burden but never once did he look around toward the Englishmen. Eventually he turned to the right, alongside a rough stone wall dotted with tiny green lizards basking in the hot sun. Wiping his sweat streaked brow, the man followed a gently winding road back down towards the riverbank.

Without warning he left the road and walked into the dappled shade of a dense grove of orange trees. Cedric carried on walking, waving behind his back to warn the others. Archie and Tom darted to their left into a filthy alleyway and keeping low behind the wall bordering the orange grove, were able to see the man emerge from beneath the trees and continue to make his way up a dusty, boulder strewn track. After a few hundred yards he reached the door to the courtyard of what appeared to be a derelict farmhouse.

'You got t' take yer 'at off to 'em, they're good these bastards fer sure. Keep their sens tucked away, ney fuss, ney bother, so as nowt will show they're even 'ere!' Tom groused angrily.

They linked up with Cedric around the next street corner. He had found a place from where he could observe the front door to the old house so Archie sent him back there. If anyone left the house then he would attempt to follow them. Meanwhile, Tom and Archie returned to the alley and once more using the low wall as cover, passed unobserved by the side of the house.

They safely reached a dense wood of ancient, gnarled fig trees covering a slight rise in the ground. Crawling on their bellies over the hard, dusty ground they broached the peak of the tiny hill. Peering with infinite care through the long spiky grass, they were afforded a clear view of the rear quarter of the house. Sitting at a rickety looking table were three men, tucking in to the food recently bought in the town. Under the shade of an ancient vine tumbling over a sagging pergola, the men looked relaxed and content.

The house had once been a magnificent structure, three stories high with dormer windows set into a steeply pitched roof. From beyond the house came the rush of fast flowing water where at one time there had been a mill attached to the farm. The noise they could hear was the race, where once the great wheel had turned.

There was much animated talk at the table, with the easily recognisable Pascal clearly taking the lead. As the sun rose higher into the sky, Archie and Tom lay in the shade, watching and waiting. High above, a hawk circled on thermal currents and Archie mused on the possibilities of flying up there with the bird and what a perfect view he would then have of his enemies.

With the meal finished, the heat from the sun became too much for the Frenchmen and they retired to the house. Soon the heat became intolerable for the watchers too, so Archie decided to withdraw.

Back at the cantina they found Perks and Lyell were still out in the town, so they took the chance to rest in the cool shade of their rooms. It was several hours later that Archie was woken by a gentle tap on his door, followed by the entry of two, very hot and bedraggled Englishmen.

'Good God, you two look all in. I trust you had the success we did?' Archie asked before quickly relaying the adventures of their morning.

'We have found the Villa de Santa Rosanna. It's across the river on the edge of town, it seems we must have passed it on our journey today,' Perks began with a satisfied grin on his dust streaked face. 'It's a very substantial house indeed, with a walled courtyard and extensive open ground to the rear. There are orchards and gardens on three sides and it's surrounded by dense woodland. From there we were able to observe the comings and goings quite easily. There must be guards or at least an escort for the Chancellor but we saw none on patrol. There are several ladies present and we saw Klaus, Manuel that is. The atmosphere seems relaxed but from what we could see, the house is vulnerable to a brazen attack, if that's what the French swine intend.'

'Okay, it's been a good morning's work chaps. Now I think we all need to rest a while. Meet back here at four o'clock and we will see if we can prevail upon the lovely Armanda to provide us with some tea,' Archie concluded before showing the two men to the door.

Later that afternoon they held another council of war over sticky cakes and thick, sweet coffee, Archie's notion of heaven on earth. Ideas were bounced around for nearly an hour before they finally settled on what they agreed was the only workable plan.

'Right gentlemen to round up, this is what we are going to do. We're agreed it's not possible for any of us to approach Klaus at the Chancellor's house. However, if by any chance the party should come into town then we must take our chance and grab him. Failing that, we'll watch the Frenchmen closely, though I still cannot believe that they would have the sheer audacity to snatch him from that villa.'

There was a general murmur of agreement from the others but Perks remained uneasy and felt obliged to voice his concerns.

'If the French get him first then not only do we have to see where they take him, assuming they don't just murder him but then we have to rescue him from them. I still think we should try to snatch him from the villa but I will go with the consensus.'

'You're right of course but the risk of getting caught by the guards at the villa is too great. We go as agreed but if nothing happens tonight then we'll have to reconsider. So, Sam and Cedric off you go to the villa and we three will do our best to monitor the French,' Archie said, with what he hoped was an air of confidence.

'I have a surprise for you all, a little contribution to the war effort that I've been working on,' Lyell said, with a very pleased look on his face. From his small knapsack, he produced a tube of stout paper about eight inches long, twisted to a close at either end. A short length of fuse from an old matchlock gun he had found in the house protruded from one end.

'We used to play silly buggers with these when I was at Harrow school, 'he added, somewhat sheepishly. 'Just keep a smouldering taper to hand, touch the short fuse and throw it. The musket balls inside will ensure it strikes head down and nine times out of ten, the black powder inside will ignite with the biggest smoky flash you've ever seen. A great distraction if thrown into a room, I assure you.'

'Impressive, well done,' Archie told him whilst turning the crude device over in his hands. 'Right, let's get our stuff together and move out. Charles would you go to the kitchen where you'll find some food laid out for us. I've told Armanda that we are going hunting, which is close enough to the truth and thanks to Seve we have three fine fowling pieces which should come in useful.'

By the time the early evening had at last begun to take the edge off the heat of the day, the two parties had slipped from the hotel, substantial backpacks helping conceal their firearms and carry their other provisions. To the casual observer they would pass as hunters perhaps but an early encounter with the French agents would end in their exposure and bloodshed would surely follow.

Perks and Cedric had left slightly ahead of the others and within forty minutes were settled down just inside the tree line, behind and slightly above the Villa de Santa

Rosanna. The gardens and surrounding areas were deserted but occasionally they caught a melodic chord of music played on a guitar and now and then a peal of laughter. The house was clearly at dinner.

The other three had made their way by a circuitous route to the tree capped rise to the rear of the farmhouse occupied by the French agents. During their discussions it had become clear that they would be able to observe anyone leaving from this side alone, obviating the need to split up. Archie had a nagging worry that the Frenchmen would leave in total darkness and be missed, so had a half formed plan to close right in to the buildings later that night.

He struggled to get comfortable lying on the bone-hard ground but by using a blanket and his pack it was tolerable. With his hunting piece prepared, two pistols, a short sword and his stiletto concealed under his belt, he felt ready. He forced his breathing to slow and felt his heart rate settle as the watery feeling in his bowels subsided slightly. Men will die tonight he thought with a growing certainty; he just hoped it would not be him or his companions. Any doubts he had were washed away by a sudden vision of a young man, writhing in agony tied to a chair, tortured for no good reason by a sadistic swine who was just two hundred yards from where he now lay.

Hours passed with no sign of activity at the old farm, not even a reassuring sound to confirm anyone was home. As twilight came so did the insects, mosquitoes buzzing angrily overhead and ants that appeared from nowhere to crawl over him, their tiny feet irritating and itching but fortunately they did not bite. In the slowly descending darkness he could just make out the other two men lying further down the slope, motionless but awake, he hoped.

Without warning he noticed Lyell flinch and looking back at the farm, he saw why, a light had appeared at one of the windows. Someone was at home he realised with immeasurable relief. The sun had slipped behind a band of dark clouds on the far horizon and a beautiful pink-grey light diffused the harsh landscape. With the setting of the sun came a slight drop in the temperature and some small relief from the mosquitoes.

Nervous energy coursed through Archie and he was forced for perhaps the third time, to crawl deeper into the trees and relieve himself. Breathing deeply, he made his way back to the edge of the trees and was surprised to see how dark it had now become. Only the outline of the buildings could now be discerned but light now showed at two windows on the ground floor and one on the second.

At the Villa de Santa Rosanna, Sam Perks was having a very unpleasant time with the mosquitoes but just before the sun slipped behind the clouds, he had caught a glimpse of his agent walking in the gardens, in the company of the Chancellor himself. The two men appeared to be smoking and were deep in earnest conversation, heads close together, the Chancellor, a man in his sixties, walking with the aid of a stick. With the coming of darkness, lights showed at many of the villa's windows and the occasional sound reached the two watching men.

By what Archie estimated to be nine o'clock, the lights still burned at the old farmhouse but at the same time, Perks and Cedric were watching a household making ready for bed, as one by one downstairs lights were extinguished and light began to appear at several of the upper windows, only to dim as shutters were closed.

As Archie suppressed a satisfying yawn, a door was flung open and the shadowy forms of two men could be seen standing outside the farmhouse. After less than two minutes they returned inside but the door was left wide open. A short while later all but one of the lights was extinguished and three men left the house. They began walking down the riverside track quickly disappearing into the gloom. Archie quietly packed his things and stiffly rose to his feet.

In the darkness the Frenchmen made their way alongside the river until they reached a narrow road, still little more than a dirt track. Strung out behind them and trying to make best use of what cover there was, Archie and his party followed, as closely as they dared. Moving quickly but quietly from the shadows, to the corner of the next building, Archie just hoped they could not be seen. Ahead, the Frenchmen were becoming harder to spot in the dark, so he fervently hope the same applied for them.

The Frenchmen crossed a field in the very last of the light, a thin mist swirling around them as they began to merge with the background, their images periodically disappearing all together. Archie led his strung out group around the fringe of the field, moving quickly so as not to fall behind, working on an assumption that the French agents would never dream they were being followed.

Reaching the far side of the field, he clambered over a small stone wall and walked cautiously down the narrow track on the other side. He now had a primed pistol in his hand, the light so low now that he could barely see his own way ahead. He knew they must almost be upon the villa but in the dark he could see nothing of the Frenchmen.

Sam Perks however could see them, quite clearly in

fact, for they were standing less than two feet from where he lay. The French agents were holding a whispered conversation and Perks fervently wished his understanding of French was better. He had observed French spies being interrogated so had picked up a little of the language but nowhere near enough to follow the conversation taking place next to him.

After a few moments the Frenchmen moved away toward the villa, still just visible in silhouette, marked out by one solitary light at the top right-hand corner of the third storey. Two of the men moved toward the rear of the house and disappeared into the inky blackness of the night. Perks could just see the third man standing some way off from the building until he too was swallowed up by the darkness as he sank to the ground.

Perks lay motionless with his heart hammering in his chest, an irresistible urge to move, distracting his concentration. During their seemingly endless discussions, they had agreed that if the Frenchmen intended to murder Klaus in his bed then there was little they could do, save for avenging him. There was however a consensus that kidnap would be on the French agents mind, not murder. Not straight away at least!

Perks heard a faint noise behind him and caught the briefest hint of movement against the sky line. He strained his eyes until they hurt but could see no more, though his instinct convinced him that Archie and his men were with him in the trees. A gentle breeze kicked up a little dust and carried with it the bleat of a distant goat. The moon was still concealed by the clouds that had come with the dusk and the black of night was complete.

Just then Perks heard footsteps heading toward him,

clumsy sounding and rushed. He peered ahead, straining for the merest glimpse of what was unfolding before him. He could see nothing but a hissed comment and the footfall seemed suddenly much closer. In an instant the men were on him, three passed to his left and one to his right. One member of the group stumbled but was supported by his partners and then having missed standing on Perks by scant inches, they were gone.

The three Frenchmen and the fourth party, who Archie assumed was the unfortunate Costa, almost blundered into him also. For one heart stopping moment, he was sure he had been seen but then in an instant they were past, three men walking briskly and a fourth clearly stumbling along, his hands probably secured behind his back.

Archie moved cautiously in the direction the men had last been headed. He could not follow in the pitch black of a moonless night but he knew the destination had to be the derelict farmhouse. The return journey in the dark was a nightmare of stumbles and near misses. Once, some way up ahead, he heard a body crash to the ground accompanied by a muffled curse. In the silence that followed, only the sound of a dog barking shattered the illusion that they were totally alone in the world.

Eventually Archie reached the farmhouse once more. There was no sign of the French agents and the only sound to break the night was the constant rushing of water through the old mill race at the rear of the buildings. Concealed once more in the tree line, he was relieved to see a light appear at a window and then after a second or two, both shutters were closed.

His ears strained to pick up the sounds of his companions, who he hoped were trying to find the agreed rallying point, a large stone gateway some one hundred yards left of his position. The occasional sound reached him, a stone disturbed, the rubbing of clothing against a tree perhaps, then a murmured word or two. Rising stiffly, he moved cautiously toward the gateway, now just visible against a slowly clearing sky. There they were, huddled in the dark, his loyal companions.

'They have him, we must move now before it's too late,' Perks began the instant Archie arrived.

'We will, don't concern yourself Sam, Costa will be fine for a while. Everyone get yourselves ready and then we'll move as agreed,' Archie whispered.

There followed a frantic five minutes as weapons were prepared and backpacks adjusted. Once they were settled, Archie felt moved to give them one last speech, if his parched throat would allow him.

'This is a fine thing we do tonight. We owe a brave man the chance of life and we'll do a great service to our King. Men are going to die here soon so just make sure those men are the enemy. Let's go.'

Silently they moved towards the house, fearful that a concealed sentry was waiting for them in the impenetrable darkness of the farmyard. They made the journey without incident. Tom and Perks spread out left and right while Lyell and Archie moved toward the shuttered window with Cedric trailing five yards behind them. Through a small gap, a sliver of yellow light could just be seen. Archie eased his eye to the gap between the shutters and looked into the room. A lantern burned on a small table set between two cots. Clothes and other personal items were strewn around the room but no one was present.

Silently they moved past the back door to the next

shuttered window, the roar of the mill race concealing any small noises they made. Archie peered through the tiniest of gaps in the shutter, careful not to touch it, as it was unsecured. The room beyond was a kitchen, furnished in roughly constructed wooden cabinets, along with a large range and a few chairs arranged around a large table. Tied to that table was Manuel Costa and he looked utterly terrified, with every good reason to be.

Pascal stood close by, a huge knife in his hand, simply staring at the bound Spaniard, not attempting to question him yet. The other two Frenchmen stood nearby, sharing a bottle of wine and looking somewhat apprehensive. Archie had seen enough and quickly returned to the others.

'Quickly now, as agreed, first prepare Charles's little toys. Don't throw them toward the far side of the room or you'll hit Costa,' he urged them all. 'Tom and Cedric take the window and as long as the back door remains unlocked, we'll take the door. Remember we can spare no one, even if we are given the chance!'

With much fumbling, the men took their smouldering tapers and with weapons at the ready, moved off. Archie waited until he could see the shadowy impression of the two men at the window, before trying the back door. With just a small creak of protest it opened and they slipped inside. They moved slowly down the dark hallway toward the yellow lantern light spilling from the open kitchen door. The voices of the Frenchmen carried easily to them. One of the men was in full rant, berating the prisoner for betraying the revolution. Pascal for sure, Archie concluded.

Reaching the threshold, Archie took the paper tube and applied the taper held in the grip of his false hand to the short fuse sticking from its top end. It immediately began to smoke and glow red hot. Taking a deep breath he glanced at Lyell, who held his own device up. At his nod, they both hurled the flares into the room. As pandemonium broke out they heard the shutters flung wide and a single shot ring out.

Crouching low, Archie entered the kitchen to be greeted by a scene straight from hell itself. The room was full of white smoke which made his eyes water and piercing screams assaulted his hearing. One of the Frenchmen had been hit by a flare and was alight from head to toe, thrashing madly in one corner. Another of the French agents lay on the floor, blood gushing from a gaping chest wound.

Pascal stood motionless as if in shock, close by Costa and still with the long knife in his hand. Archie hurriedly fired his pistol, his shot clipping Pascal at the top of his shoulder, spinning him backwards. Archie rushed further into the smoke filled room just as another shot rang out from the window, this time catching Pascal full in the face. With blood pouring down his shirt-front, wild eyed and obviously in unspeakable agony, he looked desperately for an avenue of escape. Lyell fired a shot into the head of the still burning Frenchman who fell to the floor, the flames spreading quickly from his body to a large wooden dresser. Pascal seemingly oblivious to his dreadful wounds spun on his heel and dived headfirst through the open rear window of the kitchen.

Archie raced across the room even as Pascal's horrified scream still cut the air. As Archie thrust his head through the window, there was a sickening thud and a splash from below. He looked down, perhaps thirty feet to the turbulent waters of the mill race, now illuminated by a bright moon. Pascal's broken body was momentarily visible as it was swept over the stones and into the river below.

Archie forced himself away and through the smoke and flames he ran with the others, along with the newly liberated Spaniard, to the safety of the farmyard. The group stood in a panting huddle, not sure whether to laugh or cry. Elated by their success and high on adrenaline, the group of men sobbed and held each other, too breathless for coherent words. It was Tom who finally broke the mood.

'We need t' get outta 'ere now, the 'ole 'ouse is gonna go up, look!' he urged, whilst backing slowly away from the building.

'Come on, let's get going,' Perks gasped, utterly exhausted by the violent events that he had just experienced. 'That blaze is going to attract attention, so we've got to get to safety.'

Perks and Cedric took an arm each and helped the trembling Spaniard to walk, as the little party briskly left the farmyard and crossed the rough field toward the riverside track leading back to the town. The bright moonlight made for swifter progress but left the men feeling very exposed in its harsh white glare.

Moving quickly, they made it safely to the quiet streets of the town's outskirts and the Spaniard having recovered somewhat, was now able to walk unaided. He and Perks were in animated conversation and Archie turned to them, catching sight as he did so of a pall of smoke drifting across the face of the moon. An orange glow, increasing in intensity as it became visible over the roof-tops, was testimony to the ferocious fire that would ensure no evidence of tonight's drama would survive.

'I need to know Perks, the shipment, does he have the information?' Archie asked anxiously.

'Yes, it should arrive first or second week of October, at the port of Cadiz,' Perks answered.

'Fantastic,' Archie said with a broad smile on his face and then he thanked Costa in his slightly stilted Spanish. Costa was keen to know what would happen next and Archie tried to reassure him that all would be well. As they walked back to their lodgings, now separated into two groups to try to appear less conspicuous, Archie felt himself trying to fight the adrenaline fuelled euphoria. He was fearful of being lulled into what would be a premature feeling of victory until the information and Manuel Costa were safely in London.

As they approached the cantina, the sounds of music and laughter carried on the night air from the open windows. Armanda had explained that there would be dancing that night and implored him not to miss the show. As they made their way to the rear door, they split up again, with Lyell and Perks walking quietly inside with Costa before heading straight up the back stairs to their rooms. A short while later the others slipped inside and stealthily made their way back to their rooms too.

Archie flopped onto his bed and took stock of the situation. The feeling of elation was almost unbearable. This was a truly outstanding victory. They had crossed the mountains to make up for lost time, found agent Klaus and the enemy's lair. That was an amazing achievement in its self but to observe the French kidnap Costa and then affect a rescue was a crowning glory.

He rose and stripped off before washing with the ice

cold water in the ever present porcelain bowl. Splashing the water over his dusty face, he closed his eyes and ran the events of the night over in his mind's eye. Lyell's flares had been a godsend but what great men he had around him, all working unquestioningly and in perfect unison. He felt no pity for the dead Frenchmen, though he winced at the thought of the agonies the burning man had suffered, it was a primeval fear of all men to die by fire. As for Pascal, he felt only satisfaction that a dangerous and violent adversary was dead.

He dressed and went down the dark stairway to the cantina's bar. He was joined almost immediately by Tom then Cedric, who handed out beakers of fruity red wine which they raised to toast their success. The room was crowded, the air thick with smoke and noisy with drunken conversation. Suddenly the stamp of a heel on timber brought the talk to a stop. On a small stage, a pretty young girl in a flowing blue dress took to the stage alongside a tall, older man, dressed head to toe in black. Two guitarists sitting in the shadows set up a furious rhythmic strumming and with a crash of heels; the couple began a sensual, strutting dance, a parody of seduction and a bullfight, the hunt of man the beast, woman the willing prey.

The Englishmen were entranced by the unfamiliar music and the dancing, immersing themselves in the spectacle of noise and movement. They cheered and applauded with enthusiasm, joining the locals in tossing coins onto the stage in support of the dancers and their musicians.

After a short break the guitarists took to the stage once more. Their nimble fingers struck up a haunting, rolling melody, a kaleidoscope of sound seducing and drawing the audience in. Onto the stage came Armanda, dressed in a long multi-layered, fiery red dress, her waist cinched in by black silk and her large bosom threatening to break free from the low, lace fringed top. Her jet black hair was held up by a scarlet ribbon, her beautiful face, glistening in the heat of the room.

She began to dance, a slow swirling dance, punctuated by the occasional rhythmic clack of her heels on the hard wooden floor. Subtly the tempo of the music increased and Armanda's movement followed closely, her turns became more abrupt, her heels crashed more loudly to the floor. As she spun around the dance floor, she swirled the hem of her dress higher with each turn, exposing her legs first to the knee and then offering tantalising glimpses of sturdy, coffee coloured legs.

Faster and faster the musicians strummed their guitars, Armanda crashed her heels to the floor, spun wildly on her toes, her skirt whirling higher and higher, momentarily exposing the full length of her powerful thighs to the lascivious glare of the clapping crowd. Her face ran with sweat, her breasts shone with slick moisture, as the music, superbly controlled became ever more frantic. Faster and faster she spun and twirled, hammering her heels in perfect unison with the musicians. Suddenly she spun on one toe, her skirt ballooning around her, stamped her right foot to the floor and let out an almost orgasmic scream as the music stopped and the room held its breath for several silent heartbeats before a rapturous round of applause and whooping cheers broke the mood. Armanda, breathless and smiling, took her bow and left the little stage. Archie stood entranced and with a smile realised he had been standing with his mouth wide open throughout the entire, startling performance.

Armanda never reappeared but the dancing continued into the early hours of the morning. As much ale and wine was consumed, Archie and his companions were drawn into shouted conversations with several locals, though their limited grasp of Spanish sometimes made it difficult to be understood. Eventually the garrulous town's people began to leave and the Englishmen retired for the night as they had an early start in the morning.

Bidding the others good night, Archie let himself into his room. After a brief struggle, he lit the small oil lamp and by its glow spied a note lying on the floor, close by the door. Curious, he read the note as best he could, for it was in Spanish. With a smile and hoping he had translated it correctly, he left his room and ascended the back stairs. With a gentle knock he entered the room at the corridors end.

Armanda sat in a luxurious armchair, dressed in a black silk robe, which struggled to cover her ample form. Smiling, she rose and embraced him warmly.

'I hope you enjoyed our simple entertainment?' she purred, slowly for his benefit.

'Magnificent. Your dancing was just... wonderful,' he managed to reply.

'Was your... hunting not successful?' she asked.

'We could not bear it any longer, the err ...' he hesitated and then mimed swatting mosquitoes buzzing around his head.

Armanda laughed and slipped from his grasp, returning with two glasses of red wine. They shared some more small talk and laughed together over his imperfect Spanish until Armanda took his glass to refill it. As she returned, she slipped from the robe to stand naked before him. He ran his eyes appreciatively up her statuesque, shapely thighs, took in her large, almost spherical breasts resting on the gentle rise of her stomach, her full lips smiling as she took his hand and placed it around her waist, to rest on her surprisingly small, firm bottom. As he hurriedly undressed, her eyebrows rose a fraction at the sight of his wooden hand but she said nothing then kissed him deeply and lewdly grasped his erection with her delicate fingers.

*

He was woken by the sound of horses in the yard, with the first light of dawn barely showing through the room's shutters. Next to him, Armanda lay sleeping, her breath shallow but rhythmic, a slight smile on her face. Their lovemaking had been wild, almost violent in its intensity, her strength and demands surprising him.

One of the horses snorted and clashed its hooves on the cobbles. Hushed voices could be heard and then the horses moved off. He breathed a sigh of relief, knowing that Manuel Costa was now on his way to Portugal and safety. Archie and the other two men would leave by the mail coach later in the morning. He hoped that by separating this way their sudden departure would seem less noticeable.

An hour later and he was woken by Armanda's warm embrace. The two lovers kissed deeply and passionately for what seemed an eternity until he attempted to roll her onto her back. Startling him once more with her strength, she resisted and eventually forced him to surrender. She clambered over him, squeezing him painfully with her thighs, as her fingers twisted and tore at his chest muscles. In one smooth movement she slid up the length of his body, pinning his head between her silky smooth legs, forcing her wet sex against his mouth. She took her pleasure from his skilled tongue, swamping him in the folds of her aroused body, crying out with pleasure as he squeezed the flesh of her muscular thighs. Clawing at her taut, rounded buttocks, rasping and pulling the smooth flesh, as his tongue stroked her on and on toward a long and intense orgasm.

As she lost control he was at last able to break free, forcing her onto her back and in one powerful lunge, he slid his erection deep into her. Her supple legs he looped over his shoulders, opening her wide to the ferocious assault by his painfully hard member. On and on he rode her flailing body, barely able to hold her down as wild eyed and out of control, she writhed and bucked against him. Her hands raking at his back drew blood with her long nails.

Oblivious to the pain, he continued to thrust into her, rapidly losing his own self-control, her hands now clawing painfully at his buttocks. As he began to feel the familiar surge along the length of his shaft, she pulled his buttocks wide apart and he felt the intrusion of a long, slender finger. This drove him over the edge and he exploded into her, both of them howling and crying with pure, white hot physical release. The moment held for what seemed a lifetime before they collapsed against each other, panting uncontrollably, drenched in sweat and laughing like children. Burying his face in Armanda's slippery wet chest he tried in vain to slow his racing heart. A thought struck him and he realised sadly that these were to be his final few days in Spain.

He felt an immeasurable sadness threaten to overwhelm

him, when later that morning he bid her farewell. Surely they were just ships passing in the night but he still had no desire to leave the company of this beautiful and exciting woman. The thrill of his victory over the French had long paled now and he could not shake the thought that all they had done was win the opening skirmish of a long war, which few of them would survive. Armanda seemed quite stoical about his departure and he realised he was behaving like a lovesick schoolboy. He knew in his heart that his reluctance to leave was more a direct result of what lay before him, rather than a need to stay with this delightful woman.

Their goodbyes said, Armanda took her leave with little more than a trace of tears in her eyes. The mail coach arrived and the driver loaded their baggage before helping them aboard. Leaving the fringes of the town behind, the three men sat in silence, alone with their own thoughts. They were joined by a young priest for part of the journey but were soon alone once more as the coach cantered through open countryside. Alarm swept through them several hours later when the coach swerved violently and pulled off the road, coming to a stop in an immense cloud of dust. A troop of cavalry came past them at a fast trot, kicking up a rooster-tail of yellow dust as they rode towards the town now far behind them.

'I guess they've noticed that Costa has disappeared,' Cedric ventured.

'From what he told Perks there'll be no signs of a struggle at the villa, so the Chancellor and his staff will hopefully think he has just wandered off. It would seem unlikely that they'll think he's been kidnapped, if the French were careful,' Archie concluded as the coach lurched back onto the road.

The rest of the day passed by in a monotonous daze, as the coach lurched over rutted roads, through an endless, dry countryside with little to hold the attention. At times the heat became unbearable, the air blown in through the open windows as hot as the interior had already become. It was an immense relief when the coach arrived in the outskirts of Salamanca.

Rested, the party took to the road again early the next morning. The coach's hard wooden seats made their bodies ache once more, even before they had left the town. The condition of the road was far worse than the day before and progress slowed to a walk much of the time. In the early afternoon their progress was halted completely as they sat out a violent thunderstorm. By early evening they had reached Ciudad Rodrigo and after settling into a clean but rather rundown cantina, the Englishmen went for a walk to explore the bustling town centre.

Archie was thoroughly taken with Spain, the climate and the simple way of life appealed to him greatly. He enjoyed improving his Spanish in conversation with market vendors and patrons at a bar they found themselves in as the sun finally set. Sitting outside watching the world go by, he decided he would like to come here again one day and really get to know the place. Little could he imagine that one day he would but he would find only horror, death and destruction.

As the following morning passed into the afternoon, they passed unknowingly into Portugal. A pleasant evening was spent in the regional capital of Guarda, before they took to their beds, weary beyond reason.

It took a further two days to reach Porto on the Atlantic

coast. With their money running low, Archie decided to head directly to the British Consul's residence, where he fervently hoped he would be reunited with Perks and Lyell, not to mention the fortunate spy Manuel Costa.

It took a while to persuade the reluctant receptionist to take his note but after a nervous wait, Perks appeared and ushered the somewhat malodorous travellers inside. He guided them into a large, oak panelled office where Lyell was waiting. They greeted each other like long lost family members and at last the pent up tension of the previous weeks was finally released.

'How's Manuel holding up?' Archie enquired as Perks placed a cup of tea in a fine china cup and saucer on the table before him.

'He's fine, all things considered. He has few close family members, so is quite stoical about a life of exile in London. Having talked to the Consul, he's decided it won't be safe for me to return to Madrid either, so I will be London bound too.'

'What news of the Royal Navy? I don't even know how long it is since I arrived in Iberia,' Archie said with a puzzled frown on his face, trying to bring some order in his mind to the whirlwind of recent events.

'The frigate has visited on a weekly basis as promised and should return in three days time, so we can all relax and enjoy this fine city for a while,' Perks answered with broad smile on his face. 'There are certainly Spanish agents in Portugal, so Manuel will have to stay confined to quarters but there is no reason why we should behave like prisoners too.'

'Top idea, this is a beautiful city, 'Lyell said. 'I've been here before and there are some of the finest places to eat in

Europe,' he added, licking his lips enthusiastically.

Caught up in the relaxed atmosphere, Archie let a warm feeling of satisfaction at a job well done wash over his tired body. He knew the dangers of lowering ones guard before the job was quite complete but he was lulled by the so very English surroundings and the splendid company. Before long the conversation faded into the background as he dozed off.

That evening, refreshed by bathing and attired in new clothes that Perks had acquired for them, the little group wandered through the twisting streets of the city, constantly moving downhill until they found themselves looking out over the crowded port. Archie marvelled once more at the eternal hold waterfronts seemed to have over him.

They ate well and drank fruity but rough wine, which would wreak a terrible vengeance in the morning. Inevitably it was Perks that asked the dreaded question of Charles Lyell.

'So how did these rogues recruit you into this crazy adventure?' he asked innocently, with a genial smile on his face. Archie cringed inwardly and was about to intervene when Lyell smoothly answered for himself.

'I think it fair to say I was made an offer I couldn't refuse. I'm not sure what I thought I was getting into but I wouldn't have missed it for the world. I've travelled these parts before but never with such a grand purpose,' he said calmly though his tanned cheeks were visibly pink in hue.

'Charles is a modest man,' Archie added. 'He's an adventurer of some note and has travelled through the mountains across southern Europe and in the Americas, so he was always going to be of great use to me. Also, I think he had found his life at a bit of a dead end, so the opportunity was a godsend really.'

Tom almost choked on his drink at that final remark. He looked over at Lyell, still not totally sure what hold Archie had over him but the young man had certainly done all that was asked of him and more over the last few weeks.

As the evening passed and the wine flowed, the men slipped into philosophical reverie, as men did all over the world, on evenings such as this.

'When the war does start it will ravage Europe and consume us all,' Cedric contributed morosely. 'Maybe this time when it's over, just for a while we can live quietly without hacking great lumps out of each other.'

'Not while so many kingdoms sit side by side we won't,' Perks observed. 'Too many egos, with too many dreams of power I'm afraid.'

'Your right and let's face it, the English are as guilty as the French on that front,' Archie ventured. 'No matter how many treaties we sign, sooner or later national interest forces us into war. Maybe one day someone will conquer the whole of Europe and turn it into one huge peaceful land but even the Romans couldn't hold that dream together for long.'

'They say that 'undreds of years in t' future, people will just live together w'out fightin' each other,' Tom chipped in. 'I can't see it but y' never knows. Perhaps all of us will talk the same an' all?'

'What, Frenchies speaking Italian?' Archie said with a laugh. 'Well it's a thought but not in our lifetime, that's for sure.'

'Charles, what will you do when we get back to

London?' Archie enquired.

'That depends on you to some extent but other than that I will probably spend most of my time avoiding the marriages my mother is no doubting arranging for me as we speak.'

There was a great outburst of manly, drunken laughter at that and Archie settled back in his chair, content in good company. As he looked over his companions, black thoughts descended and all he could see were dead men. War was coming for certain and they had just helped to start it.

*

Three days later they travelled down to the waterfront in two splendid carriages provided by the Embassy. Archie was slightly on edge, sitting next to Manuel Costa during the journey. Like the others, he had a primed pistol under his coat and even the Spaniard was showing signs of anxiety after his brief sojourn on what passed as English soil. In any event they arrived safely at the quayside and were soon aboard the Royal Navy frigate, HMS Narcissus.

Introductions were made and they were shown to their accommodation, if a hammock could be so described. Costa was to share the Captain's quarters, in order to keep him away from the crew as much as possible. With the cooperation of the winds they were hoping to reach Plymouth within a week. Two to three days on the road would then see them back in London.

As the sails began to fill and the ship made its way out to sea, Archie stood alone on deck. He had an uneasy feeling in the pit of his stomach, which turned into a painful gnawing doubt, as in the distance he saw the sails of two more ships. Disquiet began to turn to panic, as the memories of his fateful trip aboard HMS Leander flooded back. Phantom pains shot through the nonexistent fingers of his left hand and he clutched the hard, wooden limb in anguish.

'An escort no less, quite an honour indeed,' Perks announced, appearing quietly at his side, just breaking Archie's thoughts before he had embarrassed himself dreadfully. 'Two more frigates returning to England, so we should be safe enough I reckon.'

'I guess so,' Archie replied shakily. 'I had a bad time serving with the Royal Navy a few years back you know?'

'Cedric told me, it must have been quite appalling,' Perks conceded. 'What was it like, the battle I mean?'

'It's indescribably horrid. Below decks the noise is beyond comprehension. I think the worst part is not being able to see what's coming. Faceless gunners on another ship fire a cannonball you can neither see nor hear coming, until the hull splits open and shards of timber rip into you,' Archie answered with a visible shiver.

'We'll be fine this trip,' Perks said, resting his hand on Archie's shoulder. It was all Archie could do to manage a wan smile.

*

In the end, it was a dull and uneventful voyage. The winds were favourable and the small ships rode along under a great expanse of sail. With the sun shining and the nights humid, they spent most of the time on the open deck dozing. The highlight of the voyage was the arrival of a group of dolphins that kept them company for much of an afternoon, sometimes jumping clear of the water as they rode in formation with the little flotilla. As suddenly as they had arrived, they were gone and the ships were alone again in the vast expanse of the sea.

With the first glimpse of Plymouth Ho, Archie felt mixed emotions, glad to be home but sad that the adventure was at an end. With a shy grin, he thought to himself that it really was time to grow up. As they drew closer to the coast, he was struck once more by the English countryside's endless shades of green. The first smells of land wafted out on the stiff breeze and amidst the furious activity all around him, Archie felt embraced by a wondrous calm.

Once ashore, they were taken straight to an Admiralty building within the dockyard. A curt but efficient Captain took charge of the little party and they were soon taken off to a coaching inn on the outskirts of the city. There they spent a pleasant evening before retiring in anticipation of an early start.

By dawn's early light, two coaches left the dirty streets of Plymouth behind, conveying the Englishmen and their charge, Manuel Costa, towards London. Three days would pass before they finally entered the metropolis. The dark forbidding buildings they passed and in some places the awful smell, a mix of effluent and decay, did little to dampen their spirits.

The two carriages separated near Hyde Park, with the lead vehicle taking Perks, Archie and Costa directly to the Admiralty. Within the ornate entrance hall, a very British one act play was to run its course before the petty lower officials granted access to the more senior officials, who had been expecting the little group all along and now had the temerity to criticise their tardiness.

After a further period of sitting in a corridor as though awaiting the headmaster, they were ushered into a small room, to wait once more. After almost an hour the three men were shown into an impressive boardroom, to stand before three admirals and an assorted group of stern faced men, only Archie recognising Sir John Marshall, sitting with a very satisfied look on his face.

What followed was to stay with Archie for the rest of his life. He was selected to relate in every detail the drama of the previous weeks. Holding his audience rapt attention, it was only with the greatest of effort that he refrained from detailing his lusty romp with the bountiful Armanda but nevertheless the story reached a suitable climax with an invitation to Manuel Costa to detail Spain's impending bullion shipments.

Within the hour it was over and they were shown to the door with mumbled platitudes and the thanks of a grateful nation. A Foreign Office official ushered Manuel Costa and Sam Perks away, leaving Archie alone. As he gazed up at the larger than life portrait of a long dead Admiral, a familiar voice interrupted his thoughts.

'You have just pulled off one of the greatest espionage coups in history young man,' Sir John Marshall announced as he walked toward Archie, hand outstretched to give him a bone crushing handshake. 'Go home and rest for a few days then write me a full report, I will enjoy reading it but will then burn it to ashes,' he added. 'No one else will be allowed to know the great deed you have done.'

'Thank you Sir,' Archie replied, surprising himself slightly by the feeling of pride swelling within his chest. 'It was a team effort Sir, Perks was outstanding and Lyell was pivotal. Can we use Lyell again, forgive his treachery?'

'He's an outrageous dandy and a perverted wastrel at

heart but undoubtedly brave and resourceful. With such an uncertain future ahead of us, we'll need such men. It will be your responsibility young man and if he betrays us I will see him hang, believe me.'

'Thank you Sir. I will ensure he knows how discrete he has to be,' Archie said firmly.

He left the Admiralty building and decided to walk home. The smelly, noisy streets of London brought things sharply into focus once more. He was home, alive and in one piece, where lesser men had died. He was elated and sad in the same moment as he knew war was coming, war on a scale the world had never seen before. In his heart he knew it was ridiculous but the pangs of guilt were strong because he had helped start it.

Eventually he reached home and was admitted by Cedric. Standing awkwardly in the entrance hall they shook hands then spontaneously embraced as many complex emotions were released. The bond that imprisonment had forged between the two men was deeply personal and unbreakable. The privations and indignities that they had suffered together had changed them forever but they had survived and the past was finished with, except for those quiet, dark moments when the nightmares returned.

'Thank you old friend, we've survived a great adventure for sure,' Archie said, tears welling in his eyes.

'Thank you for giving me the chance to be a man once more,' Cedric replied and laughing self consciously added, 'do you think men will always get childish thrills from such dangerous and deadly games?'

'I do sadly and that's why wars will always be fought,' Archie replied, with a sad and tired tone in his voice.

'Would you ask Angie to prepare me a luncheon and then I think I will sleep for the rest of the week,' he announced, slapping his friend on the back before heading wearily toward the stairs.

He ate in his study, his favourite room in the house. Surrounded by books and paintings, this was his secret retreat from the world. The wall was adorned with paintings and sketches, from relaxed landscapes to erotic works of underground contemporary artists.

Exhausted, he made his way to his bed, already turned down, the room aired but noisy. Reluctantly he closed the window and drew the heavy drapes. Stripping off, he donned a cotton nightshirt and walked almost trancelike to his large four poster bed. He slipped under the heavy, familiar sheets and as the image of Armanda came into his mind, he lowered himself onto her voluptuous, welcoming body, looked deep into her eyes and saw Cordelia smiling back at him. Sleep then took him down into its merciful black depths.

*

The morning of the 5th October 1804 dawned clear, with a fresh westerly wind whipping up a lively swell in the seas off the port of Cadiz, in southern Spain. Four Royal Navy frigates sailed across the wind, spread in a line stretching over several nautical miles. Lookouts strained their eyes as they clung on to the bucking ships, even officers struggled gamely with telescopes, each hoping to be the first to glimpse sails on the horizon.

HMS Indefatigable was leading the small squadron under the command of Captain Graham Moore. Accompanying him were HMS Amphion, Lively and Medusa, three fifth rate frigates, fast under sail and armed with over thirty cannons apiece.

After several tense hours, Moore began to pace the deck of his ship, hands clasped behind his back, in reality to stop any of the men noticing them shaking, rather than to give off a dignified military air. He was racked by self doubt over this whole mission, of which he alone was privy to the details. His Captains all knew they were sailing these choppy waters with the aim of blockading the Spanish ports but they had no idea what the stakes really were. Every minute that passed reinforced in Moore's mind that he had somehow missed their targets.

'Sail Ho! Starboard quarter!' came the cry that brought an immense burst of relief to the young officer's heart. Rushing to the ship's cockpit he followed the outstretched arms of his crew. On the horizon was the smudge of not one but three sets of sail. Issuing orders to come about, Moore took his telescope and was pleased to see four sets of sails now coming into view.

What followed was a tense game of cat and mouse, accomplished with no small measure of skilled seamanship on both sides. Eventually, Moore managed to tack his small fleet alongside the Spanish ships. A signaller instructed the Spaniards to reduce their sail and slow down. For a short while this produced no response and then as one, the Spanish vessels unfurled more sail and actually increased their speed.

By ten o'clock Moore felt he had waited long enough. He issued a quick fire series of orders and one small forward cannon was prepared. At the Captain's word a single shot flew across the bow of the Spanish ship, Medea. Almost immediately the Spanish fleet began to shorten their sails and rapidly their speed began to fall away.

Moore called for Lieutenant Ascott and dispatched the young man in a small boat toward the Medea, where he was politely received by the ship's commander, Bustamante. Through an English speaking crew member, Ascott explained to the ruddy faced Spaniard that his ships were to heave to and prepare to be boarded. With an explosive laugh of derision, Bustamante shook the young Lieutenant's hand and guided him back to his boat. At that very moment a second shot flew across the bows of the Medea.

Ascott successfully crossed the heaving seas and was hauled back on board the Indefatigable. He gave Moore the news that the Spanish intended to make for Cadiz and they requested that they be left unmolested.

As Moore pondered his next move, he noticed the Medea become engulfed in smoke and scant seconds later cannon balls slammed into HMS Amphion and Indefatigable. Amphion had been prepared for combat and returned fire immediately at point blank range and within just ten minutes, the Spanish ship Mercedes exploded in a vivid orange fireball as a hot cannon ball pierced her magazine. A handful of her crew flung themselves into the swirling sea in a desperate bid to avoid the flames, most of the rest perished instantly.

Less than thirty minutes later, two of the Spanish ships had surrendered and the fourth turned away from the battle and running hard with the wind, made a heroic escape attempt. The frigate Medusa set off in pursuit, with HMS Lively quickly dispatched by Moore to assist. The fleeing Fama and her precious cargo were captured a few hours later.

As the captured frigates were being taken over by the English sailors, Moore looked on in horror as the Mercedes broke apart and sank, along with its cargo of gold and silver bullion.

He set sail for Gibraltar with his prize, three Spanish ships and an impressive haul of bullion. Sitting quietly in his cabin, he reflected on the death and destruction that had torn apart this beautiful blustery morning. He had lost just two men, with a handful dreadfully wounded but the Spanish had lost over two hundred men to the Atlantic waters. He rose and looked out of the window in the transom, breathing deeply to quell his painfully cramping stomach. He had his orders, they were clear and unequivocal but nevertheless, England and Spain were not at war.

*

As a result of Moore's spectacular success, on the 14th December 1804, the King of Spain declared war on England. Many in the corridors of power in London were stunned and outraged that such a cavalier action by the Royal Navy had set England on a course of war with Spain. For the Prime Minister and a small group of the political elite, there was elation at a job so well done. With Spain now allied to Napoleon, the countries of the Third Alliance would surely join Britain in the active resistance to France's military ambitions.

*

CHAPTER 4

LONDON, DECEMBER 1804

With Christmas 1804 fast approaching, Archie was in a restless mood and that normally spelt trouble. The weather was bitterly cold with flurries of snow amongst the incessant rain. The streets of London were filthy, awash with a mix of effluent, slush and general rubbish. Rather like the weather, the international scene was dark and desperate.

Napoleon rested in Paris, a constant, brooding, almost satanic influence over European affairs. News had spread far and wide of his coronation as Emperor. Pope Pius VII had travelled to France from the Vatican for the ceremony but had stolen away back home the next day, embarrassed and discredited.

Archie shivered as he looked down from his study window at the wet street below. His mind drifted to far away sunny lands and for just a fleeting moment, he could smell the orange groves of Spain. Sighing melodramatically, he made his way down the sweeping staircase as a resounding knock rattled the front door.

'Morning Tom,' he announced cheerily, slithering across the pavement to the waiting carriage.

'Pah, it's so bloody dark it might as well be neet!' his driver groused.

'Soon be Christmas,' Archie countered with a mock cheerfulness in his voice. He was renowned for his disdain of the Yuletide season. As the carriage lurched out into the traffic flow, conversation was rendered impossible by the clamour of the city traffic.

Archie was en route to see Cordelia at the Hendricks family home. Recently returned from Spain after the sudden death of her father, this would be the first time he had seen her since the memorial service. She had taken his death very badly and appeared to have aged terribly, almost overnight. With the approach of Christmas he hoped she would be in better spirits.

Pulling up in front of the substantial, modern house, Tom jumped down from his drivers perch.

'What time do yer need me back 'ere Sir?' he asked, habitually touching his cap.

'Two o'clock please,' Archie replied, 'I want to see this new safe-house for myself before it gets too dark.'

'Very good Suh,' Tom replied. 'Will we be moving agin the bastards reet now?'

'Not necessarily,' Archie answered warily. 'I think we might identify a few choice enemy targets if we leave them alone but as ever it will be down to Sir John.'

With that he walked briskly through the now more persistent snowfall towards the imposing front door of the house. The door was answered on the first knock by an immaculately turned out footman. The snow streaked cape was removed from his shoulders and after a quick check in the hall mirror, he was ready to be presented.

The footman showed him into an exquisitely furnished lounge. Exuding despondency, Lady Hendricks sat before a roaring fire, still elegant in mourning black.

'Archibald, so good to see you,' she whispered, as he gently kissed her proffered hand. 'Please be seated, Cordelia will join us soon.'

'How is she Lady Hendricks?' he asked, noting the

217

terribly sad look in her Ladyship's own eyes. Grief was such a terribly wasted emotion to his way of thinking but he had little experience of close family loss. This wonderfully sensual woman, after twenty seven years of marriage would now lock herself away in mourning until she was too old and embittered to turn the head of any man, suitable or not.

'She is grieving, too hard for her own good,' Lady Hendricks answered a faraway look in her moist eyes. 'She cries herself to sleep most nights. I can hear her you know, such a sad sound always carry's. By day she accompanies me in my sorrow, perhaps she feels it is her duty.'

'It has been a terrible shock for you both, I know,' Archie offered.

'Young man, you are a rogue, a likeable knave with trouble in your veins but you're good at heart and you are what Cordelia needs right now. I beg of you please, just take the girl dancing or something and make her smile, if only for five minutes.'

'I'll do my best your Ladyship,' he replied, as Cordelia bustled into the room.

'Archie...oh Archie, thank you for coming,' she gushed as he rose and kissed her hand.

'It's a pleasure as ever old girl,' he said sincerely, sitting her down and pouring her a cup of tea. She looked up to him with a wan smile and desperately sad eyes. As Archie sat back down, he casually looked her over and was saddened by the careworn lines around her eyes, the downturned edges of her once beautiful mouth.

Gradually the conversation, despite its ebb and flow, returned to Spain and the sudden death of her father. His heart had simply stopped beating whilst out on his morning ride. Crashing to the hard cobbles, his footman testified that he was dead before he hit the ground.

Cordelia and her mother had fallen in love with Spain and were both devastated at the recent declaration of war.

'Why such a tragedy has been allowed to pass, I will never understand,' Lady Hendricks offered bitterly.

'Perhaps if the Royal Navy had not behaved like pirates, it would never have gone so far,' Cordelia railed, genuine anger flaring in her dark eyes.

'Oh believe me, there was a tragic inevitability to all of this and only Bonaparte is really at fault,' Archie replied cautiously, a feeling of unease building in the pit of his stomach.

'He's not a real Emperor either,' Lady Hendricks added disdainfully. 'That papal idiot is a disgrace to his faith.'

'We must face the fact that even the Pope goes in fear of Napoleon.'

'I suppose you're right and I know that war has been inevitable for years,' Lady Hendricks said sadly. 'We will win though, won't we Archibald?'

'He'll never get past the Royal Navy, rest assured but we will have to root him out of his lair one day, of that I'm certain and the cost will be high.'

The conversation waxed and waned as the fire gradually died down in the grate. When Lady Hendricks rang the bell to have the fire attended to, Archie began to make his excuses. He quelled sincere protests by insisting his driver would already be waiting outside in the freezing cold.

'Cordelia my dear, would you accompany me to the opening of the fair in Hyde Park tomorrow evening? If this wretched rain finally turns to snow it'll be a magnificent occasion. The King intends to lead the torchlight procession himself.'

'Oh dear me no, I couldn't leave mother all alone after sundown,' Cordelia protested.

'Nonsense my dear, I shall be fine and you will go and you will enjoy yourself, now not another word,' her mother stated emphatically and finally.

'I'll show Archie to the door mother,' Cordelia said, the merest trace of a smile, not quite concealed.

She took his arm, guiding him from the room and along the corridor towards the grand entrance hall. The sudden chill away from the fire raised goose bumps on the pair and he slipped his arm around her slim waist. Cordelia rather than pulling away, held him close as they reached the front door.

'I will collect you at four-thirty prompt,' he said, not quite releasing her. 'The torchlight procession begins at five I believe.'

'I look forward to it Archie. Oh I do so hope it snows, it makes for such a pretty scene in the winter's gloom.'

'Until tomorrow then my dear,' he replied happily, as the ever attentive footman helped him on with his cape and passed him his hat. He gave Cordelia a kiss on each cheek and just a little too tight a squeeze for high society. He felt no resistance from the young woman though, as he looked down into her sad, tired eyes.

He sprinted through the now driving snow to the relative comfort of the carriage and without a word Tom flicked his whip and the horse slipped and slithered its way carefully into the traffic. As they turned a corner, Archie heard a bellow of rage as a veritable wave of slush washed over a man's pristine trousers. He could barely suppress a schoolboy snigger as he watched the red faced man wave his cane in fury.

The carriage somehow navigated its way safely to the southern corner of Cavendish Square. The snow was accumulating just enough to lie on the gardens forming the central promenade area of the square. The bare trees were beginning to attract their own coating of wet snow as the teasing wind swirled through the spindly branches.

Clambering down from the carriage, he looked over toward the park and smiled, snow always made the world look a slightly brighter place he thought. Carefully he picked his way along the slushy pavement, slipping badly once and painfully striking a young man with his false arm. Apologies were exchanged, though why the young man was sorry, only an Englishman would know. Archie slithered his way to house number fourteen, carefully ascended the half dozen steps to the front door and knocked with the ornate brass knocker.

A man shrouded in a thick overcoat and scarf opened the door just wide enough to admit him and he quickly made his way inside. A shiver wracked his body, for if it were possible it was colder inside the hallway than outside on the street. The house was empty and forbidding, the owner sensibly living in the Caribbean with his family.

Archie followed the man up the stairs until they reached the third floor of the magnificent town house. Moving carefully into a room of dustsheet covered furniture, he approached the curtained window.

'It's the house with the two strange lanterns over the front door,' pointed out the somewhat callow young man, who had been peering through the narrow gap between the heavy curtains.

'How many guests are in residence?' Archie asked whilst taking the youth's place and looking out across the snow covered square.

'Four at present, all men aged between twenty and forty,' the young man volunteered.

'Oh, I thought there was a woman there too,' Archie asked, struggling to focus through the snowfall.

'She appears to be the owner, 'Lester Jenkins informed him. 'She goes by the name of Chantelle Richards but the land tax records show her name as Chantelle Haineau.'

'French one presumes,' Archie asked casually.

'Indeed she is,' Jenkins answered confidently. 'She came over in 1796, declaring herself to be the wife of the Comte de Gireau but the reality is she was his mistress. The Comte came over with her but succumbed to typhoid in 1801. She's quite a looker, if you like severe, hard women but she seems to have has fallen on difficult times.'

'So who have we got staying there at the moment,' Archie asked, turning away from the window, the snow making observations all but impossible.

'We've only got names for two of them, both French refugees, neither registered so we could move on them straight away if we want to,' Jenkins replied.

'No need yet, let's see if we can put some people together and follow them around a bit and see what they get up to,' Archie instructed. 'Get some descriptions and put together a portrait of what they do on a day to day basis. I'm going to be tied up tomorrow but on Friday we can look at what we have here. Maybe we can take one of them and find out what the others are up to, if anything.'

'What about the mademoiselle?'

'She can wait,' Archie said thoughtfully, 'maybe she can be turned. It would be nice to have an underground landlady on our side.'

He left the house feeling very optimistic about the potential of this discovery. All over London, agents of Napoleon were infiltrating their way into the society that still maintained a self delusion of safety. Assassins, spies and general troublemakers were holed up in safe houses, from where they were free to make their trouble and plan their attacks.

Tom managed to make his way through the traffic and chaos of a blizzard in central London and delivered Archie to the secret headquarters of the covert side of the Aliens Office. Sprinting through the snow, Archie was already rehearsing his pitch to Sir John, confident that he would convince him that patience would be rewarded in the case of this safe house.

*

The snow lay inches deep across London and the streets were in a state of chaos. Horse drawn transport was all but impossible, nevertheless Archie had with the aid of Tom's considerable driving skills, not only managed to collect Cordelia but completed the treacherous journey to the fringes of Hyde Park.

There unfolding before them was a quite magical scene, with the deepening twilight illuminated by thousands of burning torches and oil lanterns. The falling snowflakes continued to swirl in the freshening breeze, shrouding the landscape in a soft white blanket. As the merry crowd thronged into the park, their excited voices were subtly deadened by the all encompassing cushion of

223

snow.

'Oh Archie this is just wonderful,' Cordelia whispered, as she clung tightly onto his good arm. Wrapped snugly against the piercing cold with just her cherub like face exposed to the bitter wind, she looked like a child granted her first evening outing. Archie found himself equally caught up in the mood as they weaved their way through the animated crowd.

'Where will the parade enter the park?' she asked. 'I so want to see the King. Did you know that he wrote a letter to my mother when father died? That was so sweet of him.'

'I do and that's where we are heading right now,' Archie replied, smiling broadly.

The couple walked down the crowded central thoroughfare, carefully avoiding the hawkers and callers trying hard to entice them to their stalls and tents. Small children queued for swings and merry-go-rounds, whilst groups of rowdy men crowded around stalls selling ale and hot toddies. They moved past a snow-covered boxing ring, where hardy souls were stripping to the waist before attempting to overcome a giant of a man, in the slim hope of winning a florin.

'Oh Archie doesn't that smell wonderful,' Cordelia cried out, pulling him towards a hog spit-roast. Unable to resist, they were soon both tucking into thick chunks of steaming, grease-dripping pork, happily crunching through the blackened crackling.

Passing a small wooded area lit by a hundred lanterns strung from the trees, they made their way through the stalls of fortune-tellers and large dancing tents, toward the main paved avenue. Crowds lined the road more than five deep in places and Archie had to use all his strength to shoulder a way through in order that Cordelia could obtain a view, with only a few urchins between her and the road.

The roadway was lit by thousands more burning torches, their smoke born away on the breeze. The snowfall had all but ceased and as the clouds above began to break, the moon added its bright light, creating a scene so wondrous even Archie's hardened heart was thawed.

Craning his neck, he was able to see in the distance the vanguard of the torch lit procession entering the park. At its very head, six horses of the 1st Life Guards rode with great majesty and extreme care on the snow-covered road. He felt a swell of pride at the sight of the men from his own former regiment. As they approached, he could see marching behind the horses, the Yeomen of the Guard resplendent in their extravagant ceremonial dress.

'Look, there's the King,' Cordelia squealed excitedly. 'He's walking look, not riding his horse.'

'Much safer I reckon,' Archie pointed out,' this snow is going to be lethal to ride on.

The procession was about fifty yards from the couple when Archie noticed the odd sight of man in the crowd opposite pitching forward into the road. With a wry grin he thought how, even in the coldest weather, there was still time to drink far too much.

One of the horses at the head of the procession slipped just as it passed them and Cordelia jumped backwards into the embrace of his arms. He looked down at her, staring deep into her beautiful eyes as they reflected the flickering torchlight. A sudden overwhelming feeling of lust, followed quickly, if he was honest, by one of deep affection washed over him.

Out of the corner of his eye, he saw one of the Yeomen stumble, half rise and slip onto the ground once more. Looking up and to his left, he caught a ripple of disturbance in the crowd as someone pushed people aside to get back from the roadside. He glanced back toward the procession, the King was now well past his position but hundreds more merry, torch bearing men, women and children continued to pass by. Lying on the roadside, the Yeoman was attended by a colleague and members of the crowd, a rapidly spreading bloodstain discolouring the slushy snow.

Archie spun on the spot, releasing Cordelia as he plunged into the crowd, still disturbed by someone's rapid exit. His heart hammering in his chest, he pushed and even punched people aside. The crowd was just too dense to make progress, the floor too slippery to keep a secure footing. He could not see the person he was pursuing merely the disturbance in the crowd as someone pushed through.

He cursed himself for not realising what was happening more quickly. Of course that man had not been drunk and for certain the Yeoman had been felled by a gunshot too. Not caring that he was only armed with his ever present stiletto, he continued to force his way further into the crowd. The snow began falling heavily once more and the evening was now darker than ever as the moon disappeared behind scudding clouds.

Archie let out a wail of frustration when he realised he stood no chance of catching the fleeing assassin. He glared at the people nearby who were looking aghast at the panting, swearing man who had pushed them so roughly aside.

'Hah. It was my wife's lover, the bastard! I'll cut his bollocks off,' he bellowed, to a ripple of laughter and lewd rejoinders. Turning on his heel, he made his way back through the crowd in search of Cordelia. After nearly a quarter of an hour he found her standing alone, looking as vulnerable as a lost child.

'Oh Archie, what happened, where have you been?' she cried, grabbing tightly hold of him. 'That man has been shot, what's happening?'

'It was the King, someone has tried to kill the King,' he told her, his voice calmer than he truly felt inside.

'Oh my God, did you see who it was?' she asked, her eyes burning bright and intense in the flickering torchlight.

'No, nothing more than a glimpse of the back of his head or hers I guess, as they pushed through the crowd.'

'We must tell someone, quickly,' she urged.

'Come on, let's get to the head of the procession,' he ordered, taking her arm and pulling her along in his wake. By keeping back from the roadway they were able to make good progress through the lighter crowds. 'That man who fell out of the crowd took the first ball and then the Yeoman copped the second one.'

'Could there have been more than one man shooting?' she asked.

'That's just what I'm thinking and worse still there could be more of them,' he exclaimed, looking down at her as they passed the brightly lit frontage of a fortune-teller's tent. He was quite shocked to see not fear but sheer unadulterated excitement in her exquisite, once more youthful face.

They reached the end of the procession that was now milling around in some confusion. The soldiers on their cavalry chargers were conspicuous standing in a tight group and Archie dragged Cordelia unceremoniously in their direction, unsure of what he was going to say. He was surprised by their lack of vigilance until he realised that the entire Royal party seemed oblivious to the murderous deeds that had unfolded around them.

As the couple finally reached the front of the tightly packed crowd they saw the King being politely helped into a stately carriage, drawn by four of the finest horses in the land. With a shouted command, the troop of cavalry formed up behind and the small cavalcade made its way carefully over the snow covered track, toward the relative safety of Park Lane.

The Yeomen of the Guard trotted along behind the mounted soldiers, slightly ragged as they shouted to each other, trying to understand what had happened to several of their colleagues who had apparently been lost in the crowd.

'Oh my word Archie, the King's safe,' Cordelia cried, clutching him tightly to her side. 'I need a warming drink; it's been rather too much excitement for one night. Do you think that poor man will be alright? Should we not tell someone what we saw?'

'I think he'll be alright,' Archie lied easily. 'I'm sure the Yeomanry will have figured it out by now, let's just try and enjoy the evening.'

They turned back into the fairground and bought large mugs of hot, fruit punch which they both drank rather too quickly, the scalding, potent drink soon warming them from the inside out. In a suddenly lighter mood, they joined the crowds testing their skills on the penny shies. Archie successfully bowled over every skittle at one such stall even though his mind was racing as he replayed the night's events in his mind.

'Oh this has been such a wonderfully exciting night, thank you,' Cordelia whispered, reaching up and kissing his ice-cold cheek. He gave her a gentle squeeze and they moved on through the crowds. The snow was falling once more, large wet flakes, soaking their clothing and rapidly building up a thickening covering over the grass and the fairground stalls and tents.

'Oh look Archie, they're selling wassail, let's have a glass,' she insisted, dragging him toward the small, red and white striped stall. Over a low fire, a blacked pot was steaming, the aroma of spices and the heady mix of beer and sherry wine, carried toward them on the wind.

They purchased two large cups of the glutinous red liquid from a stout woman who spoke with the accent of her native Scandinavia. Together they stood under the limited shelter of a lime tree, holding each other close while sipping the hot, spiced drink. By the time they had finished they were both no longer feeling the cold. Purchasing a second cup which they downed whilst huddled together in the driving snow; Archie could not help but scan the crowds, looking for the slightest sign of trouble.

Somewhat unsteadily they made their way out of the park towards the road in what proved a vain search for a cab. With the snow now beginning to lie thickly on the ground, the cabbies had retreated for home, so the couple chose to walk with the crowds as the Hendricks home was but half a mile away. With so many people carrying lanterns, the snow-covered streets were lit as never before.

'Take me to your lovely house Archie, that's an order,'

Cordelia demanded with a little giggle, clutching his arm tightly for balance as she stumbled.

'Your mother would have me strung from the highest gallows in London,' he joked lightly, without letting her go.

'Come on spoilsport,' she mewed in his ear,' I'm not a virgin if that's what you think,' she laughed, thrilled that this evidently shocking revelation caused him to slip on the wet snow.

'Luiz was his name,' she giggled. 'Oh dear Luiz, night after night whilst mummy and poor daddy slept, he came to my bedchamber.'

'Lucky Luiz,' Archie replied quietly with a slight smile, not sure how to take this news or how much credence to give it either. 'Nevertheless, you and I have drunk too much and your mother will be expecting her pure and virginal daughter home in one piece.'

'Oh Archie please, take me to your bed,' she whispered in his ear, staggering against him. 'Take me, you know you want to you naughty man,' she chuckled.

'That I most certainly do but not when you have wobbly legs and your mother knows where you are,' he told her firmly before taking her in his arms and kissing her deeply on her lips. 'You are home,' he announced, breaking the warm and deeply passionate moment.

'Damn you Archibald Dexter,' she said with a crooked smile, as he yanked hard on the bell ringer.

Seeing her safely through the door, he set off at a steady jog toward his own home, slipping occasionally but taking the risk in order to preserve his now painfully cold toes.

Back on the gloomy street outside the Hendricks house,

a lone man stood, silent and unmoving, snow rapidly building up on his hat and cloak. The bitter cold did not seem to affect him as he stood deep in thought.

Watching from the safety of the crowds, he had observed first the innocent spectator and then the Yeoman felled by gunshots, the noise lost in the excited melee. From the mass of humanity had sprung a tall man, seemingly determined to catch the would be assassin. Intrigued, the stranger had watched as the man failed in his task and rejoined his lady companion.

By the flickering light of torches and with the crowds milling around in the heavy snowfall, it had been easy for him to follow the couple through the fairground and out into the dark streets of Mayfair. The cold was seeping into his bones now, so slowly he moved off, walking unsteadily down the slippery, snow covered street.

*

The next day, Archie woke to an unusually quiet morning, the thick covering of snow deterring many from venturing out and dampening the noise of the rest. He chose to walk through the bitterly cold streets, enjoying the crisp, cold air. Walking briskly, he lamented how rapidly the city's filth was beginning to show through ragged holes in the once pure white blanket.

Brave souls drove delivery carts and cabs, slipping and sliding on the ice and slushy snow. One unfortunate beast crashed to the ground, upending the cab, spilling both driver and passenger to ground. Archie and several others rushed to their aid and by providence none were worse for their experience.

He continued his way along the icy streets towards the office in Manchester Square. He noted with some amusement how the snow before Christmas appeared to have lifted the spirits of the populace. Even the attempt on the life of the King paled into insignificance as his thoughts turned to the other monumental events of the previous evening. Cordelia had been a revelation and he was not sure where his feelings lay, for it was fair to say that she had put his mind in turmoil.

Women such as Cordelia he had always seen as marriage prospects and therefore they made him nervous. She was nevertheless one of his closest friends and one of the most attractive young women he knew. In his mind's eye he often fantasised about taking her to bed and making her a woman. The revelation that she had romped with a lusty Spanish youth, was by turns exciting and yet somehow disappointing.

He carefully checked behind himself for a few streets before ducking inside the substantial, highly polished door of the house where Sir John Marshall's secret unit worked. The doorman took his hat and coat in the entrance hall and he strode into the outer office. Barreling towards him, red faced and clearly believing Archie to be late was Sir John Marshall.

'Good morning or is it evening, I can never tell,' he blustered with heavy sarcasm. It was in fact just eight-thirty in the morning.

'Good morning Sir and is it not glorious too?' Archie added, more in hope than expectation.

'It most certainly is not.' Sir John replied. 'Worse still is that I am late for a meeting with the Home Secretary. Someone tried to kill the King last night!'

'I know I was there,' Archie replied with studied casualness.

'Well there you are then, so I can't stand and...what...what did you say?'

'I was there Sir, I saw it happen,' Archie replied, enjoying the sight of Sir John standing, mouth wide open and lost for words.

'My office, now young man,' he hissed, hastily reversing course toward his own private rooms. As they entered, he bid Archie sit before he slumped behind his outsized desk.

'Tell me what happened. All I've found out so far is that a would-be assassin fired two shots from the crowd, fortunately for the King only hitting a Yeoman and a dreadfully unlucky bystander. It seems the King and his entourage was oblivious to their peril.'

'There were two gunmen Sir, with no doubt,' Archie began confidently. 'The first man was positioned around fifty yards from me, in the crowd on the west side of the avenue.'

'Did you see him at all and how close to hitting the King was he? 'Sir John asked his eyebrows rising high on his forehead, apparently astounded at this sudden turn of events.

'I saw nothing of him Sir, the crowds were vast and the torchlight created great pools of shadow. I think he shot across in front of the King, at an angle so he was out by a good few yards.'

'What about the second blighter, did he get any closer?'

'Yes, the poor chap who was hit had been walking immediately behind his Majesty. It appeared he took the ball high in his shoulder. I wonder if he's alright.'

'He's doing fine, as remarkably is the fish-seller from Bow who was also hit. Did you get a look at the other swine?'

'Only the briefest glimpse as he disappeared into the crowds and to be honest, with thick winter clothes, he could have just as easily have been a she,' Archie admitted.

'From what you say though, it seems there were two gunmen, so a plot rather than a lone lunatic. I'm not sure whether that's good news or bad. Okay, I really must be off to Whitehall and I am fearfully late already. When I return you can tell me all about that house in Cavendish Square.

*

The following day, with just three left until Christmas, the men of the Aliens Office had planned to follow some of Mademoiselle Haineau's houseguests. Watching from the empty house across the square as yet more snow fell, the shivering men had to wait most of the morning until anyone left the imposing townhouse. Two men left the building together and walked quickly to the corner of the square. By sheer chance a cab was passing by, which they hailed and were away within seconds. By the time the Office's cab had slithered its way precariously around the three sides of the square, there was no way of finding their target amongst the throng, sloshing down Oxford Street.

The agents returned to their original positions and settled down for a long wait. Archie had arrived by this time and was peering through the snow splattered window. Tom sat down on the square, shivering at the helm of his cab under the meagre shelter of snow adorned beech tree.

After what seemed an interminable wait, the watchers were rewarded by the appearance of two figures at the door of the house. It was a young man and a woman, swathed in heavy winter clothes that all but obscured their features.

'Tom and I will take the woman,' Archie ordered, 'the rest of you go with the man.' Striding from the room he ran down the stairs to the front door. He was first out onto the snowy street and quickly entered the flow of pedestrians as he strained to see the woman, now walking alone toward the southern corner of the square. Glancing over his shoulder he was relieved to see Tom moving slowly along behind him.

He closed to within thirty feet of the woman as she left the square and expertly weaved her way through the bustling crowds, turning onto Oxford Street. The brown slush covering the pavement was soaking Archie's chilled feet and he fervently hoped the woman was not intending to go far. He was not disappointed, with a quick glance around her; she darted into a small coffee house. He kept walking past, wary in case any other party was watching her.

After a tense few minutes, he reversed his course and finally entered the warm, smoke wreathed atmosphere of the coffee shop. There was barely room to move as the warm, snug atmosphere was an attractive proposition on such a bitterly cold day. As he attracted the attention of a young waitress, he spied the woman seated alongside the far wall, deep in conversation with a man.

The warmth of the crowded room had persuaded the woman to disrobe to some extent and he was able to study her closely. She was Archie observed perhaps in her thirties, of slender build with a pretty yet sad face, twisted into a rather disdainful sneer. She was clearly known to the hard looking man with whom she was engaged in a hushed

235

conversation, though when he casually rested a hand on her arm, she quickly removed it.

After some twenty minutes, the man drained his cup, grimacing as he inadvertently swallowed the muddy grounds at the bottom. He rose, tried and failed to plant a kiss on the woman's cheek and with a grin pushed his way none too gently toward the door. Archie continued to study the woman for a few more seconds as he struggled into his coat. She was possessed of a hard sensuality he concluded and would probably be an accomplished but reluctant lover. Shaking his head clear of reverie, he squeezed his way to the door and spotting the heavily built man moving through the crowds, he began to follow him along the busy thoroughfare.

The man paused by a wizened old woman selling roast chestnuts from a smoking brazier. Archie noted that this was more a ruse to scan the crowd behind him than to assuage any hunger pangs. He allowed himself to be swept along with the flow of pedestrians and when the man moved off again he was able to continue following him, albeit now too close for comfort.

Without warning, the man turned on his heels and entered an alehouse, which though quite cramped, still boasted a large and noisy clientele. Archie was reluctant to follow him in straight away and continued walking by. He had gone no more than thirty yards when he noticed a tall, thin man limping across the busy road, weaving between carts and carriages, slipping on the vile mix of slush and horse dung.

Archie kept walking, his breath catching in his throat as he recognised Jean Henri Thiebault. Many months ago, Marie had arranged to point him out so that the Office could identify the man who ran Napoleon's intelligence agents in London. Archie was only now seeing him relatively close up for the first time so that he recognised the gait with the head held high on the strangely long neck and was transported in an instant back to the dusty streets of Alexandria. Furious with himself for not realising this on the handful of previous occasions that he had seen the French intelligence chief, he continued walking as the risk was small but significant that he too might be recognised.

Thiebault entered the crowded tavern and forced his way to the rickety little table. Sitting, with some difficulty, he accepted the proffered ale.

'So, do you have good news for me Mr. Pickles?' the Frenchman enquired in perfect English.

'I reckon I do guv,' he replied in hushed tones,' and I just spoke to the lady you put me on to and she 'as a lad in mind to do the trick.'

'I am sure she has found just the right man for the job and as soon as Christmas is past we can move this matter along,' Thiebault assured him.

'She's a cold fish that one for sure, though 'tween you an' me I would guv, if you know what I mean?' Pickles chuckled, his face twisted into a nasty leer.

'Your perverted fantasies are of no interest to me,' Thiebault said flatly, 'and kindly do not mix business with pleasure.'

'Sorry, I'm sure guv,' Pickles retorted through a mouthful of ale.

For the next twenty minutes Pickles updated Thiebault on various plans to blackmail a number of well placed individuals across London.

'What do you want' me to do now guv,' Pickles

enquired, draining the last of his ale.

'I'll send for you early in the new year,' Thiebault replied, 'and then we will have much work to do.' With that parting comment he rose and slipped into his long overcoat.

'Do not leave for at least five minutes,' he instructed, 'and this should keep you in ale for a while.' He walked away from the table, leaving an envelope lying before the smiling man. Pickles knew it contained a substantial sum of money and slid it into his coat pocket without examining its contents.

Some twenty minutes and two more flagons of ale later, he left the warmth of the tavern and began to weave his way unsteadily through the crowds. Before long, just as a fresh fall of snow began, he turned into a newly built side street, lined with a bewildering variety of shops. Kicking the muddy slush from his boots, he entered a shop marked "Pickles Brothers – Ironmongers and Cobblers".

From across the road, Archie noted this and was able to see that the man had walked straight behind the counter and out of sight. Standing behind the counter talking to a customer was a man of such similar appearance to his target that Archie was happy that he had found the man's identity, the Pickles brothers were close to identical in appearance.

*

Christmas Day dawned cold and clear over London, with a sharp frost turning to ice the still lingering, filthy snow. For much of the city it was life as usual, though many would attend church, just as they had the previous night. For Archie it promised to be a special day, for Lady Hendricks had invited him to dinner. A feast fit for a King

238

was a certainty and an evening in the company of Cordelia was always something to be treasured. Yet as the thoughts drifted through his mind, a gnawing worry settled in the pit of his stomach. On the last occasion they had met, the effects of drink and high drama had produced an enticing but unsettling change in the young lady's character.

He lay in his bed, fretting over this situation for some time as he waited for Cedric to deliver his breakfast. He knew he would give anything for a ferocious romp with Cordelia but before the prospect overwhelmed him, he remembered her place in society did not readily allow for such behaviour without the horrific ritual of marriage first. His mind's eye began to lay out a most lusty scene before him but before he could become too distracted, a discrete knock on the door heralded the arrival of breakfast.

'Good morning,' Cedric announced, placing a tray laden with food by Archie's bedside. 'I'm afraid it's nearly nine o'clock and if you remember, you have an appointment with your father at twelve.'

'Oh believe me, that is one thing I'm unlikely to forget,' he replied with a wry chuckle.

Left alone, he began to tuck into his breakfast and once more thoughts turned unbidden to Cordelia. Try as he might he could not clear his mind of lewd thoughts and he wondered if it may not be safer to excuse himself this evening. His hand stole beneath the blankets and he grasped his rigid member, as hard and sculpted as marble, slowly he stroked its length and once more in his mind's eye he seduced Cordelia Hendricks.

Suddenly a rumble of what he first thought to be thunder then he realised was probably cannon fire, echoed back and forth across the unusually quiet city. He struggled to recall any announcement of such a celebration for this Christmas morning but thought no more of it as he hastily concentrated on his breakfast before rising to take the bath Cedric had prepared.

Within the hour he was in a cab, beginning the wearisome journey across the river and then along rutted lanes to his Aunt Mildred's house in Chiswick where his parents were spending Christmas Day. He was fortunate in his timings in that he just missed the arrival of a runner at his front door, summoning him to attend Sir John Marshall at his home without delay.

*

Several hours before Archie had woken, two men had spent an uncomfortable half hour, slipping and sliding over the frozen pavements of London. The pavements had been swept clear of snow only in the immediate vicinity of the most prestigious shops and homes. Elsewhere they were now a death trap of frozen ridges of solid slush, mixed with garbage and horse dung.

The two men were a sharp contrast in physique and attitude. One of the men was a little over six feet tall with an impressively wide pair of shoulders, upon which sat an incongruously small head. Despite the deformation of a livid scar, his was a face that seemed perpetually amused with the world around him.

His companion was perhaps the most nondescript man in London. Average height and average build, with distinctly average looks. Claude Renoir was the perfect spy, once seen, he was instantly forgotten, unlike his companion George Mitterrand whose distinctive build and broad smile had often been his undoing. Renoir was grateful though that Mitterrand had secured such comfortable quarters in the sumptuous home of Mademoiselle Haineau.

Walking southbound along Saint Martin's Lane, Renoir wondered for the twentieth time why they had to walk and not take a cab. George insisted this was safer but surely a broken leg was just as dangerous as some nosey cabby remembering them.

As daylight began to make the journey slightly easier, the two men turned east and walked along The Strand. After a hundred yards, Mitterrand ducked down a narrow alley and with a cursory glance backwards; Renoir followed him into the gloom. The two men had to move a stack of rotting boxes and an old sea chest before they could even see the doorway at the rear of a derelict bakers shop. Renoir applied a key to the new and well-lubricated lock and within seconds they were inside. He locked the door behind them, leaving the key in the lock, whilst Mitterrand found and lit a small oil lamp.

The two men picked their way carefully through the tangle of debris left behind by the bankrupt business, tripping over empty barrels and clambering over sacks of rotten flour. They reached a closed door largely unscathed and Mitterrand placed the lamp to one side, with the wick turned down low. Renoir applied a second key to the door and slowly pushed it open.

The area before them had been the shop front for the bakery and they were standing behind the serving counter. Heavy curtains were drawn across the windows and the room was cast into almost perpetual night. The heavy hessian material did little however to dull the sounds of the already busy street outside.

'Check them one more time my old friend,' Mitterrand

said quietly.

Renoir walked up to the curtains and knelt by a stack of five barrels. Each barrel was around three feet in height and a foot in circumference. He ran his fingers over them in the gloom. 'All just as we left them,' he concluded as he stood stiffly, his knees cracking in the cold frigid air.

'Come on then, let's go upstairs,' Mitterrand urged somewhat breathlessly.

With the door closed behind them, Mitterrand turned up the lamp's wick and examined his fob watch. Satisfied, he crossed the back room until he found the rickety stairs leading to the first floor. As the two men climbed, the stairs creaked fearfully but held fast. They found themselves in what had been a very humble living room, the windows again blacked out by a heavy hessian curtain. Renoir dragged over a small wooden chair and perched on the back. He pulled the curtain aside, affording himself a fine view of the street below. The two men settled down to wait, shivering despite their warm clothing, their breath fogging the air around them.

A little way to the east of the bakers shop stood a small group of hawkers, hoping to profit from a little Christmas cheer. Mulled ale and roast chestnuts produced a heady aroma to compete with a small hog being roasted over a brazier of hot coals. A cheery crowd of hardy souls braved the cold to sample the fare on offer, many on their way to or from church or simply taking the air on this frigid Christmas morning.

A few yards away from the merry little group, a man stood all alone, eating a hefty wedge of bread and pork, whilst clutching a tankard of ale. He repeatedly juggled with his foodstuffs in order to check a small silver fob watch, his attention constantly drawn towards the western end of The Strand.

Some twenty minutes later it was Mitterrand, perched on the rickety chair that spotted them coming. 'This is them,' he cried, 'I can see the cavalry.'

'Let me see, quickly,' Renoir asked anxiously, leaning over his companion and pulling the curtain back.

'It's them, no doubt about it,' Mitterrand replied testily, 'now get downstairs before it is too late.'

Renoir dashed toward the stairs, turning back quickly for the lantern. He turned up the wick then opened its case, as he scurried into the shop front. Upstairs, Mitterrand opened the curtains slightly, as the time for care was long past. This gave him a clear view several hundred yards down the street and most importantly meant that he could see the small church of Saint Stevens.

Renoir squatted in the gloom of the shop, his heart pounding and his stomach churning painfully. Mitterrand watched the approaching cavalry troopers, twelve of them, more than he expected. First one, then a second horse slipped on the treacherous road surface. The troopers fought to keep the panic from spreading, just controlling the frightened beasts in time.

Renoir fought to control his own emotions, even in the half-light his breath hung heavy in the bitterly cold air. Mitterrand could now see the first of the large, ornate carriages behind the lead troopers. Unusually, it was surrounded on all sides by even more of the immaculately dressed cavalry. Following behind were four more ranks of mounted cavalry and then the gaily-dressed men of the Yeomanry. Once more a horse slipped and all but unseated its rider but on came the little procession regardless. Three impressively large carriages were making their stately way along The Strand under the protection of an equally impressive military escort.

The officer at the vanguard of the procession tentatively advanced his horse along the slippery road. He glanced to his right and took in the view of the pleasant church of Saint Stevens. Mitterrand looked on, concentrating furiously on the scene before him.

'Now Claude, now for the love of the Emperor, now!' he bellowed, leaping to his feet and plunging into the darkness, he half ran, half fell down the stairs.

Claude Renoir dipped a taper into the flame of the lantern and then touched the taper to the end of a fuse. The fuse flared briefly and then with a crackling whoosh began to burn rapidly, throwing clouds of acrid smoke into the air. He picked up the lantern and ran from the room. Mitterrand was already by the back door and opened it as his companion ran towards him. Renoir hurled the lantern into the pile of debris, where it shattered and spread flame quickly across the empty sacks and broken boxes.

The two men closed the door behind them and walked quickly down the narrow alleyway. Mitterrand doffed his hat to a woman walking towards them as they emerged into Castle Court, continuing to walk briskly but trying not to appear in undue haste.

Back on The Strand, a frightened young trooper by the name of Wells felt his charger fall to its knees as it tripped on a frozen ridge of ice and then he was plunging face first into the road. The procession came to a halt briefly but then continued past the injured man, two Yeomen trotting up to his aid. Thus slowed slightly, the cavalcade continued eastwards towards Holborn.

A ruddy-faced Yeoman Sergeant turned the trooper over and looked down at the young man's smashed face, blood pouring from between broken teeth.

'Aye laddie that's done your looks not much good, but you'll be fine,' he said kindly.

Trooper Wells looked up as the sky suddenly turned black and fire rained down around him. Just as his senses picked up a ground shaking roar, he saw the Yeoman's body twist violently, the unfortunate man's head ripping free and flying away, to be followed by the rest of his body. Debris, fire and bodies flew over Trooper Wells until a blast of scalding hot air picked him up and rolled him over and over across the road.

When he came to, his ears ringing painfully, he tried to stand but helplessly pitched forward. The shooting pain travelling up his leg made him look down and when he saw the shaft of wood sticking from his calf, he fainted.

Barely five minutes passed before he came to once more and as he eased himself to his knees, he noticed that the carriages had gone. Despite his injuries, the young man crossed himself in thanks for the King and Queen's safety. He looked around at half a dozen or more dead and dreadfully mutilated horses lying in the road with the remains of their troopers. Those closest to the blast had been quite literally blown apart, the less fortunate had been either burnt like charcoal or ripped limb from limb, to die slowly on the filthy road. Providence had smiled on young Toby Wells and he knew it as he sobbed with heartache and agony, alone with his thoughts this terrible Christmas morning.

As the King's cavalcade had made its way along the Strand, the small crowd stood by the food sellers had moved towards the road's edge, all keen to cheer their King. The man standing alone though had moved backwards, towards the entrance to a dark and narrow side street. He finished the last of his food and moved his scarf back to obscure most of his face.

As the cavalry troopers passed in front of the ornate little church, the man had begun counting slowly, just the faintest whisp of breath visible through his thick scarf. As he looked down the street, he had watched with horror as Trooper Wells fell to the road. He continued to count as the delayed procession walked on, step after step, closer to destiny.

Despite himself, the man had jumped as the shop front exploded in smoke and flame. He saw men and horses engulfed in the explosion, shattered bodies hurled across the road, many hitting the buildings on the far side. Thick smoke whirled upwards and away from the shop itself which was well ablaze. With a feeling of horror he had seen the royal carriages being expertly turned around as the surviving troops rallied to protect their monarch.

He quickly ducked into the side street, letting rushing onlookers push by him, forcing himself to appear calm and unconcerned as he made his escape from the scene. He cursed his luck under his breath, wondering what exactly he had to do to kill this troublesome King.

Walking slowly along the quiet streets, he carefully went over the plan and its ultimate failure. It was the ice and the tumbling soldier that had been their undoing, throwing their careful timing out just far enough to spare the true target of their lethal attack. He took some small comfort from the undoubted panic such an outrage would trigger once the news spread. With luck he thought, the popular press would blame the underground anarchist movements and they would live to fight again another day.

*

As Archie rode in a cab to Cordelia's house, he was deeply troubled by the day's developments. He had eventually been tracked down by Sir John's messenger and had attended the man's comfortable home in Blackfriars. For over an hour they had reviewed the worsening situation before Archie summed the situation up succinctly.

'In a nutshell Sir,' he said with emphasis, 'we have absolutely no clues as to who may be behind this. If there had been the slightest suggestion at the French Embassy then our agent there would have made emergency contact I'm sure. The most active of their agents are all engaged in the business of gathering intelligence and most of that is economic in nature.'

'What about Cavendish Square though?' Sir John asked, casually opening a small dossier on the desk before him.

'We know very little, save to say there are at least four men who are the guests of a French exile. As my report says, she's been seen in association with this un-savoury character, Pickles. I'm sure we'll be able to find out what they're plotting but I have to say, assassinating the King would seem unlikely.'

'I find it hard to believe that Napoleon would agree to such a thing anyway,' Sir John ventured. 'After all, our response would certainly be violent and bloody. Even if we didn't try to kill him in revenge, war would be an immediate certainty.'

'We all know war's inevitable Sir, perhaps he just

wants to get it started?'

'Maybe so but we can't rule out home grown lunatics, 'Sir John insisted. 'Perhaps we should look rather closer to home. Anarchists are everywhere it seems these days.'

'They're mostly all wind and talk, nothing else though,' Archie offered. 'We can have a look at a few of the local hotheads if you like Sir. We could even round a few up and that might just scare them off before they try again.'

'Yes, we'll rattle a few cages, 'Sir John agreed, whilst fumbling for his pipe. 'I want you to concentrate on Cavendish Square for now. Put men onto all Madam's guests and you concentrate on her. It worries me slightly that she's kept herself secret for so long, yet now seems to be the topic of conversation quite so much at the Embassy. It seems to me that she might be pivotal to something important, especially at a time when someone is trying to kill King George.'

*

'Archie, you sweetheart, Merry Christmas,' Cordelia gushed before he had even crossed the threshold.

'Cordelia my dear, seasons greetings,' he answered with a broad smile, planting firm kisses on each cheek. A footman stood discretely by to take his hat and coat but Cordelia was already helping him divest himself of the heavy garments. The stern faced footman stepped forward to relieve Archie of the burden of a substantial pile of garishly wrapped presents.

'Come along quickly now, Mother is waiting for us in the drawing room,' she said and positively dragged him along the gaily decorated hallway, heading toward the rear of the house.

The couple strode through a pair of large and ornately

detailed doors into a room of gargantuan proportions. Sitting before a roaring log fire was Lady Hendricks, dressed in a dark burgundy, velvet dress, cut surprisingly low across the bosom, for a widow in mourning. Archie almost chuckled as he thought, like mother like daughter, she was secretly as brazen as Cordelia, he concluded.

'Archibald, my dear young man, season's greetings,' she said, smiling broadly as he stooped to kiss her proffered hand.

'Lady Hendricks, thank you,' he responded quietly. 'You are looking well, despite the trials of recent months.'

Lady Hendricks blushed just slightly at the somewhat presumptuous compliment. To cover her discomfort, she reached for a small brass bell at her side. The gentle tinkle summoned a servant to the room, who was instantly dispatched to fetch tea and cakes, as she bade Archie take a seat on the luxurious sofa. Cordelia sat down next to him, so close it caused her mother's eyebrows to rise in unison, a disapproving look ignored, though not unnoticed by either of the couple.

As tea was served and the fire stoked with fresh logs, talk turned to the recent events, news of which seemed to have spread like a wild fire across London.

'Oh Archie, this horror must have been the work of Bonapartist scum,' Cordelia ventured, her eyes flashing with heartfelt anger.

'Language my dear,' Lady Hendricks chided gently. 'I'm not sure they would dare, for it would surely mean war, would it not Archibald?'

'Indeed it would Lady Hendricks, 'Archie replied thoughtfully, 'but I fear it's only a matter of time anyway. Sooner or later the little man will make a move against one of France's neighbours and then an alliance will be formed to face him head on.'

'Will we be invaded Archie?' Cordelia asked, taking the opportunity to look scared and clutch tightly at his arm.

'Unlikely with the Royal Navy in the English Channel,' he assured her,' but I wouldn't hold out much hope for any of France's neighbours, even Prussia.'

'We should throw all the French out of London, they're simply horrid!' Cordelia said emphatically.

'Oh rubbish my dear, some of the ladies are quite charming and I know your father had some good friends at his club who had fled the horrors in Paris. It will be a sorry affair if we cannot offer sanctuary to decent people in time of need,' Lady Hendricks scolded gently.

'What, so some of them can try and blow the King to smithereens on Christmas morning. I don't trust any of them or want them in London. We've been fools to take them in.'

'There will always be a price to pay for civility my dear,' Lady Hendricks replied sternly, with a growing feeling of unease. This was a side to her daughter she had not seen before, though these were sentiments echoed by many in London society.

In this way the conversation rattled on, only occasionally moving to more light- hearted matters. Archie was becoming progressively more uncomfortable until relief arrived in the shape of Cordelia's twin cousins Gerald and Richard, along with their mother, Camilla Ffolkes.

As evening fell, Simmons the family butler entered and announced that dinner was ready to be served. The disparate group made their way to the brightly lit dining room and were soon tucking into a wonderful feast.

Roast goose and mountains of vegetables were washed down by copious quantities of thick, fruity red wine. Just when they thought they could not possible swallow any more food, the huge, fruity Christmas pudding arrived, ablaze with burning brandy.

Much later, as the men were left with their port, Archie noticed once more that Cordelia was in good spirits and a little unsteady on her feet. As he tried to engage in conversation with her cousins, he was already planning to escape from the house at the first opportunity.

An hour later the men rejoined the ladies in the main drawing room. A sumptuous array of cakes and biscuits had been laid out and uneasily at first but gaining in confidence, the house servants joined them around the blazing fire. Cordelia handed out presents to the servants and in a scene that even touched Archie's heart, they all joined together to sing carols, accompanied by Lady Hendricks expert piano playing.

By nine, the evening was drawing to a close and the servants fussed to clear the room, as Cordelia's relatives announced that the time had come to retire to their guestrooms. Archie took this as his cue to ask Lady Hendricks if she would ask her coachman to prepare to take him home.

'Oh Archie you should stay,' Cordelia pleaded, grasping his arm, to the obvious disapproval of her mother. 'The weather is beastly cold and the roads are so dangerous at night.'

'I'll be fine in the hands of your coachman,' Archie assured her. 'I've an early start tomorrow and besides that I've presumed upon your mother's hospitality too much already.'

'You are welcome as you well know,' she scolded, glaring at him with genuine anger.

A short while later she escorted him to the door, her arm tightly wound around his. 'I do believe you are scared of me, Archibald Dexter,' she whispered, as they reached the door with the inevitable footman standing in attendance.

'I do believe you may be right,' he whispered back. 'You are becoming something of a rebel aren't you? Be warned though, your mother has her eye upon you.'

'I don't care, I want you and I am going to have you,' she said and before he could take avoiding action, she placed her lips firmly upon his, forcing her tongue between his lips, which emboldened him to return a long and passionate kiss. From the corner of his eye, he could see the footman had found something of interest on the corner of the dresser to attend to.

Breaking free at last, Archie wagged his finger at Cordelia but was unable to suppress a broad smile. Finally escaping the house for the sanctuary of the coach, he instructed the driver to take him to the club he favoured in Haymarket

Once within its warm rooms he soon found himself embroiled in an escalating card game that saw him at a point just after midnight in debt to the tune of nearly one hundred guineas. With his mind distracted by the rapacious attentions of Cordelia, he was fortunate to be able to retire to his room for the night having lost only a little over thirty guineas. The fine French brandy he had consumed had coloured his judgment once more but with the room beginning to gently spin, he settled onto the comfortable bed fully clothed and was asleep before his head touched the pillow.

*

Several days after Christmas, Archie found himself shivering once more in the empty house in Cavendish Square. It was early afternoon but already the leaden skies meant the starlings were settling down to roost in the bare trees of the ornamental gardens. Two of the men staying at the Frenchwoman's house were out and about, followed by agents of the Aliens Office. Archie was waiting for the woman to leave.

He was impatient for something to develop because Sir John was pressing to have everyone in the house arrested. He considered the assassination attempt against the King an act of war and favoured disrupting whatever these people were planning. Archie had successfully argued that at this stage it was not even clear that the French were in anyway involved in the attempts on the King's life.

He was awoken from his daydreaming by the sudden appearance at the front door of the lady of the house. Mademoiselle Haineau was well wrapped up against the bitterly cold wind and as Archie made his way to the street, he began to wish he had taken Cedric's advice and worn an extra layer. Falling in behind the hurrying woman, he felt the ice-cold air take his breath away.

He followed her with little difficulty and before long she entered the same coffee shop he had observed her use before. By the time he made his own way inside, he saw the man he suspected went by the name of Pickles had joined her. Archie took a table close by but the level of noise was such that it was impossible to overhear any conversation.

From his coat pocket, he fished a crumpled copy of The Times newspaper and whilst pretending to read, was able to watch the two people as they continued to talk in hushed tones. At one point the woman passed two pieces of paper to Pickles, who pocketed them without a glance. A short while later, she slid a small envelope across the worn oak table and this time he did examine the contents before slipping it into an inside pocket. Archie had the briefest glimpse of the presence of money in the envelope.

This appeared to signify an end to business as the woman drained her coffee and made to leave. Clearly the man had other ideas and moved closer to her in whispered conversation. The woman's eyebrows shot upwards at one point and she began to rise but the man reached over, grasped her arm and pulled her back down. The woman's hissed retort was unintelligible buts its meaning was clear to see.

The brutally ugly man merely laughed and held her arm tighter, whilst his other hand caressed her knee through her heavy skirts. When she pulled back the man began to squeeze her arm. At first the woman resisted but then a cold look crossed her face and she locked eyes with her companion. As he squeezed her bicep with a crushing grip she showed no obvious reaction except to stare deep into the man's eyes.

Shocked by her reaction he let her go, guffawed with laughter and rose, dismissing her with a cheery wave, before roughly barging his way toward the door. The woman shook herself and stood up before heading to the door but as she passed Archie, she suddenly fell flat on her face in an undignified heap on the wet and dirty floor.

He leapt to his feet to help her to her stand, still unsure

as to why he had just tripped her. He made a fuss of her wet clothes and forced her into the empty chair at his table.

'I'm so sorry madam,' he purred in the gentle Scottish burr of his alter ego Donald Ross. 'Please allow me to buy you a coffee whilst your clothes dry a little, perhaps a small slice of pie too.'

'There is no need, an accident that's all,' she said quickly, trying to head once more for the door.

'Please I insist,' he said with a smile, whilst firmly guiding her back into the chair,' it is the least I can do after my clumsiness.'

'I really do not have the time,' she assured him but looking Archie up and down she decided he was a very good-looking young man and besides she did not want to make another scene. 'However as you are so persistent then yes, thank you,' she added, though with not the barest hint of a smile.

'Donald Ross at your service,' Archie introduced himself, after ordering two coffees and a couple of slices of veal pie from the rather grubby child who was the only waitress in the establishment. Using a false persona without his disguise was a calculated gamble but he was feeling in a reckless mood.

'That's not an accent from these parts,' she told him.

'No indeed not, I hail from the north of Scotland, where I own a number of successful fish merchants,' he replied. 'If I may make so bold, that is not an accent of this city either?'

'No, I am originally from Cherbourg in France,' she answered, studying his reaction closely. 'My father was a magistrate and the mobs lynched him, so I was forced to flee and now London is my home,' she lied easily.

'And very welcome you are too,' he replied, with what he hoped was a lightly flirtatious tone. If he was hoping for a smile in return then he was bitterly disappointed. The waitress delivered two cups of dark coffee and substantial slices of pie. He ate slowly, watching with mounting curiosity the genteel manner with which the Frenchwoman consumed her food.

'Do you have other family in London?' he asked, studying her intently.

'I have no family but many friends who have been forced to flee their homes. I fear we will be fleeing once more if Napoleon makes good his promise and invades England.'

'Pah, not a chance, the Navy will never let him pass,' Archie answered, with as much Celtic vitriol as he could muster. 'Besides, what on earth could he and his rag-tag revolutionaries have against you personally?'

'You were either for the revolution or you were against it,' she answered, for the first time a flicker of emotion crossing her cold brown eyes before in an instant it was gone. 'Even if you could care less, you were still labelled and the revolutionary councils made meticulous records, so once branded that is how one stays.'

'How do you live?' he asked, still looking for the faintest flicker of emotion in her dead eyes.

'I run a small boarding house owned by a gentleman friend, so I'm quite fortunate compared to many I know. You're not from this cold and cruel city either, don't you miss home?'

'My home is where I rest my head, for I've spent many years travelling,' he replied. 'Tell me though, would you return to France if it were possible, surely this revolution cannot last forever?'

'People have long memories,' she answered with a trace of sadness in her gentle voice, 'and many things must be done whether we like it or not to get through this life.'

Archie looked closely at her and was not sure if she was the coldest woman he had ever met or had someone or something, broken her heart irreparably. She was making ready to leave, so he made his play.

'I've enjoyed our short time together Mademoiselle and hope that our paths may cross again one day. I frequent this establishment and would be honoured if you kept me company once more.'

'You are a kind gentleman Sir but I have a busy life and doubt our paths will cross again,' she said as she rose. 'However if you should see me on your travels or catch me taking coffee here, it would be nice if you said hello,' she said quietly, with the slightest hint of a smile as she offered her small, gloved hand, which he took as he rose and kissed the back gently. Flashing her brief smile in return, he was rewarded with the faintest blush in her pale cheeks.

Alone, he reflected on the insane risk he had taken but felt vindicated. He would dress the incident up as an accident when he reported to Sir John but in his own mind he felt it was futile to keep following the woman around London's streets. He waited a full five minutes before leaving and carefully checked he was not himself being followed, before hailing a cab to home.

For her part Mademoiselle Haineau walked home through the wet streets, oblivious to the heavy fall of sleet. She kept asking herself why she had sat with the man who spoke in such a strange accent. Even more so, she asked herself why she had felt a hot flush as he kissed her hand, almost as though something had pierced her reserve and once beneath the skin had somehow infected her with feelings she no longer understood.

Picking up her pace, she rushed back to Cavendish Square where she had much work to do. That it should come to this she thought, running a boarding house for an evil man who held the power of life and death in his hands, not just hers but all those forced to do his bidding.

*

The following day, Marie left the French Embassy and struggled through the crowded streets to buy fresh potatoes and carrots. In a well rehearsed routine, her report was passed through the hands of various people until it was received and deciphered at the Aliens Office. Grasping the translation, Archie hurried to Sir John's office and told him the latest news.

'Sir, it seems that Thiebault knows as little about the attempts on the life of the King as we do,' he began. 'He's discussed the matter at some length with the Ambassador and neither of them knows who is behind the attacks.'

'My God, do you realise what that may mean?' Sir John asked, rubbing his temples in frustration. 'Our King is possibly being stalked by his own countrymen but whom for God's sake? Have we no ideas at all?'

'None at all Sir,' Archie admitted. 'There's one other disturbing consideration, Thiebault is very astute and he is concerned that he's being excluded from a top-secret operation. He's not even convinced that the Ambassador is being truthful with him.'

'There's something else you need to know about Thiebault, Sir,' he continued cautiously. 'Until the other day, I'd only seen him a few times and at some distance but I came very close to him in Oxford Street and now realise that we've crossed swords before!'

'God Lord, when?' Sir John asked, genuinely intrigued, sitting forward with his blue eyes burning with an intense curiosity.

'It was in Egypt, back in ninety-eight. When I landed with Nelson's orders for the British Consul, Thiebault was watching whilst we were very nearly murdered by a gang of locals. Later as I was escaping to rejoin the Navy, he led a platoon of French soldiers that very nearly captured us. He walks with a limp now, which I fear is the result of a musket ball I put into him as we made our way to the boats.'

'My God, you had better be very wary around him,' Sir John said with a smile, adding, 'it's a shame you didn't kill him there and then, the man is a positive menace.'

'It's very unlikely he would recognise me, by that time I looked more Arab than the locals.'

'Well let's hope so,' Sir John said quietly. 'Now what are we going to do about your new lady friend and her house guests.'

'I think she is being coerced somehow and is a good longer term prospect for turning,' Archie replied, with more confidence than he felt. 'Imagine if we can turn her Sir, every agent who lodges with her will fall into our net.'

'It would indeed be something of a triumph. What can we do about this awful man Pickles? Do you think he's a traitor or just a criminal who'll do anything for a pound?'

'The latter almost certainly I would say Sir. Give me a few more days and if possible three or four more men and we'll put a big effort into finding out what Mademoiselle's current guests are up to.'

'Okay, you have until the end of the week and if you've nothing by then, we'll get the Runners to pick one of them up, find out who he is and what he has to say for himself,' Sir John concluded.

*

The next two days were frustrating for Archie and his team, not to mention cold and very wet. The big freeze had given way to torrential icy rain, which after it washed away the last of the filthy snow then began to flood the roads and many of the basements of London.

With only two days left to go, on New Year's Day, the men had finally seen something which warranted reporting. Claude Renoir had left the house early and taken a cab. With some difficulty, two of Archie's men had followed him all the way to Knightsbridge on foot, running and dodging their way through the crowded streets, slipping and sliding in muddy puddles, crashing to the ground on more than one occasion. Fortunately the flooded roads were keeping the horse drawn traffic to a crawl.

Arriving in Knightsbridge, they observed Renoir enter a large coaching house on the Bath Road. Kelvin McNeil, one of Archie's most able men, slipped inside the crowded inn. He located the Frenchman sitting sullen faced on a rickety wooden settle alongside two old men and a small child perched on her nanny's knee. McNeil was able to watch the disparate little group board a mail coach, which was bound, so the landlord assured him for Ascot, Newbury and finally Bristol.

Cold, wet and very tired, McNeil and his partner had returned to Cavendish Square, to find Archie sitting in the first floor bedroom with no lesser personage than Sir John himself.

'Bristol!' exclaimed Sir John,' what on earth is he going there for?'

'What's the other man done today, the man mountain that usually goes wherever his smaller friend goes? Strange that he's not gone with him on the coach,' Archie wondered out loud.

'He's been out and about too Sir,' volunteered a sallow faced man in his fifties, who had been sitting unobtrusively in the corner of the room, huddled in an oversized coat, shivering with cold. 'He left just after the little one and went to a few shops on Park Lane. I don't know what he bought at the first two but he hired a couple of suits at the last one, then took a cab back here.'

'Good work chaps,' Archie said his finger to his lips as he sank into deep thought. 'Clearly something's afoot, so I think we stick with that big chap for the next few days. If the little one has gone to Bristol then he is unlikely to reappear for a week at least.'

Archie and Sir John rode together in the cab, driven by the ever present Tom. The incessant rain still fell in sweeping curtains, driven along by a cold north wind. The clouds were so dense and grey that the city was bathed in an ethereal half-light, the unfortunate souls out on the streets, little more than shadows moving in the gloom. Along many streets, a foul stinking, morass of muddy water lay inches deep across the road, in places right up to the shop fronts.

'Let's see what develops over the next few days but if nothing happens then we will look at pulling them in for a little talk. Perhaps you could engineer another liaison with

Mademoiselle Haineau or Richards as I believe she calls herself?' Sir John suggested.

'I'll try tomorrow morning. I'm meeting Charles Lyell for dinner this evening. If he's not otherwise engaged I thought I might let him see if he can find out a little more about this Pickles character. Something he mentioned whilst on our trek across Spain has given me an idea.'

*

That evening Archie dined at the exclusive Whites club with Charles Lyell. Lyell looked pale and rather ill, much to Archie's alarm.

'Charles old chap, I hope you don't mind me saying but you really don't look very well,' Archie observed, genuine concern in his voice.

'Oh I'm on the mend now but this is the first proper dinner I've taken in several weeks,' the young man replied with a tired smile. 'My family has an estate in Norfolk and there is good ice skating to be had on the frozen ditches. They hold fiercely competitive races between houses and villages. Sadly the ice isn't always as thick as it should be!'

'Oh my word, you went through?' Archie exclaimed. 'That happened to me when I was a child and I've never skated since. It was the most terrifying experience of my life and I've had a few very close shaves since.'

'I wasn't trapped under the ice fortunately but it was a bitter day with a north-east wind. Needless to say I caught a terrible fever and if truth be told I'm lucky to be here to tell the tale.'

'Well, you look after yourself my friend,' Archie counselled. 'I had a task for you but it can wait, for you should be convalescing not out in this dreadful weather.'

'No, I'm fine now,' Lyell insisted, sitting slightly more upright at the suggestion of something to do, 'I've been nursed by two maiden aunts in Kensington and I'm at my wits end. Please tell me, what is it you need me to do for you?'

Sparing some details, Archie told Lyell about the mysterious Mr. Pickles, who seemed to have some involvement with people dedicated to causing trouble on the streets of London. Reminding Lyell of their conversation in Spain, he suggested that this should give him a chance to get to meet Pickles on his own territory and test his integrity.

After dinner, the two men joined a foursome playing whist but by ten o'clock Lyell was clearly getting tired and excused himself for the evening. Archie continued to play a few hands but as the stakes began to rise he did not feel the usual passion for the gamble and soon withdrew. As he waited for his hat and coat, he idly considered going on to a special club he knew in Curzon Street. The girls there were most accommodating and shockingly imaginative but somehow the enthusiasm was just not there.

Huddled in the corner of a cab as it lurched over the dark, pot-holed streets of Mayfair, he reflected on his sombre mood. If even the prospect of the perverted delights of Ma Jones' house of ill repute could not interest him then he must be in a black mood for sure. By the time the cab jerked to a halt outside his home, he had the answer to his quandary.

Cedric had the front door open before he had even stepped down from the carriage and now stood in the rain, paying the driver. Once inside, Archie divested himself of his hat and coat but graciously allowed a frustrated Cedric to take them and place them in the hall cupboard.

'Cedric, please come and join me in my study. We can toast Napoleon's continuing poor health with some fine French brandy.'

The two men settled in front of the rapidly expanding fire that Cedric had just expertly stoked. This was one of the rooms in the house blessed with a fire in the grate from six in the morning until nearly midnight.

'Is something troubling you Sir, I'm sorry, Archie?'

'It has been but now I think I have the answer. When a man loses his appetite for the cards and female company then something must be truly amiss,' Archie observed, noting the difficulty with which Cedric suppressed a knowing grin.

'Something is in the air, something big and quite terrible. I've been in too many scrapes not to be able to sense such things,' he continued.

'Well, these dreadful attempts to kill the King have the whole of London worried,' Cedric observed, staring into the now blazing fire. 'It's only a matter of time before they get him if you ask me Sir.'

'Exactly my thoughts, exactly my thoughts,' Archie mused and then downing his brandy in one, he reached for the bottle sitting on the side table. 'I know it's going to happen again and it's going to be soon. The problem is the only Frenchies we are watching don't on the face of it seem to have anything to do with it. They're just pottering around London doing very little.'

'The papers say that revolutionaries are behind it but I don't know of any revolutionaries do you?' Cedric asked, helping himself to more of the obviously smuggled brandy.

'No but it also seems so unlikely that Napoleon would risk reprisals by killing the King,' Archie responded with little conviction. 'After all he wants to start war in Europe on his terms and when he is good and ready.'

'Maybe someone wants to push his plans along a bit. If the King were killed then we would invade France surely? Maybe someone wants to start the war sooner than Napoleon?'

Archie stared into the fire, momentarily lost in thought. Cedric had it quite right he realised. Had they not done exactly the same in Spain? By stealing neutral Spain's gold bullion, they had forced Spain into a premature alliance with Napoleon. This had strengthened the resolve of England's alliance with the northern European countries. So perhaps Napoleon himself was trying to start a shooting war or plotters within the French establishment were tiring of the endless waiting game.

He watched Cedric closely as his friend swirled his brandy in the glass, studying it intently by the fire-light. He was a truly good friend Archie decided, a friendship forged in adversity. Since returning to England, neither man had discussed the privations and torments inflicted upon them during their time as prisoners of war. That was in the past they had decided and there it would stay. Sometimes though in the long dark nights, the memories came flooding back and the terrible rage began to build inside him once more.

*

The following day, for the first time in many weeks, the sky was clear over the streets of London. Archie left the house in high spirits as the sun, though it lay low in the milky sky, managed to reinvigorate the tired, damp populace. Gangs of men were collecting the mountains of sloppy horse dung that had gone unattended during the deluge. Many shopkeepers and some servants from the grander houses were making a valiant attempt to shovel the blend of mud and dung from the frontage of their properties.

At several points on his journey, he was forced to hold a scented silk handkerchief over his face. The stench from overflowing cesspits was just too much to bear. Garbage and human waste had combined to block the central road drains, especially in the rare enclosed sections. Elsewhere the open ditch was being cleared by men and filthy young children, paid by the unfortunate residents who were living with the threat of waste flowing into their properties.

He picked up his pace, fervently wishing he had stayed at home, whilst silently giving thanks for the still biting north wind, which would he hoped prevent any outbreak of disease. For perhaps the hundredth time, he wondered why the city did not simply bury underground pipes to carry all the water and waste away to the river.

With a sense of relief, he came to the Oxford Street coffee house and made his way inside. Unable to see the Frenchwoman, he took a small table and ordered two slices of veal pie with his coffee. He found a two day old copy of The Times discarded on another table and settled down to read. He chuckled to himself when he read an article on the pace with which Napoleon was building warships, juxtaposed with an article on how Beau Brummell was being sued by Lord Dartington, after he had caught him in a compromising situation with her Ladyship.

A shadow passed before him and he looked up into the stern face of Mademoiselle Haineau. Leaping to his feet he just remembered in time to affect his gentle Scottish accent.

'Mademoiselle, what a pleasant surprise,' he said with genuine warmth in his voice, 'please, won't you join me?'

'Yes I will Sir,' she answered, with just the hint of a sardonic smile,' but a surprise?' As she sat, he took in her slender form and was once more surprised by the aura that surrounded this sad and somewhat bitter looking woman. Her face was long and thin yet possessed of a striking femininity, her skin remarkably smooth and stretched over high cheekbones above which were set deep brown eyes that held his attention tightly. He could only use his imagination to penetrate beneath the heavy skirts and thick overcoat, save that she was clearly of slight build.

'Oh I cannot tell a lie, I chose this house over others in the hope that you'd be here. I enjoyed out conversation last time and hoped to see you again.' He could not help wondering if she too had chosen this coffee house in the hope of meeting him again.

'You are a charming man but I wonder if your intentions are not just dishonourable and misplaced,' she answered with the merest hint of a smile, whilst signalling to attract the attention of the harassed looking waitress.

For nearly half an hour they talked pleasantly of the weather and the dreadful havoc it had unleashed upon the city. Archie was forced to talk on the subject of fisheries and he hoped fervently that the Frenchwoman was not about to reveal that this had been the family business. As she began to relax, he found himself warming to this stern but not humourless woman. He concluded that before the trials of surviving the revolution wore her down, she must have been an elegant and vivacious young woman.

'Has your house survived the deluge?' he asked, seeking an opening to bring the conversation around to where he wanted it to go.

'Sadly no, the water invaded my basement and caused the drains in the road to overflow into the scullery. The smell has been unbearable for days. It all could have been worse though, the family just two houses down the road succumbed to the night gas. All the servants and two of the children died in their sleep!'

'Oh my Lord how awful,' he replied, wondering how this kept happening to people. Surely he reasoned, it was obvious that sealing the house against the air outside, meant that any foul air inside was at liberty to poison those residents susceptible to whatever it was that proved so lethal.

'I have no servants and though my lodgers have helped we are still struggling to clean up. When Mr. er...Jones returns today then we'll have another pair of hands to help. Four strong men should be able to finish the job quick enough.'

'What do your lodgers do for work?' he asked in what he hoped would pass as a casual query. To reinforce the image he looked toward the waitress and signalled that he required two more cups of coffee.

'I don't really know, they come and go quite a lot. I think they work on the new buildings just across the road from here. The man they work for brings them to my house, so it saves me the trouble of finding lodgers,' she replied, a slightly faraway look crossing her face.

'That's good, at least that way you won't get too many scoundrels living under your roof,' Archie said with a gentle laugh, looking closely at her face as he added, 'and 'you were lucky to find this friend to help you get by in London.'

'He's not a friend,' she hissed, intense anger flaring in her eyes for just a moment before she recovered, 'just a business contact, but yes I'm grateful as his business allows me to live reasonably well.'

'If you need help clearing up, I have several drivers who could spare a few hours I'm sure,' he offered casually. He studied her closely, slightly flushed cheeks and a forced smile on her thin yet womanly lips as she sought to cover her mistake.

'No, no, please don't worry, we are well on the way and with so many strong hands around the house we'll be alright,' she assured him, just a little too quickly. She looked hard at Archie but saw only a slight distraction in his eyes and convinced herself that she had persuaded him not to become involved. The thought that this man might bring his workers to her boarding house terrified her but now she concluded that he was just being pleasant.

'Do you have many friends from France living in London,' Archie asked lightly, hoping she could not hear the drumming of his heart. 'I know it took me many months to find companionship when I arrived from Scotland.'

'I do see a few people from the old country but it just makes me sad, all these people sitting around lamenting for a time lost,' she replied, a strangely intense look on her face. 'Do you think there'll be war soon?'

'Yes I'm afraid so. Never before has there been such posturing between two such large power-blocks. Eventually something, probably just one trivial incident will push the two sides to all out war.'

'Maybe it won't come to that,' she said, looking him full in the eye. 'Maybe all those powerful men will continue playing their silly games and the ordinary people can just live in peace. There's such misery in the world, the lives of the little people everywhere manipulated by those delirious with power.'

'I couldn't agree more. You're a very perceptive woman, who deserves better fortune than you've been dealt,' Archie observed, a warm smile on his face. This woman was undoubtedly the enemy but it seemed to him that she would give anything for a peaceful life. Clearly her lodgers were active at something treacherous but if this woman knew exactly what then she was not going to let anything slip easily.

'I really must go,' she said suddenly, draining her coffee with a grimace. 'I have food to buy and then I must get back to cleaning my house.' With that she rose to leave but offered Archie her dainty, gloved hand.

'Thank you for your company, 'he said as he kissed her outstretched hand,' but good heavens I realise that I don't even know your name.'

'Chantelle, Chantelle... Richards,' she replied, a faint rosy hue staining her cheeks.

'Chantelle, a beautiful name,' Archie said holding onto her hand, 'and would you do me the honour of dining with me one day?'

'Oh... I really don't know, maybe...yes maybe,' she stuttered.

'Good, I look forward to it and hope to meet you again soon,' he said. 'I will make it my business to come to this coffee shop at this hour on Wednesdays and Fridays whenever I'm in London and hope to find you here.'

'I look forward to it Monsieur...err...Donald,' she replied, now failing hopelessly to conceal her blushes. Just a little too quickly she snatched her hand away and with an almost demure smile hurried toward the door.

Once on the street she walked quickly through the crowds, drawing deep breathes of cold air as she tried to slow her racing heart. What on earth was she thinking, even taking coffee with this handsome stranger, let alone agreeing to a further assignation. Where would this affair ever end and what on earth did this young man want of her? She knew for certain that her feelings towards all men had been coloured forever by the last few years. She knew in her heart that she would never enjoy a normal relationship with any man, especially the physical side of love where her needs were now few and unusual. More worrying was the potential reaction of her sponsor, the only man who she allowed into her life, upon whom she relied for everything in London.

Archie left the coffee shop a short while later and took a cab home. He was intrigued by Mademoiselle Haineau and was finding himself strangely and dangerously attracted to her. It was clear she was in the service of French Intelligence; however he was beginning to convince himself that she was not an entirely willing participant in the dangerous and deadly games they all played.

*

That afternoon found Archie huddled under a blanket watching the house in Cavendish Square. Chantelle Haineau was at home and alone as all her guests were out. His men were following three of them, the fourth was presumed to be well on his way towards Bristol by now.

He was finding it hard to keep awake, even the birds in the trees seemed to be snoozing in the cold winter sun.

Idly he watched a tall man carrying a large wicker bag working his way along the row of houses. With his battered top hat the man stood nearly seven feet tall, swathed in several dirty overcoats. Whatever he was selling was clearly of little interest, as not once had he made any head way against a series of implacable servants. Eventually he reached the house of Mademoiselle Haineau and to Archie's astonishment was given admittance.

*

At about the same time as the stranger's arrival in Cavendish Square, Charles Lyell was engaged in conversation with Alfred Pickles in his small cluttered shop.

'Well mark me word guv, this is a right tidy safe and no mistake,' Pickles exclaimed, rubbing the stubble on his chin thoughtfully.

'I know that, I bought it, the point is can you open it for me?'

'Problem is guv, I ain't any idea who you are and 'ow do I know this is yours?' Pickles responded, with just a hint of menace in his voice. He contemptuously looked Lyell up and down and saw nothing but a well bred gent and a potential source of profit.

'Of course it's mine you rude idiot,' Lyell exclaimed, attempting to look affronted.

'Says you,' Pickles growled but as he spoke he bent down and ran his hands over the door of the heavy iron safe that Lyell and his two friends had deposited in the shop. With his friends having left him alone with Pickles,

Lyell was beginning to find the man rather menacing.

'Five pounds should see the job done guv.'

'Five pounds!' Lyell exploded. 'Are you insane?'

'Up to you guv,' Pickles said with finality. 'Safes are not really my line, an' as I say, who's to say it ain't nicked. What's in it that's so important then?'

'To be honest I can't remember, it may well be empty,' Lyell answered vaguely. 'Daylight robbery,' he grumbled whilst peeling some notes off a small roll and paying the man.

Pickles insisted Lyell turn his back while he worked a series of small tools into the lock, eventually freeing a small piece of broken key and then turning the handle until the door swung open. Seeing Lyell's back still turned, he helped himself to a handful of guinea notes he found within the safe before pronouncing it open.

'Well done,' Lyell allowed as he pocketed several small envelopes that were left resting in the bottom of the safe. 'I'll get my friends and we'll be on our way. That's a useful skill you have there my friend.'

'My pleasure guv,' Pickles replied with a jaunty smile,' I got lots o' skills gentlemen find useful, ye just gotta ask if yer ever need anythin' guv.'

*

Back in Cavendish Square, Chantelle Haineau was taking tea with the street-seller in the parlour of her private apartments. Jean Henri Thicbault was most certainly no street-seller but he was always nervous about coming close to one of his agents. He was putting himself at great risk and he knew it was foolish but sometimes life was not so simple.

For some while they discussed the state of the house

and he enquired over the behaviour of her guests. She assured him that they were perfect gentlemen and in fact spent little time at home.

'It's such a relief that the rain has stopped,' she said, glancing through the window to check that the sun was still shining faintly.

'Simply dreadful, simply dreadful,' Thiebault agreed. 'The Embassy basement has been flooded too and will take several days to dry out completely. I hear that night-gas has extracted a terrible price across the city once more.'

'Oh I know, it's heart breaking, so many children, just dead in their sleep.'

'We must learn its terrible secret and prevent such wasteful deaths from happening every winter.'

'Never mind, spring will soon be here,' she said absently, finishing the last mouthful of fruitcake before placing her tea on the side table and slowly walking over to the brown leather sofa where Thiebault sat.

'Enough small talk it grows late and I know what you want,' she said in as offhand a manner as she could muster her voice breathless and somewhat faint. A change had visibly come over her, as slightly flushed and panting gently she walked slowly around the somewhat bemused looking man.

'Au contraire Madam, it is I that knows what you need!'

'I do not need anything from you and it is you that has weakness in your heart.'

As so many times before, this was how their private games began. Thiebault grasped her thin wrist and slowly stood. In a swift, practiced movement, he threw her face down on the chaise lounge. She struggled valiantly as he pinned her down and with his free hand pulled up her luxurious skirts, exposing long, slender yet exquisite shapely thighs. Unceremoniously he pulled her luxurious silk knickers down to her ankles, exposing her small pert bottom. Struggling at first, he eventually managed to disentangle his belt and began to administer a sound thrashing to the screeching woman.

Again and again his belt landed across her bottom as she screamed and writhed against the sofa. In truth she was in ecstasy, driven nearly insane with heart pounding pleasure by the humiliating, painful experience. On and on the beating went, the blows not dangerously hard, just having sufficient power to have the desired effect. She ground herself against the sofa's rough material as the rhythmic fall of the leather belt matched her own gyrations, her skin now criss-crossed with livid red wheals.

The taught muscles of her bottom only served to enhance the pain of the beating as her skin began to turn a deeper shade of red until Thiebault suddenly tired, dropped the belt and slid his hand slowly up between her silky smooth thighs, caressing the warm skin with surprising gentleness.

Everything slowed down in the small, comfortable room. His fingers began to expertly manipulate her moist sex, stimulating her toward the point of no return. As she wriggled and writhed, kicking her knickers free, she tried to spread her legs ever wider, her gasps falling into a strange rhythm with the loud ticking of the mantle clock.

Thiebault slowly slid three fingers into her and stroked her clitoris with his thumb as she began to parody the act of intercourse, thrusting herself onto his hand. Faster and faster she worked her body, the muscles in her thighs visibly flexing beneath pale skin, now covered in a light sheen of perspiration. Coming up onto all fours like an animal, she began to lose control and all rhythm to her desperate thrusts before she finally climaxed with a piercing cry, collapsing in a sobbing, gasping heap, lewdly exposed to Thiebault's gaze.

'Until next time Mademoiselle,' Thiebault mumbled coldly as he replaced his belt and walked to the door with a brief backwards glance at the woman, lying, legs splayed, half naked, trying desperately to catch her breath. Making his way out of the house he knew once again that there had not been the slightest twitch in his ruined groin and once more he cursed the damned Arab responsible for his living nightmare.

Left alone, Chantelle Haineau curled herself into a tight ball, sobbing with heartache but still immensely satisfied. She wondered if she would ever be able to enjoy a normal relationship with any man, as with a sudden horror the image of a friendly and handsome young Scottish fish merchant appeared before her mind's eye. Bursting into tears once more she held herself tighter and cried her heart out.

Her mind drifted back to when she had first travelled to London in genuine fear for her life. The sanctuary the city offered was brief and illusory. With the death of her lover she had found herself starving on the streets and with little hope left, she began working as a prostitute in a high class brothel in Marylebone.

The British upper classes seemed to have an obsession with flagellation, brought about she understood as a result of beatings by nannies and school masters. When Jean Henri had first visited her, she had realised straight away that he was French, despite his impeccable manners and flawless English. He was possessed of a varied and imaginative sexual cruelty, yet was incapable of sexual arousal. Over many months the sad yet handsome man befriended her and eventually offered her a way out of her life of degradation.

However the damage was done, her soul had been ripped apart by her lifestyle. She had come to crave the physical pain and emotional detachment of her profession and had lost the ability to love in any conventional way. As she rose on still shaky legs, she lamented on a life ruined. She had lost her past life to violent revolution and now found pleasure from pain and degradation not love and affection.

*

Archie was intrigued by the stranger that had been a guest of Chantelle Haineau for nearly an hour. He was on his feet and from the house in seconds after the man left. As the stranger walked along the north side of the square, well muffled against the cold wind, he suddenly spun on his heel and walked directly toward Archie. Furious, Archie had no option but to avert his face and try to merge with a group of elegantly dressed men, who provided fortuitous cover for him.

The two men passed without a glance but just yards apart. Further down the road, Archie spied the reason for the stranger's sudden change of direction. Clearly he did not want to be seen by one of Mademoiselle's house-guests, the same man who had recently boarded the coach to Bristol. Archie continued to walk past the boarding house and then onto Oxford Street, careful to avoid any observation from the house. Obviously the French agent had not travelled as far as Bristol on the coach, so where on earth had he been Archie wondered.

Taking a circular route, he made his way back to the Square and regained his seat, watching the Frenchwoman's lodging house. After an hour had passed he saw the larger Frenchman return to the square and was soon joined at the window by two of his men.

'Afternoon Archie,' the younger of the men greeted,' busy day again, they never sit still for five minutes.'

'What's man-mountain been up to today?' Archie enquired.

'He's just been to a shipping agent in Shoreditch. Maybe we could take a chance and ask them what this guy's business was?'

'Possibly,' Archie replied cautiously, 'and the little guy is back at the house too.'

'Really, well he can't have gone any further than Ascot then.'

'Is Ascot the only place they would let him off?' Archie asked.

'So I was told, though I suppose he could have paid the driver to let him off anywhere. Maybe he was just going to the races?' the young man volunteered.

'The races are the day after tomorrow or so I read in the Times,' Archie replied, peering out of the window once more. Two lights burned within the house, one on the ground floor and one in the top right hand window, just below the eaves. He wondered absently if that light shone from Chantelle's room, picturing her there he tried to imagine what thoughts occupied her mind in the dark hours.

'Same time tomorrow chaps, in fact sorry but let's make the start a little earlier,' Archie decided,' everyone here by eight tomorrow morning please.'

*

The next morning was bitterly cold, a white frost glistening in the lukewarm midwinter sunshine. Archie had been collected by Tom very shortly after seven o'clock and they had made good time across what had recently been coined as London's West End. Tom parked on the southern corner of Cavendish Square and Archie made his way quickly to the house being rented by the Aliens Office.

Once inside, he was joined by his men, who arrived in steady procession. By a little after eight o'clock, as planned, the men were ready for another days work. Archie took the window seat first and had only a short time to wait before the front door swung open and first the large man and then his smaller companion exited the Frenchwoman's house.

Along with two companions he sprinted for the front door. There they composed themselves in the hallway before leaving in quick succession, Archie moving immediately towards Tom and his carriage. Glancing across the square he was afforded a brief glimpse of the Frenchmen through the bare foliage of the small resident's park area. He could see that both men were carrying sizable bags slung across their backs. For once things went with perfect timing and just as Archie was approaching Tom, the larger of the two men hailed a passing cab and with some difficulty clambered aboard with his companion. Lurching precariously on its rudimentary

279

suspension, the cab executed a u-turn and headed west towards Hyde Park, small puffs of white vapour coming from the snout of the hardworking horse.

Archie was joined by Kelvin McNeil just as Tom forced his way into the flow of vehicles. McNeil was an ex-soldier from the Scottish borders and one of Archie's most trusted men. They sat in silence as Tom jockeyed for position on the busy roads whilst trying to keep the other cab in sight. The fact that the Frenchmen's cab was almost identical to all the hundreds of others on London's roads only compounded the problem.

The traffic on Bond Street was moving at little more than walking pace and Tom skillfully maneuvered them directly behind the Frenchmen. Approaching the junction with Piccadilly all their plans almost fell foul of an accident involving a brewery dray and a hay rick. Broken barrels and sodden hay caused the traffic to come to a frustrating crawl as drivers sought a way around the chaos. As Tom cleared a way through, Archie was rewarded with the amusing sight of the dray's driver felling with a single blow, a young man attempting to make off with a barrel of ale.

Eventually the traffic thinned sufficiently to allow the horses to move forward at a progressive walk and away to their right Archie could finally see the frost rimed trees of Hyde Park. Rounding Hyde Park corner itself, the cab conveying the two mysterious Frenchmen continued westbound into Knightsbridge. With the road opening out slightly, substantial residences now lined both sides and the cabs were able to pick up more speed over the well maintained, cobbled surface. Kelvin shouted a warning just as the first cab turned off the road and passed through an ornate ironwork arch, disappearing out of sight.

Tom brought the cab to a shuddering halt a hundred yards further down the road, the horse snorting loudly to voice its annoyance. Archie and Kelvin leapt from the cab and walked as quickly as they dared back towards the archway through which the Frenchmen had disappeared.

'Is this where they caught the mail coach last time?' Archie asked breathlessly as they pushed through the jostling crowds clogging the icy footpath.

'Yes it's a large coaching inn. What can we do, should we try and get aboard?'

'That would be a little awkward with no luggage and we'd have to work on the assumption they were travelling all the way to Bristol,' Archie remarked as they strode past the entrance.

'Well perhaps...,' Kelvin began to say before he was interrupted by the blast of a post horn, amplified by the confinement of the tall buildings. Neither could prevent themselves turning to stare as the magnificent mail coach emerged from the inn's yard and was immediately allowed out into the traffic flowing past. Immaculately turned out with black and maroon bodywork, the coach rapidly picked up speed, the sun flashing off the whirling scarlet-red wheels. The Post Office guard was equally well turned out in his uniform of red and gold, the polished brass of the post horn glistening under the winter sun. The power of four large horses soon saw the coach disappearing into the distance, as regular traffic struggled to make way for the mail.

'Quickly, get yourself inside and make sure they've gone with the coach,' Archie ordered, frustration straining his voice. Furious, he stomped his way back to the waiting cab.

'What do y' think them Frenchies are about now?' Tom asked as Archie slumped down on the carriage's uncomfortable seat.

'I haven't the faintest idea Tom and maybe we'll never know,' Archie complained, with one eye on the returning McNeil.

'They're both on the coach,' he announced breathlessly.

'Okay Tom, back to the office if you please,' Archie said. 'I need to ask Sir John about where we go from here.'

'Is it time to pull in that French woman and the rest of her house guests?' Kelvin asked.

'Maybe it is but we still have no idea what, if anything they're all planning,' Archie replied thoughtfully. He knew Kelvin was right, they should pull them all in and that would be sufficient to disrupt whatever they were plotting. At the back of his mind though was a burning desire to turn Chantelle Haineau into a double agent. After a moment's reflection he was less than convinced that his judgment was not being coloured by a desire to get to know the enigmatic Frenchwoman more intimately.

Frustrated, he slumped lower in his seat and glared at the passing street-life as the cab swayed and thumped its way over London's rutted streets. By the time they reached Manchester Square he was enveloped by a deep depression. A lot of work had been put in over the preceding days and he had taken a great personal risk by befriending the woman and so far they had nothing tangible to show for their efforts.

Leaping from the cab, he rushed inside, grateful for the warm fug produced by several roaring fires in the busy office now taking up most of the downstairs floor. He pointedly ignored all the staff he encountered until he was stood before the desk of Sir John's private secretary Joseph Clegg. The pale young man looked up at him with cool grey eyes and slowly stood, his ill fitting suit barely clinging to his skinny, wasted frame.

'How are you Joseph?' Archie enquired with heartfelt concern in his voice. 'You look desperately tired.'

'I've been feeling poorly recently,' the younger man wheezed. 'My chest hurts in this bitter weather but it'll soon be spring. I assume you want to see Sir John?'

'Yes please and I don't suppose he's feeling any better either?'

'No, he shouldn't be here at all,' Joseph opined sympathetically, whilst slowly pushing back his heavy chair. He knocked swiftly on Sir John's door before slipping inside and closing the heavy oak door behind him.

Archie could not suppress a chuckle at this little ritual. Clegg jealously guarded Sir John's private inner sanctum as though it were his own. Presently he reappeared at the door and guided Archie inside with an absent minded wave of his arm.

'Good afternoon young man,' Sir John greeted, waving Archie toward a chair by the blazing fire. After a wracking and painful coughing fit, he continued, 'so tell me what is happening in Cavendish Square?'

'Two of Mademoiselle's guests have left London on the Bristol mail coach. They both have substantial bags, so presumably they're planning to be away a little longer this time.'

'What did your man Lyell discover about this chap Pickles?' Sir John asked before coughing violently once more, then wiping his lips with a small silk handkerchief.

'Oh Mr. Pickles is certainly a man who will do anything for a farthing,' Archie answered casually, watching Sir John check the white material for the dreaded signs of blood. There was none that Archie could see but the ever-present threat of consumption stalked the people of London during hard winters such as this.

'We'll have to keep an eye that one for sure,' Sir John said, before a protracted coughing fit wracked his body.

'Sir, you should be at home tucked up in bed or you'll develop pneumonia, an acute fever at the very least.'

'Maybe you're right but if young Master Clegg can drag himself into work then so can I,' Sir John replied in a tone clearly designed to bring this conversation to an end.

'Perhaps we can bury you side by side then,' Archie ploughed on regardless.

Sir John managed a throaty laugh before a coughing fit shook his body once more. Archie rose and opened the small cupboard that he knew contained Sir John's secret supply of medicinal drink. Pouring a small brandy into an inappropriate cut glass tumbler, he politely refused Sir John's gesture that he should pour one for himself.

'So, all we know is that these men are keeping themselves busy but not obviously doing anything seditious,' Archie continued.

'We'll keep an eye on them but not devote quite so much time to them,' Sir John concluded.

Archie rose and headed for the door. Reaching for the handle, he turned and asked,' Sir, just out of interest, where's the King?'

'He's at Windsor Castle, overseeing the redecoration works would you credit? It looks as though he's decided to make a home for himself and the Queen in at least one part of the dreary old place.'

'Well he should be safe there at least, so I will bid you good-day.'

'Good-day to you young man and yes I'm sure the King will be fine, though he'll probably lose his shirt at the races tomorrow!'

'The races? Which races Sir?' Archie asked slowly.

'Ascot, the King is attending the program of racing at Ascot tomorrow.'

'Oh my Lord, Ascot is the first scheduled stop of the Bristol mail coach!'

'Good God man, are you certain,' Sir John shouted, leaping to his feet, spilling finest brandy onto his shirt.

'Indeed I am and when the smaller of the Frenchmen caught the same coach a few days ago, he was back in Cavendish Square the next day so he can have gone no further than Ascot.'

'Damnation, what on earth can we do to help? The guard on his Majesty has been strengthened but we must warn them somehow. If we send a messenger to Windsor it's unlikely they'll get there before the King leaves for Ascot early tomorrow morning.'

'We must try Sir,' Archie stated emphatically. 'We can send an escorted messenger to Windsor immediately. They must ride through the night. Perhaps a troop of cavalry could make the journey in time?'

'Is there nothing more that we can do?'

'Let me take a couple of our men and ride for Ascot,' Archie pleaded. 'We'll need to find fresh horses somewhere but if we ride through the night we should be there by early morning.'

'The barracks at Hounslow should be able to help you,' Sir John exclaimed, mounting excitement straining his hoarse voice. 'I'll write you an order to give the commanding officer and instruct him to provide you with an escort for the remainder of your journey.'

'I'll take McNeil and Tom as they're both downstairs as we speak. If you'll excuse me, I'll have Tom arrange the horses. We need to begin our journey as quickly as possible, whilst there are still a few hours of daylight left.'

Without delay Archie ran down the stairs to the building's basement and quickly updated his two friends. Neither man questioned him on his plan but immediately began to prepare for their desperate journey.

*

The late afternoon light was fading fast as the pale yellow orb of the winter sun began settling toward the horizon. Already the city's buildings were creating patches of frigid shadow across the still busy streets. Archie and his two companions trotted steadily through the heavy traffic. They had made good time across Hyde Park by ignoring the established roadways and forging a line straight across the grassland.

With the sun hovering just above the horizon, shining blindingly into their eyes, they made good time along the ruler-straight lane that took them across the village green of Shepherds Bush and on towards the riverside town of Brentford. With night beginning to fall, the sky cleared and air became desperately cold. As the nearly full moon began to rise, Archie crossed his fingers and hoped for a clear, bright night through to dawn's first light.

The three men did their utmost to preserve the wind of their exhausted horses, only breaking into a trot when the road was straight and level or better still descending. They were crossing open countryside on the fringes of Hounslow Heath, when the moon was suddenly obscured by a silver whisp of cloud. Instinctively the men slowed to a walk, even their now acutely sensitive night vision, affording little penetration of the gloom.

Archie glanced backwards, straining to see into the darkness beyond his companions. For some minutes now, an uneasy sensation had begun to settle over him. He could not shake the feeling they were being watched. Suddenly away to the left, through a small copse of birch trees, he caught a fleeting glimpse of movement. The shadows under the trees changed shape, separated then merged once more. He blinked furiously and tried to focus but all he could see under the starlight were the still branches of the leafless trees. Breathing regularly to steady his racing heart, he grinned to himself and looked up to see the moon slip from behind the cloud, flooding the scrubby heath-land once more with its stark white light.

Picking up into a steady trot, they breasted a slight rise and passed quickly into the tree-lined sunken road that would lead them directly to the cavalry barracks on the heath's northern border. As the light faded once more, he saw again a disturbance in the shadows ahead, as bizarre shapes moved with a strange, ethereal quality. In the dappled moonlight he fancied that the spectres had assumed the shape of horsemen riding towards them.

He was snapped back to a dreadful reality by the ear splitting crash of a pistol shot and the accompanying blinding flash. The three attackers were upon the agents in an instant, presumably bent on robbery and if required, murder. What the highwaymen had not reckoned with was the response of their intended victims, which was shockingly swift and devastatingly violent.

Tom reined his horse to a stop and as the leading highwayman charged up to him through the gloom, he drew a prepared pistol from its saddle holster and fired at point blank range into his assailant's face. The man pitched backwards in the saddle but the horse's momentum caused it to slam into Tom's mount, unseating the hapless robber and sending him crashing to the hard ground.

Kelvin McNeil kicked his horse on and turned into one of the attackers. With no room to maneuver in the narrow lane, the two horses collided almost head on. McNeil lashed out, catching his attacker in the face with his forearm. The blow elicited a high pitched cry but McNeil silenced it with a second vicious punch, so squarely did it land that he felt bone break in the soft face, as the rider toppled from atop the large horse, only to be trampled by both animals. Another, clearly feminine scream was cut sickeningly short with a stomach churning crunch.

The final attacker tried to rein in his steed as he realised that they had selected the wrong victims this night. An expert at riding with one or no hands on the reins, Archie met his attacker head on. In one fluid motion he dropped the reins, slid his saber, carried for just such an eventuality, from its scabbard and rammed it into his attacker's torso. With a gruesome squelch the blade, impelled by the motion of two horses, passed clean through the man's abdomen before being wrenched from Archie's grip. Slumped over his horse's blood soaked neck, the dying man was carried away into the dark night.

The three agents urged their tired horses into a reluctant

canter and continued down the dark lane. Adrenaline coursing through his veins, Kelvin was unable to suppress a whoop of delight. It was some time before the men, emerging once more onto open heath-land, were able to haul their panting horses to a stop and take stock of their situation.

'My God, what next,' Archie gasped, 'is this ever going to be easy? I thought the Government was claiming such robberies were on the decline?'

'Bloody 'ighwaymen,' Tom spat, preparing his pistol once more,' 'anging is just a waste o' good rope.'

'Not highwaymen,' Kelvin ventured quietly, 'one of them was a woman!'

'Well let's get on and hope they've no friends in these parts,' Archie said, whilst scanning the moonlit moor around them. 'By my reckoning we can be no more than a mile from the garrison.'

With nothing left to say, the men persuaded their horses to walk steadily but not too slowly along the frustratingly winding track, twisting out ahead of them in the moonlight. Archie took the lead and despite their recent brush with death, he felt truly, wondrously alive. Under the harsh light of the moon, the heath was a mystical almost magical place of deep, threatening shadow and silver lagoons of low heather. A barn owl flew down the track towards them, swerving effortlessly at the last instant and disappearing into the night, just another hunter out on the moor.

Walking alongside their exhausted horses, an hour passed before they reached the imposing buildings forming the cavalry barracks of Hounslow Heath. Remounted, they cautiously approached what they took to be the guardhouse. Beside the gate stood a small wooden shack but no light shone forth and it appeared deserted. Bringing his horse to a halt, Archie caught the faint scent of tobacco smoke drifting from within the guardroom.

'Hello, you men, stand-to this instant,' he shouted in his best parade ground bellow. Grumbles and oaths came from the darkness, accompanied by a brief flash of light then the glow of a lantern, as three soldiers staggered out of the tiny hut.

'What the 'ell?' a tall, painfully thin man demanded.' Put your 'ands up the lot o' yer!'

'You rogues, stand to attention this instant!' Archie growled. 'My name is Captain Dexter, 1st Life Guards and you three will be flogged by dawn's grey light if you don't come to attention right now!'

Tom and Kelvin could barely suppress a chuckle as the sentries, still fumbling with uniform buttons and weapons, formed a line and came to a perfect attention. Both men knew from hard experience, that if an officer adopted just the right tone then a British soldier would march through the very gates of hell for him.

'We are on a mission for King George himself and you reprobates will take us to the garrison Adjutant at once,' Archie continued, whilst already moving towards the locked and barred gate. The Lance-Corporal of the guard ran on ahead and began beating an urgent tattoo on the solid oak doors.

'Sullivan…Sullivan…open the beggaring door you idiot,' he hollered. 'There's officers 'ere and they 'as business with Captain Frith.'

With much banging and crashing and not a little cursing, the doors were unbarred and opened on well-oiled hinges. Archie led his party inside and stiffly dismounted.

'You lot help my men to tend to the horses,' he demanded, 'and you Corporal, take me to the Captain straight away.'

'Sir, of course, so if yer would follow me Sir,' the Corporal said quickly, now very eager to please, though not relishing the prospect of waking the bluff Irish Captain from his slumbers.

The Corporal led Archie across a small courtyard and showed him inside. Using the lantern to find their way, they passed down a seemingly endless series of corridors, their footfall echoing off the cold, stone walls. Eventually they left the building once more and skirted their way around the edge of a large parade ground. Away to their left, Archie could smell and hear the sleeping horses in a vast stable block. Approaching a second dark building they were briefly challenged by another sentry and then admitted without further enquiry.

A sleepy eyed Staff-Corporal came staggering down a roughly carpeted corridor, struggling to fasten the top button of his tunic.

'What the 'ell is going on and who the 'ell is this?' he demanded of the Corporal.

'Captain Dexter to see Captain Frith, as soon as you like Staff, if you please,' Archie instructed the bewildered man, his tone broking no dissent.

'Er yes Sir,' the NCO stuttered,' though the Captain don't like his sleep disturbed Sir.' He cast a disapproving look over Archie's dishevelled, civilian appearance but refrained from comment.

'Me neither Staff I assure you but this is most important, so lead the way there's a good man.'

He followed the NCO along a maze of corridors and then up a flight of stairs. Pulling himself up to his full height, the shaven headed soldier knocked gently on a door. After a couple of minutes there had been no response so Archie hammered on the door just as a bleary eyed man pulled it inwards and stepped outside.

'Bonaparte had better be in the streets of Dover, Staff,' he growled and then noticing the muddy civilian for the first time, he came instantly awake.

'What in the name of God's going on here?'

'Captain Archibald Dexter, late of the 1st Life Guards and most damnably sorry to have disturbed you at this ungodly hour but I ride on a mission to protect the King,' he offered in the kind of pompous tone that he hoped would impress the burly Cavalry officer. Standing in his undergarments, long johns and fleece top, the Irishman still cut an imposing figure, almost as tall as Archie and twice as broad.

'Would you be now? You'd better come in and explain yourself. Perkins run along and arrange for some coffee would you. Come in…come in,' he urged, leading Archie into his cramped quarters.

'This note will I hope assure you of my authority,' Archie explained as Captain Frith poured them both a generous glass of whiskey.

Frith read the note provided by Sir John, not failing to notice the official seals of both the Home Secretary and Foreign Secretary, which the head of the Aliens Office was able to employ whenever he needed his word to be accepted as some kind of higher authority, answerable to virtually no man.

'Would these be the same fiends who tried to blow his

Majesty into the next world on Christmas Day?' Frith asked, handing back the note.

'They were certainly working as part of the same group and they also tried to shoot his Majesty at the winter fair in Hyde Park.'

'Good God! What do you need?' the Captain asked, refilling Archie's glass. 'I can give you a troop, maybe two if you give me thirty minutes to rouse them.'

'His Majesty is already well protected but the presence of your men will perhaps be an added deterrent. Other than that, I need fresh horses for both my men and I. We can recognise the assassins, so we must get there at all cost.'

'Have a seat old man, you look done in,' Frith urged, gesturing toward a battered armchair. With that he hurriedly dressed then bustled from the room, shouting orders into the dark and empty corridors. With admirable speed the garrison came to life and within half an hour a young Cornet was presenting himself to Archie.

'Cornet Hurst, Sir,' the young man announced as he stood to attention in the doorway. 'My platoon stands ready below and we have fresh steeds for you gentlemen. Captain Frith has put me at your command Sir'

'Thank you Cornet,' Archie said, coming reluctantly to his feet. The warmth of the whiskey had almost sent him into a dcep sleep. He looked young Hurst over and saw a handsome, soft faced young man probably still in his teens, slender of build, yet standing nearly six feet tall.

By the time they reached the stable-yard, the rest of the troop were already mounted and ready to go. Their chargers were snorting clouds of white breath into the cold night air, their heads thrashing against their bits, obviously raring to go off into whatever action awaited them.

Reassured by the young officer that he knew the way to Ascot, even in the dark, Archie was happy to bring up the rear with his two companions. The quiet of the night was shattered by the clatter of hooves as they made their way at a brisk walk across the yard then out of the garrison's rear gate. After passing through a small hamlet made up of perhaps a dozen hovels, they struck out across the heath under the comforting white glare of the moonlight.

Dawn had broken by the time they reached the outskirts of the village of Ascot. Struck by a sudden inspiration, Archie sought out the coaching inn and found it nestled alongside a millpond, adjacent to the main road from London. Taking two troopers and Cornet Hurst with them, the three agents entered the inn and quickly roused the proprietor. He was able to assure them that the two Frenchmen were not staying at the inn but after conferring with a timid young scullery maid, announced that the two men had most certainly disembarked from the mail coach yesterday.

'Bloody 'ell, yer was right,' Tom said quietly. 'Now what the 'ell do we do?'

'Can we intercept his Majesty before he gets to the racecourse Sir?' Hurst volunteered.

'We could certainly try but by all accounts his Majesty is a stubborn man and he may not take heed of our warning. No, I think we must ride to the races and try to protect his Majesty from whatever danger he faces. You can present yourself to the Captain of the Royal Guard and try to impress upon him the danger these French agents pose. Meanwhile, we three will do our best to find the murderous swine before it's too late.'

With the races not scheduled to commence until eleven that morning, Archie had the innkeeper feed the soldiers and his own party. The surly man's initial reluctance evaporated with the appearance of several guineas and presently Archie was sat with Hurst alongside Tom and McNeil tucking into ham and eggs. The troopers were not forgotten and were soon tucking into their own breakfasts out in the stable yard.

Fed and watered, the men and horses set out on the road a little after nine o'clock. They made good time over a well-made road that became progressively busier as they approached the racecourse. A sizeable crowd, many riding in a bewildering array of carriages and carts, were steadily making their way along the road under a clear blue sky. The sun was low on the horizon, only just peeking over the bare treetops and offered little warmth but everyone seemed in good cheer.

Many more men and a few women were walking along the muddy verge, determined to wager what paltry amount of money they had earned through hard toil, in the usually vain hope of bettering themselves. As Archie weaved his way through farm labourers and shop keepers, he marvelled once more at the potency of gambling's addiction.

Amongst the crowds of would be spectators were carts carrying all manner of fairground entertainers and vendors of various ailment cures and curios. From the rear of one particularly large covered cart, a group of girls catcalled and flashed their breasts at the soldiers, promising erotic delights for a florin.

Eventually the racecourse came into view around one final bend in the road. In truth it was little more than a gently sloping field, already dotted with tents and carts where merchants prepared their wares. Beyond a thick rope line was the race-track itself and in the distance could be seen the racehorses and their riders, already preparing for the first race.

Passing through the gateway, Archie stood in his stirrups to gain a better view. The majority of the spectators would be watching the races from the level of the muddy field but a privileged few would enjoy rudimentary seats on a tiered grandstand. To the left and slightly forward of this was a separate dais with a brightly coloured canvas awning. This he reasoned must be the Royal Box and was undoubtedly to be the scene of today's fateful drama.

The three agents left their horses in the care of a young boy and made their way to the empty viewing platform. A cursory examination was all that was required to ensure that no gunpowder packed barrels were attached to the rather flimsy, white painted structure.

Cornet Hurst returned within minutes, in the company of the Clerk of the course, a rotund little man, kitted out in a twill patterned suit, complete with mud spattered riding boots. His ruddy complexion and vein riddled nose spoke of a man used to the outdoor life and the contents of a bottle of strong liquor.

'Graham Pedrick at your disposal Sir,' he announced, whilst coming very nearly to attention. 'Your man tells me there may be trouble afoot today?'

'I sincerely hope not but there are likely to be men here today who may wish the King grave harm and we must be ready for them,' Archie replied calmly.

'His Majesty is due here in a little over an hour, should

I inform the Captain of his Guard?' Pedrick enquired.

'Yes please and I would be grateful if you would point him in my direction at the first opportunity,' Archie answered, whilst looking around anxiously at the steadily growing crowd. Despite the winter cold it was clear the races would be popular.

'Have your men tend their horses and their own needs Mr. Hurst. My men and I will begin scouring the crowds for these French renegades. Once the King arrives I will persuade his guard to allow your men to bolster their numbers.'

'Very good Sir,' Hurst replied with a smile and a jaunty salute before trotting off to rejoin his troops. Archie could not suppress a smile as he watched the young man bound away and wondered idly if the young man had even started shaving yet.

The three agents moved off in separate directions to scour the steadily building crowd, desperately seeking a familiar face amongst the thronging masses. On a sudden whim, Kelvin made his way towards the entrance, reasoning that as long as the Frenchmen had not yet arrived, then he would surely spot them there.

Archie found himself drawn to the fairground where stalls were being hastily erected, their owners hoping to relieve the crowd of their money before the bookmakers had the chance. Colourful stalls offered everything from cure-all medicines, to cloth caps to fend off the biting wind gusting across the exposed fields. Tents were being erected all around him as he weaved through the distracted crowds. Callers were already hard at work endeavouring to attract customers inside to have their fortune told or their lusts satisfied.

For nearly an hour he searched in vain for the two Frenchmen amongst the crowds. As he was heading back toward the entrance he heard a long blast on a trumpet, followed by a ripple of applause and cheering, sprinkled with a smattering of boos. Above the heads of the crowd he could just make out the arrival the King's cavalcade.

Moving as swiftly as the dense crowd allowed, he made his way toward the royal dais as the coach carrying the King came to a halt alongside. Mounted cavalry troopers and Yeomen of the Guard, newly dismounted from a convoy of carriages, hastily formed an honour guard. By the time Archie arrived, the King and his entourage were making their way onto the dais, now surrounded by the guards. Archie began to search for Cornet Hurst who he hoped would gain him an immediate audience with the Captain of the Guard. He quickly realised that there were simply too many people milling around for them to have any hope of finding the Frenchmen until they made their move.

Archie knew it was important that they plan quickly and arrange the best possible protection for the King. Caught up in the swirling mass of humanity, he was jostled and pushed as the crowd parted to allow the carriages to move away from the grandstands. It was with some relief that he spied Hurst standing in conversation with a cavalry Major. Just a short distance away, the King and his consorts were seated with servants in attendance, distributing steaming hot toddies to the royal party.

Archie felt an urgent tug at his sleeve and turned to see Tom standing at his side, clearly agitated.

'The Frenchies are 'ere Sir,' he told Archie in a hushed tone, his head swivelling as he scanned the crowds.

'Where did you see them?' Archie asked excitedly, joining Tom in studying the sea of faces around them.

'The big un came out yon brothel tent with flags on it; I reckon that's where they bin 'iding out.'

'We've got to get the King out of here now,' Archie said bluntly, already thrusting his way through the crowd. 'It would be suicide to try anything here, so they must have a more elaborate plan in mind. I have to get to Hurst and that Major right now.'

Archie shouldered people aside as he forged a path to the steps leading up to where the King was seated. Approaching the apparently impenetrable barrier of Yeomen, a sudden disturbance to his right attracted his attention. A large man had knocked two of the Yeomen over backwards against the wooden structure of the dais and in a heartbeat Archie recognised him from the streets of London.

George Mitterrand staggered as he fought to regain his balance, whilst drawing a brace of pistols from beneath his coat. Looking up at the fat, ruddy face of King George, all the hatred in his heart welled up to cast away the terror he felt at his certain death coming in these next few moments. He aimed his first pistol at the face of the man whose Navy had killed his father and two brothers at Aboukir Bay. As he fired, his view was momentarily obscured by the smoke from the shot but as it cleared he saw the young woman seated behind the King fall backwards, her clothes soaked in her own blood.

He aimed his second pistol straight at the King and fired just as a blur of colour moved across his field of vision. Cornet Hurst took the ball full on in the chest and was dead before his body fell across the horror struck

King's lap.

Archie was moving toward the hulking Frenchman as he drew his own pistol but Tom fired from where he stood, his shot thudding into the large man's shoulder, turning him right around. Now at point blank range, Archie fired into the man's chest, felling him as though pole-axed.

'There look,' Tom cried desperately, pointing towards a man climbing onto the far corner of the stand, 'it's the little un!'

A Yeoman swung his pike at the man, slicing open Claude Renoir's stomach but not before he was able to fire in the King's direction. The range was too great though and a slim, pale looking man seated to the King's left took the ball in the arm, screaming hysterically before he stood and effectively blocked a further shot. A cavalryman leapt onto the grandstand and stabbed the Frenchman in the side with his sword, pulling the long blade free, leaving blood pouring from the open wound. The cavalry Major fired his own pistol, hitting the dying Frenchman in the thigh. Claude Renoir slumped to his knees, covered in blood, a cry of pained anguish escaping his lips yet still raising a second pistol. The sword of the cavalry trooper swished through the frigid winter air and all but decapitated the man, a vivid spray of blood covering the people seated close by.

As he died, Claude Renoir saw the beautiful faces of his wife and daughter for one last time, as they had been before they drowned in the cold Atlantic waters, taken down in a ship sunk by the Royal Navy.

The Major took the King by the arm and guided him toward the stairway, being joined as he went by three of his troopers. It was clear to Archie that the quick thinking

Major realised he had to get the King to safety and that meant away from this now wildly panicking crowd. The Major led the way as the King and the troopers rushed down the stairs. The phalanx of Yeomen parted and hurriedly tried to form a protective cordon. The screaming, hysterical spectators were all rushing to escape from the sudden, horrifying violence. All except one man Archie realised, who was pushing his way forward against the tide of humanity.

Archie moved as quickly as he could but was still fifteen feet from the tall, well built man as the gun held in his hand came into view. The large pistol came up just as the King reached ground level, his guards oblivious to the new danger. Shuffling forward, dragging his lame left leg, the assassin closed on the King.

'Vive Napoleon!' Archie yelled, desperate to distract the gunman by any means. The ploy worked as the man hearing his mother tongue, turned and stared in disbelief at Archie. The stare was returned as Archie looked in horror at the ruined face of Antoine Pascal, otherwise known as Sean O'Brien.

Reacting first, Archie raised his second pistol, taking in the twisted face, scarred and with one closed eye socket, the eye blown away by a pistol shot, in a far away Spanish farmhouse. He fired, his shot slamming into Pascal's shoulder, blood and flesh spurting through the torn cloth of the man's coat. The impact spun him backwards into the screaming crowd as Archie fumbled for his ever present stiletto.

He pulled his knife free and made to throw it straight at the repulsive face staring malevolently back at him from the crowd. Cocking his arm to throw, he heard the loudest bang he had ever thought possible, followed by a blinding pain and then darkness, utter, total darkness.

*

The world was rocking and pitching in a bone-shaking, violent and unpredictable manner. Archie tried not to move because the last time it had induced a violent attack of vomiting. The floor on which he lay suddenly pitched upwards with a violent crash against his face, the pain it caused adding to the almost unbearable throbbing in the back of his head. He knew he had to sit up if only to avoid being jarred against the rough wooden floor once more.

With a supreme effort of will, he rolled onto his back and slowly sat up, almost toppled over once more by a new bout of nausea and the rocking motion of whatever instrument of torture he was imprisoned within. Reaching out with his hand in the gloom he found that there was a raised seat to one side of what he slowly realised was a speeding carriage.

Using a soft sack as a kind of ramp, he was able to lever himself onto the seat and noticed for the first time, the small barred window set into the rear door. The window offered a restricted but welcome view of the bleak winter countryside as they made great speed along a badly rutted road.

He leant back against the hard wooden side of the carriage and rested his feet upon the lumpy sack spread across the carriage's floor. With his eyes shut, he tried to fight the throbbing agony in his skull. He gently ran his fingers over the back of his head, through matted hair, stiff with dry blood and once more pain lanced into his brain.

Clearly he had been mistaken for one of the assassins, firing a gun whilst shouting in French had perhaps not been the best idea he had ever had. That said he knew that the distraction might just have saved the King's life.

The memory suddenly came back to him like a thunderbolt. Pascal! How on earth had that evil man survived that terrible wound, let alone the fall into the old mill race? More to the point Archie thought, is he still alive and what of the King?

At that moment, the old sack on the floor coughed and then began groaning pitifully. Archie could not fail to recognise the cursing that then ensued.

'Tom old man, take it easy, take it easy,' he implored.

'Me bloody 'ead,' Tom groused as he struggled to sit up. 'When I find that Yeoman bastard I'm gonna break his 'ead into a thousand bits!'

'Like me, I reckon you owe him my friend,' Archie chuckled. 'We could've been impaled on the end of a pike by now! As it is if the King's dead then we may not even get a chance to explain our position to save us from the noose.'

'No worry... King's fine. I saw 'im being bundled into 'is carriage and taken off wit Cavalry.'

'Thank God for that. Now all we've got to do is get out of this mess. Did you see who the third man was? Antoine Pascal, that swine from Spain!'

'God preserve us, no way, are yer sure Sir?' Tom asked incredulously.

'Oh yes it was him alright. His face was a mess and he could barely use one leg but yes indeed it was him.'

'Did you kill 'im for sure this time then?'

'I don't know but I certainly hit him hard.'

'Not an easy man t' kill that 'un,' Tom observed thoughtfully.

'Indeed not,' Archie replied, a sick and uneasy feeling gripping his stomach.

The carriage continued to crash and thump over the unmade road for what seemed like days to the two incarcerated men. In reality it was only a little over an hour before they came to a juddering stop. Anxious, agitated voices sounded through the thick wooden walls and more than once a dirty face peered in through the bars of the small window.

'Listen you men, my name is Captain Archibald Dexter of the Life Guards and I'm an agent of the Aliens Office in London, now open the door you bloody fools.'

'You shut it you Frenchie bastard or I'll string you up myself right now!' a filthy, unshaven man with few teeth spat through the small opening.

'Listen to me you young fool, we are as English as you are,' Archie pleaded.

'Oh err such airs and graces now,' the man sneered, 'but they all 'eard you shouting for your bastard Bonaparte, you scum.'

With that, the bolts were drawn and the door swung open. As the two men staggered out, blinking in the suddenly bright light, they were forced to run the gauntlet of kicks and punches as they were dragged into a small austere, sandstone building. Archie fought the temptation to resist as they were bundled into a small cell by what appeared to be a rag-tag bunch of militia men, loosely under the control of a Sergeant of the Yeomen Guards.

'Sergeant, you will fetch the officer of the day or I will see you broken to the ranks,' Archie yelled with some measure of desperation, as the door was slammed closed. He had the small satisfaction of seeing a flash of doubt cross the man's face just before they were plunged into darkness once more.

Huddled on the stone floor, they tried to sleep, shivering with the intense cold. No food or water was offered to the two men and the hours dragged by, broken only by fitful sleep. Archie consoled himself that it was nothing personal and he would have behaved exactly the same way towards men he believed had attempted regicide.

He was convinced only a few hours had passed by, yet it was early the next morning when the cell door was thrown open and blinking into the light, he looked up into the grinning face of Captain Frith. Standing behind him was a dreadfully dishevelled but relieved looking Kelvin McNeil.

'Good God, are you two alright?' Frith blustered, helping them to their feet. 'Sorry it's taken so long to find you, no one seemed to know where you'd been taken to.'

'Is the King safe?' Archie asked, trying to ease the stiffness from his chilled limbs.

'Perfectly, thanks to you,' Frith exclaimed clapping Archie on the back. 'The Queen's maid was not so lucky or poor Cornet Hurst, but his Majesty is well.'

'What was his first name?' Archie asked sadly. 'I didn't even learn the poor lad's name.'

'James and he turned nineteen on Christmas day,' Frith replied, looking at the ground uncomfortably.

'Oh my word, the waste of it,' Archie mumbled. 'Nevertheless a hero and we must ensure that he's decorated as such.'

'You have my word on that,' Frith assured him. 'It might just bring his mother some small comfort and what a service to his country, to die for his King.'

'Indeed but he's still dead at just nineteen,' Archie muttered to himself. 'Kelvin, what happened to the tall man at the steps?' Archie asked urgently, grabbing at the man's arm as they walked down a long, cheerless corridor.

'I don't know but he surely ain't dead, unlike t'other two. If the shot didn't kill 'em, the trampling the crowd gave 'em surely finished 'em off. The third man must 'ave got away.'

'Damn it to hell,' Archie cursed. 'We have to find him or he'll try again until he succeeds.'

'Who are these swine anyhow?' Frith asked, as they pushed past the somewhat cowed looking militiamen and stepped outside, where to Archie's surprise he found the sun shining brightly.

'Two of them were French agents who've been holed up at a safe-house in London for weeks,' Archie explained, as the four men boarded a large carriage that lurched into motion the moment they sat themselves down. As they careered out of a small courtyard and onto the muddy road outside, they were joined by a troop of cavalrymen.

'The third man, the one who seems to have escaped, is an agent by the name of Pascal, who was supposed to be dead and buried in a land far away,' Archie continued. 'We must get back to London as soon as possible and hunt him down like the dog he is. Believe me if we fail to find him then he'll try once more to take the King's life.'

'London's a vast city, where will you begin?' Frith asked.

'We'll start with the safe house in Mayfair,' Archie replied and with a faraway look added, 'Mademoiselle will have some questions to answer before she goes to the gallows.'

The small party fell into a weary silence as they made haste along the rough road to London. The journey was broken at the barracks in Putney where the men were fed and the horses changed before they continued to race the setting sun toward the smoky horizon and London's crowded streets.

Captain Frith dropped them in Manchester Square just after night had fallen. Archie offered him his profuse thanks and bid him a safe journey to the barracks at Chelsea. It was with some trepidation that he made his way into Sir John Marshall's office but he need not have worried for the man looked dreadfully ill and rather than rising, he simply waved Archie toward a chair by the roaring fire.

'Sit down and please tell me that what we've heard is true, the King is unharmed?' he asked in a deep, phlegm filled voice.

'The King's uninjured Sir but sadly a maid in the service of the Queen and a gallant young Cavalry officer were killed,' Archie explained, pouring himself a brandy and topping up Sir John's glass.

'What of the would be assassins?' Sir John enquired.

'The two men from the house in Cavendish Square are dead, shot by us and then beaten to death by the crowd. A third man escaped, Antoine Pascal, whom I thought I killed in Spain.'

'Good God, how on earth has that bastard survived?' Sir John shouted hoarsely.

'I don't know but I intend to ask Mademoiselle Haineau tomorrow then I shall escort her to the gallows personally,' Archie replied flatly, staring into the blazing flames of the fire.

'You may want to reconsider, 'Sir John said quietly. 'Within the last hour we've received further word from your agent inside the French Embassy. This man Thiebault, who you believe controls the whole French intelligence operation in London, still, has no idea who's trying to kill King George.'

'How can that be Sir?' Archie asked, now intrigued. 'What exactly did the message say?'

'Thiebault has been trying to find out who's behind these attacks and the Ambassador is petrified that there will be reprisals. He's requested a militia guard be placed outside the Embassy, to protect it from a mob that's been gathered there ever since the first attack on his Majesty.'

'Well he placed the two men inside Mademoiselle's safe house, so how can he not know what they're doing?' Archie asked doubtfully.

'According to your agent, Thiebault visited the lady today, when rumours of yesterday's incident at the races broke. By the way it's the Government's plan to keep this latest incident out of the popular press to prevent distress and disorder. The owners are co-operating so if we're lucky it will be accepted as nothing more than gossip by the populace at large.'

'Upon his return to the Embassy, Thiebault briefed the Ambassador on what he'd learned,' Sir John continued. 'Those two men were sent to London by his masters in Paris, in order to carry out Thiebault's orders in relation to corrupting an officer based at Horse Guards. However, it seems from what the lady has told him that they were free-lancing too and often left her house in order to meet someone but she has no idea who. Thiebault it seems also had no inkling what they were up to much of their time.'

'Working for Pascal no doubt about it,' Archie observed. 'Pascal has clearly been operating outside Thiebault's network, which is why we've not seen anything of him. I still think we should pull in that woman and to hell with diplomatic niceties, let's have a word with Monsieur Thiebault as well.'

'The woman yes but not Thiebault,' cautioned Sir John, through yet another coughing fit. 'That will cause a serious issue for the Government and we must tread carefully. For now, we must find Pascal and I'll ensure the King doesn't leave the palace until we do. I've an appointment with the Home Secretary this evening when I can ensure that the King is protected properly this time. After the shooting in Hyde Park I had thought the message had got through. The journey by carriage on Christmas Day was an elaborate decoy so God knows who thought a day at the races was a good idea.'

'Good heavens Sir that was mighty prescient of you. Oh my word, those poor souls who were killed in the explosion...for nothing,' he continued sadly. 'With respect Sir, you should be in bed not dining with gentlemen of the Government,' Archie added with genuine concern.

'Don't fuss, I'm on the mend, slowly but I just need to shift this congestion in my throat,' he insisted, clearing another clump of phlegm for effect.

'If you'll excuse me Sir, my men and I are exhausted and tomorrow promises to be another long day,' Archie said whilst stifling a yawn.

'Of course, get yourself home and I'll see you in the morning, 'Sir John replied as he rose. 'Jolly well done, you and your men won't be forgotten for your sterling efforts protecting the King. In the morning we'll decide what to do with the residents of Cavendish Square, because it seems to me that either Mademoiselle Haineau is part of Pascal's plans or if not, then she's unlikely to have the first idea of his whereabouts.'

'Nevertheless Sir, I think it may be time to close her particular safe house down once and for all.'

*

Archie stepped wearily from the cab that had taken him home through the dark streets of London's West End. He looked upon his front door with a mixture of warmth and relief. As he struck the polished brass knocker, he tried to work out what day of the week this was.

'Good evening Sir,' Cedric greeted him and ushered him indoors.

'Good evening to you my friend,' Archie replied, yawning theatrically as he was helped out of his coat. 'Be so good as to prepare a bath for me, I'm exhausted and I think I'll go lie down for a while. I'll tell you all about the last few days adventures later,' he continued in a monotone, moving slowly toward the stairs. Cedric noticed the matted blood on the back of Archie's head but chose to say nothing.

Two hours later, Cedric woke him and after shaving, he was soon relaxing in piping hot water, scented with salts and perfumed oil. Lying back in the steaming water, he reflected on this luxurious indulgence that was enjoyed by few of the wealthiest men in London.

Cedric knocked gently and entered with a decanter and glass. He poured Archie a generous measure and withdrew. Archie noticed two letters propped against the decanter and after drying his hands, opened the smaller of the two, as he recognised Cordelia's gently sloping handwriting. He sat bolt upright, slopping water onto the tiled floor as he began to read.

Dearest Archie,

Please do the bidding of this beastly man, I am so afraid for myself and Mother. We are frightened but unharmed as yet. I beg of you, do as he says.

All my love always, Cordelia.

He fumbled in desperation to open the second letter with his one good hand, addressed simply to 'Dexter'.

Archibald Dexter,

No more will you be a thorn in my side you English cur. Not a day goes by that I have not seen your face in my mind's eye but such was the damage to my mind, that I could not recall how I knew you.

I saw you interfering once more in Hyde Park and though I easily recalled dear Cordelia, still your face was an illusory nightmare.

Now though I have you my friend. The pain of the shot you have lodged in my shoulder brought it all back to me and now I will have my revenge.

Cordelia will die in two days time, along with her mother. I promise you she will remain well until that time but only you can prevent her death.

You have until Friday, Archibald. By midnight, either King George will be dead or Cordelia and her mother will die painfully and very slowly.

My men will be watching your every move.

AP

'Protheroe... Cedric!' Archie yelled, slipping and slithering his way naked toward the bathroom door. 'Get my clothes ready now! I have to go out.'

Cedric looked only slightly aghast at his naked master towelling himself dry on the landing, before hurrying off in search of clothes. While Archie dressed he explained the contents of the notes to his horrified friend.

'What on earth are you going to do Archie?'

'Well I'm not going to kill King George but neither am I going to let that maniac harm Cordelia,' Archie replied with what he realised was ill founded confidence. 'Get a cab and go to Whites, where I'm sure you'll find Charles Lyell,' he ordered. 'Bring him here and broke no argument from him. I'll prepare some pistols and by the time you return I'll have the semblance of a plan.'

'Should you not contact Sir John first,' Cedric suggested.

'Not just yet, first we must find out what the situation is and whether we can act quickly enough to save the situation tonight,' Archie urged. 'Now go, quickly as you can.'

He took several deep breaths as he continued to stare at the front door, long after Cedric had slammed it shut. He fought the urge to be sick and in an attempt to keep busy he rushed to his study and began to prepare a number of pistols. When that was completed he flung himself into a leather chair, closed his eyes and tried to calm down. He just could not accept that his secret life had caught up with him in such a terrible fashion. He had thought himself so careful, that he was almost immune from his two lives ever touching, let alone colliding in such a nightmare.

With his eyes closed he massaged his aching temples and Cordelia sprang into his mind's eye. She looked pale, drawn and utterly terrified. Pascal's ruined face then swam into view, laughing insanely as he moved inexorably toward Cordelia. Opening his tired eyes, miraculously the vision evaporated in an instant. Could he really just sacrifice dear sweet Cordelia? Whatever else he was going to do, he most certainly would never be able to bring himself to kill his King but he did not feel he would ever live with the shame of allowing this girl to die.

Impatiently he began to pace around his study, plans and schemes swirling through his mind, as he frantically tried to work out what Pascal was planning. For the fifth time in as many minutes he checked his watch and wondered where on earth his two companions were. It was nearly half an hour before the two men arrived, breathless and wild eyed.

'How on earth has that scoundrel Pascal come back to haunt us?' Lyell asked as he shook Archie's proffered hand.

'The Devil looks after his own, my father always says,' Archie offered. 'Now we must get on and find out what the situation is at the Hendricks home. Charles, have you ever been there?'

'Strangely enough I have, on more than one occasion when I was a youngster.'

'Good, then you'll have some idea of the house and its layout,' Archie said, whilst leading them to his study. Once there, he handed out the pistols and ammunition, while his companions took their choice of daggers and small swords that he had lain out on his desk. He sent Cedric in search of a cab while they donned heavy coats and waited anxiously by the front door.

'I'm sure we'll find her Archie, try not to worry too much,' Lyell said quietly, not even convincing himself.

'I promise you this Charles, if she's harmed in any

way, I will kill Pascal and that slippery character Thiebault too.'

'Then we shall all journey to Paris and kill the jumped up little Emperor too,' Lyell joked.

'Maybe we will at that,' Archie replied, the tone in his quiet voice chilling Lyell to the core, as he realised with a grim certainty that his friend was deadly serious. The darkening mood was broken by the timely arrival of Cedric and his announcement that he had secured a cab.

The cab picked its way through the gloomy streets of London's most fashionable district. Carriages jostled for position, passing through impenetrable darkness and occasional pools of pale yellow light, cast by the sparse street lamps. On the pavements, well to do residents walked briskly in the cold night air, heading perhaps to friends and neighbours for drinks and a convivial dinner. The three men in the cab travelled in silence, each preoccupied with their own thoughts.

Archie rapped on the cab wall when they were two hundred yards short of the Hendricks home. He tipped the driver outrageously to ensure that he waited in position for their return and the three men made their way along the edge of the road, toward the group of trees that grew by the gates of the imposing house.

Archie scanned the dark shadows of the street and studied the barely visible faces of the few pedestrians still making their way to whatever social engagement they seemed to be late for but found no hostile intent or concealed watchers. As the trio reached the gate, they continued without breaking stride but surreptitiously studied the front of the mansion.

A cold chill seeped into Archie's soul as he saw not

one single light emanating from the house. Not even the porch lights had been lit for the evening. Even had the family been away, the remaining servants would have lit the house's lights to deter intruders.

'Okay chaps, clearly something's terribly wrong here and we're going to have to get inside,' he said, picking up the pace and taking the next left side-road.

Within minutes they had reached the rear gates to the house, the smell of the stables wafting toward them on the gentle evening breeze. Unable to open the large, wrought iron gates, Archie helped first Lyell and then Cedric onto the top of the stone wall and was in turn hauled up by the two men. Catching their breath, they stared up at the rear of the house, shrouded as it was in a blanket of darkness. Somewhere below them, a restless horse whinnied in the stables and above the clatter of the sparse street traffic, a tawny owl hooted to be answered by the shriek of its mate, somewhere high in the lime trees in the grounds of the house.

As quietly as they could manage in the impenetrable gloom, they made their way to the rear of the house. By feel alone, Lyell was able to find the door to the scullery and gently he turned the polished brass knob until surprisingly, the door quietly opened. The click as Archie pulled back the percussion lever on his pistol made the others jump then without hesitation he silently moved inside.

Guided by fingertip touch alone he managed to negotiate the scullery without mishap but in the next instant he walked head first into the edge of the door.

'We need some light or we'll still be searching by dawn,' Lyell hissed and he began to blunder around the room in search of a lantern. By good fortune he found one and then some paper which he made into a taper. Working quickly in the dark, he removed the shot and most of the powder from his pistol. With the taper in just the right position he discharged the weapon. The blinding flash and ensuing flare of heat from the pan ignited the taper and he quickly had the lantern alight. Within the house nothing stirred save for the ticking of a distant clock.

With Archie and Cedric following at a safe distance, Lyell led the way up the stairs to the main entrance hall and then began a careful search of the house. Eventually they found Cordelia's rooms, empty and like the rest of the house, nothing appeared disturbed.

They descended once more to the ground level and with some trepidation approached the last un-tried door. It was clear now that Cordelia and Lady Hendricks were not in the main part of the house, so that left only the cellars. Just as Archie tried the door and realised that it was bolted top and bottom, a low desperate wail came from beyond the thick wooden barricade.

Heart racing, Archie threw the bolts and opened the door. Charles Lyell, a pistol held somewhat unsteadily before him, carefully advanced with the lantern in his free hand. At the foot of the stairs a woman cried out in fear then a man pushed forward in front of her, a broken bottle in his hand.

'Come on then you swine, get it over with you bastard,' he shouted, with a slightly unsteady voice.

'Simmons is that you?' Archie asked.' It's Archie Dexter, are you all right down there?'

'Oh thank God Sir, 'Simmons replied, coming slowly up the stairs on what appeared to be very shaky legs.

'Tell me what happened man,' Archie asked while helping the elderly man up the last of the steps.

'That man O'Brien came to call on Miss Cordelia, Sir,' Simmons began, as he was joined by half a dozen other bewildered looking domestics of the household. 'When he first arrived I felt so sorry for him, he had or so he insisted, been in a dreadful accident at sea. That story lasted only five minutes though and before we knew it we were locked in that hole at gun point. Miss Cordelia and her Ladyship were tied up and taken outside to a waiting carriage. The Lord alone knows why or where they've been taken Sir.'

'Who was driving the carriage, did you see?' Lyell asked, while the shocked servants lit more lanterns from his and a young boy began to light a fire in the scullery grate.

'It was a woman would you believe?' Simmons spat angrily. 'I noticed her when Mr. O'Brien arrived. She was a fine looking woman mind you, slender and very poised.'

'Mademoiselle Haineau!' Archie hissed under his breath.

'You know who she is?' Cedric asked.

'Indeed I do and I know where we are going to find her too,' he added. 'When we do she'll lead us to Cordelia or else she won't survive the journey to the gallows, on that you have my word.'

*

Silently and swiftly, Archie and his companions entered the empty house in Cavendish Square. Once inside the cold dank hallway, the men made their way carefully up the stairs and into a rear bedroom. With the door safely closed they lit a lantern from a taper brought from the Hendricks house and then Cedric began to light a fire.

Tom had been summoned and had journeyed with them to Cavendish Square.

'If Miss Cordelia an' 'er mother are in that 'ouse then we 'ad better get over there right now surely?' he urged.

'We don't know for sure that they are being held there Tom but we do know that Frenchwoman is going to be there. If Pascal is in the house then we must tread very carefully because he'll not hesitate to kill the Hendricks in an instant.'

'So what do you want to do Archie?' Lyell asked quietly. Archie watched the boyish faced young man in the flickering light and he appeared to be the calmest of them all.

'We have a long night ahead of us,' Archie predicted, ' so let's start establishing a watch on the French house and perhaps Cedric, you could go out and find us some food from somewhere, home if necessary.'

Archie and Charles Lyell made their way carefully into the upper front bedroom and slowly drew back the curtains by around two feet. Looking out across the square they were just able to see the Frenchwoman's house, shrouded in darkness, not a single light showing from any of its windows. A lone cab clattered around the square before pulling up outside her house. Adrenaline coursed through the veins of the watching men as two people, shadows in the dark night, stepped down from the cab. Disappointingly they walked briskly to the front door of the adjacent property.

Throughout the frigid night the men took turns to watch across the square before taking their turn huddled before the fire in the back room. As dawn's steely grey light began to permeate the gloom, a single light appeared in the room that Archie had long since decided belonged to Chantelle Haineau. It was with mixed emotions that he realised that the woman was surely going to die, if not this day then at Newgate shortly after a brief trial. Despite the fact that she was undoubtedly the enemy, he had become somewhat irrationally entranced by her.

On a whim, he came to a sudden and hurried decision. Quickly he gathered his men together in the dark room.

'We're not waiting to see how this pans out,' he said quickly, a tremor of excitement in his voice, fire burning in his eyes as the moment for action dawned.

'Tom, we need an excuse for you to knock on Mademoiselle's front door. We'll enter from the rear of the house and when she returns we'll take her.'

'There's a bakers just round t' corner,' Tom offered, 'I can get a basket o' bread and just go on the knocker if yer like. Are you sure yer don't wanna wait and see if Pascal's in there?'

'There's only one light showing,' Archie pointed out, casting a glance toward the house once more. As one, the men turned and looked through the branches of the bare trees in the square's tiny park and saw there was but one small light showing. The grey light of a winter's morning diffused through the grimy window and the men were able to study the lines of worry etched into Archie's face.

'Okay Sir, let's just do it,' Tom said quickly, catching the first signs of dangerous indecision crossing Archie's face. Exhausted and with dark rings under his eyes, Tom realised that Archie was all but done in by the whirlwind events of the last week. It really was now or never he decided or the moment would be missed.

'Okay chaps this is what we'll do,' Archie announced,

clapping his hands together, making every man present jump ever so slightly. 'There's a rear mews from which we can gain entry to the building. Tom, go and get your bread and meet us on the far corner of the square but keep out of sight of the house windows. Here's enough money for all that you need. Should Pascal happen into the square we will take him but we must keep him alive, for a while!'

'Everyone, prepare all your pistols before we leave,' Lyell reminded them, a little superfluously.

Within five minutes, Tom had left the house and shortly afterwards the others exited one at a time. They walked around the square, unable to resist glances toward the house where all their destinies were about to be shaped. Tom joined them shortly, attired in a white apron and carrying an impressive basket overflowing with loaves, freshly baked and sending out delicious wafts of the most tempting aromas.

As Tom began to work his way down the row of houses to establish his credibility, the others made their way quickly to the mews at the rear of the square. Keeping tight against the back wall, they counted their way down until they were just short of the rear door to the Frenchwoman's house. Fortunately, the alleyway was deserted and nobody was looking out from any of the houses. Archie clearly heard the rap of the heavy brass knocker on the front door. With a mute thump an internal door closed and he chose that moment to try the rear door, exhaling loudly upon finding it open.

The three men stole quietly into the small kitchen and Archie moved quickly toward the partially closed door leading to the rest of the house. A coal fire burned in the grate to one side of the kitchen and a range was beginning to warm as the fire within it raged.

Footsteps sounded in the hallway and Archie moved to one side as the other two men spread out, pistols at the ready. The footsteps grew louder and he heard the woman singing quietly to herself. She came through door, two large loaves in her arms and walked straight into him.

'What on... Monsieur Ross... I, 'she spluttered, confused and then terrified as she saw the other two men.

Archie's hand shot forward and grasping her mouth tightly shut, he forced her backwards over the edge of the kitchen table. She squealed and writhed, trying to fight back with a surprising strength. As he forced her further over backwards, her feet came clear of the floor, reducing her capacity to resist further. He placed his wooden forearm over her throat and turned to his companions, who though appearing shocked, were closely covering the helpless woman with their pistols.

'Go out into the hall, no further and stand guard. Now!' he hissed.

The two men exchanged looks but did as they were ordered. Once in the hall, they quietly closed the door behind them. Archie looked deep into the terrified eyes of Chantelle Haineau, noticing the fading bruise over one eye and pressed slightly harder down onto her throat.

'I'm truly sorry it's come to this Chantelle,' he said, so quietly his words barely carried to the gasping woman. His good hand squeezed her face mercilessly, giving her no chance to cry out. Her legs kicked feebly as she began to struggle for air, Archie's whole weight, pinning her to the tabletop.

'Believe me when I tell you that I find you a strangely enticing woman. I was hoping to enjoy finding out exactly what made you the person you've become. Now regrettably it's time for your life to end, how easily and in what manner, is for you to choose.'

Gasping against his hand, the woman tried once more to struggle but a slight increase in pressure of the solid wooden prosthetic began to slowly choke the life from her body.

'I want to know where Cordelia and Lady Hendricks are and I want to know now,' he said slowly, almost gently, as though they were in a lovers embrace. In a perverse parody of lovemaking, the woman began to writhe against him as she fought for her last breaths. The downward pressure of Archie's prosthetic arm slowly began to extinguish her life.

*

Antoine Pascal was in a buoyant mood, feeling at last that the ultimate revenge was close at hand. As he walked along the bustling street, even the pain in his leg that he was forced to drag along behind him every hour of every day, seemed to fade ever so slightly. The cold wind made his face ache damnably but for once he could not care less and he maintained a respectable pace, the tapping of his walking stick ringing out on the pavement. Even the blinding pain from the raw wound in his shoulder had been dulled by the effects of opium and the thick bandages had at last stopped the bleeding.

Walking into the small park in the centre of Cavendish Square, he realised for the first time that he did not hate the English nor their King but rather the target of his lust for revenge was that man who had taken his body and broken it to pieces in that distant Spanish farmhouse. He still could not understand how he had survived the fall into that swirling millrace but he wished with every beat of his heart that death had taken him that warm summers night.

Returning to Paris he had sought out his two lifelong friends, men whose lives had also been destroyed by the cruel actions of the British. With nothing left to live for, they happily accepted his gold and agreed to engineer an assignment to London. Once there, they would work for French Intelligence until Pascal was ready to use them. Between them they would make war inevitable and ensure thousands of Englishmen would die in a war everlasting.

Approaching the front door of the house, he wondered if Archibald Dexter really would take the life of his King, in order to save a young woman and her mother. Pascal did not think that he would but was in no doubt that the Englishman could never live with the horror of knowing that he was responsible for the death of the two women. Die they most certainly would and this very night. He would kill the older woman first and then he would enjoy the pleasure of Cordelia. With a cynical laugh he decided to cut her throat at the height of her pleasure and of course his own. Maybe he would let the older woman watch her daughter die first. Driven to insanity by his thirst for revenge, he felt not one moment of doubt, as in his mind's eye he saw the rape and murder of his prisoners.

The time had come to remove all trace of his presence in London and that process would begin with Chantelle Haineau. She had unwillingly served him well but had outlasted her usefulness. Physical violence had only partially cowed her but the revelation that he knew the whereabouts of her sister, still living in Boulogne, had broken her to his will. Once she had been disposed of then he would take care of Cordelia and her mother straight away he now decided, as he shuffled up to the front door of the Frenchwoman's house.

With a quick glance behind, he walked up to the sturdy oak door, fumbling for the key Mitterrand had obtained for him. Satisfied he was not been watched, he quietly entered the hallway and gently clicked the door shut. He stood motionless, alert and tensed, ready for action but the house seemed still, the only sound coming from a crackling fire in the scullery. To the right of the scullery was the staircase and he moved silently to the first step.

With agonising slowness he began to ascend the heavily carpeted stairs. His shattered leg made stealth painful and slow as he tried desperately to avoid the inevitable creaks and squeaks of the flexing timbers. It had been providence indeed that Haineau's remaining house guests had left London for several weeks.

Gasping for breath and his body rigid with the agony flaring in his crushed knee joint, he made his way along the first floor landing. A few yards short of the next flight of stairs, the tiniest of noises from behind a deep burgundy coloured door caused him to pause and listen intently. Gently and almost with affection, he ran his fingertips over the smooth painted surface, smiling slightly before slowly moving on.

He only reached the top of the next flight of stairs by taking much of his weight on his walking stick. Trying to catch his breath whilst making no sound made him dizzy with stress but eventually he regained his composure and the blazing torment in his knee began to slowly subside.

Carefully he placed his ear against the first door that he encountered on the landing, listening intently for signs of life beyond. Holding his breath, he fancied that he could hear the rhythmic ticking of a hearth clock and he was sure the faintest sound of snoring. With infinite care he turned the door's smooth brass handle and inch-by-inch opened the door. The gentle light, filtered by heavy net curtains gave the room a warm and welcoming feel. At the far side of the room before a glowing fire, stood a leather armchair that held the sleeping form of the house's landlady.

Step by small step, he inched forward, painfully lifting his twisted leg to avoid making the slightest sound. With a nerve shredding crash, the door slammed shut behind him. Jumping with fright and turning in one jerky motion, Pascal staggered and then fell backward as his weakened leg gave way under him. The bright flash and ear-shattering bang from a pistol fired at almost point-blank range sent his senses reeling.

Archie looked on in horror as Pascal fell to the floor, the sight of the mantelpiece mirror shattering, clear in his peripheral vision, testimony to the fact that he had missed his unexpectedly falling target at a range of less than three feet.

Dropping the now useless pistol and advancing on the fallen Frenchman, he struggled to pull a curved dagger from beneath his coat. Recovering with astonishing speed, Pascal began to rise with a growl of agony and in one fluid movement slashed a backhand swipe at Archie with his cane. Archie sidestepped and avoided the attack with some ease, grinning at the crippled Pascal desperately defending himself with a walking stick. The grin faded as a four-foot length of the cane flew free through the air, exposing a vicious rapier blade of the same length.

Archie tried to advance before Pascal had the time to recover his balance and use the deadly swordstick to his advantage. Closing on the rising Frenchman, he blocked the sword as it swung toward his head and slashed at the man's body with his knife. The short blade missed by several inches and Pascal punched Archie in the face then swung the sword in a low arc and stabbed toward Archie's stomach. Only by turning at the last second did he avoid the blade's lethal point. Instantly he stabbed at Pascal, piercing his forearm and eliciting a terrible scream of pain but as Pascal instinctively pulled away, with the blade lodged against bone, he wrenched the knife from Archie's grasp.

Archie leapt back in desperation, his eyes darting around the room for anything that would serve as a weapon. Pascal regained his composure, despite the dagger sticking obscenely from his forearm, blood pouring from the wound onto the floor. Taking an almost formal stance, he thrust forward at the very centre of Archie's chest, just as his back hit the wall, with no further space to retreat.

Archie swept up his arm with instinctive desperation and parried the blade, the tip just tearing through his clothing and deeply cutting the skin over his ribs. The hard wood of the prosthetic jarred Pascal's hand and shocked by the force of the blow against the sword's blade, he was knocked off balance ever so slightly. Archie lashed his foot out and slammed his boot against Pascal's knee.

He screamed in unbearable agony and fell to his knees, dropping the sword. Archie dived forward and grasped its handle, just as Pascal launched a frenzied series of punches to the side of his head. Archie fell forward, stunned and hurt but he had the sword's wooden handle in the grip of his good hand and rolled over onto his back, whilst lifting the blade upwards.

Carried forward by the momentum of his attack, Pascal fell over Archie's prone body and impaled himself on the end of the long, straight blade. As his mouth opened wide in a silent scream, his weight continued to pull his body down onto Archie until the blade passed clear through his abdomen, pierced his spine and exited his body in a bloody shower.

Horrified, Archie struggled to extricate himself from beneath the manically twitching body, which in its death throes was pumping copious quantities of blood all over him. Struggling free, he jumped to his feet and looked down as the Frenchman twitched once more and then with an almost tired sigh, he died.

The door burst open and Tom charged into the room, pistol at the ready. Behind him, Cedric was wrestling with a screaming and scratching Cordelia. Archie kicked the door shut to spare the young girl the awful scene within the room.

'Stay out Cordelia,' he bellowed, 'I'm perfectly all right and it's all over.'

'Archie... Archie,' she wailed from beyond the door.

He slipped out of the room, closing the door behind him and lost himself in the wildly passionate embrace of the hysterical young woman. Crazed with relief and unleashed stress, she showered him with kisses and pulled his lips painfully against her own as tears streamed down her pale face.

'Cordelia, calm down, come on sweetheart, it's all over,' he pleaded, watching an equally relieved looking Lady Hendricks approaching up the staircase.

'Is it really over Archie,' Cordelia asked, 'is that horrible beast dead?'

'Very dead my dear,' he assured her quietly, as the adrenaline rush began to fade and the pain of his wounds began to hit him in waves. 'Cedric old man,' he asked weakly,' take the ladies downstairs and prepare some hot water to bathe my wound,' noticing for the first time that he was bleeding heavily from his side.

'Oh my God, Archie you're hurt,' Cordelia shrieked, rapidly becoming hysterical once more. She was liberally covered in blood herself now, though Archie knew most of it belonged to Pascal.

'It's a scratch nothing more,' he endeavoured to reassure her. 'Now go down to the kitchen and help Cedric please.'

'Come on my dear let's go and I'm sure Archibald will be down to let us sort out his wound shortly, will you not?' Lady Hendricks said calmly, whilst none too gently taking her daughter's arm.

Archie re-entered the private lounge of Chantelle Haineau, to see Tom helping the woman to her feet. He untied the silk scarf gag that had prevented her from crying out and after a nod from Archie, began to untie her bound wrists and ankles.

'You bastard swine,' she spat through swollen lips,' I promised to co-operate, there was no need to truss me up like a turkey.'

'It's chickens that we truss,' Archie replied with a grin,' and trust only goes so far.'

'Oh my God, that's horrible,' she squealed, noticing for the first time the blood soaked corpse of Antoine Pascal. His body was twisted grotesquely and held off the ground by the handle of the swordstick. Congealing blood soaked his clothing and already his skin had turned grey in death.

Archie looked at the trembling woman as she began to be overtaken by the shock of the last few hours. He could not decide why but he found the woman so compelling that he knew there and then what he must do. She had almost seemed to accept death at his hands and then seemed to undergo a profound change of mind, begging him to let her live if she helped him save the women. When he agreed, she took him to the first floor bedroom for a tearful reunion with Lady Hendricks and Cordelia. She had then revealed that Pascal was expected imminently and Archie had made an instant decision to lay a trap. Now he had to try to turn this terrible mess to his own advantage.

'Is there any chance of you receiving visitors in the next few hours?' he asked the woman, who was now sitting staring into the fire, wringing her hands together in her lap.

'No, I'm not expecting guests and I usually only receive my instructions once a week,' she answered absently.

'Listen to me woman,' Archie said harshly; kneeling before her and grabbing her painfully sore wrists so hard that she yelped with sudden pain. 'We have to move quickly if we're to salvage this situation. You've promised me you will co-operate and if you don't then there is nothing I can do for you!'

'I know… I will, I promise and after all, what choice do I have?'

'None whatsoever I'm afraid,' he agreed, trying to keep his voice low in order to calm the shocked woman. Over her shoulder he watched the ever dependable Tom straightening Pascal's corpse. With a stomach turning slurp, he pulled the bloodied sword blade back through the man's abdomen and then to Archie's surprise, left the room.

'You know what the deal is,' he whispered soothingly, 'and I promise that I will do all I can to make it a success. You work for me now, I have you body and soul, do you understand?'

'Yes... of course, I understand... what else can I do?'

'Nothing at all, other than go to the gallows as a true patriot of France, the country that ran you out of its lands in terror. Nothing is forever and one day your beastly revolution and that ludicrous Emperor will be consigned to the graveyard of history.'

'Just tell me what you want of me,' she replied, fear now being replaced by a tired acceptance.

'We'll clean up here and leave you to carry on as before. Change nothing in your routine and do everything Thiebault asks of you.'

At the mention of Thiebault's name, she twitched as though in sudden pain. Fear returned once more to her eyes as she tried desperately to figure out how he could have known Thiebault's name and what did he know of her perverted relationship with the man?

'I know many things,' Archie assured her as he saw the vivid shock in her eyes. 'You'll continue to accommodate his people as before, live your life and be thankful for each new day. All that will change is that, utilising a system I'll devise, you'll keep me informed of everything that goes on in this house. Do you understand?'

'Yes... I'm to be your spy in return for my life.'

'That's right and be grateful for this chance. Many thousands will die in the wars that are coming but one day all this will be over and survival is all that really matters not misguided loyalty.'

Nodding in agreement, she curled up and began to sob gently. He gave her a reassuring squeeze on her shoulder and put several logs onto the fire to dispel the sudden chill that had gripped them both.

Tom and Charles Lyell came into the room carrying a large rug they had found in one of the rooms below. With some difficulty they managed to roll Pascal's body up in it and between them were able to carry it out onto the landing.

'Lady 'endricks and 'er daughter 'ave left in a cab Sir,' Tom said, as he wiped blood from his hands. 'Cedric 'as gone with 'em and will return with one of t' family's larger carriages, which we can use to dispose o' this wretch.'

'Archie, you are summonsed to appear at the Hendricks household for dinner this evening,' Lyell told him with a grin. 'I believe Cordelia has an urge to thank you properly.' He then began to carefully pick up the shattered pieces of the mantelpiece mirror.

'Don't be so bloody juvenile,' Archie replied, unable to suppress a broad grin of his own as he prized the musket ball from the wall and looked around for something to fill the hole.

He took one last look around the room and was satisfied there were no signs of the life or death dramas that had been played out earlier. Chantelle seemed exhausted and still in shock as she continued to stare into the blazing fire. She would be fine he concluded.

With a growing feeling of apprehension he realised that he still had one onerous duty to perform. He would have to leave his faithful companions to conclude the clearing up operation, whilst he took himself off to see Sir John Marshall and explain how come in the last few days, he had saved two of London's most eminent ladies of society, killed a murderous deranged French assassin and turned a pivotal French agent. With a grin and a resigned sigh he accepted that he could expect a dressing down of epic proportions but perhaps a little grudging gratitude too.

EPILOGUE

As he had predicted, Sir John Marshall's fury at him for acting alone to deal with the threat to Lady Hendricks and her daughter was indeed tempered by his twin victories in ridding the world of Antoine Pascal and recruiting a potentially devastating double agent, in the form of Chantelle Haineau.

Over the following few days, Archie and his men set up an elaborate system of contacts to allow their latest recruit to pass information to them safely. By the end of that first week she had been told by Thiebault to expect three new lodgers within days. The intelligence war between England and France was clearly increasing in its intensity as war loomed on the horizon with a tragic inevitability.

Cordelia had welcomed Archie at her home the night after her rescue and only by skilled sleight of hand had he avoided her over-amorous attentions throughout what had turned into a very long evening. He had finally made good his escape beyond midnight but knew he would have to keep his wits about him over the coming weeks, lest he became embroiled in an emotional tangle he could ill afford.

Journeying back to his home that cool winter evening, he reflected on the future and the storm that was surely going to blow through the countries of Europe. Many reputations would be made and many more lives lost he was sure but whatever the outcome, the world would never be quite the same again once this cataclysm was over.

**

HISTORICAL FOOTNOTE

In 1798, Napoleon invaded Egypt, landing almost unopposed save for a few ineffective yet brutal assaults by Bedouin tribesmen. He took Alexandria with ease before settling his fleet in Aboukir Bay. Admiral Brueys placed his ships in what he believed was a strongly defensive position should he be compelled to fight at anchor. A shallow island at the entrance to the bay was reinforced with mortars and artillery. As the Royal Navy entered the bay and engaged with the anchored French ships, this gun emplacement seems to have had little or no recorded effect on the battle.

The defeat of the French fleet at what became known as the Battle of the Nile was almost complete. However, a Royal Navy frigate, HMS Leander, sailing to Naples with Nelson's dispatches was overhauled and captured by a surviving French warship, her surviving crew being taken prisoners of war.

In 1804 a Royal Navy squadron consisting of the frigates Indefatigable, Amphion, Lively and Medusa successfully intercepted four Spanish ships carrying bullion to the port of Cadiz. Under the command of

Captain Graham Moore this action by the Royal Navy, on the face of it an act bordering on piracy, successfully brought to an end the phony war between France and much of northern Europe and from that moment onwards war was inevitable.

The Aliens Act 1793 was a desperate attempt to control the considerable numbers of French and other potentially hostile foreigners taking up residence in Great Britain following the upheavals of the French Revolution. Within the Aliens Office set up to administer this law was a smaller unit tasked with countering the colossal efforts of French Intelligence operating within Great Britain. Having so generously offered sanctuary to those seeking asylum, Britain would struggle to control those elements now seeking to bring about the nations downfall.

Georgian London was a place of great contrasts, where immense wealth and privilege sat alongside terrible poverty. Disease and poor public health plagued the capital through deep, cold winters and blazing hot summers. Open sewers combined with hundreds of tons of horse dung deposited daily on the streets created a vile atmosphere.

While the poor struggled just to exist, bolstered by the vices of crime, alcohol and tobacco, the wealthy enjoyed their own diversions and depravities. Gentlemen's clubs were places where fine food and excessive gambling could be enjoyed in luxury and privacy. High-class brothels and walloping houses flourished as the upper classes appetite for perverse entertainment knew no bounds. Opium and hashish was imported in considerable quantities from the four corners of the globe. Still a capital offence, homosexuality flourished in underground "molly houses" and other secret establishments. Hedonism was a very much more public affair within certain social groups before the arrival of Victorian values and hypocrisy drove most vice deeper underground.

ABOUT THE AUTHOR

N. J. Slater is a writer from England. An Agent of the King is his first novel. Follow the further adventures of Archibald Dexter in Peninsular Spy. Also by N. J. Slater, The Black Knight, a thriller set in Victorian London.

30238046R00212

Made in the USA
Middletown, DE
17 March 2016